Copyright © 2021 by MJ Fields

All rights reserved. No part of this publication may be reproduced, distributed, or transmitted in any form or by any means, including photocopying, recording, or other electronic or mechanical methods, without the prior written permission of the publisher, except in the case of brief quotations embodied in critical reviews and certain other noncommercial uses permitted by copyright law.

This book is a work of fiction. All names, characters, locations, and incidents are products of the author's imaginations. Any resemblance to actual persons, things, living or dead, locales, or events is entirely coincidental.

John Ross
m Maggie

Molly Alex Tessa Kendall Jake

ROSS

BLUE VALLEY SERIES

Josie Ross-Fields
div

Troy

ROSS

Jack Ross
div

Jasper *d.* Jason *d.* Jade

ROSS

Landon Links — *div* Kate
m Audrianna Lucas

Alexandra Ally

LINKS

USA TODAY BESTSELLING AUTHOR
MJ FIELDS

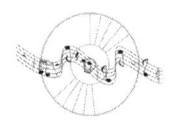

Blue Love Playlist

I'm In A Hurry- Alabama
Hey Jealousy- Gin Blossoms
Runaway Train- Soul Asylum
I'll Never Get Over You - Exposé
Cryiń- Aerosmith
Falling In Love With You- UB40
Even Flow - Pearl Jam
Here I Am - Russ Taff
Rain - Madonna
Dreamlover - Mariah Carey
What's Up? - 4 Non Blondes
Love Song - Tesla
Better Man - Pearl Jam
She Doesn't Know She's Beautiful- Sammy Kershaw
Lightning Crashes- Live
Black - Pearl Jam
Little Miss Can't Be Wrong- Spin Doctors
What You Give - Tesla
I'm Not Alone- Russ Taff
Love Me Anyway - P!nk

Piece of My Heart- Janice Joplin
Any Man Of Mine- Shania Twain
Don't Go Breaking My Heart- Elton Jon
I Love Rock Ń Roll - Joan Jett & The Black Hearts
Please Forgive Me- Bryan Adams
I Get Around - 2 Pac
The Joker - Stevie Miller Band
I Touch Myself - Divinyls
Against All Odds - Phil Collins
Leather and Lace - Stevie Nicks,
Edge of Seventeen- Stevie Nicks and Don Henley
Love and Affection - Nelson

Blurb

He's the boy you hate to love, and love to hate.

Lucas, the star quarterback, seems to have it all—super star athletic abilities, expensive clothes, cars, and women who will stop at nothing to be his, if only for a night.

Tessa is a young woman who lives her life always doing what is right. She tries desperately to hold herself accountable to the demanding expectations of her family, and everyone around her, while remaining virtuous.

However, when two worlds collide, sparks fly and ignite in a fiery passion that neither Lucas nor especially Tessa are ready for.

A troubled home life is exposed. Past flings fight for attention. Exes wreak havoc. And the odds continue to stack up against them.

Will the fire and passion of first love win, or will it destroy them?

This is love, not a fairy tale.

The *Blue Valley* series is not your typical love story. It is a journey through one's past ... maybe even a story resembling yours, or someones close to you.

It's our story.

PLEASE NOTE: this series was previously released as The Love series (MJ's very first works) and has been through a complete rewrite, which consists of a change from narrative to first person/ dual POV and forty thousand words worth of new content.

To The Reader

PLEASE NOTE:
this series was previously released as The Love series (MJ's very first works) and has been through a complete rewrite, which consists of a change from narrative to first person/ dual POV and forty thousand words worth of new content.

Warning: *Highly Emotional!*
This book contains volatile characters in real-life situations that may be triggers to some readers.

CHANGE

Chapter One

TESSA

Five, I start the countdown as my feet pound against the cracked sidewalk just out the back door of the old farmhouse. When it slams shut behind me, bounces back open, and slams again and again, I cringe.

The door ... Something else that has long been neglected due to the fact there's always more important things to do around the Ross family farm than fix a busted spring.

"Tessa Anne Ross, easy on that door!" I hear my mom yell from the window in frustration as I round the lilac tree and hit the driveway.

I run even faster now, eyes on the field beyond the shop

where Dad is constantly fixing up the old equipment to keep things running.

Four. I inhale deeply as I run between the fields of sweet yet dusty-smelling hay, feet pounding against the hard, uneven, rutted dirt driveway.

Dad said it was a "*Good year. We're blessed to get a second cutting.*"

To the family, it means extra money, but it also means more work.

Faster.

Three. I push myself harder as I approach the corn. Rows and rows of it. It was also a good year for corn, which means, mid-September, the harvest begins … More work.

There is no outrunning the work to be done, but soon, really soon, I can better wrap my head around all that this "good year" has brought the Ross family.

"Two," I pant out as my feet hit the overgrown grass mixed with colorful blue and white flowering weeds. Beautiful, yet still weeds that now cover the ground that used to be meticulously cut. A place where the five of us—me; my older sister, Molly; older brother, Alex; younger sister, Kendall; and younger brother, Jake—would spend summer lunches, picnicking with Mom and Dad on the grass. Even after Mom was in community college, finishing her nursing degree then working, Molly continued the summertime tradition—sun tea and sandwiches on a checkered blanket —until she went to college.

Not anymore.

Not stopping at the once loved and now abandoned spot, I head into the woods, pushing through the burdock bushes, not caring if I get them stuck to my clothes or in my hair, stepping over and on the ferns that blanket the ground, passed the unkempt pathway, panting as I continue.

I make my way down the steep hillside to the place I go to be alone, to think, to scream, to shout, to cry, and to wash away all my worries.

"One!" I yell up to the sky to hear my echo through the woods as I stand on the edge of the creek, toeing off my sneakers then pulling off my socks while watching the birds fly from their resting places. Carefully, I step into the cool water and look upstream, trying to control my breathing as I take in the sight before me.

The falls …

Finally, I feel like I can breathe.

Curling my toes in the water to feel the rocks and find my footing, I carefully trudge upstream, toward the cascading water, the mist hitting my heated face, cooling it in the sweltering late-summer heat and humidity, a welcome feeling.

I carefully climb the slippery rock until I'm finally at the point where it evens out. Then I turn and scoot back on my butt until I'm under the heavy flow of water and cry.

I cry because of change, I cry in frustration, and I cry because I know something awful is brewing at home. My parents have always had little arguments—that's normal—but a couple weeks ago, I overheard the word "Separation" fall from Mom's lips and "Absolutely not" was Dad's immediate response. Since then, not one quibble. Heck, not even a funny little jab about Mom overcooking the meat, which would bring on her normal "Learn to cook for yourself, John Ross" reply.

Now she's busy organizing the house, which means emptying every nook and cranny, including each closet and cupboard. Dad is consumed with farm work, as he has done every summer since I can remember, dodging rain and summer storms while crop season is in full swing, but this time ... even more so. And he's irritable, which is not at all like him. It may be because my brother, Alex, and I have been skipping out on helping as much around the farm as we have in previous years, and this year, even more was planted. At first, it was due to fall sports tryouts and now practices.

Alex is playing football for the first time ever, and in our senior year. He played peewee with our cousins, Jasper and Jason—also his best friends—but five years ago, they were killed in a car accident. Alex stopped playing and was held back a year in school. Then, a year ago, when Jake started playing, tossing the ball around with him, he mentioned wanting to try out yet never did, because things were always too busy. That was another argument I overheard. Mom was insisting that Dad encourage him. It was his last year in high school, after all, and Mom wanted him to come out of his shell before college. He has been ... withdrawn. I was, too, after the accident, but Jade, my cousin and best friend since birth, their sister, she needed a distraction, too.

Me. I'm her distraction.

And lately, I've been distracted myself.

I scoot back behind the falling water and wipe away the tears mixed with water droplets, angry at myself for being so upset that my parents are having problems when things like accidents and dead cousins are also a part of life.

And so is work, I think as I slide down the rock, determined to stop feeling sorry for myself.

* * *

Once on even ground, I take my time walking back. As I get closer, I hear the all-too-familiar sound of the hay elevator. Even though I'm exhausted from the four-hour field hockey practice in the heat and humidity, I need to do my part. But I will take my time getting there.

From a distance, I see the normal hay crew, all friends from school looking to make an extra few bucks. Ryan, also a senior and playing ball for the first time since the accident—he and Jasper were extremely close—and Frankie and Mark, both play soccer and are juniors. They come from broken homes, and I swear they use the farm as an escape. Odd how I have to escape from this place while others find respite in it.

Since I've been a bit off my game, Jade has found a new distraction. I'm not going to lie and say I don't find it a good disruption in the angst that seems to be my life, because I totally do.

After field hockey practice, Jade and I wait to catch a ride with Alex and watch as all the new players come out, freshly showered. The hottest ones always seem to wear white hats.

Tomorrow is the last day of practice before the long Labor Day weekend break, and then … school starts.

School will be different this year due to State and Federal budget cuts to the education system. Some of the rural schools in Central New York have been closed since the end of last year. Therefore, Blue Valley Central School District has gained about fifty new students. Jade and our friend, Becca, call the newbies "implants."

More change …

* * *

Blue Love

"It sure is a hot one today." Jade wags her brows as she fans her face.

I roll my eyes and she nods at the white hat boys ambling out of the locker room doors.

"Should we invite them to the pond to—"

I quickly cut her off with a sharp, "No."

"Oh, come on, Tessa," she grumbles as she follows me to the passenger side door of the old truck. "Fresh meat, not related, not working for your father, or mine, and we haven't known them since before their faces cleared up and their voices and balls dropped."

I swing the door open, and she grabs it before it hits the shiny black Pontiac Trans-am, that looks way out of place here in Blue Valley's parking lot.

"Interesting way to meet some new hotties, but I'm sure Uncle John wouldn't like the insurance claim if you dent up that car." She jokes.

I hear a loud whistle and look toward it. Alex nods to the back of the truck, I groan as I slam the door, walk around the back, and climb in, Jade follows.

"I'd rather be back here anyway." She smiles as she leans against the cab smiling at the guys walking past us.

"Got your suits on?" Alex asks as he throws his gear in the back.

I nod.

"Good."

* * *

"Why not?" Jade splashes water at me.

"Why now?" I respond as I swim backward and kick my feet, splashing her back.

"Like I said at the school, none of them work for your

dad on the farm or have swung a hammer for my dad." She swims after me. "And truth be told, none of them knew my brothers, so maybe they won't look at me like some broken little girl who needs saving."

"Who looks at you like that?" I huff, pulling myself up onto the raft.

"You know who," she says, doing the same.

"Ryan Brookes doesn't look at you like you're broken."

Sitting beside me, she nods at him and Alex, standing on the bank. Ryan's arms are crossed, black hat pulled down, and yeah, he's staring in our direction.

"Care to eat those words?" she huffs.

"Alex is looking at us the same way," I defend Ryan, who is glowering at Jade like he always has.

"Is not," she huffs.

"You ever think maybe Ryan *likes* you?"

"Oh, that would be fun, making out with someone who thinks of my brothers every time he looks at me." She lays back on the floating deck and closes her eyes.

"Jade, I don't think he'd—"

"Yeah, well, maybe *I* would. So, no. Just no."

I lay back, too, and then reach over, grab her hand, and give it a squeeze. "Okay. So, we wait for college"—*or marriage*—"just like we always said we would."

She turns and looks at me, then past me and nods up the hill. "Why wait to go to the market when the market has come to us?"

"Oh great," I grumble as I hear the stereo system blasting Alabama's "I'm In A Hurry."

"We're still country, Tessa." Jade snickers as she sits up. "And a little bit rock and roll."

I watch as Alex's teammates barrel down the hill.

Jade starts to stand up, grinning. "Here come the *white hat boys*, Tessa."

I yank her back down. "Weren't we working on getting rid of our farm-girl tans?"

"Good idea." She lays back down and pops a knee up. "Looking relaxed seems so much less—"

"Desperate? Yeah."

Laying on our stomachs now, we watch—one of us less obvious than the other—as all the implants hop out of the back of the truck and throw off their shirts.

"Lord have mercy," Jade groans as they begin to run to the pond.

Ryan and Alex beat them in and begin to swim toward the raft, where they climb up and shake off, water spraying droplets on our sun-heated skin.

"Assholes," Jade hisses.

"Nice mouth," Alex mumbles.

"Well deserved." Jade sits up and wipes the water from her arms as some of the others climb up.

I immediately notice a couple of them looking at my chest, making me incredibly self-conscious with my choice of suits.

I hate my boobs. I hate that they decided to sprout over the summer even more.

Giving them a nasty look, I stand then dive in.

"Wait for me!" Jade calls from behind me, and then I hear a splash as she jumps in.

I see a couple of the guys, ones who clearly spend a hell of a lot of time at the gym, standing on the bank still; shirts off, of course. Without looking at them, I hurry to the picnic table, grab my tank top, and throw it on. Then I grab Jade's and look back to watch her slowly walk out of the water, reaching over her shoulders and pushing her boobs out as she squeezes water from her long, black hair.

When I see her smirk at the two, I toss her tank top in her face.

"Gee, thanks for the heads-up." She laughs.

"Come on." I stomp toward the truck.

"Where are you pretty ladies heading off to?" one of them asks while the other snickers.

"Places to go," Jade says in a voice I seriously don't recognize.

"Ouch," the same voice says, feigning insult.

I throw open the door and yell to Alex, "I'm taking the truck. Catch a ride."

Jade jumps in as he calls back to me, "Okay, TT."

I huff at his use of my "nickname." TT for Tessa the Terrible.

"What's the hurry?" Jade asks as I turn the key.

"You're ridiculous," I tell her, throwing it in gear then hitting the gas.

She looks out the back window. "Look at them. I think ridiculously naughty would be fun."

"Gross," I grumble as I watch her giving them a flirty little wave.

In the rearview mirror, I notice one of them waving back. The other, the broader one, with the kind of hair that obviously gets cut once a week, covered in the damn white hat, brim pulled low, all I can see is how square his jaw is.

"Jesus, Tessa." Jade grabs the wheel and jerks it, straight-up saving us from driving through the blackberry bushes. "Focus."

How embarrassing.

Entering the clearing, we see a black Pontiac Trans Am with T-tops.

"I wonder which one of the two that thing belongs to?"

"Why do you think it's one of theirs?" I ask, knowing damn well why—it fits.

Blue Love

Jade looks over her shoulder as I pass it. "And vanity plates."

"Telling," I quip.

"L-L-I-N-K-S 1." She giggles. "My guy is too sweet to be that showy. Yours is—"

"Oh, hell no, they aren't Motley Crew for Lord's sake. It's not a you-give-me-Tommy-Lee-and-you-get-Vince-Neil kind of situation."

"You don't like blonds," she defends herself.

"And you know this how?" I ask, pulling out onto Harvest Road.

"Because you said you didn't. Remember *Top Gun*? You demanded Maverick because Goose was blond, and so was Alex?"

I can't help but laugh because, indeed, that was the excuse, but the reality is I liked Maverick because he was edgy and, as Aunt Anne would say, full of piss and vigor. And, yeah, he was a bad boy.

"Even before that, you called Han Solo, and I got Luke Skywalker. Not that I'm complaining but … you set a precedent."

I laugh again. "Indeed, I did."

After a few seconds she smacks me. "Oh my God, you have a type."

"I've never even had a boyfriend; how do I have a type?"

"Well, I guess it's time we put my theory to the test."

"Not a chance," I say, hitting the gas and causing her to squeal and grab the oh-shit handle.

* * *

"What did you do this weekend? I didn't see you once," Jade asks, sliding in beside me on our regular, Ross family church pew.

It wasn't the entire weekend; it was just one day that seemed a lot like a week.

"Cleaning," I clip quietly.

"Had to get rid of the old clothes so we can do some school shopping tomorrow," Mom says, obviously hearing me. "Jade, you're more than welcome to come, too."

Kendall leans forward. "You should come. Mom is taking us to the mall and said we can go to County Seat and get some Guess Jeans," she whispers, knowing Dad has a fit at the price of the clothes there. "Lerner and Gap, too."

"Then I'm in."

Uncle Jack slides in beside his daughter. "You're in for what?"

"School clothes shopping with Aunt Maggie?" She grins.

"And how much is this gonna cost me?" He sighs.

"A lot, Uncle Jack." Kendall grins. "A whole lot. Especially if Jade wants Z Cavaricci jeans."

"Z Cava-what?" Uncle Jack asks as the choir begins.

Day One, Senior Year

Chapter Two

TESSA

Looking at myself in the mirror, I'm unimpressed. I don't like how I've developed, nor do I like the new clothes that Jade and Kendall insisted I get. Well, maybe if they weren't peeking under my door like they did in the changing room, coaxing me out and crooning over how "beautiful" I looked, I would like them. But the thought of wearing them to school? No way. I mean, *really?*

I tug at the bright colored shirt and wonder what the hell I was thinking allowing my middle school sister, who went nuts over the Jelly shoes, to give me fashion advice. Or is it that I'm using the term "fashion advice" at all?

Last year, I was shopping in the boy's department in Hills Department store and getting Levi jeans at Homer Men and Boys, which was definitely more fun than the County Seat or Lerner. I will admit that I liked Gap, but seriously prefer the boy's section. None of the clothes in that area showcased the "girls."

My hair looks amazing, sun-kissed and hanging to my waist, and with the growth spurt came the waves. Mom says it's all related to my "changing hormones."

Gross.

"Tessa, honey, time to come down. Breakfast is getting cold, and the bus will be here soon," Mom yells up the stairs.

"Dammit," I grumble as I peel off the jeans and stupid shirt. A shirt that has freaking shoulder pads in it.

Like, what designer woke up one day and had a light bulb moment that involved thinking it would be awesome if everyone looked like a linebacker?

I grab a pair of khaki shorts that hit just above the knee and a light blue, baggy tee to cover up these damn boobs. Then I exchange the fancy bra for a sports bra that is too tight but holds my boobs in and do a quick once-over.

Perfect, I think as I step back.

Out of the corner of my eye, I see the last family portrait we took—two years ago at Aunt Ann's at The Cape—on my dresser, and my worries do a one-eighty. Screw the clothes. Mom is extremely emotional, and Dad is almost nonexistent. He didn't even come in for supper the past two nights. I know worse things are going on than shoulder pads and boobs.

I run down the stairs just in time to see Kendall and Jake walking to the end of the driveway to meet the bus, Mom following them with a camera.

She yells back to us, "Alex, Tessa, get out here; I need a picture."

"Why don't you make them ride the smelly old bus, too?" Jake snips.

"They're seniors, young man." Mom smiles at him,

eyes full of emotions, and not of the happy variety. "When you're a senior, you can drive to school, too."

"Why can't we ride with them?" he grumbles.

"Only room for three," Mom explains while Alex and I stand beside them. "Now, smile. The bus is heading down the hill."

After waving them off, Jake sticks his tongue out at us from the bus window, and the three of us laugh.

When we all turn toward the house, Mom looks toward the shop, where Dad is standing, wiping his hands with a grease rag.

She swallows hard and looks back to us. "Now a picture of just you two, my seniors."

"Gonna be late if we don't leave to get Jade in just a minute, Mom," Alex says softly, a look of concern in his eyes that I don't think has a thing to do with being late.

Mom clears her throat. "Just one."

"Of course." Alex puts his arm around me, pulls to his side, and says, "Smile, Tessa."

Once out of the driveway, I ask him straight-up, ready to have the conversation, one that I haven't burdened him with in fear it would push him back inside that shell of his, but knowing he's sensing something, too, I know we're both ready. "What's going on?"

"We're going to get Jade, and then—"

"You know that's not what I'm talking about."

"Not one hundred percent sure, but we'll be fine. Always are."

The rest of the short ride, the storm that I've sensed brewing is now inside the cab of the old Chevy, but the clouds are not breaking … not yet, anyway.

* * *

Sitting outside Uncle Jack's, Alex sighs loud enough to pull me from my thoughts.

"What?"

"You gonna go grab her?" he asks, sounding impatient, which is not at all typical.

"Yeah, sure." I turn away and open the door just as Jade flies down the porch steps.

Jade is what I would consider classically beautiful. She is older than me by a few months, having turned eighteen in May. She's tall and developed way before I did. Her hair is long, black, and thick. It always has a perfect, smooth wavy look to it.

Uncle Jack and her mom divorced two years ago. After the accident that took the lives of Jasper and Jason, Aunt Janet got hooked on pills. Everyone knows that she cheated on Uncle Jack. Not everyone, but close family, knows it was in their bed.

Honestly, I wish I didn't know. Even more, I wish Jade wasn't with her father when they came home early and found her, and the piece of shit.

Janet hasn't been the same since the accident—that's what Mom told me—and she still isn't. I don't understand how Mom can possibly see her side in this. What she did to Jade and Jack, because of her grief, is selfish. They also lost them. And now they lost her, too.

She only lives a little over an hour away in Watkins, but Jade doesn't see her. I wouldn't either, if I were her.

After pushing the door open, I slide over in the seat as Jade, smiling from ear to ear, hoots then yells, "We're finally seniors!"

Alex puts the truck in drive, shaking his head as he says, "Yeah, and we'll probably be late our very first day."

"Have a great day, baby girl," Uncle Jack calls from

somewhere inside. Then he yells, "Hold up!" running out of the door and waving her sweater in the air. "You forgot half your wardrobe."

"Gee, thanks, Dad." She forces a smile.

"Anytime, Jade." Uncle Jack gives her a tight smile then shakes his head. "You all have a good last first day at Blue Valley."

"Thanks, Uncle Jack." I wave.

Pulling out of the driveway, Alex laughs. "He wants you to cover those things up, Jade."

She reaches across me, smacks him, and then sits back.

With everything going on, I look at Alex, who is smiling, and can't help but do so myself.

Five years ago, he gave up on school. Didn't even talk for a few months. Well, only to Jade or Uncle Jack, or if forced into a conversation. He was also held back a year. Now my brother is the valedictorian of our class and, from what I hear, in the starting lineup on the field.

What he said before, on our way to Jade's, "We'll be fine. Always are," I'm going to believe. Both he and Jade are proof that, no matter the storm, we Rosses can get through it.

* * *

Hopping out of the truck, in the student section of the parking lot, I realize that we are once again beside the black Trans Am.

"L-L-I-N-K-S 1." Jade giggles then whispers, "Your man is here."

"I'm totally going to pretend you did not just say that," I grumble as I hoist up last year's backpack, that Mom managed to make look almost brand new, over my shoulder and hurry toward the entry.

Looking around, I notice how full the parking lot is, and the cars look to outnumber the trucks. Nice cars, too. Too nice.

The halls are more packed, just like the parking lot. And, like the cars, the clothes on the implants definitely stand out.

I tug at my shirt as I walk past the first few lockers, and a group of girls snicker. I look up to see that some of them are pushing blue and white pom poms in their locker.

"Oh my God, look at them." A blonde—obviously not a natural one, as she either used lemon or sprayed Sun-in and baked outside—fake-gags as Jade and I walk past them.

"You missed your roots," I tell her.

Jade nudges me. "Oh shit, we missed cheerleading tryouts."

"Our hair isn't bleached out enough," I grumble as we pass even more people.

I watch Jade turn around and walk backward. I crane my neck to see if that wretched bitch is following us and see exactly where she's looking.

The white hat boys.

"That's too damn bad," she says.

"Too bad? Thank God! I wouldn't be caught dead cheering for that bunch of boys with God complexes, in a short skirt with frilly poof balls in my hand, especially if I had to make my hair look like theirs."

The same dark-haired boy from the pond is now smirking at Jade again. The other one ... is looking me up and down, making me even more uncomfortable in my own skin than I already do ... in my own damn school. It pisses me off, too. When his teeth, that are whiter than his damn hat, rakes his lower lip, my stomach flips and my face catches fire.

Blue Love

I think I'm going to be sick, but ... I can't look away.

His green eyes are locked on mine, mischief playing in them.

Pissed at my confusion, him ... both, I ask, "What the hell are you looking at?"

Bleach-blonde huffs, "Oh, hell no, Links. Not happening."

He rolls his insanely green eyes and turns to her. "You're not even supposed to be here. Walk the fuck away."

Having no desire to be involved in any of this conversation, I walk to my locker, where Jade is already unloading her backpack and hanging a mirror.

"You're remodeling already?"

"Damn straight." She laughs, shrugs off her sweater, and tosses it in her locker.

"You good?" Alex asks me while opening the door to his locker and hanging his backpack.

I hang my own backpack in my locker. "Perfect."

"You sure? Because I saw a little TT coming out back there." He shuts his locker door.

From behind me, I hear a drawn out, "Damn ..."

Looking over my shoulder, I see him looking me over again. Then he gives me a slow wink as he walks past and whispers, "Nice eats."

"That's my sister, Links." Alex steps like he's going to go after him, and I step in front of him to stop him as *Links* opens his locker.

The other guy smiles as he looks Jade over. "Very nice."

"Step off, boys," Alex growls.

"Lucas." His friend nods down the hall.

"You may want to watch it. You're on *my* team now." Lucas Links, L-L-I-N-K-S 1, owner of the black Trans

Am, and apparently several white hats, slams his locker shut.

"I've been on theirs for over seventeen years," Alex snaps.

"Ease up, Ross. Just enjoying the scenery." Lucas winks at me.

I force myself to look him up and down, just like he did me. When my eyes meet his insanely green ones, I force myself to give him a disgusted look and tell him, "You have a better chance of seeing God."

He laughs and, unfortunately, it's a good one. Then he looks back at me and yells over his shoulder, "Challenge accepted."

Hell. No.

***

Sitting in the auditorium with Jade, while waiting for the principal to do the beginning of the yearly announcements, I watch as she looks in her little compact mirror and begins fluffing her hair.

"For the love of God, do not try to look like them. Your hair is perfect."

"Always room for improvement," she says before applying lip gloss.

Ryan's sister, Becca Brooks, and the newest addition to the Brooks family, sit beside me.

The Brooks family takes in foster children, which I admire. Even more so, I love that this one is a girl who looks to be our age. I recognize her shirt—a denim button-up. It was mine, my favorite. Because of my boobs, I can no longer wear it. It was in one of the many bags that Mom dropped off when we cleaned out closets.

The Brooks family are kind and accepting of everyone.

Blue Love

Each person is made to feel like they belong and are truly a part of the family, regardless of the circumstances that brought them to their home. Mistakes are forgiven, slates wiped clean, and love is given without expectation or explanation. They're kind of amazing.

"Tessa, Jade, this is my friend, Phoebe." Becca pulls her schedule out of her Trapper Keeper. "Let's compare."

I smile. "Hey, Phoebe, welcome to Blue Valley."

She smiles softly. "Thanks."

"You're lucky to be starting today. Now they'll think you came from Stoneville High."

"Not sure that's any better," Phoebe says, pulling her notebooks to her chest, as if to hide behind them.

I look around and laugh, attempting to make light of what I imagine is a difficult situation. "I'm gonna have to agree with you on Stoneville."

Jade catches on. "You just be Phoebe with the super cute Meg Ryan hair and flawless skin."

To that, Phoebe smiles softly.

"And that smile, perfect," Jade adds.

I redirect the conversation. "All right, let's compare schedules."

We quickly figure out we're all in the same lunch and Honors classes together. Becca and Jade have P.E. and Study Hall together. Phoebe and I share the same P.E. and Government class.

"Looks like you and I will be in every class together," I tell her. "It'll be fun."

She nods, sits back, and releases a breath that I imagine she's been holding in for days.

Just then, the newbie football players sit in front of us, and as they sit down, Jade nudges me and wags her eyebrows. I roll mine at her then look away.

L-L-I-N-K-S 1, who is sitting directly in front of me—I

can tell by his shoulders and the broad back that don't belong on a high school student—turns and looks back at me.

I look away immediately.

"Tessa"—Jade kicks my foot—"he was checking you out."

Thankfully, the auditorium starts to fall silent, and I look up at the stage.

Mr. Camp, the school principal, taps the mic then begins. "Welcome back, students. As you know, we have merged with other schools this year due to state budget cuts. I know you will welcome the new Blue Valley students with kindness. This school belongs to all of us, so let's make sure we treat each other with respect as we all transition into our new normal."

He then gives the typical first day speech, goes over the rules, upcoming sign-ups, games, the pep rally and, of course, the fall festival.

The entire time, I focus on Jade's smitten look. For a moment, I allow myself to be happy for her. She deserves happiness, but she also deserves respect, and I'm not sure someone like him would give her that. Which, of course, puts me in protective mode.

Lost in my thoughts, I realize that it does not go unnoticed that L-L-I-N-K-S 1, Lucas Links, Lucas, or, to make it easier, I will now use LL at his mention, is looking back at me, his self-appointed "challenge." I don't like that he thinks he can play games with me. I also don't like that, for some reason, it makes my heart beat a bit faster, or that his eyes are the color of the trees, or that he is incredibly built … any of that. But, what worries me the most is that I have never backed down from a challenge, and I have a feeling neither has he.

When the assembly finally ends, I'm the first to stand

and head out of the auditorium. Jade, Becca, and Phoebe follow behind me as I head to the signups.

Jade writes her name on the sign up for chorus.

"Jade Ross." LL's friend winks at her. "Now I have a name to go with that pretty face."

Smooth, I think and can't help but laugh as Becca, Phoebe, and I sign up, too.

* * *

Sitting in English, listening to Mr. Mandel give out a list of the semester's required reading, I overhear a group of implants whispering behind me. The name Lucas Links catches my attention. I try to force my ear elsewhere, but the dark-haired, green-eyed, square-jawed man-boy has obviously piqued my interests.

Chewing on my pencil, my thoughts wander. He's tall and built, not lanky like the majority of boys our age. His clothes fit him flawlessly. His shirts hug his pecs and biceps just enough that you know they're there. And his butt … hmm … football pants would surely look great on him, but probably no better than his dark jeans that rest perfectly on his hips. He seriously has the nicest ass.

Get a hold of yourself! I silently scold myself.

But Lord help me, I think as I lean back and listen.

"He's so fine … Have you heard what he did in the storage closet."

"I heard he could make a girl orgasm just by talking to her."

"I am going to have him just once before graduation. Since he and Sadi"—must be the blonde with zero social skills—"split up, he's on the market."

"I heard that boy was hung."

Oh my … My chair tips back, and I not so gracefully

grab the desk, barely catching myself from falling on my ass.

Serves you right, Tessa.

After righting myself, I look around to see who may have witnessed my moment of idiocy.

No one, thank God.

* * *

"I talked with Coach V. He said, since you just transferred, and if you are interested, you could join the field hockey team."

Phoebe looks up from her schedule with hopeful eyes. "I wouldn't have to try out?"

"I mean, you may not start at first, but we can practice and get you caught up. Then maybe—"

"I'll have to ask Mrs. Brooks." *Her new foster mother.*

"We can go to the office. Mrs. Murry would let you use the phone to call home."

At the use of *home*, her eyes do some nervous flutter thing, and I immediately feel like a jerk.

"I didn't mean—"

"It is what it is, right?" She shrugs. "And yeah, if you think she won't be upset, I think I'd like that. But I don't have a uniform and—"

"Gym clothes for practices, and there are plenty of uniforms in the storage locker."

She smiles genuinely now; I assume the ease of not having to ask an almost stranger whose home you just moved into causes some anxiety. "Then yes. Definitely yes."

I open my locker and shove my books in before Study Hall, which is right before lunch, and something falls out of it.

I pick up the paper and open it.

*Tessa Ross,
You're lovely.*

"Did you get a note?" Jade asks from behind me.

"Yeah. Weird. I have no idea who it is." *I mean, I have a suspicion, but it couldn't be.* I hand her the note.

"It's from Lucas. He asked for your number, too!" Jade giggles.

"And you gave it to him?" I gasp.

"Tommy asked for it nicely, so I gave him both of ours."

"Jade, seriously?"

Right now, I feel a lot like one of our barn cats getting that fourth belly rub, the one that lets you know they seriously only wanted three. But, instead of hissing or scratching my best friend and cousin, I slam my locker and walk away.

I have spent my life involved in the farm, my family, our church and, over the past few years, worrying over Alex and Jade. With the heavy hanging over me at home, now is *not* the time to allow my stomach to get all tied up in knots over a boy, no matter how incredibly good-looking he is.

Let's not forget the conversation I overheard about LL, because that is definitely not what I want in my life.

When I'm ready, I'd like to date a guy who, like Jade mentioned, hasn't worked for my family. I'd like to fall in love, not become he sees me some sort of challenge, and definitely not just because his best friend makes Jade all giddy and flirty.

I certainly don't like the way I felt when LL looked at me. And I don't like the fact that the note, now fisted in my hand, makes me feel like I'm Supergirl holding kryptonite when I should be throwing it as far away from me as I can.

There is, however, something about him that unnerves me. Or maybe he just gets on my nerves. I don't have the time or the luxury for being weak. Not now when Alex and Jade finally seem to be breathing again and not with the dark cloud hanging over the farm.

I walk to the trash can and toss the note.

Practice

Chapter Three

Tessa

I thought the only thing I could truly love more than my hair is finding gratification from helping my loved ones — but, turns out, I also have this uncanny ability to blur those that take up too much space in my head, for the rest of the day, I do just that.

Phoebe Maxwell has the most amazing smile, and she's lit up most of the day. She's over the moon excited that she will be playing field hockey with Becca, Jade, and I. During gym class, Coach Val let us grab her gear, and she and I happen to both wear size seven shoes, so we cleaned up my old cleats, and I gave her my new ones. She tried to object, but I told her that the old ones were my favorite, anyway—they were all broken in. Aside from that, I loved that she was getting something only a little bit used, as I just wore them around the house to try to break them in.

I don't know her story, nor will I pry, but it seems to me that a girl like Phoebe deserves some good in her life. If being part of a team and wearing only a partially- used pair of cleats makes her smile like that, she's definitely the kind of person I want to surround myself with. The bonus, in which I do not share, is that no one on the team has seen them, so they'll never know. Not that it matters to possibly anyone but me, but it does matter to me. I'm not sure how, but I know she and I are going to be great friends.

Walking out of the locker room door, a little bit of that blur disappears, knowing we're in close proximity and getting closer every second to that football field, in which we have to pass to get to our practice.

Walking past the football players and cheerleaders, we hear a whistle, followed by, "Nice skirt, pretty girl."

I look at Jade, because I know that voice—LL's sidekick—and see her raise a finger over her shoulder.

"Damn, Tommy, was that your girl?" LL's unmistakable voice booms in fake shock.

"You're breaking my heart, pretty girl," Tommy calls after her.

I look back and see him drop to his knees.

I elbow Jade and tilt my head back, knowing she'll love it.

Jade turns around and gives him a quick smile, whereas I jog ahead.

***

Today at practice, we ran the perimeter at the state park that borders the school's property, including the one hundred plus stairs, two times. So, as much as I thought Phoebe and I would be great friends, I'm thinking she's going to hate me after this practice. Hell, I hate me right now.

When we return to the locker room, Coach V is waiting.

"This is like basic training, ladies. It'll show us who is varsity field hockey material and who isn't. If it's not for you, don't bother coming back tomorrow. Half of you will make it through the next two weeks, and the others will walk away. It's not for everyone. We're looking for skill and heart. That's a wrap." He claps. "See you all tomorrow." Then he leaves the room.

I look at Phoebe who, God love her, is still smiling.

"Let's shower at home?" Becca asks.

"Okay." Phoebe nods.

"I'm seriously starving," Becca admits.

"See you tomorrow." Phoebe smiles at me as she grabs her bags.

Jade smiles at her. "You got heart, Phoebe. Now let's see your skills tomorrow."

Like seriously, it's infectious.

"Oh, I'll bring it," she calls back as she follows Becca.

Jade looks at me. "We love her, right?"

"Even more so now. She's got some sass in her."

* * *

Showered and dressed, Jade and I walk out to the back parking lot to see if Alex is still here. When I don't see the truck, I realize that he probably thought we were catching a ride with Becca.

Suddenly, I hear a car racing toward the sidewalk then the sound of brakes and …

"You crushed me, pretty girl," Tommy shouts from LL's car as they pull up next to us.

Jade laughs as Tommy jumps out of the car, shirtless, holding his hand over his heart as he falls dramatically to his knees.

Okay, up close, I kind of like his smile, too. It's … sweet.

The engine to the Trans Am revs, and I decide to ignore it as I dig in my bag for … absolutely nothing. However, I do pull out a note that reads:

You look hot, Tessa.
LL

I roll my eyes, ignore it, and shove it back in my bag.

"Is that how it's gonna be, Tessa?" LL leans over and rests his elbow on the console between the seats, flashing his perfectly white half-smile.

"Oh, I'm sorry, was that from you?" I ask sarcastically.

"You're not used to this kind of attention, are you?" he asks, trying to hide his amusement. "You need to get used to it, Tessa Ross. I'm going to be watching you."

"Sounds kind of stalker-ish, LL."

"No, Tessa, just someone who admires your assets." He looks me up and down.

"Wow, does that normally work for you?" I turn away, annoyed and embarrassed.

"Jade, you ready?"

Jade is kneeling down, laughing at Tommy, who then

stands, pulls her up, and asks, "Can we give you ladies a lift?"

"Sure. We were going to probably walk to Tessa's house, but now I guess we don't have to."

"Thanks for accepting."

"Yeah, thanks, Jade," I grumble as Tommy opens the door and slides in the back.

"Looks like you're up here with me, Tessa Ross." Lucas states the obvious.

"Oh my, I feel—"

"Honored?" He grins.

I get in and sit. "Not the word I was looking for, but whatever."

I cross my arms over my chest and hear him chuckle.

Ignoring him, I look back and see Jade's face lit up as she smiling at Tommy who points to the clouds through the T-top, resting his head on her shoulder. Then I turn and look out the window, secretly wishing I could crawl out of it.

Lucas revs the engine then hits the gas, flying through the now near-empty parking lot and hanging a crazy fast right on Main Street as I scramble to put on my seat belt.

A few blocks down, he grumbles, "Fuck."

I look at him then follow his gaze. Immediately, I see that blonde, Sadi, half a block down, looking toward us.

"Don't ask questions, just bend down and hide," he almost demands.

I do what he asks immediately then get pissed at myself for doing so.

"Okay, the coast is clear," he says much softer this time. "Sorry, Tessa. Crazy ex."

Pissed, I spit, "That won't happen again."

His green eyes flash in something like amusement, but different. Something ... way different.

"That cloud looks like a monkey," Tommy says from the back seat. "Do you like animals, Jade?"

"Yes. Why?" Jade stills.

"Just wondering. I want to know everything about you. You're perfect on the outside. I just want to know you. Is that all right?"

"I guess so. Since you asked so nicely."

"I told you, Jade. I always will."

As we get closer to the farm, I feel incredibly uncomfortable.

Jade leans forward and taps Lucas on the shoulder. "Could you pull up this road and let us out? I don't want my aunt and uncle to get upset about us riding with you guys without asking first."

Lucas pulls over, reaches across the car, and pushes the release on my seat belt. His hand lingers for a second on my leg, and my skin tingles with adrenaline. I even feel my entire body begin to heat.

"I think you're hot. You'd have to agree I'm not hard on the eyes, either. Just think about it. I would love to spend time with you, Tessa Ross." He squeezes my leg, and I jerk back.

"Thank you for the ride." Uncomfortable, I shove the door open and jump out. Jade follows.

"Come to my game this weekend?" Tommy asks Jade.

"My cousin plays. Of course, I'll be there."

"Oh, that's right. Well, when I make a touchdown and hold my hand like this"—Tommy grins, making his fingers into a J—"you know I'm thinking of you, pretty girl."

Jade blushes, and I almost laugh, because I think this is the first time I've ever seen that. But I don't, because I'm pretty sure I am fire engine red from the tips of my toes to the top of my head.

Blue Love

Once Lucas pulls away, Jade laughs. "He's *so* cute and funny, and he really likes me!"

The rest of the quarter mile walk up Old Stage Road, grinning from ear to ear, Jade gives a recount on the two-mile ride, as if I wasn't in the same vehicle. Hell, I'm pretty sure she thinks she was on her own planet.

I love that she's happy, and I love that she doesn't even notice I'm kind of a mess, so I listen intently.

That borrowed happiness dissipates, though, as soon as we walk into the house and I see two old suitcases by the door.

Jade gives me a questioning look, and I do what I always do—I wall up and act unaffected, minimizing the stress it may cause Jade to see me emotional, thus making her forget that, for the past five minutes, she was happier than she's ever been.

I shrug and let the numbness overtake me.

The lingering clouds are about to break, a storm is about to rock Ross Farms, and I have to be stronger than ever. Strong for Jade, for Alex, for Kendall, for Jake—basically for everyone.

But can I be?

"I think I saw Dad's truck out back, in front of the shop. I'll call you later?"

I nod as she hugs me tightly before walking out the door.

Standing at the sink, I see Mom holding Jake's and Kendall's hands as they walk from the barn to the house.

* * *

The blur proves to be penetrable as we all sit around the table. I'm not sure what I expected. These are my people, the ones I hold the nearest and dearest.

Dad stands at the head of it, and when he places a sad smile on his face, my heart immediately hurt.

Lots of words are spoken, but the short version is that things changed between my parents. The playfulness between them ended some time ago. I know this. Even before the past month, I caught Mom crying in the bathroom more than once. And, deep down, I knew that the thorough cleaning was not the normal organizing of the house that takes place in the fall.

When my knee begins bouncing under the table, I'm overwhelmed with the want to run, to avoid what's coming next.

Dad takes a deep breath and tells us that he and Mom need a break from one another. That it has nothing to do with us, the kids. The part that nearly causes the dam to break is that Mom already has an apartment ten miles away and is going there tonight. I didn't expect that so soon, and I feel betrayed because, out of all of us, I spent the most time with Mom over the past few months, and she said ... nothing.

Dad continues, "We decided it would be best for you all to stay here for the week so you can settle into the new school year."

Dad looks at me and doesn't say anything. And, although I've been strong ... so strong over the past few years, he's looking at me like he did when I was younger. It's no secret that when I allow myself to feel, I become a bit hard to handle. Even I'm aware of it.

My chest tightens, and I feel my breaths become harder and faster.

Dad begins talking again. "You are not choosing when and where you go between our places. You're still our children, so we make those choices. Maggie and I agree that's too heavy a cross for you all to carry, so there will be no discussion or choices about this. It's for the adults in the situation to make. Maggie's going to get the apartment set up and ready for the weekend. Then we'll discuss how the weekends will work."

"Or weeks," Mom says.

I've never seen Dad pissed at Mom, or hurt by her, for that matter, because it's never happened. His eyes now, though, they flash both feelings at the same time.

Sensing things are about to get heated, something Dad said neither of them wants, Mom stands, eyes shining with unshed tears, and holds out her arms. "Come give me a hug, and I'll get on my way."

* * *

As soon as Mom leaves, I put my shoes on and head outside. The door slamming causes the first tear to fall.

Five. My feet pound on the cracked sidewalk, and I swear to God above I'm going to fix that damn door myself. Then, in the next breath, I hope it never gets fixed, because it's just a damn door.

I also couldn't care less that my feet hurt from running for almost two hours at practice and my body is exhausted.

Four. I inhale deeply as I run between the fields of hay now laying on the ground, because Dad cut it at some point over the weekend. Or, hell, maybe just today and did so when he knew his family was falling apart.

Dad said it was a "*Good year. We're blessed to get a second cutting.*" I wonder if he's still feeling that way, and I wonder if the extra money really means a damn thing.

Faster.

Three. My feet scream at me as I pass the rows of corn

and wonder if we're going to be okay or, if by mid-September, all semblance of normalcy will be gone.

No one died, like in Jade's family, but after the accident, after her family was altered, Aunt Janet fell apart epically. And, for a couple years, Uncle Jack's business nearly crumbled. Then Jade stopped seeing her mother altogether.

Two. I pant as my feet hit the overgrown grass and take no caution in crushing the mixed blue and white flowering weeds beneath my feet. Because I will spend the next few weeks clearing this spot, because God above knows, I'm going to need to come back here much more than ever before.

I head into the woods, pushing through the burdock bushes, leaping over the ferns, past the unkempt pathway. I make my way down the steep hillside not nearly fast enough to get to the water, to see the falls, to plead for it to wash away this hurt, this anger, this pain. To beseech it to make me feel like nothing will ever be the same again. To beg for its strength, because I'm going to need it, maybe more now than ever before.

"One," I yell up to the sky and hear my broken voice echo through the woods as I stand on the edge of the creek.

"What the fuck?" I scream, and it feels so good to scream such a word that I do it again and again and again as I stomp through the water, my shoes still on.

Afraid the force of the water will break me apart if I sit beneath it, I sit next to the waterfall instead and throw stones as I watch the water crash down over the rocks.

I cry, I scream, I pray, I look for more rocks to throw, and I close my eyes.

I'm unsure if I dozed off or just spaced out, but when I

open my eyes, the sun is starting to set behind the towering pines.

It will soon be bedtime and, as much as I don't love the idea of heading back, I know that Kendall and Jake will need me now more than ever.

Trudging up the hill, Alex's words, '*We'll be fine. Always are,*' whispers in my head. And I know for sure I will make damn sure we are.

When I reach the edge of the woods, I see Cory, Molly's boyfriend, holding her as she cries. I clear my throat, not wanting to witness a make-out session, if it gets to that, as I walk toward them.

"You okay, Tessa?" Cory asks.

I nod and start to jog home, happy that Molly has Cory, that I have one less person to "hold up."

Walking into the house, I notice the answering machine flashing and hit *play* as I take off my drenched sneakers.

"*Hey, Tessa, it's me, Jade. You wanna talk, I'm here.*"

Word clearly has already gotten out.

The next. "*Me again. To clarify, just like you were there for me, I'm here, okay?*"

The next. "*Hello, this message is for Tessa. I was wondering if you could give me a call and remind me of what our government assignment was for tonight.*"

The voice is familiar, but LL isn't in my Government class.

Whatever.

I hit erase, and the phone immediately rings.

"You wanna grab that, Tessa?" Dad yells from the living room.

"Sure, Dad," I yell back, surprised he's inside.

I answer, "Hello?"

"Tessa, do you have a pen?"

Not sure who is on the other end, I grab one from the counter. "Yep."

"Jot down this number."

"Go ahead."

"Three, one, five, five, five, five, one, two, one, two."

"Okay, got it. Can I ask who's calling, please?"

"Shot to the heart." He chuckles.

My back straightens with immediate recognition.

"You there, Tessa Ross?"

I open the door, drag the cord out to the mudroom, and then shut the door behind me.

"Look, *LL*, I didn't give you my number, so how about you lose it? And we don't have any classes together, so lose the lame excuses to call here, as well."

"Actually, we do have classes together. A few."

"Oh my God, you are so full of garbage."

"Changed my schedule because I got stuck in the same classes with my ex. Government, Bio, and—"

"I have things to do. There was no Government homework."

"Tessa, you're not making this shit easy, you know." He sighs.

"You need to move on, because I'm not easy at all. And—"

"Not looking for easy with you."

"Oh, right. You've made this a challenge for yourself. Don't bother. I don't have the time, and I am not the least bit interested."

"Lie to me, but not to yourself, Tessa Ross. See you in school tomorrow. Use my number whenever you feel the urge. It's a cell phone."

"Am I supposed to be impressed by that and your fancy black sports car?" I immediately regret it.

He laughs quietly and deeply. "Baby, I don't need those things to impress. Just happen to have them."

Flustered, I say, "Goodnight, LL."

"Sweet dreams, Tessa. See you in them soon."

I open the door and slam the phone down.

"Who was on the phone?" Dad calls from the other room.

"Wrong number," I say as I make my way to the living room. "I'm gonna shower."

* * *

After showering—my third of the day—I wrap up in my robe and head out through the living room and up the stairs to get my pajamas on, then head back downstairs.

Dad is on the phone, and Kendall and Jake are sitting on the couch, both looking extremely sad.

It breaks my heart to see them like that.

"What are we watching?" I ask, wedging myself between them.

Kendall crosses her arms. "Not ER."

"It's on after our school bedtime," Jake mumbles.

I look at the TV as the commercial ends. "So, it's Home Improvement, then."

"Dad's favorite," Kendall whispers as she leans against me.

I wrap my arm around her and Jake. It takes Jake a minute before he caves and lays his head on my shoulder.

"This sucks, Tessa," he grumbles.

"I know right now it does, but we Rosses are strong."

He says nothing.

"Jade called, left two messages to check on us. I think we should call her back and let her know we're just fine."

"After we do that, can we sleep in your bed with you tonight?" Kendall asks.

"Well, that may be a little tight, but maybe we can all get our sleeping bags and sleep on the back deck."

"Could we really, Tessa? On a school night? Won't Dad be mad?" Kendall asks.

"Look at him. He won't even notice." I make a joke about it, but it's not a joke. He's been so distant. "But that's why this is going to be so cool," I whisper then tickle them.

* * *

After Kendall and Jake fall asleep on the deck, I head inside to grab my bag and a flashlight to get ahead on some reading.

Alex is in the kitchen, getting a glass of water.

"Where did you disappear to?"

He looks at me over his glass, and I nod once.

"Right. You and Molly, I suppose?"

He swallows his water then sets the cup on the counter. "She's our Mom, Tessa. Just checking in on her."

I'm pissed, more than I thought I would be.

"Yeah, well, she left us. How do you think Dad feels about you going there?"

"He thought it was a good idea."

"Right," I huff as I grab the flashlight from the cabinet and my bag from the hook by the back door. "Goodnight."

"Tessa, it sucks, but it'll work out," he says to my back.

More so than Mom leaving us, it hurts that I feel like I've been stabbed in the back again tonight. The one Alex just drove into it is so much deeper.

"Yeah, I'm sure it will."

He grabs my hand and tugs me back. I turn around and scowl at him.

"Don't go TT on me." Before I have a chance to reply, he hugs me. "We'll get through this."

"You keep saying that. It doesn't—"

Hugging me tighter, he says, "Those words mean something, Tessa. It's what you've said for five years now, so don't kick dirt on them."

Tears begin to fill my eyes again, and I finally hug him back. "Okay. Okay, I promise."

He steps back. "How are Kendall and Jake?"

"Tucked away in sleeping bags, sound asleep on the deck."

"Want me to sleep out there?" he asks.

"We're good."

Outside, I shine the flashlight in the bag and see the note LL somehow snuck in my bag. Then I see the one I crumpled and tossed in the garbage at school.

My stomach tenses, and then … it flips.

I shove them back into my bag, zip it up, and set it on the deck before leaning back in the chaise. Looking up at the sky, I watch the stars twinkle and dance.

Not a cloud up there tonight. The storm seems to have passed. How does that happen on a day like today? It makes no sense at all.

I whisper in a direction in which I don't even know, because I'm unsure who the words belong to, but I do know they must be spoken.

"You're giving me mixed signals."

I allow myself to silently cry about the whole situation at home. I honestly don't understand it. And when the pain from overthinking it hurts too much, I think of the hottest white-hat boy, L-L-I-N-K-S 1, LL … Lucas Links, and my thoughts immediately fall to the way he looks at me, the fact he's written me notes, his eyes, and how much I'd like to feel him hug me, engulf me in his arms, and yes, his lips.

The thoughts make me feel dizzy, and the emotions make me tired, so I close my eyes.

* * *

I wake as the dawn breaks and startle when I realize where I am, and then I blush when I remember where my dream took me.

He was smiling at me, the most attractive smile in the world. And then he kissed me, and his dream kiss felt so real that my lips are still tingling.

I run my fingers over my lips and imagine how it would feel while I was awake. Would it be as warm, as soft, or as sweet? Would I kiss him back like I did in my dream, and would it make me smile the same? Would his green eyes show kindness and not malice? And why was I wearing a ring?

I guess none of that really matters, but I do know that when I close my eyes, as I am doing now, I can still see my smile like it was playing on a movie screen. And I can see the one he gave me in return. The look in his eyes was kind in my dreams, not like the reality.

I had a ring on my finger.

"Tessa?"

My eyes pop open, and I watch Kendall yawn and stretch.

"Good morning."

"Did Mom come back?" she whispers as she sits up.

I shake my head and smile softly as I push my sleeping bag down and get out quickly, watching her lower lip tremble. "Which means extra chocolate chips in your waffles. Let's go."

Jake pops out of his sleeping bag. "Me, too?"

"Of course, you, too."

We all rush inside, dragging our sleeping bags.

"I got these. Go get dressed and brush your teeth. I'll make breakfast."

I watch as they both bound into the bathroom to get ready to face the day. And I close my eyes, trying to recall my dream.

When it doesn't happen, I shake my head and realize just how ridiculous I am.

Walking into the kitchen, though, I can't help but wonder, *What was that about?*

In My Dreams

Chapter Four

TESSA

Unnerved by the dream with the kiss and the ring, and having quickly rationalized that it was provoked by the notes, the call, and obviously the fact that my parents' marriage is ending, thus the ring, I have no desire to run into Lucas Links today.

Luckily, I have today and tomorrow to avoid him, and then the weekend is here.

Knowing the forecast is calling for heat and humidity, I French braid Kendall's and my hair, and then I help her pick out a sundress as I grab my Ross Farms tee with the sleeves cut off and a pair of denim cut-offs. After a quick once-over, I'm unsure if the shorts are too short, but since they're mid-thigh still, I'm okay with my choice.

I grab a pair of silver hoops and my cross necklace, putting them on while wondering if it's a bit much. On a scale of one to Jade, I feel I'm safe.

* * *

The fact that Jade was uncharacteristically rushing out the door as soon as Alex and I pulled in and didn't even make us wait for a second for her to come out of the house is telling, and the fact that Alex is ... Alex and not wanting to be late, we left early to get her. And this is why we're now fifteen minutes early to school. And it just so happens that so is the black Trans Am.

Walking past the locker room, I see Tommy standing at the bottom of the stairs, obviously waiting for Jade. I'm sure his friend is going to step out of the men's locker room door, directly across from the stairs, any second.

Before she can say anything, he says, "Good morning."

Alex glares at him.

Normally, I'd stick around, but I need to get out of here.

I call after Jade, who is already shaking her ass as she walks toward the stairs, "I'll be up at the lockers in a minute."

She blushes as she waves and starts up the stairs, pausing when Alex and Tommy exchange words.

Going to Coach V, using the excuse to talk with him about the game schedule, making sure I keep the conversation going until the first bell rang, therefore gaining a hall pass and completely avoiding the Lucas Links situation, I then run through the hall to get to my locker.

When I open it, a note falls out. I quickly pick it up and shove it in my bag. Then I grab my books for the next three classes, hoping to avoid him.

***

Fourth period Economics is the first class I have with Lucas Links and, as with each class today, I have snuck in with the bell, just to ensure I don't get stuck sitting next to him. As luck would have it, Phoebe is sitting next to the door in the back row, and the seat next to her is vacant.

"Mind if I sit next to you?" I ask, not waiting for a reply.

"I mean, sure, but you don't have to," she says sadly.

It hits me then that I didn't sit with her in second and third period. It also hits me that there is no way in hell I'm admitting my entire second day of my senior year has been spent avoiding *him*.

She leans over and whispers, "Is it because you want your cleats back? Because if—"

"No. God, no." I reach over and give her hand a squeeze. "I'm just …" I stop and shake my head. "Things aren't good at …" I snap my mouth shut because "things are not good at *home*" is definitely the wrong thing to say to someone who is in the foster care system. It would be incredibly rude. "I—"

"It's okay. You don't have to explain." She turns and looks to the front of the class.

"I promise I will when I understand it myself, but Phoebe, it has absolutely nothing to do with you. I promise."

"It's okay. Really it is."

Mr. King clears his throat, and I look up.

"Miss Ross, would you like to teach the class today?"

I slide down in my seat when everyone chuckles and shake my head. "I've heard you're a good teacher. I'll let you have a crack at it first."

I hear a deep chuckle then feel eyes burning into me as the class busts up laughing. Luckily, so does Mr. King.

"Let me know if I screw up, will you, Miss Ross?"

"Sure." I smile as my face turns red, and then I glance left and see green eyes, white teeth, and a dimple.

No. Just no, I think as I look away.

Unable to pay attention—seriously, who has shoulders like that?—I watch the time, and a minute before the bell, I whisper to Phoebe, "When the bell rings, we run."

She looks at me then in his direction and back to me, a sly smile crossing her sweet face. She nods once. "Understood."

* * *

Walking into the cafeteria with our lunch trays, we walk toward Alex, and I overhear a part of his and Mike's conversation.

"How are you guys doing?" Mike asks.

"Fine. Just busy," Alex answers, worry etching his face. "After practice, we need to get the hay in the barn. Not much got done yesterday, ya know."

"We can help," Mike offers.

A look of relief and gratitude softens his features. "That would be great."

I hip-check him. "Thanks, Mike."

He lifts his chin. "Course."

Jade is giddy, and even before my butt hits the seat, she starts whispering, but rather loudly, about Tommy this and Tommy that.

Becca and Phoebe immediately get wrapped up in her excitement. Me? I try, but I'm worried she's moving way too fast. I can't bear to see her get hurt. And yeah, I also really freaking hope *he* didn't change his lunches along with his class schedule.

They listen to Jade read notes she has received from Tommy. She is freakishly happy.

A moment later, Tommy walks in and bends over Jade's shoulder, grabbing a carrot off her tray. "Hey, pretty girl," he says before shoving the carrot in his mouth and winking at her.

The chair next to me is pulled away from the table, and I don't even have to look to see who it is.

Then the deep low voice whispers, "You're avoiding me."

Not looking at him, and completely ignoring the way the hair pricks up on the back of my neck when he speaks to me, I say, "I have a busy schedule."

"Gonna want to start freeing that up, Tessa Ross."

The blonde cheerleader, the one who I now know is Lucas's ex, Sadi, walks toward the table, glaring at me and Becca, who happens to be sitting on the other side of him.

Becca looks down, and by the look on Sadi's face, even after yesterday, she looks shocked I'm not doing the same.

"She's not very smart, is she?" I whisper.

Lucas chokes on his water, and I have to bite the insides of my cheeks to stop from smiling.

Sadi stops beside Tommy, who is oblivious to the exchanged looks or anything other than Jade.

He smiles and says, "Hey, girls. This is Jade."

"Seriously?" Sadi sneers as she glares at me and sputters, "Sitting at the kiddie table now?"

I roll my eyes, and I swear steam rolls from her ears as she stomps away.

"Nice meeting you, um ... ladies?" Phoebe yells after her and her friends, and we all laugh.

"So, Tessa, what do I have to do to win your brother over?" Tommy asks, squeezing Jade's shoulder.

"Good luck." Jade giggles as she looks up at him.

"No one will be worthy of Jade. She's the princess," I inform Tommy.

"And, how about you, Tessa? How does one win you over?" Lucas asks.

Becca and Phoebe quickly turn and look at me, and I know damn well this is going to be a conversation I won't be able to avoid later.

Glaring at him, I stand as the bell rings, and as I walk away, Lucas laughs.

I swear I can feel his eyes on me as I exit the cafeteria.

* * *

Walking out of the school for practice, Lucas and Tommy whistle as we hurry past them to head to the Glen to run our asses off, I'm sure.

I catch Lucas watching Tommy, amused as he smiles at Jade. She, of course, smiles back.

"It's a hot one, boys; make sure you stay hydrated," their coach yells as he walks onto the field.

"Head in the game and not on the ass, Tommy." Lucas pats him on the back then directs him to the field.

Feeling a bit of relief yet something nagging, as well, that he hasn't given me any of those looks that makes me feel uneasy, I glance back, and he does the same.

Shit, shit, shit. I turn quickly and hurry ahead of the others.

I hear Tommy laugh and say, "Head in the game and not on the ass, Links."

* * *

I knew Alex would be leaving as soon as he could get off the football field, and I intentionally lulled behind, taking my time showering and also holding a long conversation with Coach V so that we'd miss catching a ride with Becca ... and Lucas Links.

Jade is a bit annoyed, but all I have to do is bring up Tommy and she starts telling me about the notes *again*. She does so for three miles.

I want to be happy for her, I truly do, but I'm also scared as hell she'll get hurt, and I can't imagine anyone hurting her. She's been through enough.

Cresting the hill, I see the driveway littered with vehicles.

"We've got work to do today." I sigh.

"Hot as hell, too. We should grab them some water. Unless you have sun tea brewing."

Mom always has sun tea brewing, but not me.

As soon as I open the door, Dad, who looks exhausted, asks, "You know where the water cooler jugs are?"

I nod.

"Alex brought some hay help. We may have to feed them. There's a lot of work to be done."

"We've got this, Uncle John." Jade hugs him.

"Thanks, Jade." He pats her back then squeezes my shoulder as he walks out the door.

Washing my hands next to Jade, I hear her gasp then laugh.

"What?"

"Look at all those cars."

"I think you need an eye exam." I look out the window. "I see a bunch of trucks, but no ..." I swear my jaw hits the stainless sink, and Jade laughs. "That cannot be—"

"It so is." She grins.

My stomach turns, and worry creeps in.

There is too much to do, too much going on to get distracted, and he is likely to do that to me. Hell, he already has. And I wouldn't consider him a good temptation. I liken him to the apple in the Garden of Eden. And now ... Eden's apple is on the Ross farm.

"You're home!" Kendall says as she and Jake come running out from somewhere in the house.

I grab a towel and dry my hands quickly before hugging her, and then Jake actually allows me to hug him, too.

I sneak a kiss to the top of his head then step back, asking them both, "How was school?"

They tell me about their day—thankfully, they seem to have both had good days—as I grab the water jugs from the pantry. Jake goes on and on about gym class and getting first place in the football throw. I give him a high-five then grab the first of two jugs filled and pull it out of the sink, set it on the counter, and twist the top off the other.

"Fill that, and I'll grab hamburgers and hot dogs out of the freezer.

"Kendall and Jake, will you guys go out back and grab a couple dozen ears of corn?" I ask as I walk back to the mud room and grab a bushel basket.

Kendall smiles. "We have company?"

"Never a dull moment," I say. "Make sure it's sweet corn and not cow."

"I know the difference," Jake huffs.

"I know you do, Jake." I wink.

"Come on, Jake!" Kendall yells as she grabs the basket.

"Hey, wait for me!" He runs out behind her, and I watch out the window as they hurry toward the field, carrying it between them.

"What's going on out there?" Molly asks as she walks out of the family room.

This morning, she said she was going back to her apartment in the morning and had stayed in town while Cory was home.

"We have to feed and water the dogs." I nod to the window. "Hot dogs."

Molly laughs as she looks out.

* * *

When the first load is done, Jade and I are almost to the back of the farm.

We set the basket full of cups and the three jugs of water on the open tailgate then begin filling the cups with ice-cold water.

As soon as the elevator stops, Alex, Mark, Frankie, Ryan, Tommy, and then Lucas slide down the hay elevator, all dripping with sweat.

Jade walks right up to Tommy and hands him a cup of water. And what does he do? He pours it over his head then shakes his hair as he pulls his drenched shirt over his head.

"Much better." He laughs.

She nods. "Totally." Jade then grabs another cup and hurries past everyone else to hand it to him. Her expression? Undeniably giddy.

Not that I could disagree. He is quite perfect. Great definition in his chest, and his abs are well-formed. His smile seems genuine, too.

I watch as her eyes trail down his abs and she bites her lower lip when she looks back up at him.

I hand out the rest of the cups and, embarrassingly enough, notice that Lucas hasn't come to grab one.

Glancing around, I see him sitting on a haybale, wiping his face with his shirt that is now off. Tommy is hot. Lucas is … gorgeous.

I grab a cup, fill it, and then walk it over to him.

"Thanks, Tessa."

"Thank you for your help. It's nice of you." I smile quickly.

"And she can smile," he jokes. "All I have to do is sweat my ass off throwing hay. Good to know."

From behind me, I hear Jake and Kendall yelling my name as they run toward me. "Tessa, Tessa, we have the corn. Can we help you make dinner for all the guys?"

"Sure." I muss up Jake's hair. "Can you start husking the corn? I'll be over in a minute to help."

"You making me dinner?" Lucas asks, and I turn to make a smart-ass comment when he winks. "Our first date."

Shocked silent, I stand there like an idiot as he drinks down his water. Then he stands up, nearly nose to nose with me. I feel like I can't breathe as his green eyes capture mine. I swear my heart skips a beat. Then something in his eyes changes.

When I can't hold in a breath a second more, I exhale.

Lucas smiles but softer this time as he steps back, looking me up and down with an expression that seems conflicted. Then he turns and scales the elevator.

Standing in the loft's opening, I can feel his eyes on me as I hurry to the house to pack up the food.

I stop and let Dad know, "I'm going to cook the burgers and dogs at the pond. I'll take Jake and Kendall with me."

"Thanks, Tessa." He nods.

After the third load is done, we take out more water

jugs then load up the truck. As I climbed in the cab, I look up again and see him watching me, eyes ... intense.

* * *

Walking up from the camp in the woods, carrying the last large pan of burgers and dogs we cooked in the family cabin tucked in the woods on the property, I hear splashing and laughter just beyond the tree line. Once in the clearing I see them all, and when I say all, I mean every one of them, in the pond.

After setting everything out on the huge table that Dad and Alex made last year, I walk over and ring the chow bell, the one Mom and I bought at the country farm store as kind of a joke, because Jake and Kendall were nearly impossible to get out of the pond when we were ready to eat.

Jade stands next to me, a grin I fear will remain on her face until he breaks her heart, which I'm hoping will be before he breaks her cherry, thus ruining our childhood promise to each other and ourselves, as they all swim in.

Watching Lucas step out of the pond and wiping the water off his insanely handsome face, I completely understand how one could get swept up. I force myself to look away and grab a towel for Kendall and Jake.

Within minutes, plates and the tables are full. Dad and the kids sit next to me, all of us watching the old and new hay help eat, laugh, and chat amongst themselves. The conversation is mostly about football.

I steal a glance toward Lucas as he is doing the same. This time, I summon enough courage to hold his eyes, not wanting to look away, to look like a thief, expecting him to look away first, yet he doesn't.

I know of his reputation, none of the things about

Lucas have been whispered about, leading me to believe he's ashamed of who he is. The hot, popular, rich football player, who's had sex with several girls, and a line is forming as we speak of girls at Blue Valley High, all wanting a piece of him. He also just broke up with a girl who, even without a frothing mouth, was obviously rabid.

Even if I had a million falls left in my lifetime, I would never stand in a line for a boy. Nor do I want to be with someone for the sake of convenience, which seems like this is to me. I suppose it's normal to want to couple up. Convenient that two sets of best friends would want to do so. I don't think relationships should ever be based on convenience, either.

"Can we make s'mores?" Jake asks.

Lucas smirks, his dimple deepening, eyes sparkling, knowing somehow that he's going to win this ... stare off.

"Yeah, of course."

I roll my eyes and look away as I head to grab the graham crackers, chocolates, and marshmallows.

"Remember I like mine burnt?" Jake says as I pull the flaming marshmallow out of the fire.

"Jake, it's literally flaming." I laugh before blowing it out.

Through the smoke, I see Mom's car pulling down the driveway. I look at Alex, who shrugs.

Dad appears at my side. "She's your mom, kiddo. Go say hi."

I scowl at him. "Why is she here?"

"Taking the kids tonight. Alex has a game Saturday, so she wanted them an extra night. I know she wants you to come, too."

"When pigs fly," I huff.

"Go say hello, Tessa Anne."

I glare at him.

"Now," he insists.

Forgetting we have a table full, I stomp forward, stopping just far enough away that I don't have to actually interact with her.

"Tessa, she's still Mom," Alex whispers.

I cross my arms over my chest, just finally realizing I am about to be the only one who hasn't seen her new place. It hurts. It hurts a lot. And hurt turns to anger when the realization hits that I'm the one who busted my ass helping her pack under the false pretense that we were "cleaning." Anger turns to rage, and I grind my feet into the ground, as if that alone will keep me from having to go any closer.

When she walks toward us, I feel trapped, though I'm in the middle of one hundred acres of wide-open space.

When she hugs me, I don't return it, and then she moves on to Alex. After that, she asks, "When will you two be stopping by?"

"When will you be coming home?" I snap, and my feet that I planted and had felt like lead, no longer do.

Five, I think as I turn away, but there is no door that will slam shut. There are people; some staring at me.

Shit! I scream in my head when Lucas Links stands up and steps over the bench.

"Tessa," Mom calls from behind me as I run toward the pond.

"Give her time," I hear Alex try to calm her.

Four, I think as I pass the table.

Three. I kick off one sandal as I run toward the pond.

Two. I kick off the other.

One. I throw off my tank top and dive into the water.

As soon as I surface, I hear a loud and familiar voice yell, "Cannonball!" and then a squeal as the water splashes over my head.

Blue Love

One arm over the other, I swim toward the floating dock as fast as I can, hoping to expel some of the emotions built up inside of me and pull myself up. Jade is not two seconds behind.

"You all right?"

"Yep, just pissed."

"Focus on something else, Tessa, like the trees." Jade points toward the boys. "Those tall, thick, strong trees."

Laughing, because if I don't, I know my anger, that's at the point of boiling right now, will turn to tears. I smack her hand. "It's not polite to point, you know."

"You're going to be okay, Tessa. We'll keep you busy," she promises, and then Frankie and Ryan dive in.

* * *

After a few rounds of King of the Raft—more accurately, Queen of the Raft, because I managed to be the last standing every time—we all swim in.

Of course I notice Lucas and Tommy helping to carry firewood up from down by camp, which means Alex is building a fire.

I'm glad we'll be staying here for a bit. I can't even imagine going back to the house, with more than half the occupants now gone. It just isn't normal.

Alex threw Jade and me towels when we finally came out of the pond, and yes, the cold spring-fed water did help to settle the anger.

Drying off, I watch Dad walk over to Lucas and pat him on the back. "Thank you, boys, for the help. I'm going to head home. Anyone need a lift up the hill?" When no one accepted, Dad chuckled. "All right then, you have two hours, tops. You need to get some rest for the big game tomorrow night."

"Dad, could you call Uncle Jack and let him know where we are?" Alex asked.

Dad nods and waves to Alex as he walks toward me.

"You get it all worked out?"

I shrug.

"See you at home."

Home, I think … *Home*.

Dad nods and waves as he walks to the truck.

* * *

Throughout the night, I find myself thieving glances at Lucas, and each time I do, he's doing the same. By the time the sun is setting, it doesn't feel as wrong, and we both even smile at each other.

For Jade, and the distraction, I may be able to play this game … maybe.

After Alex puts out the fire and the others are leaving, Jade motions to Tommy and Lucas. "Ride with us."

Alex looks at me with annoyance and concern showing, even in the dark.

I roll my eyes. "See you at home."

He nods then walks to his truck.

Once in the driver's seat, Tommy and Lucas jump in the back, and we follow Alex up the dirt road and stop by Lucas's car.

Alex reaches his arm out and waves as he pulls onto Harvest Road.

I watch as Lucas walks to his car, leans in through the open top, grabs something, and then walks toward us.

Jade slides out, and I force myself to do the same.

Walking over toward me, sweatshirt slung over his shoulder, Lucas holds out a familiar-looking envelope. "Can you give this back to your dad and let him know that we had a great time." He then takes his sweatshirt and tosses it over my shoulders.

"I'd love to help peel you out of those wet clothes, but something tells me you're more than a first date girl. And Tessa, it was a great first date."

"Bold move, LL." I hold up the sweatshirt. "And even bolder presumption."

"Nothing presumed. We swam, we ate, we stared at each other over a romantic fire." He smirks in amusement over that last part. "That's a date."

"You are so full of yourself."

"Sure *of* myself," he corrects. Then, as he steps toward me, he whispers, "My boy Tommy is going to ask Jade out for dinner and a movie. I'm guessing that won't go over well unless you and I go, too." He grabs his sweatshirt off my shoulders and, in a swift move, pulls it over my head. "Shouldn't be a big deal to us, since we've had our first date already, but it's gonna be to them, so play along, will you?"

I'm ready to call him out on his arrogance once again, as I push my arms through the sleeves, when I hear Tommy, reminding me that Lucas and I are not the only ones here. Thankfully, it's dark because, if not, he'd surely see me blush.

"Pizza and a movie tomorrow night after the game?" Tommy asks Jade.

"Well, we'll see. I think it'll take a lot more of that free help to win Alex over," Jade flirts … blatantly as hell.

"Thank God we're past that awkward stage," Lucas whispers jokingly before finally stepping back, allowing me to breathe.

"Thanks for your help"—I hold up the envelope—"but this was earned."

He rolls his glorious green eyes. "You have seen me shirtless, Tessa Ross. I lift more than that in my sleep."

I roll mine back. "You need to get that ego in check."

"I already put it into perspective; I wouldn't want to have to wrestle with it again."

Again, for the second time today, I bite my cheeks so I don't laugh, and he walks away.

He looks back and catches me looking at his ass.

"Squats." He chuckles. "It's all about the squats."

The entire ride, I listen to Jade recap the night, and it's not as annoying this time. It's kind of like reading a different point of view.

When we get back, Alex is waiting for us.

He looks us both up and down and shakes his head. "Nice sweatshirts."

Jade grins. "I think it was nice of them."

I hand him both Lucas's and Tommy's envelopes as I walk toward the house and say, "Yes, it was. See you tomorrow, Jade."

I grab a glass of water as I watch them drive out of the driveway, counting down the days before I can finally drive after nine so Alex doesn't have to take Jade home every time we hang out.

I would never have wished on one shooting star for the feeling, the warmth, the butterflies that overcome me with the thought of the nights to come where we will be hanging out with the implants ... the white hat boys, but right now, I will bask in them.

Sweatshirt Weather

Chapter Five

TESSA

I woke up wrapped in his sweatshirt and couldn't help but inhale his scent—warm and outdoorsy and comfortable, so comfortable.

A light knock on my door has me pulling the thick cotton away from my nose just in time as Dad walks in.

"Tessa, you up?"

"Yep." I sit up and look at the alarm clock, realizing I only have twenty minutes to get ready. Normally, that's not an issue, but now it seems a burden. "Quiet here today, huh?"

"Too quiet." He looks sadly at Kendall's empty bed then back at me. "So, your birthday is in a couple days. I thought maybe Saturday night you'd want to invite some friends to stay at the camp. I know it's last minute. Things have been a little hectic around here, and I'm sorry I didn't get to mention it last night. But it's all set. Alex and a couple of friends will be in tents outside to chaperone."

I can't help but smile.

"I have to deliver a load of hay to New Jersey Saturday evening. Leaving after the game. Your mom will be stopping up to check on you."

"Forget it then," I grumble, flopping back on my bed.

"You're still my kid, Tessa, soon-to-be eighteen or eighty."

"Alex will be there, Dad. I really don't want to see *her*, especially with my friends around."

"I'll see what I can do, but Sunday after church, we're all going to have dinner together for your birthday. She's your mother, and regardless of what's going on with us, she does love you. No arguments. Got it?" he says sternly.

I throw back the covers and slide out of bed. Stomping past him, I head down to the bathroom.

I shower then blow out my hair, which is a horrible idea since it now resembles the implant cheerleaders. I quickly braid the sides of my hair back, leaving the rest hanging, then fasten the two braids together.

The bathroom door opens a crack, and Alex yells in, "We're out in five."

"I'm hurrying." I sigh as I grab a pair of jeans and the Pearl Jam T-shirt I got at the concert Aunt Josie took Jade and I to over the summer.

I look at the sweatshirt in a pile on the floor, and my hand itches to grab it, but I decide that would look completely desperate, and I am certainly not that.

* * *

Blue Love

Outside my locker, I invite Jade, Becca, and Phoebe to stay over Saturday night at the camp after the game. All four of them answer with a resounding *yes*.

Part of me is glad, and another part is disappointed throughout the day that Lucas keeps his distance. It has, however, given me the chance to watch his interaction with the female fan club that just seems to be around him at all times, which is something I would not want in my life.

I do, however, like that he's a constant presence and that his eyes hold less malice and more of something else, something unrecognizable.

After practice, I ride with Alex to drop off Jade, and then we get snacks for the sleepover.

Dad and Alex go to bed early, but I'm unable to sleep, so I do laundry as I watch *Picket Fences*.

When I pull out the last load, I get pissed at myself when I see the Blue Valley sweatshirt and, on the back, instead of Ross, it says Links.

Holding it to my nose, I inhale and ... he's gone.

After putting away the laundry, I stand in the doorway and look at my empty room. For years, I've dreamed of having my own. But, right now, it doesn't feel like mine.

I grab my pillow and a blanket and head down to sleep on the couch.

When I wake, Dad is about to head out to meet the guys to load the truck and Alex is cooking eggs.

"You do know that's a chicken's entire weeks' worth of work in that pan, right?"

Ignoring me, Alex looks at Dad. "Season's changing."

Dad sets his coffee cup down. "Is that so?"

Jokingly, he nods toward me. "We can always tell when we're closing in on deer season around here."

I smack him.

After Alex gobbles down his eggs, he leaves to go do one of the things Alex does to calm his nerves or relax—either fish, clean guns, or maybe his old go-to, which is chin-ups in the old barn. I get to cleaning, and after cranking up the family boom box to listen to this week's top one hundred—starting late of course—I run up the stairs to write down the first song of the countdown I hear.

I grab my blue spiral notebook, flip to the blank page, and wait excitedly, because Jade and I consider music to be much more reliable than the magic eight ball and the first song sets the tone for the week ahead.

"Number thirty-three on this week, climbing from last week's number forty-six, "Hey Jealousy" by The Gin Blossoms."

After a few seconds of listening, I put a big star by the song, knowing it's one that I will try to catch on the radio and tape onto a cassette, or buy next time I hit Record Town. If I like them, I'll grab the tee-shirt, too.

The next song is not my cup of tea, and I already wish I'd taped the Gin Blossoms as I begin to dust my room.

Number thirty-one makes me think of Mom and Dad, but as it goes on, it really makes me think of Sadi and how maybe, if she was less a bitch, sent him a mixed tape of songs like the one by Expose, he would be more receptive to working out whatever issue broke them up. But I also think, screw her. She's a nasty bitch, and he's lucky to be rid of her.

The only other song that has me dropping the broom or dust rag to write down with a star is "Cryin'" by Aerosmith. The rest of the countdown continues, but "Hey Jealousy" plays in my head the entire time I clean until a song I remember Dad playing comes on, Elvis's "Can't Help Falling In Love," remade by UB40. Then I get emotional.

Looking at the clock, I realize it's time to shower, but

first, I need to call Mom and tell her I'll be picking up the kids for Alex's game.

Except, I have no clue what her number is.

Fighting the urge to run down to the falls, knowing I don't have the time, I head to the shower.

Afterward, I walk out in my robe to find Alex standing in the middle of the living room.

"You done with the shower?"

I nod then ask, "Do you know if Mom has a phone yet?"

He nods. "She and Dad both got cellular phones. Both numbers are on the corkboard by the phone."

"They got what?" I gasp.

"Cell—"

"It was a rhetorical question. Those two won't even get a freaking cordless because they think whatever we have to say to our friends should be able to be said in front of the family."

"Things are changing."

"They certainly are," I huff as I walk to the kitchen.

"House looks good, Tessa," he yells to me.

"It took thirty-three songs," I grumble.

* * *

After Mom told me that she would be bringing the kids, my mood went from bad to worse, and I end up pulling into the game a little bit later than planned.

Finding parking is an issue. Apparently, the entire town is now showing up to football games.

I easily find Jade, Phoebe, and Becca sitting on the bleachers, a few rows behind the cheerleaders.

Great, I think as I make my way up to them.

Sitting, I comment, "Nice seats."

Jade elbows me and I can't help but smile for her as I look at the field and see Tommy making a J with his fingers.

"He's just"—she sighs, and her head falls onto my shoulder—"everything."

I look at the clock. Only two minutes in, and the Blue Valley Saints are already ahead by six.

The game is nothing like the few I've attended over the past few years when trying to get Alex involved in the game again. It's fast-paced and there is little standing around. Lucas Links cannot throw a bad pass if he wanted to, and between Tommy and Alex, they catch every one of them.

I swear I get teary-eyed watching Alex.

"He's really good," I tell Jade.

Jade grins. "I told you he's everything."

"I wasn't talking about Tommy." I roll my eyes.

"Yeah, your guy ain't too bad, either."

"She wasn't talking about Lucas," Phoebe says. "She's talking about the other guy killing it out there. You know, your cousin, her brother?"

"Oh my God, I totally love you." I lean over to give her a hug.

Jade blocks me. "Hey, remember who your best friend is here."

Phoebe and I both laugh.

With each touchdown Tommy makes, he holds up his "J" and smiles at Jade.

It's cute, but not nearly as cute as when Alex returns a punt and runs eighty yards to score a touchdown then holds up his hand in a "J," points at Jade, and shakes his head. Jade laughs when she sees Tommy look down, covering his face.

"Busted." Phoebe laughs.

It's not until Alex's big play that I realize Mom is

behind us when Jake and Kendall both freak out right along with me, and then they climb down to sit next to us.

It's not until then that I realize Sadi is cheering in front of me and throwing nasty looks at us whenever she can.

I choose to ignore her as best as I can.

However, Phoebe surprises us all when she yells, "Your face is going to freeze like that, girl."

Sadi glares at her, yet continues cheering.

The game ends with the Saints winning by twenty-one points. It's the first game that the Saints have won at home in over a decade.

Everyone, including us, rush the field. Jade scans the crowd for Tommy, and I watch as she runs up to him. It's then I find Alex and hurry toward him.

Tommy looks uncomfortable as hell, knowing Alex is on to him and Jade, and when Alex grabs his shoulder to stop him from meeting her, Tommy hangs his head.

"You wanna hug, Tommy boy?" Alex teases, nodding toward Jade.

"Dude, sorry, but I definitely do." Tommy sighs.

Totally out of character, and apparently high on the win, Alex jumps up and wraps his arms and legs around Tommy, hugging him and knocking them both to the ground.

The boys laugh, even Ryan, who reaches out his hand to pull them both up.

It warms my heart seeing Alex having fun again, and it does the same seeing Ryan take to Tommy.

"We're going to walk away now, Tommy Boy, but we'll look back in ten seconds," Alex warns.

Tommy smiles as he runs up to grab Jade. He picks her up and hugs her while twirling her around. "Pretty girl, I think you're a good luck charm. Can I kiss you before your cousin's ten seconds are up?"

"Since you asked so nicely." She smiles then kisses him first.

Kendall and Jake congratulate and hug Alex, not giving me a chance to do the same.

Then Kendall gasps and points. "Hey, Tessa, that's the boy that was at our house last night."

"Hey, hay guy." Jake laughs at his own joke to Lucas, who stands in a crowd of cheerleaders. "You played awesome."

I immediately feel my face redden, but Lucas smiles at him warmly as he walks toward us and gives Jake a high-five.

"Awesome game!" Jake exclaims.

"Thanks, little man. Do you think your sister liked the game?"

"You bet she did. She smiled a lot more today than usual."

"Jake," I whisper-hiss.

Alex walks next to me and nudges me. "What did you think?"

Embarrassment leaves immediately, and I smile up at him and give him a huge hug. "Great game. I'm so freaking proud of you."

"What about me, Tessa Ross?" Lucas asks from behind me.

Without looking back, I answer, "You guys played well together."

Alex pats Lucas's shoulder. "We did."

Finally, I look at him and swear on everything that is holy that sweat-drenched is definitely his best look.

"What's this *hay boy* shit, Lucas?" Sadi yells from behind us, and then I feel hands on my back as she shoves me into him.

Lucas catches me and steadies me while telling her, "Back off, Sadi. I told you weeks ago that we're done." He looks down at me, hands still firmly on my hips, gripping harder as I try to turn, because I am going to whoop her ass.

His green eyes are no longer filled with the joy from the win. He looks … sad?

"You okay?"

I no longer want to kick her ass; I want to teach her a freaking lesson.

"I'm fine."

I turn around and look at her. "You need to watch your mouth in front of kids, especially these ones."

"Kiss my ass, farm girl," Sadi retorts, reaching out to shove me again.

Before I even have a chance to react, Lucas reaches around me and catches her hand. "One last time. Back off, Sadi."

"You boys enjoying the homegrown Prosti-tots now?" Sadi hisses.

"Let's go." Alex grabs my arm, but I pull away.

"I'll catch up in a minute."

"Tessa, you are the captain of the field hockey team and—"

"Alex, I'm good," I assure him.

Alex shakes his head as he walks away with the kids.

"Now that the kids are gone, I'm only going to tell you this once. If you ever put your hands on me again, I won't hesitate to do the same to you."

I look at Lucas. "You done with her drama?"

Eyes sparkling, he nods.

"All right then."

"Your threats don't scare me, bitch," Sadi yells from behind the people now standing between her and me.

I turn and look up at him, knowing exactly what I'm going to do, and nerves be damned, I will not back down.

I whisper, "I'm going to kiss you."

"And I'm going to enjoy it," he whispers back.

I hold on to his biceps and push up on my toes as he wraps his arm around me, lifting me up. I take his face between my hands and lay my lips on his.

When he presses his lips firmly against mine, I begin to pull back, but he catches my lower lip between his teeth, and I open my mouth slowly while he gently explores it with his tongue. When he pulls it out and presses his lips once, twice, and then three times against mine, I realize my feet are now touching the ground and I force myself to step back.

He takes my hand, and then we walk off the field together.

Passing Alex, he looks angry. Next to him is Jade and Tommy, who both smile at Lucas.

Out of the corner of my eye, I see Mom and know she's upset as she says something to Alex, throwing her hands in the air, then comes storming toward me.

I brace for her, knowing I'm not going to back down.

"What are you thinking, young lady? That is not the way you were raised!" she yells.

Lucas starts to pull away, but I tighten my grip on his hand and calmly say, "That's right, Mom, it wasn't."

I smile and step to walk past her when she grabs my arm.

"Tessa Ross, don't you walk away from me!"

"It was only to put some stupid girl in her place, Mom!" I yell back just as loudly. "And, as far as how I was raised," I continue to yell, "actions speak louder than words. *You're* the one who taught me how to walk away!"

I look up at Lucas as he rubs circles with his thumb on

the back of my hand. Then, while she's still too shocked at the way I spoke to her to reply, we walk away.

Jade runs up to me and hugs me.

"I'm fine," I assure her and step back.

"We're going to shower. Will you be here when we get done?" Tommy asks Jade.

She looks at me, and I nod.

"Yes, we will," she tells him.

As soon as they join the team and head to the locker room, I am hit with the realization that my sister and brother probably saw the argument, and that is not something they are at all used to.

Seeing them standing outside the car, I run to them and hug them. Kendall is in tears, and Jake looks so scared it breaks my heart.

"Don't cry." I kiss Kendall's cheek then pull them both into a hug. "I'm okay, you're both okay, and Alex kicked butt today."

Smiling, I step back. "Have fun with Mom tonight. I'll see you all in the morning."

"For your birthday?" Jake asks.

"Yep, and I want chocolate cake, got it?" I force myself to look at Mom and nod. "With chocolate frosting."

She nods.

"What do you want for your birthday?" Jake asks then continues, "We're going shopping when we leave here."

"Blank cassette tapes, for sure."

"What was your favorite song on the countdown?" Kendall asks, causing me to get angry again because that's something we love to do together on Saturdays. And then we always get together whether it be on the phone or in person with Jade to discuss.

"Hands down, 'Hey Jealousy,' and my second—"

"'Runaway Train?'" She grins.

"Yeah." I nod, smiling as I feel my eyes heat.

"If we don't go now, we won't get to the movie store before it closes or all the good movies are gone," Jake whispers to Mom.

"I won't hold you up." I muss up his hair then force myself to look at Mom. "See ya, Mom."

"I love you, Tessa Ann," Mom, who is clearly shaken, says softly.

At first, I don't want to say it back, but I don't want this to affect Kendall and Jake, so I respond, "I love you, too."

And I do, but I'm so freaking pissed.

* * *

By the time I get back to the truck, Lucas and Tommy are walking out.

Lucas walks up to me, looking truly concerned, which doesn't sit well with me. "You okay?"

I look away. "I'm fine." The butterflies begin dancing in my belly. "Sorry about all that. It's just—"

"Don't be." Lucas takes my hand, walking us away from Jade and Tommy.

When he stops, he turns and looks at me, his eyes narrowed slightly. "Not that your point- proving kind of kiss wasn't great—it was—but I'd really like to try it again. You know, a kiss for us, not for the hundred people who were standing around."

I feel my eyes widen as he lifts my chin with just a finger, and then I smash my eyes shut, unable to look at him and not feel ... dizzy.

He kisses my lips gently then moves to my cheek then back to my lips. He then slides his tongue across my lower lip before sucking it between his full, soft, hot lips.

I inhale a sharp breath as my head spins and attempt

to step back, but both of his hands are softly yet firmly holding the sides of my face, and he is pushing his tongue inside my open mouth again, gently exploring.

I attempt to break the kiss, and not because I don't like it, but because I do. Too much. However, he cups the back of my head, and I finally decide to allow myself to truly kiss him back.

When I rub my tongue against his, he groans as he slides his hand down my head, coming to rest on my lower back, as our tongues caress one another's.

It's him now who attempts to pull away, lightly dragging his teeth down my tongue. Then he releases it and kisses me softly again, this time without tongue, parting his lips slightly so they cover mine once more, and then over and over again.

I like that, too, but I desperately want his tongue again.

Catching his lower lip between my teeth as he did mine, then slipping my tongue between his parted lips, I slowly explore his mouth until my head is spinning. But again, it's Lucas who pulls away.

Needing to catch my breath, and fearful my weak knees may buckle, I slowly allow my eyes to flutter open and am quickly struck with the reality that we are not alone.

Face aflame, I close my eyes, and he pulls my head against his chest. I can feel his heartbeat against my cheek.

"Damn, Tessa," he whispers. "So hot."

Unable to reply and not wanting to do anything but live in the moment, the glorious moment after my first kiss, I sigh, and he pulls me even closer now.

Someone clears their throat, and Lucas and I both look over to see Jade and Tommy looking at us.

Face red, Jade's voice squeaks when she asks, "You ready to go?"

I step back and look at Lucas.

He smiles and nods toward my truck. "See you tonight, birthday girl."

Still on cloud twelve—his jersey number—I walk over and climb into the truck. Then I look at Jade as she climbs in. Neither of us say a word as I start the truck and put it in drive. Then I see his sweatshirt sitting there on the seat, folded.

I pull up next to his car, where he and Tommy are leaning against it. I toss the sweatshirt out the window, and he catches it.

"I washed it."

"Why are you giving it back?" he asks, a slight V forming between his dark brows.

I shrug. "It doesn't smell like you anymore."

His delicious lips curve up, and the V vanishes as I pull my shades down, lift my chin, and then hit the gas.

"Holy. Shit," Jade gasps as we pull out onto Main Street. "And again, I say, holy. Shit."

"I don't want to talk about it." I reach up to turn on the radio.

"No need. I'm pretty sure I *felt* it." Jade laughs, and then so do I as I turn up the radio and Pearl Jam's "Even Flow" blasts through the truck's cab.

Not a word is said about the kiss as we drive up the hill and pull into the driveway, but Jade breaks the silence when we walk into the farmhouse.

"Did Lucas tell you that Alex invited him and Tommy to camp with them tonight?"

"What? You're kidding me!"

Jade laughs. "Oh, that's right, he wouldn't have had a chance to tell you anything with his tongue lodged down your throat."

"Jade, seriously, why? Did he say why?" I begin to panic.

"Nope. All I know is that they had to agree to go to church in the morning with us." She laughs.

I gasp, "And they did?"

"Yeah, Tommy had to call his parents to make sure it was all right to miss church with them, and they said yes." Jade beams like this is a good thing.

Feeling completely like the fool that I am, I walk around in circles, flipping out inside, because I thought I had until Monday to deal with my actions.

Finally, I stop and start toward the stairs. "So much to do."

"No, we're all set," Jade calls as she follows me up the stairs.

I empty my school bag on the bed and grab a duffle from underneath.

"I need to pack."

"I swear to you that Alex and I have it covered." She laughs as I throw clothes in my duffle then head back down the stairs.

Jade and I go through the house together, gathering flashlights, blankets, and snacks. Then I stop in front of the liquor cabinet and grab a bottle of peach Schnapps.

Jade shakes her head. "What are you doing, Tessa?"

"It's my birthday party, and I may want a drink. I may also want my favorite cousin to have a drink with me." I shrug like it's an everyday occurrence. It's not. But today is far from every day.

"I don't think that's a good idea, Tessa—"

"It may not be, Jade, but it's my eighteenth birthday and, apparently I'm breaking all the rules."

BIRTHDAY GIRL

Chapter Six

TESSA

When we pulled down the road toward the pond, there were fresh tracks leading down past the pond toward the camp.

Jade grins. "The white hat boys are here."

"Speaking of, did you notice the blooming bromance between Ryan, Tommy, and Lucas?"

She pushes out her lower lip and says, "Yeah. That makes me happy."

"Me, too." I smile as we approach the narrow roadway through the trees and see tents set up.

"The boys must have been here and gone." Jade says as I pull up beside the camp.

"Let's unload then, shall we?" I push the door open and hop out.

Inside, we clean up a bit. It's dusty in here and needs a good cleaning. But that won't happen, not today, anyway.

"I'm going to wipe things down. You mind unpacking the bags and hiding the Schnapps?" I ask.

"Are we really going to drink?"

"Maybe." I laugh, grabbing a cloth from my bag and wetting it under the sink.

We unload the truck and are setting up inside with music blasting when Alex, Tommy, Lucas, Becca, and Phoebe walk in with their arms full of grocery bags, so Jade turns it down.

Tommy winks at her, and then the guys start talking football.

"We heard about this the entire way here from Ryan," Becca grumbles.

"They won," Phoebe says with a smile. "Let them have at least another minute before we shut them down."

I laugh. "I swear I like you more and more every day."

"Don't worry, Jade." She puts her hands in the air. "I know where I stand."

"That's good." Jade attempts to give her an intimidating look, and we all laugh. "What can I say? I suck at mean."

While they continue to talk, I grab a cardboard box that someone must have broken down and wipe the dust off it before tearing the bottom free then pull a marker out of the camp junk drawer and start to turn things around.

When I finish, I set it on the counter.

Lucas is the first one to notice it, and he chuckles.

I arch a brow, and he fakes surprise as I clear my throat to get their attention.

Alex laughs. "What's that supposed to mean?"

"My dearest brother, today, we watched an almost three-hour game. I have to suffer having a chaperone that is just a year older than I am, who invited friends to join him. While you're in here for the next eighteen hours, it's Doe Camp. No testosterone-driven kill stories, no farting, no burping, and absolutely no more football today."

Alex shakes his head. "Is that so?"

I nod. "As a matter of fact, I've decided you're not my chaperone tonight; you're my servant. You may find yourself painting our toenails."

"I am absolutely positive that's the most I've ever heard you say." Lucas laughs.

"If you would keep your tongue out of her mouth long enough, you may find she's quite the conversationalist." Jade giggles.

Alex covers his ears. "I don't want to hear anymore, but it best not move any further than that."

"Seriously," I gasp as I scowl at Jade and Alex. Then I feel green eyes boring into me and look over at him, shaking my head. He smiles.

"All right, boys, the princess has spoken, so let's go cook some grub," Alex concedes.

"What's for dinner?" I ask.

"It's a surprise," he answers as they all walk out the door.

"What's this about a tongue down your throat?" Phoebe immediately asks.

"Let *me* give you all the details." Jade sighs, covering her heart. "I had a front row seat for the second act."

Jade gives them the account, kindly leaving out the parts about the fight with Mom after the game. Then she talks forever about how much of a gentleman Tommy is, unlike his best friend's hedonistic self—her words, not mine.

"Did you like it, Tessa?" Phoebe asks. "I mean, did he kiss okay? Did he taste nasty? Did you want to push him off you?"

The way she asks kind of breaks my heart. No kiss should feel like that.

I shake my head. "He tasted hot and sweet, a little like cinnamon. To be honest, I didn't want him to stop. I wish it could have lasted even longer."

From behind me, I hear someone clear their throat, and by the looks on the girls' faces, I know who it is. There is absolutely no way of backtracking now.

I groan, palming my face.

"Dinner is ready, ladies." His tone? Clearly amused.

The girls start filing out, and I try to get it together to follow them. When I'm almost in the clear, an arm juts out in front of me, stopping me from leaving.

"Let me pass, Lucas. Let me walk out of here and pretend you didn't hear that." I hate that my voice sounds shaky.

"Look at me, please," Lucas whispers softly.

I do, to avoid feeling any more like a child than I do right now.

"You are so cute right now. Can I ask you a question?"

I square my shoulders and look him right in the eyes. "Only if I can look away so I don't throw up on your feet."

He tries to hold back his laugh but fails.

"You're an ass," I hiss, trying to duck under his arm.

He grabs me and positions me in front of him, but he's gracious enough, so my back is to his front. "Is that better?"

I nod.

"Okay, now my question: how many guys have been lucky enough to kiss you?"

I think for a minute then answer firmly. "Five."

He laughs out loud, and I elbow him hard in the gut.

He grunts, and with amusement still in his voice, he chuckles. "Tessa, don't be angry with me."

How could I not be, you ass?

"One more question?"

"Sure, and when you're done, there's a gun in my closet and bullets in the drawer over there. Make it a quick shot to the temple, would you?"

"Oh, for fuck's sake, it's not that bad, is it?"

"Not for you," I huff.

"How many were not related to you?"

What an ass.

"None of your business." I pull away from him, but he reaches around me, his hand now splayed across my belly.

"I want to know." His voice is suddenly gentler.

"Fine. None. That was my first real kiss, Lucas. Are you happy?"

"I'm so fucking happy," he says, his breath hot against my neck. "I've kissed a lot of girls, and you are, by far, my favorite. So curious, so receptive, and so incredibly hot. Thank you for answering my questions. Will you look at me now?" He lets go.

"I don't know," I answer honestly as my heart rapid-fires in my chest.

"Can I take your hand and walk with you to dinner?"

"No, you can race me." I lunge toward the door and rush outside.

Laughing, he follows me but stays behind.

When we get to the table, Lucas sits next to me. When a dish is passed, Lucas spoons the food onto my plate.

We have all my favorite dishes—crab legs, with corn on the cob, and an assortment of salads.

When dinner is done, Becca and Phoebe grab blankets and lay them on the ground near the bonfire, and us girls sit together and talk as music plays in the background while Alex and Lucas stand by the fire.

I look around and notice Jade and Tommy have been missing for some time, but obviously saying such will make Alex aware. I wonder if Lucas is chatting him up to divert his attention. Honestly, I'm not sure how that makes me feel.

Then Jade walks out of the dark, holding up my pale blue notebook. "I brought the book."

My Birthday Wish book.

"Oh, hell no." I start to jump up, but Becca holds me down.

"We do this every year."

"In my freaking bedroom," I defend myself.

"Fine." Jade laughs as I jump up and grab at the stupid thing. "We can do this at Doe Camp ... after cake."

* * *

After they all sing "Happy Birthday," which is totally embarrassing on its own, and I blow out the candles, it gets even worse.

"Presents before cake!" Jade announces.

I cover my face with my hands. "Jade, I'm not twelve. It's seriously not necessary."

When it's immediate family, I enjoy gifts. I especially like giving gifts. Receiving in a situation like this, I hate them. Not because they aren't appreciated, because they are. I just never feel like I can justly express enough gratitude, and it makes me feel pretty much the same as the dream when I got on the school bus naked—terrified.

I feel *his* eyes on me and glance at him from between my fingers. The corner of his mouth twitches up in a shit-ass half-grin. I roll my eyes, and then he grins.

"Mine first!" Jade exclaims, setting the hot pink package, with a little gift tag on it that says, "*Happy Birthday,*" in front of me. "Open it!"

I unwrap the paper and peel the tape closure on the box. Inside, beneath hot pink tissue paper, is a gift certificate for the movies, my favorite winter activity, and the Pearl Jam cassette. Beneath it, a framed picture of her and me at the concert this past summer.

"Thank you so much." I hold the picture close to my chest.

The next two are cards; one from Phoebe and one from Becca. Phoebe's contains a gift certificate for a manicure.

"You'll have to go with me."

"I'd love that." She smiles.

I smile back. "Me, too."

I open Becca's card, and there's a gift certificate for a pedicure.

"Looks like we'll all be getting mani-pedi's together?" I ask Becca.

"Most definitely."

"Thank you all so—"

"Mine next." Tommy slides a card in front of me.

"Oh my God, you didn't have to."

"You only turn eighteen once. And eighteen has been the best year of my life so far." He smiles at Jade.

I open his card and see a gift certificate for Greek Peak, a ski resort a few towns over.

"Not much to do around here in the winter," he explains.

"I love it." I smile, setting it in the pile. "Now cake—"

A large package, covered in shiny blue paper, is placed in front of me. "One more."

"You didn't have to." I blush. *I freaking hate blushing.*

"From what I hear, he shoved his tongue in your mouth so, yeah, he did," Alex says, and I throw daggers at him with my eyes. He shrugs. "Just stating a fact."

"And I am just going to ignore you," I grumble, carefully peeling back the paper.

I sigh when I see a quilted backpack, in different shades of blues and greens.

"Thank you," I whisper as I look at it.

"You should unzip it," Tommy advises.

So, I do.

Inside the bag is a teddy bear wearing a football jersey. *Adorable.* The fact that I already know it smells like him makes me smile. Beneath it is the sweatshirt I returned to him just a few hours ago and a note that says: *READ ME LATER.*

"Thank you so much, everyone. I truly appreciate it."

And I hope they know I do.

"Group hug!" Jade cheers.

After cake and making a fire in the fireplace, the guys make their way out, and at Jade's insistence, we open the book and read every embarrassing wish I wrote for year seventeen—where I see myself in five years, and then ten.

"A handsome husband who adores me and dances with me when the kids go to bed," I read. "Three kids, two boys and a girl, and—"

"This is adorable." Phoebe claps. "Do you have names?"

I say no, but Jade rats me out.

"One boy has to have the name CJ."

"Oh my God, shut up, Jade." I laugh.

"Oh no, now you have to tell us: why CJ?" Becca insists.

"I have no idea," I lie.

"Her first crush. Some kid she met on a mission trip—"

"It wasn't a mission trip, and it wasn't a crush," I interrupt Jade.

Becca laughs. "See? She totally knows."

"Do tell," Phoebe, bless her heart, asks with all the sincerity in the world.

"A kid at VBS, when I was like five. I don't know his name. I think it started with a C."

"And she shared her lunch with him," Jade finishes.

I mean, not exactly, but it was so long ago that the details are sketchy at best.

The rest of the night, we play cards and laugh while listening to music and laughing some more as Jade and I take turns changing the words to the songs, personalizing them a bit. It's a perfect night, a welcome distraction from the tension, both good and bad, going on in my life.

* * *

Unable to sleep, thinking about the letter in the backpack and knowing the girls are asleep, I quietly sneak out the back door with it in hand.

Sitting on the back porch, I open the envelope and pull out the letter. Before I even have a chance to start reading, though, I hear something in the distance.

I quickly hold up the flashlight and see Lucas standing about ten feet away.

I cover my mouth so I don't scream out into the night.

"Seconds ago, you were smiling, and now there's a V forming between your brows, Tessa Ross."

"You scared the hell out of me."

He starts walking toward me, and I look down, unable to look him in the eyes.

Blue Love

"And you can't look at me. Why?" he asks, sitting next to me.

"I don't know," I mumble.

"I'm not that hard to look at, am I?" He rubs the side of my cheek, and I jump. "Wow."

"Sorry." I force myself to look up at him.

"I love your smile," Lucas whispers, and I look away.

He takes the note from my hand and moves behind me, scooting up behind, legs outside of mine, and pulls me closer. He then wraps his arms around me and holds the note in his hand in front of us as he whispers. "So?"

"I haven't read it yet."

"So, read it now."

"Okay, I skimmed," I admit.

"All right, so the cliff note version is no different than the novel. I want to date you exclusively. What do you say?"

Sweet Jesus, I think then attempt to answer calmly. "I don't want to jump into a relationship that's going to fail or that I can't give one hundred percent to."

"Then don't," he says matter-of-factly. "Don't let it fail. I see what's going on in your life, and it sucks. I get it. But we could be good together. I have very strong feelings for you that I don't want to push under the rug until a better time that may not ever come. After the football game, I know you're feeling me, too. But, if I'm reading you wrong, let me know, and I'll stop pressuring you. But I know damn well that you and I can be a good thing. I think we both know it." He pushes my hair away from my neck, pressing his soft, hot lips to my bare skin and causing goosebumps to rise beneath them. "So, what do you say, Tessa? Will you let me make it to the top ten on your list of favorite things that happened when you were seventeen?"

I elbow him, annoyed that he was listening to girl talk, but not as hard as last time.

He chuckles. "Can't blame a guy for wanting to get to know everything about the girl he plans to make his number one favorite thing that happened when he was eighteen."

"Do you really have a list?" I ask curiously.

"Never had a reason or inclination to make one. Give me that reason now."

The sincerity in his statement, the tone in his voice, the warmth of his body so close to mine, causes my feelings to form words and flow out. "I'd like that."

His lips at my neck, he exhales, and something about its depth makes me believe it means more to him than I could imagine.

He folds up the letter, sets it somewhere, and then he somehow turns me so I'm on my knees, facing him.

Okay, so I'm sure I had some part of it, but yeah ...

Hands on my face, he pulls me toward him and kisses my lips, tugging at my bottom lip with his teeth, and I open to him. His hot, sweet tongue glides against mine, and I whimper as tingles tickle my skin. He puts his arm around my waist as I grab his shoulders, squeezing them, and he groans into my mouth. Needing to be closer, I end up on his lap, and now *I* deepen the kiss.

When raindrops hit the tin roof of the cabin, I regretfully pull away, but Lucas pulls me back and kisses me harder and doesn't stop until we both need a breath. My heart is beating so fast that it feels as if it could come out of my body.

Lucas pulls my head to his chest. Ear resting over his heart, I can hear his beating just the same. Then he lifts my chin and places a soft kiss on my forehead, my nose, and then my lips.

"Happy birthday, Tessa Ross."

Thunder rocks the woods, and we both jump up.

"See you in the morning." He kisses the top of my head then heads back toward the dark, and I make my way back inside.

When I walk into camp, I see the digital clock reads: 12:02. It's officially my birthday.

I know the last few pages will be filled with a lot of angst for age seventeen, but the kiss and Lucas will make the top ten list. I also know that I will definitely be writing all these feelings going on at this moment into year eighteen immediately so that I never forget them.

Lightning crackles outside, lighting up Doe Camp, as if the sun has risen, and I see Jade rush inside.

Our eyes meet, both of us shocked to see the other. Thunder booms, and Jade jumps and screams, and then we both bust up laughing.

"What on God's green earth is going on?" Becca asks, sitting up and rubbing her eyes.

"It's raining," Jade responds, hurrying to me.

At the same time, I say, "A storm woke us."

Phoebe sits up. "Oh no, the boys are in the tent."

Again, Jade and I begin laughing.

"Why is that funny?" Becca asks.

Just then, the boys stumble in.

"Looks like we're crashing in here," Alex announces.

Lucas smiles at me as he follows Alex inside, carrying a sleeping bag, one that still has tags on it.

"We'll take the loft." Alex's nods toward it, and they follow him.

Lying beside Jade, staring at each other, both of us smiling from ear to ear, the rain begins pounding on the tin roof and, like a lullaby, it lulls me to sleep.

***

The morning is quiet, near silent except for the birds chirping. But, if you listen closely, I'm sure four hearts could be heard beating faster as the four of us steal glances—all of us now thieves—while cleaning up.

By six thirty, Alex had breakfast on the table—scrambled eggs, toast, and bacon. By seven, Phoebe and Becca headed out to get home to get showered and ready for church. By eight, the camp was cleaned, and we all said our goodbyes. Lucas and Tommy rode with Alex to the top of the hill, and as we drove by them, they were getting into his Trans Am.

"Tommy said Lucas's father bought him that this summer. Must be nice to get a brand-new sports car handed to you, right?"

"I'm more of a four-wheel drive kind of girl." I laugh then ask the burning question, "How was your night?"

"It was amazing, Tessa. He's amazing. He's funny, too, and we kissed a lot. I swear my head is still spinning. He asked me to be his girlfriend, and I said yes. I mean, why wouldn't I?"

"You wouldn't." I grin.

"How did your night go?"

I laugh. "Pretty much the same."

***

Standing with the choir, Jade and I immediately notice Lucas and Tommy walk in with Alex, all three wearing suits. They are as handsome as can be, even though I will admit that I prefer jeans, tees, and white hats. I swear my face catches fire when I see Dad behind them.

His brow arches when he sees me, and I lift a hand. He nods.

"Nice poker face," Jade whispers, and I elbow her.

Lucas whispers something in Tommy's ear, and then they look up at the high ceilings. I'm not a lip reader, but I could swear Tommy says, "Looks sturdy enough." Then they both chuckle.

I watch as they make their way to the third pew on the left, where our family has always sat. Then Lucas is shaking Jake's hand then … Mom's. She smiles at him, but it's in no way from the heart.

When the pianist starts, the choir walks in. Once seated, I make sure I look anywhere but at Lucas.

I'm not embarrassed to be in choir. I love our church, and music is an important part of my life, but I certainly try my best to avoid looking at the boy who makes my heart beat faster and whose smile provokes my own. I've seen said smile in the mirror, and I swear I look like a dork when I think about him.

The pastor asks for announcements, and Dad is the first to stand. When he reaches down for Mom's hand, she takes it, and then they stand together.

In that, I feel hopeful that maybe this is, in fact, just a break.

I force myself not to slouch down in my chair as he says, "Our Tessa is celebrating her eighteenth birthday today."

The entire congregation, in sync, wishes me a happy birthday, and I smile and wave. "Thank you." Then, my eyes land on his, and he mouths, *"Happy Birthday, baby."*

My heart skips a beat, and I spend the next several minutes of my time focusing on keeping my face from doing what it does in the mirror and overanalyzing the term *baby*. However, none of the moments between thoughts last more than mere seconds without looking back at him.

Until … the sermon begins. The topic? adultery. Then my eyes pretty much stay fixed on my lap.

When it's time for "Joyful Noise," Jade, me, and the other two junior choir members stand then walk to the front of the church. Becca sits at the piano.

I squeeze Jade's hand, sensing her anxiety about not only her first solo, but it being in front of Tommy.

"Just be in the words, Jade."

She nods, and then Becca begins to play "Here I Am."

Jade starts out quietly, but when she's mid-solo, she's singing like I know she can—loud and beautifully.

When mine starts, I'm not at all nervous as I sing. I have sung a million times; the first as a child while attending vacation Bible school in Cape Cod when I stayed with Aunt Anne.

When the song ends, Tommy stands up, whistling and cheering.

Jade's face turns red, and then typical Jade, she laughs, smiling at him.

***

When I walk out into the fellowship hall, someone grabs my shoulder.

I look back and see Pastor Zach smiling. "Happy birthday, Miss Ross."

"Thanks, Zach."

"The big eighteen, huh?"

"Yep, officially one year closer to nineteen."

He throws his head back and laughs. "Have you given any thought to the wedding?"

"Things have been pretty busy, so I really haven't even had a chance to look at the date."

He hugs me. "Heard the road is bumpy right now."

"Yeah." I give him a squeeze back.

From behind me, I hear, "I'm Lucas, Tessa's boyfriend," and then I feel a possessive hand grip my hip.

Chuckling, Zack steps back and shakes his hand. "I'm going to assume you're part of the reason Tessa hasn't gotten back to me?"

Looking at Lucas, I immediately sense he's angry.

I push his hand from my hip and step to the side. "Lucas and I actually just decided to date." I say firmly.

Lucas narrows his eyes at Zack. "Exclusively."

Zack holds back a smile and nods. "Nice meeting you, Lucas. Talk to you soon, Tessa."

As soon as he leaves, I whisper annoyedly, "You can't come to my church and act like that."

"Me?" He laughs maniacally. "Like seriously? I came here to be with you, and you're hugging some guy right in front of me? That's not how I want my girlfriend to act."

Before I have a chance to say anything, he takes my hand and pulls me through the crowd.

Once away from the masses, I yank my hand back and set to putting him in his place.

Before I have a chance, though, Jade is by my side, asking, "What were you and Pastor Zack talking about?"

Lucas's eyes widen as I answer her, "Before the *interruption*, he was asking if I looked at his wedding date." I look at Lucas. "He and his fiancée asked me to sing at their wedding."

"Awesome, Lisa must be so happy." Jade, being on cloud Tommy, misses the fact that I'm annoyed at Lucas.

"I'm sure they are." I turn and walk away before I flip

out on Lucas. And because I'm fuming, I'm not thinking at all when I walk over to Dad ... and Mom.

Mom hugs me. "Tessa, you sang beautifully. See you at the house in a few?"

Right, the family birthday lunch, I think as I nod.

"Let me hang my robe, and I'll go home."

Walking down the stairs, I am fully aware that the guys are following Jade and I.

"Want to see the eleventh and twelfth grade classrooms? They're pretty cool," Jade asks them.

Coming up with an excuse to do anything but be around him, I tell Jade, "I'm going to the bathroom. I'll be right in."

After I pull my choir robe off and splash water on my heated, angry face, I open the door to find Lucas standing there, arms crossed, leaning against the wall.

"I'm sorry I acted like that. I just can't stand to see another guy touch you."

"First of all, you don't know me, and I certainly don't know you enough to do this ... this ... thing." Overly emotional, I stutter. "My family is falling apart. With that, school, hockey, choir, church, and trying to keep things normal for my little brother and sister, I'm not ready for this thing with you. And what the heck were you thinking?" I snap my mouth shut when I realize my anger has boiled over.

Lucas pushes off the wall and wipes away the stupid tear that falls.

"I messed up, okay? I apologize. But seriously, don't be sad. The same stuff was going on in your life last night, and you weren't upset like this. But this *thing*, as you call it, Tessa, can be the distraction you need. I've been through the family crap. Let me help you. I *want* to help you. I'm

Blue Love

sorry. Please say you'll forgive me?" he asks, searching my eyes.

"Just don't get angry at me when you have no idea what's going on. And like, before you grab me in public, I should be given the opportunity to tell my family we're dating."

"I already told my mom." He says it like he won some sort of challenge, or race against me.

I roll my eyes but smile. "Ask me questions when you have them. I've never done this—I've never been anyone's girlfriend—but I can tell you that I'm nothing if not trustworthy and honest."

Without notice, Lucas kisses me.

Without thought, I open my mouth.

Without a warning, Jade scolds me.

"Tessa!"

We both jump away from each other as Jade stomps down the hallway.

Feeling as if I just got busted by my mom ... again, I quickly tell Lucas, "That can't happen again here, okay?"

"If you say so," he says, eyes twinkling.

* * *

After a dinner of chicken, salt potatoes, a salad, and feeling like the last few days were a bad dream as we all sit around, talking about the first week of school, I am stuffed.

Mom stands up and nonchalantly asks, "So, Lucas Links?"

"Asked me out," I answer.

"He what?" Alex gasps.

Kendall smiles. "Lucas is your boyfriend?"

I look at Molly, who smiles.

"Yeah, I guess he is."

"That's so cool." Jake grins. "Maybe him and Alex will be best friends now, and he won't miss—"

"Not sure they'll be best friends, but I do hope they can become good ones," I cut Jake off, worried that Alex will get quiet again.

"Already liking Jade's guy better. At least he had the decency to ask me if it was okay that he dated her," Alex grumbles.

"Yeah, well, I don't think I have to ask permission to have a boyfriend. Never saw that in the rule book."

"May not be," Dad pipes in now, "but there will be some new rules added now."

"That's seriously not fair. Molly didn't have rules."

Dad arches a brow. "Molly dated Cory. Known that boy all his life."

"Well, I think it would be weird if I dated him, too, don't you?" I smart back.

Molly laughs. "You think?"

"I'm not dating Cory. He's old." Kendall laughs, too.

"How about cake?" Mom says, placing it on the table in front of me.

"It's beautiful. Thanks, Mom."

"We helped, too," Jake adds.

"Well, thank you, too. Do you think it tastes as good as it looks?" I wiggle my brows at him.

We eat the cake and ice cream, *as a family*, and then it's time for presents. Mom and Dad give me a new hockey stick, one that I admired at the sporting goods store when we were shopping with Mom. They also give me money.

My brothers and sisters give me another pair of new cleats and blank cassette tapes.

"How did you know?" I ask Mom.

Blue Love

"Mrs. Brooks." She smiles proudly at me as we clear the table together.

"I would like you to come stay with me one day this week. Is that doable?" Mom asks, causing the perfect birthday bubble meets reality dart and burst.

"I guess so. I have a game Tuesday. Maybe after that."

* * *

By eight thirty, Jake is zonked out on the couch and Kendall is fighting to stay awake so she doesn't miss the rest of *Louis and Clark*.

Yawning, she rests her head on my shoulder. "He looks kind of like Lucas, right?"

"If I squint my eyes real tight, maybe."

"Doesn't throw hay as fast as that boy or Alex." Dad laughs.

"He's got me on football, though, so I'll call us even." Alex shrugs.

The phone rings, and I sigh as I start to get up. "I'll get it."

"I got it right here," Dad says.

When he holds up a cordless phone, I almost die.

Mimicking him, I laugh. "I thought hell would freeze over before we got one of those damn things."

Kendall giggles. "He said it wasn't a birthday present; it's a family gift. I think he did it for you."

"He definitely did it for her," Alex agrees.

Dad answers the phone. "Ross residence." He holds the phone out. "It's for you."

I look at Kendall. "Be right back."

She nods as I take the phone.

"Hello?"

"Hey, baby." If the words didn't give it away, the voice certainly would have.

"Hi."

"Am I calling too late?"

I look at Dad as he stands. He doesn't look upset.

"No, I guess not."

"Still pissed at me for being an ass?"

"Nope," I say, making my way out to the deck.

"Seven words lead me to believe otherwise." He sighs.

"Seven words?"

"Now nine."

It dawns on me that he's actually counting my words. "Gotcha."

"Ten."

I step outside onto the front porch and close the door behind me. "Eleven."

"Aw ... she's quick," he says, a smile in his voice.

"Audience. Now I'm outside."

"Nice." He clears his throat. "So, let's start over. I'm sorry I was a dick. Just didn't like seeing some other guy's hands on you. I'll try not to jump to conclusions next time."

"Good."

"Just make sure you give me the same courtesy, okay?"

"Um, sure?"

He chuckles then asks, "How was dinner?"

"Good. Weird. But good."

"So, what does Tessa Ross do after nine o'clock on a Sunday night?"

"Not much, you?" Lame. I am so freaking lame.

"Can't say as if I remember anything in the past, but tonight, just laying here, thinking of you and hoping this is going somewhere good."

"So, you suffer from amnesia?" I joke. Again, lame.

He laughs quietly. Or, is it politely? Probably that.

"One could wish."

"Maybe two could," I whisper.

"We'll work on that together."

Together. I'm not sure if that scares me or makes me happy.

He continues, "I didn't get much sleep last night."

"That was some storm."

"The storm was just a moment. Slayed me laying above you, but not touching you. Laying there thinking about those lips and not being able to taste them … nearly killed me."

I feel the blush begin, and I have no idea what to say.

"You with me?"

"Uh-huh."

"Good. Do me a favor?"

"Uh-huh," I repeat because, apparently, I am quite the conversationalist.

"Take that bear with you to bed tonight and think about me and not that other stuff?"

"Yeah," I whisper.

"See you in the morning, baby."

Baby.

"Sweet dreams."

"They sure will be," he says softly.

Twelve

Chapter Seven

TESSA

Standing at my locker, talking with Jade, Phoebe, and Becca, I see heads turn, and they do so in a big way. I look down the hall and see the cause of it.

The white hat boys.

But it's not just the hats.

Lucas is wearing a pair of faded jeans that hang on his hips, held up by a black leather belt and a matching black Polo shirt, yet still the white hat. Tommy is in knee-length khaki cargo shorts and a white tee.

Jade smiles. "There's our guys."

"Check out the girls," I whisper in annoyance.

Jade laughs. "And the boys."

Blue Love

A sea of congratulations on Saturday's win fills the halls, and I grumble, "Them, too."

Grabbing her first period books, Jade whispers, "Chill, Tessa. He obviously only has eyes for you."

Hands grip my shoulders as he says, "Good morning, Tessa."

Annoyance has left the hall, and I feel that silly grin wobble on my face as I try to get my shit together as I turn toward him.

He takes my hand. "Can I walk you to class?"

"Sure, but you better lose the hat before you get it taken away."

He takes it off, reaches over me, and then sets it in my locker. He takes my hand and shuts my locker door.

Now all eyes are on us and, although I enjoy singing and being on stage, I do not enjoy this. I especially don't enjoy the looks I'm getting from the girls, and not just the implants, but people I've known for years.

"You'll get used to it."

I look up at him curiously.

"You're dating the quarterback; let them look. Hell, let's make 'em squirm."

He doesn't even give me a second to respond before his hands are on my cheeks and his lips fall over mine. He sweeps his tongue across my lips, and I open enough for him to ... slip his cinnamon gum into my mouth.

"Check them out now," he whispers in my ear.

I just stare at him, completely dumbstruck that I, Tessa Anne Ross, just tongue-kissed a boy in the middle of Blue Valley High's "Make-Out Hall," a place that I vowed never to put myself on a public display ... like I just did.

He grabs my books from my hand, tucks them under his arm, takes my hand, and gives it a squeeze. Suddenly, I do not care about the onlookers at all. And, if I'm totally honest with myself, is this any worse than a packed football field on a Saturday afternoon?

"You better now?"

Pushing the piece of gum between my teeth, I look up at him, and he smiles. It's seriously the best smile, too.

"You left something in my mouth."

His eyes flare. "Tessa, don't say that."

I look at him, confused, and he shakes his head. "Never mind."

* * *

Throughout the day I realized I needed to, at the least, come off cloud Lucas for classes—both of those we had together, and the ones I had without him, in which I thought about him the entire forty-three minutes—so that I don't flop senior year. But lunch was even worse. Like make-out hall, all eyes seemed to be on us. He seemed unbothered by it, and I crossed my fingers, hoping I would get used to it, as he suggested several times throughout the day.

After practice, we all hung out in the parking lot for a good thirty minutes before I remembered I had responsibilities waiting at home and my first game tomorrow.

I also realized that, as much as I loved kissing Lucas Links, his hugs were epic, as well, which scares the hell out of me.

* * *

Once home and hearing Kendall talk about Mom's place, namely the bathroom being so small that it only had a shower, I called her and asked if I could stay the night tonight. She seemed excited, and when she asked me why the change, I didn't want to admit to her that I liked a long soak after my games, because that would not start our "visit" off on a good foot, so I told her I didn't know.

Then I call Lucas and let him know, because Mom has a cell and not a house phone.

"Where's her place?"

I tell him, and he offers to come pick me up in the morning, so I don't have to ride the bus.

"It's no big deal," I say as I shove my uniform into my duffle bag.

"It's actually on my way."

"Doesn't Tommy ride with you to school?"

"He has his own car; just likes mine better."

"Really, it's no big—"

"I'll see you at seven," he cuts me off.

"I think Mom will leave around then."

"Okay … Seven fifteen."

I throw my undies in my bag. "I don't think it's really that big a deal."

"Perfect. See you then." Before I can object, he says, "Take the bear, baby. Goodnight."

"Sweet dreams, Lucas."

"They're only sweet because you star in them."

***

Walking up the stairs to Mom's place on Walnut Street makes me feel sick to my stomach. It feels wrong on so many levels.

When she opens the door, smiling, I try to match her energy, but apparently, I fail.

"It's better inside," she assures me as she steps back.

Walking into the tiny two-bedroom apartment, I

thought I was prepared, but I'm truly not. I'm not sure it's the apartment-sized kitchen with barely enough space on the counter for a coffee maker, making it abundantly clear that there will be no cookies baked at Christmastime here, or the stark white of it mixed with the lingering scent of Clorox.

This isn't Mom. Nothing except maybe the Clorox scent even resembles her.

"I'm calling the decor minimalistic."

"Accurate description," I say, setting my bag on the floor.

"I made soup and salad. Have a seat."

"I already ate."

"It's your favorite—French onion," she says, opening the tiny oven.

I sit.

The soup is the only thing, so far, that resembles, even a little bit, the mom who was still living with her family less than a week ago.

"What do you think?" she asks, setting her spoon down.

Looking at my half-eaten crock of soup, I answer the only way that won't be offensive. "The soup's perfect. The same as …" I stop.

She reaches over the tiny, round table and puts her hand on mine. "Change is never easy."

"You don't say," I mumble.

"The thing you need to remember is that we're all going through it."

I pull my hand back and pick up the spoon, and not because I'm the least bit hungry. I just need something to do with my damn hand that doesn't include her. "But we all didn't choose it."

"Right," she says then picks up her coffee mug and asks, "Tessa, do you really like that boy or—"

"Lucas is my boyfriend, Mom." I spoon up some soup.

"He's cute, Tessa. Just please remember what you were taught and who you are."

"I got it, Mom. I'll try to remember that none of it means anything, because after twenty years, it won't matter anymore."

"Tessa, you don't know what I've lived through for those years. I don't expect you to be happy about it. I do, however, expect you to be respectful of me and respectful of yourself always."

"Right. Of course." I push back from the table. "I have homework."

"I can clear the table or—"

"Honestly, I'm tired. Just show me the"—*closet*—"bedroom."

She points left. "This room has bunk beds." She points right. "This one has a double." Then she points to another door. "The TV room and the bathroom is in there, as well."

After a cry in the "bathroom," I pull myself together then join Mom on the daybed that she uses as a couch, and we watch *Evening Shade* while I do my math homework.

By eleven, I know she's only awake because I am. "Go to sleep. I'll lock up."

"Do you know which room you'd like?"

"I'm guessing the bunk bedroom is for us, and the double is—"

"Actually, when I eventually get all four of you here, this"—she pats the space between us—"will be mine."

"That's nuts, Mom."

"No, it's my choice." She smiles in what I think is an

attempt to show me that she's happy, but it does the opposite. It breaks my heart.

Laying on the bottom bunk, looking up at a picture I assume Kendall shoved up there, one of the seven of us, I get even more emotional. I reach down and pull the Teddy bear from my duffel and inhale the scent of Lucas's cologne. It's earthy and woodsy, which feels comfortable, but the added something altogether edgier makes me feel things that I am not comfortable feeling.

* * *

Mom left well before seven, giving me time to look around. After seeing her plastic containers full of her clothes under the "couch" and the box of pictures, many of her and Dad, I feel hopeful that it's temporary.

When there is a knock on the door, I begin panicking, because it's only ten after and I planned to meet him outside.

Opening the door, I feel mildly embarrassed, but it is what it is. "You're early."

"Drove by last night to make sure I knew where I was going. Saw your mom's car, and it wasn't here when I drove by, so I decided to surprise you."

"How do you know what my mom's car looks like?"

His lips curve up. "I've met Mrs. Ross and her car twice. The pond, when you took a swim, and the game."

Stepping back, mildly embarrassed at not only the apartment but my stupid question, I shake my head. "Right. Well, please excuse the place."

"I've seen worse. We have about thirty minutes before we have to leave. What do you want to do?" Lucas asked.

"I don't know." I cross my arms over my chest and look around.

"Baby, look at me. You never have to be nervous around me."

I look back up at him.

"That's better. Now, what do you want to do?"

"Kiss you, because it feels good." *No way did that just come out of my mouth.* "Okay, that was so wrong and—"

"Look at me, baby." He takes my hand as he sits in one of the kitchen chairs.

I turn and look at him. "That is kind of our thing, though. I mean, right? I know your mouth, but I don't know a thing about you other than you play football and are an implant at Blue Valley High."

"Implant?" He chuckles.

"You got put here, so ..." I wave my hand in front of me, the one he's not holding, the one his thumb isn't softly brushing across, back and forth, as if to wipe away that whole conversation, knowing that would probably lead to the whole *white hat boy* conversation, because clearly, I'm not only rambling outwardly, but also inwardly.

"I have an idea." He pulls another chair out with his foot then nods for me to sit.

I do so, while still holding his hand.

He leans forward, resting his elbows on his knees and looks up at me. "You ask me a question to get to know me better. I get to kiss you after I answer. It's a win-win."

I close my eyes and shake my head. "I don't know about that."

He squeezes my hand. "You need an audience to kiss me, Tessa Ross?"

"Oh my God, no," I gasp.

"Good to know." He sighs a bit, which is so un-Lucas-like. "So, what do you say?"

I look at the clock but nod, because I like that he seems

to want this, maybe more than me. "I say we only have fifteen minutes."

"Then you better make the best of it." His eyes are sparkling, which makes him look, well, his age. It's cute, a stark contradiction to his normal, insanely hot.

"Okay, but we can't be late for school." I do that stupid smile, which seems to make him chuckle.

He hooks his ankles around the chair I'm sitting in and pulls me close. "Knee to knee, right here."

I nod, and he again graces me with one of those sweeter smiles.

"Ask away," Lucas said.

"Parents divorced or married?"

"Divorced since I was three. Now my turn." He leans in and kisses me.

Eyes still closed, I ask, "Who do you live with?"

"My mom. My father lives in New Jersey. We see each other a few times a year. My turn again."

This time, I lean forward and kiss him lightly on the mouth.

When I start to pull away, he catches my lower lip with his teeth, his big hand gripping the side of my face, his fingers threaded through my hair, stopping my retreat.

"My answer was much longer and more detailed than that kiss. Give me more." He kisses me quickly and nips my bottom lip before moving back.

"So, the deeper the question, the longer the kiss, huh? Okay, let's see." I tap my lips, as if in thought. "Parents remarried or not? Siblings or no siblings?"

He laughs. "You're tough, Tessa. After I answer this one, you may want to take a deep breath and ready those lips."

I bite my cheeks to stop from smiling. In turn, his green eyes smile without his lips turning up as he answers.

"My parents divorced due to infidelity. My mother remarried first, to someone younger. They lasted three years. He had a pill issue and, apparently, that was contagious and expensive. Drinking is more budget-friendly. My father has remarried three times. The girls get younger every time, except the soon-to-be-ex-stepmother is older. He has two kids with wife number four, both girls. One is two, the other three. I see him on occasion, never really felt like any of his houses were homes. He owns a construction company. He likes to buy my love, thus the new car. which, at this point, I'm okay with."

I'm not sure why, but him being so open and vulnerable makes him less godlike and more real to me. Therefore, I lean forward, take his face, and I kiss him.

I slide my tongue between his lips and strokes his. He wraps his arm around me and pulls me closer, causing me to have to stand in order not to break this kiss. He slides his hands down to my hips, and I find myself on his lap, lips never leaving his, and he groans.

Needing to breathe, I move from his lips to his cheek, and then to his neck.

His voice rough and strained, he says, "Tessa, baby, you need to stop."

Embarrassed, I try to jump back. "I'm sorry."

"Don't be sorry. I love how curious you are. Drives me crazy," he says, fingers tangling in my hair. The other hand is still on my hip, his fingers digging in lightly. "Makes me want to do things to you." He closes his eyes.

"You want to do things to me?"

"God yes, Tessa. Not one thing about you turns me off."

I lean in, thinking I'd rather kiss him than have that conversation, but he leans back, looking ... shocked.

"Tessa, what's going on with you?"

"Is that a question?" I lean in. "If it is, don't I get to kiss you?"

"You get you're playing with fire, right? I'm on fire right now."

"Shall I be the fireman?" *What the hell is wrong with me?*

"Holy fuck, Tessa. I thought you were a virgin and shit. I mean—"

"I'm sorry, I didn't—" I quickly move off his lap and stammer as I rush to the bathroom, "I mean … wow. Oh my God, I was just trying … I'm sorry."

Inside, I lock the door, and it's a good thing, because he's trying to open the door.

"Dammit, Tessa. I'm sorry. I didn't mean to upset you. Please, open the door. I wasn't trying to upset you. I apologize, baby … Please, open the door."

Wrong choice of rooms to hide in. I now understand the term *claustrophobic*, so I open the door. With his hands on each side of the doorframe, I skate under his arms.

"Will you please take me to school? I don't want to be late."

As my feet hit the kitchen floor, he grabs me around the waist. "I said I was sorry. I just thought, because you'd never been kissed, you were a virgin, and then you started talking about role playing. I thought you wanted to take this slow. I'm sorry."

"I am a virgin, you asshole. You were my first kiss. But I haven't been living under a rock for eighteen years. So, yeah, I am a virgin, not an idiot," I snap.

He laughs, and I elbow him, harder than the first time, and he lets go.

I hurry to the door and open it. "If you're not going to take me to school, then you should leave now."

When he doesn't reply, I square my shoulders and force

myself to look at him. He leans against the kitchen counter, all four feet of it.

"Tessa, I've never met anyone like you. And when you're straddling me on my lap and kissing me, your kisses do things to me. I want you." The last part, his voice sounds like gravel. "But I am trying to respect you and not … well … you know, push things along." He takes a deep breath and runs his hand over his face. "Damn, Tessa, you confuse me."

"I don't want to be late. Can we go, please?"

"No." He steps up to me and grabs my shoulders. "Not until I know we're okay."

"We will be. I'm just"—I pause, resting my hands on his hips and looking down—"embarrassed."

He pulls me into him, hugging and kissing me tenderly on the head. "I'm sorry, Tessa."

"Me, too."

He kisses my head again then steps back, takes one of my hands, uses the other to grab my book bag, and walks us out the door.

When we get to his car, he opens the passenger side door.

To stop the awkward silence, as I slide in, I ask, "So, this from your father?"

"Yep, to replace the one he bought for my seventeenth birthday," he answers before shutting the door.

"Replace?" I ask as he gets in.

"Yeah."

"He must have been really trying to buy your love that day."

He laughs as he starts the car then pulls out before taking my hand.

"How many girlfriends have you had?"

"Tessa, do you really want to have that conversation

now? 'Cause I'm thinking maybe we should wait until we can play our game again."

"Now, please."

"I really don't know. Lost count." He starts to turn on the radio, and I grab his hand, stopping him.

"What was the longest relationship?"

"Do we have to do this now?" he asks again, looking out of the corner of his eye nervously.

"Yes."

"Eight months."

"Was it Sadi?"

"Yes."

"Did you have sex with her?"

"Tessa ..." he sighs out.

"I want to know."

"I cannot believe I am answering this, but yes, I did."

"Was she your first?"

"Really?" he asks as he pulls into town.

"Please?"

He clears his throat. "No. I've had a lot of sexual partners. My first was when I was fourteen."

I gasp.

"See? We shouldn't have had this conversation now."

"How many?" I ask, voice squeaking.

"Sadi was number twelve."

I hate math, but did he really say *twelve*? And did he really say *fourteen*, because that's like an average of three per freaking year.

As soon as he parks, maybe even before he actually puts it in park, I jump out.

He catches up quickly and grabs my hand. "They were all before you, Tessa, and none were at all like you. You're just ... better. I don't have time to explain it now, but I will after school. Please, just don't be mad."

Blue Love

I give him a weak smile and a peck on the cheek. "I'm not. See you at lunch."

The first bell rings, and I run like a thoroughbred at the Kentucky Derby.

"Why are you so late?" Jade calls from behind me as I rush down Make-Out Hall.

"Long story. I'll catch you up later," I call back.

* * *

Sitting in class, listening to the whispers behind me, the same girls who were talking on day one, I look out the window, thinking about the number—the dirty dozen; twelve, his jersey number—and what Mom said to me. *"Remember what you were taught and who you are."* The problem is, when I'm around him, I just don't want to remember any of that, but on the flip side, I don't want my first time to be with someone who's just going to move on to the next person as quickly as he seems to.

From the whispers in the hallway, those behind me now, and his admittance, I'm quite sure that's what I would be to Lucas Links—thirteen.

Rained Out

Chapter Eight

TESSA

Tuesday's game was called due to severe thunderstorms, and practice was canceled because the football team was taking up both the gym and the weight room.

It was a good excuse to put some much-needed space between us.

He still walked me to class, held my hand, sat with me in lunch, and near me in the classes we shared, but he was acting differently, too.

When he called that night, and basically all week, I made up excuses as to why I could only talk for a couple minutes, thus avoiding deep conversations that would lead to any talk about his sex life and my lack thereof.

Blue Love

I mean, truth be told, we'd only been together a few days, and it probably shouldn't have gone as far as it had gone so quickly. Also, I couldn't easily use that as an excuse to back away, since I was the person who brought it there.

On Friday after school, we had a short practice, because Blue Valley High's first Friday night under the lights game was tonight, and when I say first, I mean the absolute first in the history of Blue Valley football. We never had lights before, and the only reason we did now was because an anonymous donor had donated them.

I managed to talk Mom into letting me bring Kendall and Jake with me and keep them overnight, but of course, it came at a cost—Tuesday night at her place.

I would not be sharing that information with Lucas. I mean, if we're still together at that point, I'm pretty sure he's going to jump off the Tessa train and hop a more ... experienced one.

* * *

"What was the score again?" Jake asks as we walk on the field toward Alex and Lucas, who are surrounded by a slew of female fans.

"Thirty-four to fourteen, Saints," I tell him.

"Alex, Lucas," Jake pushes through the crowd toward them. "Awesome game! Good guys win!"

I watch through the crowd as he proceeds to give them both high-fives.

"They certainly are *good*." Some red-haired girl in the crowd of *Sadians* smiles seductively in their direction.

I watch as Sadi looks at Lucas. "I know personally that the quarterback is very good."

I watch his reaction—an annoyed eye roll—and then he scans the crowd and his eyes find mine. He smiles in that way that makes me smile back, and not the one I know makes me look like a weirdo.

Sadi follows his line of vision and sees he's looking at me. "Here come the prosti-tots."

My blood boils immediately, and I want to kick her ass all over the field.

"Tessa, baby, they were all for you!" Lucas yells so that Sadi can hear him.

Way better than kicking her ass, I think. Smirking as I watch him push through the crowd to me, where he kisses me sweetly on the cheek, picks me up, and spins me in a circle. "My good luck charm."

The cheek?

"I'm gonna get these two home. Make sure you head that way soon," Dad says from behind me, and I wonder if that's the reason for the cheek kiss.

"Nice game." Dad shakes Lucas's hand.

Lucas nods. "Couldn't have done it without the rest of the team."

"I know a thing or two about the importance of a man's team," Dad says, eyes slightly narrowed.

"Understood." Lucas nods.

"Dad," Alex says, jogging over to us, "you think the ice cream shop is still open? I could go for a brownie sundae."

Kendall and Jake both yell, "Yes!" and Alex tosses me the keys.

* * *

Waiting for the boys to shower and come back out, Jade shows me some Polaroid's she took during the game.

"I got some good ones of Lucas, too." She beams, handing a few to me. "The last one is my favorite."

Blue Love

I flip through them and get to the last one. It's of him holding me up in the air, me smiling down at him as he smiles up at me, during the spin.

"Now you need to bring your camera to the game so you can get some of Tommy and me."

Our aunt Josie gave us both Polaroid instant cameras for Christmas. I wasn't really good at remembering to bring mine to anything, except the falls. Jade knows this.

"I promise to make a point to do so."

Out of the corner of my eye, I notice a big blonde blur and her friends, who don't go to school here, walking toward us.

"You think he likes you, Tessa?" she yells to me.

I nod and try to reel in the anger. "Yeah, I do."

"You're just the flavor of the week. I'm the only one who lasted more than a month with him. He's going to get sick of you, farm girl."

"For the record, he and I have already discussed his past, um, how shall I say it?" I tap my finger to my lips and hold up a finger. "Oh yes, mistakes? Yeah, that's a perfect word for it. He's done with you. You should try to let that sink in. I'm not the reason you two broke up, so maybe you should get off my case."

"It's never over between him and me. He'll be back," Sadi says, "and you'll be on your ass. Just like the rest of them."

Looking her up and down in disgust, I spout off, "Maybe you should get a bit of self-respect. Seriously, why the hell would you want me, or anyone else, to know you've been a revolving door for him? You're pathetic, and you've done that to yourself."

"Don't look at me like that, bitch." Sadi swings on me.

I quickly move out of the way. "That all you got?"

She then lunges, grabs me by the hair, and I swing,

making contact with her face. She falls to the ground and attempts to bring me down with her. She fails.

Jade grabs me and yanks me back. "Tessa, don't."

"She deserves so much more than that!"

I see Lucas and Tommy running toward us and, apparently, so does Sadi, because she starts acting like a wounded animal and cries. "Did you see what your little whore did to me?"

"Yes, and I saw how it started." He takes her arm and yanks her toward her little black car. "Go home, Sadi. We aren't doing this shit, not ever again."

Her friends pile in with her.

"What is that thing? A fucking clown car!" I yell.

"Oh no, she said *fuck*," Jade gasps. "Tommy, she said fu—"

"It's a BMW, *farm trash*."

I start toward her. "I'm gonna kick her ass all the way back to hell where she—"

Tommy wraps a firm arm around me, and I'm sure it's to hold me back as he chuckles. "Easy, tiger."

She pulls out, and I watch as Lucas stands, arms crossed, looking at the car as if he's ... wounded.

I shrug Tommy's arm off my shoulder. "I'm gonna go. Can you give Jade a ride?"

Tommy looks at me as if he understands. "Sure thing."

* * *

I don't bother pulling out the main entry, not wanting to have to drive by him and see the way he looks at her. Because I'm likely to get out and knee him in the nuts. So, I use the maintenance road and head out the back way.

I see the line outside the ice cream shop around the corner and am glad I'll be going home to an empty house where I can try to chill the hell out before they get home. If it wasn't dark, I'd run to the falls.

Pulling in, I notice headlights following me and realize I won't have that kind of time.

Once parked, I hop out and start toward the house when I realize it's not Dad. It's *him*.

"Screw that," I growl as I move faster toward the house.

I'm not even sure he gets the car in park before he jumps out.

"Tessa … wait!" I hear him running toward me. "Why are you angry with me?"

"I saw how you looked at her. I'm not stupid. You care about her. Go be with her and leave me alone." I try to sound pissed, but it comes out more pathetic. "I told you that I don't have time or want—"

"Tessa, come with me." He grabs my hand and starts to basically drag me toward the barn.

"Get your hands off me. I can walk." I try to yank my hand away, but he just keeps pulling me behind him.

Inside the barn, he lets go and sits on a bale of hay. "Just give me a chance to explain. Sit with me."

"I'll stand, thank you very much," I snap.

"Okay, listen. I'm going to trust you with something, Tessa, because I know who you are and that I can. Maybe you'll start seeing I'm the same. But no matter what happens, this is between you and me."

I cross my arms and tap my foot.

"Sadi and I dated for about a month before we had sex. She was really good at playing head games, and it drove me crazy. I told her I loved her, feeling she needed that, and at the time, I thought I did. We were together for four months when she got pregnant." He scrubs a hand over his face. "I wanted her to keep it, wanted a family of my own, and she said that's what she wanted, too. But she had an abortion when I was at football camp, so I broke things off."

I hold my hand over my nauseous belly. "I'm sorry, Lucas."

"I hooked up with a girl, and we dated for about a month. Sadi threatened suicide. We got back together. We broke up, and she started seeing someone else. I was hurt, which was her intention, and we got back together for the final time. She was"—he pauses—"*is* a complete bitch. I broke things off again and started sleeping around."

He sighs. "I guess I do care, Tessa. I don't need someone ending their lives because of me. But I don't love her. I feel sorry for her. Pity her. I know what I want and what I don't want. She's obviously fucked-up about it. I'm not. I'm sorry if that hurts you."

Feeling a bit dizzy, I walk over and sit beside him. "That's a lot to absorb, so I'm sure it's incredibly hard to live. I'm sorry."

"I'm sorry you got hit because of me."

Folding my arms around my midsection, feeling a bit ashamed, I look down. "I hit her in the face. That was a first for me."

He wraps an arm around me and tucks me into his side. "She attacked you. It's called self- defense."

We sit in silence for a long time, because I have no idea what to say to him, and I'm sure he doesn't want to talk about it anymore than he already has.

When a car slows down, almost stopping in front of the house, I start to stand.

He tightens his grip. "I think that's her car. Baby, I'm so fucking sorry for dragging you into this shit."

"We *farm trash* are tough stock," I joke as the car pulls away.

"Don't ever call yourself trash. And don't pick on the farm thing. Kinda what sealed the deal for me wanting to be with you. Like your dad said, he has a little team here."

"Yeah," I agree, and then remember how broken that team is right now. "Maybe."

"No maybe about it. It's a fact."

She drove back by, slowing down a bit again.

"I shouldn't ask you to be part of my fucked-up life—hell, I should tell you to run—but I'm crazy about you, so I'm going to ask you to stick with me."

I lean into him, and he exhales a held breath.

"Do you think we should keep our distance and—"

"No. Hell no. She does not get to take you from me, too."

Tears build behind my eyes as I wrap my arms around him.

"Christ, Tessa, do not—" He stops and lifts my chin. "If it's too much, I promise that—"

I shake my head. "I don't want that, either, but you looked so sad, and—"

"That wasn't sad. That was me wanting to get her the fuck out of there before you or I lost our shit. One of the girls with her, the redhead, her father owns the sports station in Ithaca. He's covered me for three years now, and I can't mess that up this year. Not when college scouts are already showing up, and we're only two games in."

"College scouts?" I ask.

He smiles, and it's not the sweet one. It's the cocky, confident one. "Yeah, in case you haven't noticed, I'm pretty good at this football thing."

"You're hard not to notice." I smile back. "Especially now that you're all lit up on the field."

"Let's be real here. It could be pitch dark and I'd still shine."

He kisses me, and I think to myself, *He's pretty good at that, too.*

After a second kiss, more intense this time, I sit back. "They're going to be home any minute."

He stands and reaches out his hand to pull me up.

At his car, I get a hug, a really good hug.

"Call me when you get home?" I ask.

"Yeah, of course."

"Drive safe."

His eyes smile as he slides in. "Will do."

Walking toward the house, I look back. "Oh, and by the way, I was never a very big football fan, but the quarterback is awesome and superhot in those tight pants."

* * *

Sitting at the table, eating the hot fudge sundae that they brought home for me, the phone rings. I pick it up.

"We may as well super glue that to her hand," Alex jokes.

I stick out my tongue at him and answer, "Hello?"

"Made it home, baby." His voice is deep and much more relaxed.

"Thanks for letting me know."

"Of course."

Holding the phone to my ear with my shoulder, I grab my sundae, walk to the door, open it, and then make sure it's closed behind me. "Thank you for trusting me."

"Do me a favor and give me the same back."

"Always be honest with me, and I always will." I sit down and set my sundae on the porch.

"Always, huh?" he says with a smile in his voice. "You

make my head spin, Tessa Ross. Gonna be real honest with you and tell you I'm falling hard and fast."

Falling hard and fast, I think as the stupid smile spreads across my face.

"Awkward silence. We okay?" he asks.

Feeling a bit dizzy, I close my eyes and sit back. "Of course."

"Okay then. Goodnight."

"Lucas?"

"Yeah?"

I whisper, "Me, too."

He laughs softly. "Seriously making me sweat that out?"

"Sweet dreams." I smile, even though he can't see it.

* * *

Mom picks up the kids and tells Dad that she'll have to bring them back early because she was called in to do some overtime at the hospital, which causes him to get stone-faced. He never liked when she took on extra shifts, and that is clearly one thing that hasn't changed.

Once they're gone, I begin cleaning. I crank up the family boom box and ignore the song currently playing as I grab the dusting polish and cloth.

"Falling from number fourteen to number sixteen on this week's chart is 'Rain' by Madonna."

I drop the cloth and spray then head up the stairs to get my notebook. This song gets a star.

The phone rings, and with the music being so loud and the vacuum cleaner running, I'm surprised I hear it.

I answer, and Jade yells, "Are you ready?"

"For?" I ask, shutting off the vacuum cleaner.

"Number one. And I swear it's going to be a sign,

because as I told you before, Casey Kassem is seriously a prophet from God above."

I shake my head and laugh at her. "I'm more a Dick Clark girl, but—"

Jade squeals, "I told you! It's totally a sign!"

Then she begins singing along with Mariah Carey's "Dream Lover," and I can't help but join in.

When the song ends, she says, "Okay, I have to go, but I'll be down around six."

"Okay?"

"Oh, shoot, I forgot to tell you; our guys are taking us on a double date." She squeals again. "It's already double dad approved!"

"What!"

"Kisses," she sing-songs then hangs up.

And now I'm freaking out on the inside.

Double Date Trouble

Chapter Nine

TESSA

Jade hugs me tightly as soon as she walks into the kitchen where I am just putting things away from cleaning, which happened to be overkill today but expunged a massive amount of nervous energy.

"I'm spending the night."

"Okay." I laugh, stepping out of her way.

"Come on; we have prepping to do," she calls to me. "And you need a shower."

While I'm showering, Jade does her hair and makeup, telling me all about week one with Tommy. She tells me about the notes, the poems, and that he calls her *pretty girl*. The last part, I knew, which totally reminds me of a parrot, but Lucas calls me *baby*, so it is ... whatever.

"He goes to church every Sunday with his parents and sisters, who are older than him. His parents own a chain of convenience stores in Ithaca and towns farther south of it. He works at some of them part-time. And Tessa, I know he's the one. I can feel it."

I turn off the water, wrap my hair, and grab a robe.

"You aren't saying anything. You don't think he's the one? You—"

"No." I push the shower curtain back and step out. "I didn't say that. I just hope it's a feeling in your heart and not because Prophet Kassem has spoken."

She shakes her head. "Last night, when he was holding you back, and the way he was sweet to you. Then when you left, he was worried; that's what sealed the deal. No boy will ever be okay for me unless they love you, too."

I hug her, because, well, she's seriously amazing and because I hope, for her, that he is the one. "Forever lasts a long time, so go slow, okay?"

"Now you." She grins.

"We kind of played a game." I start to tell her all about Mom's place.

"A game?" she asks, as if it's scandalous.

I feed into that but can't help laughing as I joke. "Naked Twister, and he won. You should see the rules for what the loser has to give up at the end."

"Tessa, seriously?" She swats my arm. "Tell me!"

"Okay, I told him that I liked the kissing thing but really wanted to get to know him. We compromised. Each question answered got a kiss. It was very … enlightening."

Jade grins. "You are so bad, Tessa."

Then I tell her about our conversation on the phone last night.

"He's falling fast and hard? That's so cute. Too bad he

Blue Love

has baggage, huh? And the baggage followed him here, too. That's a total downer."

"Sadi has major issues. But I'm not worried about it. We'll be fine, or we won't. We'll see." I look in the mirror, searching for her reaction. She's concerned, but at least she doesn't think I'm being delusional. "What are you wearing tonight?"

"Not sure. What are you thinking?" Jade asks, continuing to primp.

I shake my head and giggle. "Something that shows off the goods I've been hiding all summer. I have boobs now, Jade. And I have you tonight, so I'm safe."

She claps. "I think you should wear your long, black skirt with that hot pink V-neck top, and your black, cropped jacket with your cowgirl boots, hair down and straight. I'll put some makeup on you, too."

"Okay, but only light makeup. The clothes are going to be stepping far enough out on a limb. Full makeup would seriously push me right off it."

"I can do that."

"And what are you wearing?"

"This." Jade pulls out a red, knee-length halter dress and a black denim jacket. "With black heels."

"Beautiful."

"Okay, now get your hair dried, and then I'll use my magic makeup wands to enhance your natural beauty."

I roll my eyes but do as she says.

When we're done getting ready, we look in the mirror.

"We look dope." Jade smiles then bends down and ruffles through her bag before pulling out her camera. "Let's try to take a picture in the mirror." She holds it up.

I laugh. "Seriously vain."

"I'd take pictures of myself all day if I could get rid of the glare and know that the angle was right."

The camera spits out the picture, and she starts fanning it. When the gray fades, there is totally a glare.

After two more, she sets the camera down. "Someday, someone better figure this shit out. Tommy always asks for pictures of me."

We walk out to the kitchen, hand in hand, a united front against, as Jade calls them, the double dads, and their possible disapproval.

When neither flips, I can't lie and say it wasn't a little disappointing.

"It's about time." Jake sighs in exaggeration as he stands up and walks past us.

Kendall grins. "You two both look so pretty."

Dad musses up her hair. "Where did my little Tomboy go?" But he's looking at me.

* * *

When Lucas and Tommy pull in, we both beeline for the door to make sure to avoid an embarrassing "Dad cleaning the gun" situation.

Lucas doesn't even look me over—also a bit disappointing. He looks me straight in the eyes as he holds the door open for Tommy and Jade.

"He's got to be uncomfortable back there," I whisper to him.

"Yeah, well, I want you by me," Lucas says, pulling his Tom Cruise in *Top Gun* style sunglasses over his eyes.

He holds my hand as we drive and doesn't say much at all. I seriously hope "disappointment" isn't the theme for tonight.

Pulling into the parking lot of Dock Side, I get butterflies.

"Fancy," Jade says, leaning between the seats as she looks at the restaurant.

"You Ross girls deserve the best," Tommy says as Lucas parks the vehicle and kills the engine.

Once Tommy unfolds himself from the back seat and takes Jade's hand, Lucas locks the door and reaches for mine.

I step back.

"Tessa?" he asks.

"Look, I know I'm new to this dating thing, and dates in general, but if they don't involve conversation, or at the very least—" I smash my lips together before I say, *Tell me I look nice, for heaven's sake*, and shake my head. "Never mind."

"No, not never mind. Sorry I haven't said much, but the thoughts running through my head are not that of hearts and flowers. Actually, I'm a bit thrown." He motions up and down to me. "Christ, are you trying to kill me?"

"What?" I half-laugh.

He steps forward, erasing the space between us, and grabs both my hands. "You still want honesty?"

Unable to speak, I simply nod.

"You're fire right now, which is some bullshit. So, instead of telling you how fucking good you look, I've been conversing with my dick this whole ride."

"Wha-wha-what?"

"*Sit, boy. Down, boy. Stop straining your neck to look at her, boy. Play dead, boy*. Shit like that so I don't walk into this place with a hard-on."

I swear my mouth is hitting pavement.

"You and I are taking it real slow. I'm more than good with that. But that doesn't mean you can just walk in a house less than twenty-four hours ago, in jeans and a baggy sweatshirt, and then walk out that same door like a runway model and expect me to not get worked up. I'm not perfect, Tessa—certainly not good enough for you—but I'm trying."

Still, I can't find words.

"We good?" he asks firmly.

I nod.

He turns around, my hand in his, walking with a purpose toward the restaurant, where Jade and Tommy are waiting for us. Finally, I find my words.

"Then you better untuck that shirt and put away that ass."

He almost stumbles as he looks back, his jaw now unhinged.

I walk past him, square my shoulders, and whisper, "Virgin, not an idiot, and certainly not blind."

As soon as we walk in, we are led through double oak doors, through a bar, and onto the back deck that overlooks Cayuga Lake, next to an outdoor fireplace.

The hostess takes the little card that says *"Reserved"* off the table and smiles at Tommy.

Lucas and Tommy pull the chairs out for Jade and me, who share smiles as we sit down. The hostess then hands us the menus and excuses herself.

"You look great every day, but wow, Jade, just wow." Tommy smiles as he looks her over.

"You sure? You didn't say anything this whole time, and I thought—"

Looking at my menu, I say it is as serious as a heart attack, "He was talking to puppies."

Lucas laughs. "Dogs, baby, not puppies."

"What?" Jade asks, confused.

The waitress appears at the perfect time, setting a bottle of wine in the middle of the table then four glasses of water before us and asks, "Do you need more time, or are you ready to order?"

"We'll need a few more minutes," Lucas says.

I look over as Tommy's eyes rake over Jade.

"Pretty girl, look at you. You turned into *Pretty Woman* tonight."

Jade chokes on her water.

Patting her back, Tommy asks, "You okay?"

Jade whispers, "You do know that *Pretty Woman* is a movie about a hooker, don't you?"

"Um, no. You know I didn't mean that, right?" Then he leans in closer and whispers, but we still hear him, "You watch porn?"

"No!" Jade gasps as she stands and walks to me, hand extended. "Can we go to the bathroom, please?"

Once in the bathroom, Jade tells me what Tommy said. I don't have the heart to interrupt her and tell her that I heard it all. And honestly, it's way more funny coming from her retelling. Laughing, I tell her about the parking lot.

We both use the restroom, wash our hands, and once we get it together, we rejoin our guys.

Both of them stand and pull out our chairs again, and we sit, feeling much less alone in our awkwardness.

"Funny, right?" Lucas whispers in my ear as he pushes in my chair.

"Sure is."

We order dinner, and the waitress opens the bottle of wine, offering a glass to each of us ... minors at the table. Jade and I look at each other, clearly both wondering what to do.

"We're all set for now," Lucas tells her, and she sets it down.

Once she leaves the table, Lucas and Tommy excuse themselves to use the restroom, and Jade and I both giggle.

"They think we're twenty-one," Jade whispers.

"Because we look so dope," I use her phrase from earlier.

When she laughs a little too loudly, as Jade does when she is nervous, I whisper, "Shh …" as I look around.

In looking around, I notice something odd. A woman who looks a lot like my mother is sitting in the dark corner of the deck … with a man.

It can't be!

On closer examination, I realize it *is* Mom, and I also notice him holding her hand.

"We just need time apart …" "You don't know what I've lived through for those years."

Everything Mom has told me, and I assume my siblings, is a lie. Everything I've been brought up to believe—a joke. Everything I have avoided with Lucas, because I was almost ashamed of … the feelings I've all but convinced myself were nerves … Hell, I even told myself they were butterflies! Well, they weren't just in my belly. Everything was bullshit!

I look away and vow to refuse to live like this anymore, refuse to hold myself to her standards, ones in which she doesn't even hold herself to. Then I grab the bottle of wine, pour myself a glass, and drink it down before Jade can even say a thing.

It tastes dry and disgusting, but so what? Maybe my fucking taste buds have been brainwashed, too. Then I pour myself another.

"Tessa," Jade whispers, "what are you doing?"

I ignore her as I down the second glass, looking at Mom, part of me hoping she sees me. I reach for the bottle again, and Jade reaches for it, too. I'm quicker and pour myself another.

"What the hell are you doing? This isn't like you."

Blue Love

"I'm being naughty." I hold up the glass. "And liking it."

The first swallow causes my stomach to lurch, but I force myself to finish.

Reaching for the bottle again, so does Jade ... again.

"If you touch that, I'll scream, and we'll all get in trouble. Leave it alone."

I pour the fourth glass, almost emptying the bottle, as Lucas returns.

Afraid he, too, will try to stop me, I lift the glass and gulp it down.

"Oh my God, Tessa," Jade whispers.

I look back at her and see that she's not looking at me. She sees Mom.

"Tessa, let's go to the bathroom." Jade stands. "Now."

I sway a bit when I stand and focus really hard on my footing, as well as attempting to shove hurt behind pissed in my head, and my heart.

Once inside the bathroom, Jade hugs me. "Oh, Tessa, I'm sorry."

"Fuck that." I bark out a laugh.

When Jade opens the bathroom door, I ask, "What are you doing?"

She holds the door shut but leans out and talks to someone.

"If that's her, let her come in here. I have a few things to say to *her*."

Jade steps in and shuts the door. "Do you have to pee?"

"Pee." I laugh. "Pee!"

"Okay, let's go."

Dizzy, I'm so fucking dizzy that I watch my feet as I walk out into the restaurant's hall. Focused, so focused that, when fresh air hits my face, I look up and realize ...

"Why are we outside?"

"Many reasons. One being your mom is in there."

"Your aunt." I laugh. She doesn't.

"Another, you're a minor and, oh yes, let's not forget you signed a sports contract promising not to freaking drink!"

"Hey, ladies," I hear Lucas and feel that stupid grin spread across my face.

"I'll go get Tommy. You watch her." She scowls at me before I turn away.

Once she's gone, I turn and look at him.

He's looking me over, eyes narrowed. "You good?"

I step toward him and link my hands behind his neck. "You tell me." Then I kiss him. Not only do I kiss him, but I pull myself up and wrap my legs around him while kissing him.

"Easy, tiger." He laughs in amusement. "Jade, what the hell is going on?"

"Jade?"

I look behind me, still wrapped around him.

She rolls her eyes. "Well, obviously, my cousin is drunk, and just so you know, this is a first for her."

I lean in and whisper, "You're going to be my first."

His eyes smile, and then ... Jade pulls me down from him.

Music starts playing in the background, through outdoor speakers, and I decide it's time to dance, between cars, in the parking lot.

"Lucas, come dance with me, and I'll tell you all about it." I curl my finger at him, thinking I'm being all sexy, and not caring if I'm not.

"Jade, can you get my purse? Grab some money out and pay for my first bottle of wine. Oh, and be my best friend and grab me another?"

Lucas hands Jade his credit card. "I got dinner. Skip

the bottle and go help Tommy out of this jam. If there's any problem because of the wine, come get me. And leave a good tip. That should help avoid the problem."

Lucas walks toward me as Jade heads into the restaurant.

"Baby, what's going on?"

"I'm dancing, and I want you." I grab him by the waist of his slacks then laugh because the word *slacks* is seriously hilarious. Slacks. Oh, right. "I mean, I want you to dance with me, or something, with me."

"How about we talk over here for a minute first?" He takes my hands and walks us to a bench surrounded by pretty flowers.

"I don't want to talk." I plop down on his lap. "I want to dance or kiss your incredibly sexy face." So, I do, and he kisses me back.

"Tessa, I love this, but you're drunk." Lucas's voice is deeper than usual.

"Yes, I am, but I know what I want, and I'm sitting on it. Do you know what you want, Lucas?" I take his hand and slide it from my waist to my ass. "This, right?"

He nods slowly. "But not when you're loaded, and not with an audience. Your cousin and Tommy will be out here any minute."

"Then, how about these?" I pull his other hand up to my chest.

"Tessa"—Lucas pulls his hands away slowly—"stop, please. You're killing me."

"Ya know, I think I will be really good in bed." I keep his hand on my chest. "Or right here on the bench." I laugh.

When he doesn't move, or even respond, I lean in to see what green his eyes are. "Why so serious, Lucas? This is supposed to be fun, right? And, just think, you got to second base on our first date."

He stands up with me in his arms and begins moving.

My body, the one I've lied to, heats in places I've ignored.

Then my feet hit the ground as he unlocks his car. He opens the door and sets me inside.

Laughing, I ask, "Will you chill? I am eighteen."

To that, he shuts the door and walks around to the driver's side.

He doesn't get in, though. Tommy and Jade do, and then he gets in and tosses his shades on the dash.

When he pulls out, he heads in the direction of home.

"I'm not ready to go home."

"You don't say," he grumbles, yet he still heads that way.

"I have to pee. Can you pull over?" At a stop light, I try to find the door handle.

Lucas reaches over and puts his arm in front of me. "In a minute. We'll pull into the park up here, all right?"

"Sure, I would love to pee in the park." I giggle and hold his hand. "Pee in the park."

A few seconds later, we're pulling into the parking area, and as soon as he stops, I jump out and throw my coat on my seat.

"I hear music. After I pee, I am going to dance with you, Lucas … dirty dance." And then I head toward the first building I see.

"This way, drunkard." Jade grabs my hand and pulls me in the opposite direction.

Walking past the guys, I hear Tommy ask, "She okay?"

"Apparently not. I have no idea what brought this on, but drunk Tessa can get me in a whole lot of trouble."

Lucas laughs, and I can't help but feel relieved. Not fully, though, because I really have to pee.

When we walk out of the bathroom, I feel much better. I think, anyway.

I see Lucas holding on to take-out containers and hurry as I skip toward him. He smiles.

"I squatted and peed because public toilets carry germs and diseases. By the way, Lucas, do you have any STDs?"

He shakes his head.

"Good to know. I wiped and washed my hands, and now I'm ready to find that music and dance. We need to find where it's coming from. Let's go."

He grabs me. "Hey, I want you to do me a favor, okay?"

Smiling, I nod.

"I want you to take these two pills and drink this." He hands me the pills and a bottle of water.

"If it's a date rape drug, I can assure you that you don't need it. I want to remember the first time you're—"

Jade covers my mouth, and I pull her hand away.

"I'm a bit tipsy, so maybe a refresher tomorrow?"

He doesn't respond, so I decide *screw it* and start toward the music again.

He grabs my arm again.

I look back. "Change your mind? Because, seriously, anything you want, Lucas. And I mean *anything*." I pop the pills in my mouth and swallow them back. "Satisfied?"

"Not yet." His voice is huskier than before. "Will you sit and eat with me? Finish the start of our date here? A picnic?"

"Sure, I will." I spot a tree and hurry to it, sit down, and pat the spot next to me.

"Looks like Lucas is who Tessa wants to take care of

her right now, Jade. Can you and I walk over there and eat?" Tommy asks.

Jade sighs. "Sure, just not too far, though."

"Hell no. Go have fun. Break rules. Get to second base and catch up."

"Tessa," Lucas says, sitting beside me and placing the food containers between us.

"I want to feed you. I wanna sit on your lap as I feed you, okay?"

Lucas closes his eyes momentarily. "That would be nice."

I hike my black skirt up so I can sit facing him, take a fork, and twirl it around in the pasta. As soon as I pick it up, it falls off, so I try again.

"Nope, you will not win," I scold the pasta then try a third time. "Slippery little bastards, I'm gonna get you."

I pick up the spaghetti with my fingers and shove it in his mouth. "See? I don't lose."

His eyes are smiling as I pull my fingers away and watch him chew.

"You're so hot." I wipe some of the sauce that I dripped on his lips and sucked it off my finger.

He shifts, and I *feel* him. "Your dog woke up."

His eyes widen, and I feel sexy.

I wiggle a bit on his lap, and he closes his eyes and groans.

"That feels very good, Lucas." And it does. It feels tingly, so I move again.

He grabs my hips, stopping my movement as he swallows the pasta. "Tessa, this is not—"

I quickly take another handful of pasta and shove it in his mouth. He nips my fingers when I pull them away, and I feel my nipples stiffen.

Looking down, I see them beneath my tank top. Then I

Blue Love

run my fingers over them and gasp. I do it again then decide I'd like to feel them without my shirt covering them up, so I pull my shirt up to look at them.

Caressing my bra, it feels even better.

I look up at him and whisper, "Bite these, please."

"Fuck, Tessa, I want you so badly right now, but you're drunk. Therefore, I need you to cover yourself before I explode."

I grab his face and tell him again, "Bite now, please."

"Tessa, I'm going to tell you one more time—"

"I bet they're big enough that I can do it myself. Huge boobs." I scowl, looking down at them then back up at him. "So, what's it gonna be? You or—"

"Pull your shirt down, or I'm going to get Jade over here, understand?"

"Okay, *Dad*." I grin, and before he can start talking again, I shove more pasta into his mouth, pull my finger out, and lick the sauce from them.

Lucas begins to choke.

"Are you okay?" Jade asks.

I pull my shirt down. "Double dates, overrated."

I hand him a bottle of water. "Put this in your mouth and suck it down."

"Everything okay?" Jade asks again. Closer now.

"No, not really." I look back at her. "He won't touch my boobs, and Jade, they are great boobs. Look!"

"Tessa—enough!" Jade snaps.

"You need to lighten up. Have a drink. That'll help. Look at me."

"Tessa, get up and come with me," Jade demands.

"Are we gonna find the music?"

"Yes, we are," Jade says, forcing a smile.

"Good, because I want to dance, Jade, and we're

gonna dance." I stand then hurry past Jade to get to the music, but she grabs my hand.

"These aren't running shoes."

"Cool. Now let's go find out if they're dancing shoes."

A few feet away, there's a sign that reads, "*LIVE BAND*," and an arrow pointing to the right.

"Thank God, because a dead band would suck." I laugh.

Jade laughs, too.

"Eighties music!" I smile as I twirl around on the wooden dance floor, and when I stop, I do it in perfect fashion.

I squeeze Lucas's arms. "Hot damn, Links."

"*Hot damn, Links?*" I look up and see it's not Lucas. It's Jade.

"Girl, you have some guns." I laugh.

"If I ever drink and act like this, please promise me you'll hide me from all humanity."

"Fine, but only if you promise to dance with me now."

"Oh, my good Lord, fine." She twirls me in a circle, and my stomach feels a bit off.

"No more twirling, either."

We dance, we sing, we laugh, but we do not twirl.

From behind me, Lucas says, "Can I have this dance?"

"Yeah, but watch your toes," Jade jokes. Well, I think she's joking, anyway.

"Hey, I'm a good dancer."

She laughs. "Best in the world."

I look up at Lucas as he slides an arm around me. "I'm a good dancer."

"Yeah, baby, you are."

"Also, I called Jade, Links. You should feel her guns." I step back. "Jade, come here. Let Lucas feel your guns."

She laughs. "Piss off."

Blue Love

I swing around and see Sadi standing close to us, but maybe I'm just drunk.

Screw it. "Hey, Sadi! How are you?" I laugh and wave at her.

Lucas turns me around. "I think we should get back to the car."

"No way. I want to dance. Look, Lucas, my friend Sadi's here."

"Tessa, you're drunk. We should go," Lucas says more seriously.

"Buzz kill."

He rolls his eyes and shakes his head.

"Please dance with me, Lucas." I jump up in his arms.

"One dance, and then we leave, okay?"

The band plays Tesla's "Love Song," and he pulls me in tighter. We begin to sway and, within seconds, Tommy and Jade are right beside us.

"'*So, you think that it's over,*'" Jade sings to me, and this is when we join the eighties Live Band ... unofficially, of course.

When the chorus begins, I raise both arms in the air and sing the entire thing. "'*Love is all around you ...*'"

I about pee myself when Tommy begins playing the air guitar, but not at him, because he is seriously good it.

"'*Love will find a way. Darlin ...*'" we all sing together.

The next song is "Eternal Flame" by The Bangles.

"Baby, do you know this song?" he whispers in my ear, sending tingles through my body, and I nod. "Sing to me, please."

Holding his face, and with those amazing green eyes, I sing the whole song. When it ends, he kisses me in the sweetest way.

"Get a room!" Some rude bitch yells in an annoying as hell voice, and that rude bitch's name is Sadi.

"Don't let her ruin this moment."

"I won't." I wrap my arms around him, push up on my toes, and kiss his neck.

"Check that out," Lucas whispers as the next song begins. "Jade isn't even trying to punch her in the eye."

I step back, a bit shocked. "Probably because she didn't attack her."

"I know, baby. I'm just joking."

Hurt. Yep, that hurt. I hiccup, and that hurts, too. "I don't feel well."

"Let's get out of here." He takes my hand, and I'm seriously not sure if I want him, too.

"Hey, Tommy, we're going to head back to the car."

"Oh, Tessa, he likes it in the front seat ... with me on his lap!" Sadi yells.

"That won't be happening. I'm not on birth control yet, Sadi. Don't want to take any chances," I yell then flip her off.

Lucas's jaw drops. "Tessa, don't be a bitch."

My immediate reaction is to strike him, just as he has done to me. And when my hand does just that, I cover my mouth in shock. But, when he glares at me, I get pissed again.

Storming away, I hear Sadi's wretched voice again. "Feisty little one, isn't she?"

Within seconds, I'm in his car and pissed, so fucking pissed that I am ready to cry, and that is not happening.

Somewhere off of Route Thirteen, my mouth fills with saliva, and my stomach turns.

"I think I'm going to throw up."

Lucas turns down a dirt road, pulls over, and I nearly fall out the door and begin vomiting immediately.

My hair gets pulled away from my face, and it doesn't stop.

"Oh Tessa," Jade whispers soothingly as she holds my hair.

When nothing more can possibly come up, I stand on shaky legs, a complete and total mess, with Mom's words running through my head.

"Jade," Lucas yells from the car. "Here's some water, a toothbrush, and toothpaste."

Embarrassed, I don't dare turn around. "Did she get any on her?"

I look down at my tank and skirt. Then I look at Jade, my lip now trembling.

"A little," Jade answers, rubbing my back.

Doors open and shut behind me as I brush my teeth and Jade pulls my hair into a ponytail and fastens it.

"We're going to change these clothes, okay?" Jade says quietly.

I pull my tank over my head as she pulls down the skirt.

Teeth chattering, a sweatshirt goes over my head.

"So cold," I say, hugging myself.

"Step in," Jade says, so I do, and quickly.

"Do you have an old bag that I can put these in?" Jade asks as I squat down and cover my legs with the sweatshirt to try to stop my teeth from chattering and my body from shaking.

I hear doors open and shut.

"Okay, come on now," Jade says, pulling me up.

I hear a phone ring, reminding me that he has a cell phone. He answers it.

As Jade hugs me to warm me up, Lucas tells someone, probably Sadi, "Give me twenty, and I'll meet you."

And then I cry.

"It's going to be okay, Tessa. You'll feel better in the morning."

"No, I won't." I wipe my eyes and decide *screw it*. I don't even care if he sees me. I'd rather that than to freeze.

I slide in the car, and he immediately asks, "You okay?"

Emotions change and, again, I'm pissed. "No, I'm not. You called me a bitch," I snap then begin to hiccup again.

"I said not to be a bitch, Tessa. There's a difference. And you slapped me, so …" He shrugs as he pulls onto the road and turns around.

"Really? Is that how it went?" *Hiccup.* "Because I distinctly remember you were sticking up for her and called me a bitch. Of course I slapped you! Call me a bitch again and see what happens next time."

"Tessa, you're drunk. Stop," Jade pleads from behind me.

"Jade, he loves her," I sing-song. "He wanted to be her baby—"

"Now you're being a little bitch," Lucas yells. "Just shut up!"

The Aftermath

Chapter Ten

TESSA

No one says a word for the rest of the ride home, not until we drive by the farm.

"Lucas, you missed the turn," Jade whispers.

"Alex is meeting us at camp," Lucas seethes.

"You called my brother?" I yell, voice breaking.

"No, I answered his call while your drunk ass was being changed on the side of the road." He hits the gas.

"And we're done."

"Yeah, you think you get to call it after that shit?"

"Both of you, shut the fuck up!" Jade yells.

Shocked, I look back at her.

"Nothing nice gets said in moments like these, Tessa.

Not one damn thing, so shut up." She shifts her eyes to Lucas. "You, too."

When we pull off of Harvest Road and onto the dirt road leading to camp, the headlights shine on Alex standing with his arms crossed. He looks pissed.

Lucas throws the car into park and turns to me. "You stay."

Alex walks toward his window. "She okay?"

"Just let her sit there for a minute, Alex," Jade says sadly. "We went to dinner and she saw—"

"I know what she saw, Jade. I've known for a few days that Mom was seeing someone. Dad told me."

I'm not sure I've ever felt so much anger, rage, and fucking betrayal in all my life, but I am sure I heard what he just said.

I throw the door open and run toward him. "You knew, Alex, and you didn't tell me? Dad knew?" I scream. "What the fuck is wrong with you two?" Batting away tears, I trip and fall over a fucking rock.

"Shit," Lucas says, now beside me as he grabs me and helps me up.

"Is she drunk?" Alex yells at him.

"Yes, I am! I'm loaded, Alex. And guess what else? I showed Lucas my boobs and asked him to bite them, and I wanted him to!"

Alex reaches for me, and Lucas puts himself between us. "Not now, man. Leave her alone. Not now."

"You need to leave, Lucas. I'll deal with her. You've done more than enough," Alex says through clenched teeth.

"Don't talk to him like that! He was well-behaved. You should be patting him on the back. He wouldn't touch me!" I scream at him, tears now falling like a summer storm.

"Tessa, enough." Lucas wipes at my tears. "Alex, I got this, man. Give it a minute, please."

Lucas then picks me up, carries me to the other side of the car, and set me down next to him.

"I'll be back."

Willing myself to stop crying, I listen as he tells Alex about tonight, starting with the restaurant and the wine, moving on to the way I was coming on to him and the fact that he was a perfect gentleman. He asks Alex about the man with Mom, and he tells him that he works at the hospital with her.

When Lucas returns, he squats in front of me. "Drink this and listen up. I didn't call you a bitch at the park. I said *not to act like one.* I trusted you with my deepest, darkest secret and expected you to keep that secret. Now, I'm not a Sadi fan, Tessa, but that was mean. Cruel, actually. I have watched you for over two weeks. Admired the hell out of how you treat the people you love. The girls on your team all look up to you. Your softness and some of that sass is what drives me crazy about you. I didn't see that tonight. I know you're hurting, and I'm sorry I can't fix it for you, but don't ever slap me across the face again. Got it?"

"You called me a bitch in the car," I whisper.

"You were way out of line."

"Don't call me that again, even if I deserve it. Got it?"

He stuck out his hand to shake. "Deal?"

"Deal." I try to smile, but even my face knows better.

"You ready to see your brother yet?"

"No," I snap.

He sits next to me and pulls me against him. One arm wrapped around me, he uses the other hand to gently pull my head to his shoulder. "Talk to me, Tessa Ross."

"I don't dare say a thing, because if I do, and you get mad, or worse, reject me again, then—"

"I wanted to do everything you asked me to tonight, Tessa. You get those thoughts out of your head, the ones of me not wanting you, and get pissed. You get to the point your cheeks are burning with embarrassment thinking I want you any less, I'm telling you don't even go there, because you have no idea the thoughts I have about what I want to do to you every night—hell, even in my dreams. And let's not leave out the morning shower. Your tits are beautiful. Perfect, actually. It just wasn't right. I don't want to have sloppy drunk sex with you, not for your first time." He kisses my head.

"Well, I wasn't asking for sex. I was asking you to ... Well, you know what I asked."

"Not when you're drunk, Tessa. Only when you're sober and very alert, and not for a long time." He lifts my chin so I'm looking at him. Even in the dark, I see his eyes are soft. "Drunk women are good for one thing. You are better than that, and I want no regrets with you." He kisses me softly on the lips. "Now rest."

* * *

Squinting, I awake in a field, in a sleeping bag, and in his arms. The minute I lift my head, I feel like it's going to explode. I have no idea how I even got here.

I deserve this, I think as I sit up.

"How are you feeling, baby?"

"Like an elephant stepped on my head," I groan.

"I guess you drank too much, huh?" Lucas slides out of the sleeping bag, stands up, and extends his hand.

"What happened? I mean, I remember drinking and seeing my mom, but the rest is a blur."

"You really want to know?"

The dawn starts to break and, let me tell you, it's no friend of mine.

"Ouch. I need to sit."

"Maybe you should ask your brother. He knows everything." Lucas chuckles.

I sit back down as bits and pieces come back, and then I hold my head. "Or maybe you should just tell me."

After Lucas recaps last night's events, not seeming pissed off in the least, I ask, "Are we okay?"

"We"—his green eyes sparkle as bright as the sun, and that doesn't hurt my head at all—"are fine. Growing pains. We'll figure it all out."

"Lucas?"

He smiles as if to ask *what*.

I shake my head. "Never mind."

He leans in and whispers, "Your face gets pink when you're thinking naughty thoughts. So, whatever you're questioning, don't. And baby, I can't wait to meet the girls on a more personal level."

It hurts to smile, but it can't be helped, especially since he totally just read my mind.

"You ready to talk to your brother?"

"No. No, I'm not."

* * *

As soon as Lucas gave me the recap, I remembered everything, and I especially remembered that I'm pissed at Alex. I can't even look at him, let alone answer his annoying questions. But I'm also not going to fight with him, because it's still early enough that Dad's still in bed. And at least I can get some sleep before Alex tells Dad.

I jump out of the truck, run into the house, up to my room, where Kendall is asleep, and slip into bed.

When I wake up, I need to use the bathroom.

Walking downstairs and into the living room, Alex and Dad are sitting on the couch.

"Stomach bug?" Dad asks as I walk past him.

"Uh-huh."

After eating some toast, I decide to soak in the bath, and to avoid Dad and Alex, I stay soaking until the water grows too cold.

When I walk out of the bathroom, wrapped in a robe, I stick my nose in the air and head upstairs, completely ignoring the fact that Mom has now joined Alex and Dad in the living room.

"Tessa, we need to talk," Mom calls after me.

The cordless phone, that was, in fact, by my side all the times, rings as I'm throwing on a pair of jogging pants.

"Hello."

"Hey, baby. How are you feeling?"

"Better. You?"

"Missing you."

I smile.

"You feel up to meeting my mom? She'd like to meet you and barbeque."

"What?"

"I've met yours, now it's time you meet mine."

"Well, mine is here right now, waiting for me to get dressed"—I pull a shirt over my head—"so we can *talk*."

"So, the girls are free right now?"

"The girl ..." I stop immediately, and he laughs.

"You blushing?"

"Maybe?"

"Get through your talk, and I'll see you at five."

"Lucas ..."

"Bring swim wear. And don't overthink this."

"I'm probably grounded for life."

Blue Love

"You're not. See you soon." He hangs up.

* * *

Head held high, I sit down in a chair opposite the couch, where Dad and Mom are sitting. Alex in the middle. It does not go unnoticed that she looks extremely uncomfortable.

"Talk."

"I have been on one date with the man you saw me with last night."

Dad interrupts, "But has had lunch with him twice at the hospital."

Mom sighs. "Obviously, your father knows everything about it. I don't feel it's something that you should be concerned about."

Before I lose my shit, I ask, "Where are Jake and Kendall?"

"With Uncle Jack and Jade, fishing," Alex answers.

Now I lose my shit. "Why do you need to go on dates, Mom? You're married and have five kids, for crying out loud!"

"Tessa, this is between your parents, our relationship, not that of our children's. You don't get to make the decisions here. Things haven't changed. We both still love you," Dad says sternly.

"Thank you, John," Mom says.

"Are you freaking kidding me? You're okay with this?" I yell at him. "Hey, Dad, why don't we just start pimping her out?"

"That's enough, young lady." Mom stands abruptly. She hugs Alex then walks over to me. "I will see you at your game on Tuesday."

"Don't plan on it, *bitch*."

She immediately slaps my face, and before I do something worse than calling my mom a bitch, I jump up and run to the bathroom.

Tears fill my eyes as I look in the mirror, a handprint adorning my face. Then I suddenly start laughing and, for the life of me, I can't stop.

"Tessa, you okay in there?" Alex asks from just outside the door.

"Hell yes!" I continue to laugh.

"Open the door."

"It isn't locked." I laugh louder.

He walks in and looks at me. "I'm sorry I didn't tell you first."

I continue laughing. "Don't you see? This gets us off the hook. No more straight and narrow, Alex. Now we can let loose and have fun."

"No, Tessa, that's not right, and you know it." He hugs me, and it immediately turns my laughter into tears.

"Why? Because she said so? Look at her now, Alex! All of our life, we have done what she says, and now look! At! Her! Seriously, we've been taught all our lives that God's law and family are what matters the most, and we've done a really good job following that. And now look at her! Look at her!" I sob. "I will not do a damn thing she says. She's nothing but a phony. And what the hell is he doing? Letting her date other people? What the hell is that? So, no, Alex, I won't follow their rules. I'll do what feels right and good."

Alex holds me tighter. "Tessa, you're their child, not their judge. Keep that in mind."

I look up at him. "This makes no sense."

"Not much has over the years, but don't you fall apart." He pulls me in for another tight hug.

***

The phone rings, and I jump up to answer it.

"Hey, baby, be there in thirty."

Shit, shit, shit.

"Okay."

I jump out of bed, grab clothes out of mine and Kendall's shared closet, and realize I haven't a clue as to what the temperature is.

Still wrapped in my robe, I run down the stairs and yell, "Alex, what's the weather like?"

"Sixty-five degrees and sunny. Why?" he answered.

"I forgot I was invited to dinner at Lucas's at five. He's on his way, and I'm a wreck."

"Did you ask Dad?"

Ask? I think with a huff.

"No, can you tell him for me?"

Looking in the bathroom mirror, I am horrified. My face and eyes are all puffy and red, and I swear I can still see Mom's handprint on my face.

I turn on the cold water and splash myself over and over. Then I run a brush through my hair and consider putting it up in a bananas clip, but then I remember hate them and grab a butterfly clip, which I also dislike, but I have to do something with my hair. I brush it out and clip the sides back.

Grabbing Jade's bag, that is still here, I use her foundation to try to cover up the red, and I even swipe some mascara on my lashes, even though I've always thought mascara looked silly. I gotta say, though, I kind of love how long my lashes look in black.

Next, I run upstairs and grab the black, knee-length shorts and throw on a gray cami and a darker gray cardigan.

I see a pair of Molly's sandals—black thongs—and grab them before running down the stairs, where I rush to the bathroom to brush the hell out of my teeth as I look myself over.

"You're good." I nod to my insecurities staring back at me in the mirror and, for once, I mean it.

I hurry out to the kitchen, expecting to have a disagreement with Dad. Instead, I find him sitting with Lucas.

Where is Alex?

"Feeling better, Tessa?" Dad asks.

Good Lord, what has Lucas told him?

"Lucas said he thinks maybe it was the food. His stomach has been off today, too. You'll be home early, right? It's a school night." Dad stands up, kisses my cheek, and then walks into the living room.

Leaning back against the counter, I sigh.

Lucas chuckles. "You ready to go?"

"Yes." I head for the door.

"Hey, you going to grab some shoes? I could carry you, but …"

"Ha-ha."

"Grab a swimsuit, Tessa," he calls as I head back to the bathroom to grab the shoes.

"Don't you think it's too cold?"

"Don't sass me, girl," he says, smiling.

When I come out, he's not in the kitchen.

"He went out to say hello to your brother," Dad calls to me.

When I walk outside, the door slams once, twice, three times, and I cringe. But then when I look back and see him … I really don't give a shit.

I love seeing him from a distance. It gives me the ability to take him all in, and there is a lot of him. He's wearing light-colored jeans, a black tee, and that damn white hat, leaning against his car, smiling. His clothes, I know are probably expensive, but they're not over-the-top or showy. They're simple, yet he's far from it. In this case, the man is definitely making the clothes.

"You gonna stand there all day, Tessa?"

I shake my head and walk toward him. He opens the door for me, takes my bag, and I slide in.

Once on the road, Lucas asks, "You feeling okay?"

"No, I feel awful, and I look like death."

He grabs my hand. "You look great. How did things go with your mom today?"

"Awful. I hate her."

"Those are harsh words."

"Sorry. I was just taught one way, and they can act another all of the sudden? It's not right. I called my mother a bitch today, and she slapped me across the face. I know I deserved it, but it still pissed me off."

"In less than twenty-four hours, we have both called someone a bitch and been slapped for it. Word's like a trigger. We should avoid it, huh?"

"I'm so sorry. I don't even remember." I grab his hand.

"I'm messing with you, baby." He kisses my hand then clears his throat. "You're about to meet my mother, a functioning drunk since I was three, sober now for two months, who, when she's drinking, brings different men home all the time. I'm fine, haven't always made the best choices, but I'm fine. I don't like what she does, but I'm respectful to her, and it has worked so far. Let this situation work for you, Tessa, and you'll be all right."

"I'll try," I say uneasily. "I'm getting really nervous about meeting her."

"You'll be fine. Just don't judge me based on her." He squeezes my hand, and then silence falls between us as we're probably both internally considering our situations.

We drive up a big hill and pass several small homes. At the top of the hill sits, almost majestically, a newer Colonial. It's magnificent, much different than the farm. But, like the farm, there is nothing beside the house for as far as the eye can see.

Even before he pulls in, I know it's his home.

He pulls up in front of a three-car, attached garage and hops out.

I open my door and step out as he rounds the front, my bag in his hand.

"I'd have gotten that door."

I smile at him then look around at the open fields and the forest behind the home.

"Come on." He takes my hand and walks around back.

A sidewalk leads through a flowery path to a black, vinyl privacy fence. Lucas opens the gate, and I smile when I see the inground pool.

"This is amazing."

"It's cool. The pond is amazing."

I step inside the gate and see a hot tub, an outdoor kitchen, and his mom standing at a huge grill. Her hair is long, curly, and black, like his. She's also perfect in her outfit, not a cardigan and knee-length shorts. She's wearing a black tank top with a wrap around her waist.

When she turns, she smiles and, just like Lucas, she has perfectly straight, brilliantly white teeth.

"Mom, this is my girlfriend, Tessa. Tessa, my mom, Kate," Lucas introduces us.

"You are stunning," falls out of my mouth, and then I feel myself immediately turning red.

"And you are precious." She sets down the tongs and walks over to me, takes my hands, and looks me up and down. "And gorgeous. Lucas, can we keep her?"

He smiles. "That's the plan, Mom."

Blue Love

"It'll be about thirty minutes. How about you two take a swim? The pool is nice and warm."

"Sounds great. Come on, Tessa. I'll show you the bathroom." He grabs my hand, and I follow him in through the French doors.

He points left. "The kitchen." Then to the right. "Dining room." We walk on the hardwood floors to the front of the house, which is massive, with huge windows.

"Bathroom's upstairs."

"Wasn't much of a tour." I laugh nervously, following him to what I know is bound to be his bedroom.

He walks me to one end of the hall and opens the door. "Mom's room."

He's about to close the door, and I am definitely buying time when I step in. "I love the color. And the room is huge. Is that a king-sized bed?"

"Yeah, have a look around."

So, I do.

The king-sized, cast-iron bed is against the far wall. The wall color a deep wine. Her bathroom is also large, with a shower and separate Jacuzzi bathtub, granite countertops, and a double vanity. The toilet is in a tiny private room, opposite side the enormous walk-in closet. It has light purple walls and stone-colored tile.

"Not much more in here, baby," he says, clearly amused.

I nod and turn around. He takes my hand and walks us back down the hall.

"Three bedrooms, and a shared bathroom."

He opens his door. "Casa Links. Get acquainted, Tessa Ross."

His room is identical to his mother's in size, except the walls are gray and the room has wooden floors. His bedding and curtains are black. The bed is a king-sized, four-poster in black. In one corner, a full trophy case, with a weight bench in front of it. I walk around and look in his large closet, which happens to be bigger than mine and with more clothes than Kendall and I have combined. On his large, black dresser sit a couple of pictures.

"Your sisters?" I ask, and he nods.

There are three prom pictures; one was with Sadi, and I really didn't care to look at the other two. His room is spotless, just like the rest of his house.

His bathroom is a bit smaller than his mother's, with only one sink and a large walk-in, tiled shower.

"Your home is beautiful."

"It pales in comparison to you," Lucas says, completely serious. "And those pictures, they can go. I want those frames filled with you," he says, raising an eyebrow.

Nodding, I look down.

"Let's get dressed," he says, taking off his shirt, and I can't help but look up. When I do, he smirks and winks. "You like what you see?"

I feel the burn hit my cheeks but answer honestly. "Yes."

He walks closer, bends down, and kisses my lips, softly at first, and then he takes my face and deepens it. My body arches into his, and he immediately steps back. Almost ashamed, I look down.

"You like what you see, Tessa, so stop looking down. Look at me." He unbuttons his pants, and they slip to the ground. "Don't look away."

"Your mom, Lucas," I whisper.

"She's not coming up here. Trust me; we could be in here until midnight, and she wouldn't even knock." He steps out of his jeans and walks toward me in his white boxer briefs. Again, he kisses me, this time longer and harder. Then he trails his lips down my neck, and having nothing else to grab, I decide on his biceps.

He begins pushing my sweater down and off my shoulders. I become tense, but when his lips meet mine again, I feel the tension slip away. His hands now on my waist, he moves them softly up my sides and breaks the kiss to pull off my cami. Then his lips crash against mine again.

His kisses are intoxicating. His tongue, addictive. And my body responds to our closeness, my nipples pebbling, and a knot growing in my stomach, just below my belly button, and it's definitely not butterflies.

As we kiss, he skillfully undoes my bra with one hand, while he tightens the other on my hip. As he slips one strap then another off my shoulder, licking where the strap just lay, he then does the same to the other side.

My erect nipples now rub against the bulging muscles of his abs, and I whimper at the friction, the connection, the jolting pleasure caused by both.

Lucas kisses me harder as he unbuttons my shorts then slowly lowers the zipper, and they fall to the ground. I free my feet from the fabric pooling around them and lean against him, feeling his erection just above my belly button. Digging my nails into his shoulders, I then push up on my toes and kiss him hard, like he was kissing mine.

He skates his hand down the side of my body, gripping behind one of my knees then lifting it around his hip to grind against me.

The knot moves lower and is replaced by a pulsing feeling, and exquisite heat pools between my legs as he grinds against me again.

Hands on his shoulders, I pull myself up and wrap both of my legs around him, hooking my ankles against his muscular back. Then he lays me on his bed.

Hovering over me, he kisses my neck as he rocks

against me, my legs spreading to accommodate him, and then I shake my head, trying to break the Lucas-induced trance.

"Oh God. Lucas, stop, please."

"You don't like this?" he asks, looking down at me smugly.

"Too much ... I like it too much." I squirm beneath him.

"It's not time yet. Just wanted to feel my favorite girl against my skin. How does it feel to you?" He lowers his body against mine again.

"Lucas," I plead.

He pushes himself up, and my greedy eyes take him in. "Exactly how I felt last night, Tessa." He slides off the bed and stands, drops his boxers, and my eyes nearly fall out of my head. "And that's how I felt when you showed me your perfect tits."

"You're such a dick," I say as he turns and walks away, giving me the full view of his amazing ass.

"We're perfect for each other. Fucking perfect," he says, walking toward his bathroom.

He is ... perfect. Not that I have anything to compare him to, but the few nude men I've had seen in movies, and the articles I curiously read ... his dick ... huge and so hard.

I close my knees and groan, my body throbbing even more just thinking about it. Then I realize my panties are ... damp. Another first experience.

He walks out in his swim trunks. "What are you waiting for, baby? Let's go swimming."

I sigh heavily. "I don't want to move."

He laughs as he grabs my bag then takes my swimsuit top from it, tossing it over his shoulder. Then he bends over and grabs my hands to pull me up.

He puts my top on, and then, with a devilish grin, he hooks his thumbs in my panties, and I jump back and slap his hands away.

"I showed you mine. Now you have to show me yours."

"Mine is very angry at you." I scowl at him. "Now, turn around."

"I'm not looking." Lucas laughs, and I look directly into the mirror to see he's grinning as he looks at me in the mirror.

"I see you looking at me." I grab my bag from the floor then hurry into the bathroom and slam the door.

I can't help but laugh at myself for being snippy with him, because the reality is that I'm seriously confused by my body's response to everything he does and the comfort I feel being practically naked in front of him. In this case, confusion doesn't seem to be a bad thing. Oddly, it doesn't even feel terribly wrong anymore.

I quickly change into the rest of my suit then head out the door.

He is trying not to laugh when I walk out, and I try not to smile. We both fail.

I lift my nose, stomp past him, and head out the door, down the stairs, out the patio doors, and then I dive into the pool, hoping to cool my damn jets.

As soon as I surface, he does a cannonball directly behind me as I swim across the pool to the stairs.

"You still mad at me, Tessa?" Lucas asks, giving me puppy dog eyes.

"Yes, I am. I think you're trying to torture me."

We both laugh.

"Did you like what you saw?" he asks quietly.

I splash him with water. "Of course."

"Your tits? Perfection. There are a million ways I want to touch them when you're ready. Tell me, baby, what did you want to do with me?" he whispers, his sweet, hot breath hitting my neck, making my hair stand up there.

I arch my eyebrow and whisper in what I hope is a sultry tone. "First, I want to touch it, then maybe rub it up and down ... slow, soft strokes. Maybe rub it against my panties because it felt good when you did." Looking into his now dark green eyes, I wet my lips. His eyes are now hyper focused on my mouth, giving me more ideas. I lean forward and whisper, "I kind of wanted to run my tongue up and down it and ..." I lick my lips again, since he's still looking at them.

"So fucking—"

"Then I really thought I'd like to ..." I pause with purpose then say all gravely, "bite it off." As planned, I then lunge forward, push off the stairs, and swim underwater, all the way to the other side of the pool.

When I come up, I hear him laughing a full belly laugh, and it sounds a lot like a song, one that I would write in my book and put a star next to. Hell, put two.

"Lucas, honey, dinner's ready!"

"Gonna have to give us a minute," he says back, his voice right behind me now.

I turn and look at him as he nears. "I really like your laugh."

"I really like everything about you."

"Even pissed off?"

"I'll take it if I have to in order to keep you."

Okay, he gets all the stars.

After a minute, which I realize is his "cooling off period," Lucas pushes his body out of the pool, arms bulging, back bulging, ass ... his ass is *everything* as water cascades over him. For a minute, I am rendered immobile when I realize I haven't run to the falls in need of an escape even with everything going on since his kiss.

He's the falls.

"Baby"—he leans down—"hand."

I look up, and he's smiling, towel wrapped around his lower half, and another slung over his shoulder.

I take his hand, stupid smile spreading, and I don't care.

I sit, wrapped in a towel in one of the outdoor dining chairs, shivering as Lucas, at his insistence, plates food for all of us.

"Honey, get Tessa a sweatshirt." His mother, Kate, smiles. "She's cold."

Lucas winks then walks into the house.

As soon as he's gone, she looks at me and whispers, "He likes you, Tessa, a lot. He's only invited one other girl over for a dinner."

"Sadi," falls from my mouth like a bomb.

Stupid mouth.

"I never liked her. I liked you the minute you walked in through the gate."

"Thank you."

Lucas walks outside and puts one of his sweatshirts over my head, and I can see his mother smiling as I push my arms through the sleeves and Lucas pulls it down.

He kisses my nose. "Better, baby?"

"Yes, thank you."

"Mom, I brought you a sweater." Lucas drapes it over his mother's shoulders and kisses the top of her head.

Plates are set before us. Grilled chicken, perfectly seasoned, alongside grilled vegetables and seasoned rice.

Lucas's mother shares stories about Lucas and talks about how he's going to go pro someday, and the pride in her eyes and voice are undeniable. He looks at her with obvious love.

When she talks about his childhood, from insisting on

no training wheels for his bike to the day he was going to swim across Cayuga Lake, lengthwise, which is thirty-nine miles, he laughs that amazing belly laugh.

"He was five, Tessa." She hold up five fingers. "Luckily, we talked him into doing just the nearly four-mile width."

I see nothing of the monster I had pictured in my head, and the way Lucas looks at her, I know, at that moment, neither does he.

When we finish eating, he insists on clearing the table, and when I get up to help, he stops me.

"I got this. Sit and relax." He then takes the plates in the house.

"Tessa, he adores you." She grabs my hand. "Thank you for bringing his smile back."

Lucas clears his throat, and I look up.

His light and happy disposition suddenly changes. "You ready to go home?"

His mother looks at him, lets out a slow, deep breath as she closes her eyes, then opens them and smiles at me. But, this time, she doesn't look all that happy.

"It was very nice meeting you." She stands and hugs me, then turns and smiles again, sadly, at Lucas.

It takes moments for him to appear with my clothes, and it becomes obvious that I'm not changing before I head home.

Walking hurriedly to the gate, I ask, "What's wrong?"

When he doesn't answer, I grab his hand and softly demand, "What is wrong?"

"Nothing, baby." Lucas pulls his hand away and runs his fingers through his hair as he opens the car door.

"That's not true. You're upset about something. Tell me," I whisper as I slide in the passenger seat.

When he gets in, he says, "I don't want to talk about it."

The tires squeal as he backs out, whips the car around, and then heads down the driveway. Hell, he doesn't even slow down when he hits the mouth of the driveway.

"Please, slow down."

He doesn't.

"Please, Lucas, you're scaring me."

He turns a corner, and the car skids on some loose gravel before going into a three-hundred-and-eighty-degree spin.

When the car comes to a stop, hands shaking, I grab the door handle, jump out, and start walking.

"Tessa, come back here," Lucas yells after me.

I keep walking, faster now, *definitely needing the falls*.

I hear gravel crunching beneath his tires and pray he's going to turn around. When the car stops behind me, I hear him running up from behind. Then, without warning, he grabs me around the waist, lifts me, and carries me back toward the car.

"Not fucking happening, *Links*." I attempt to wiggle from his arms. When that doesn't work, I kick at him.

He's strong. I am, too, but pissed and still shaking, he's able to turn me around and set me firmly on the hood of the car. The heat of the engine warms me, but I will not take comfort in it.

"Let me go. Now."

He holds tighter.

"What the fuck? You're scaring me!" I shove him, and it's like trying to move a fucking brick wall. "Let me go."

He does, and my body begins to tremble as I slide down the hood.

He grabs me again and pulls me into him.

"Lucas! Let—"

"You're shaking," he says in an oddly soft voice, and it enrages me.

"I'm in a fucking wet swimsuit under a sweatshirt. Of course I'm shaking! I need my damn clothes!" I shove him again, and this time, he steps back.

I storm over to the car, fling the door open, grab my bag, pull out my shorts, step into them, throw on the stupid thong sandals, and start hoofing it home.

"Tessa, you're five miles from home. Get in the car. I'll drive slow, I promise," he calls after me.

I throw the finger over my head and keep walking.

He follows me all the way home but turns around in the driveway then peels out.

GAME ON

Chapter Eleven

TESSA

Heads turn and the whispers begin, alerting me that Lucas is walking down the hall.

"Our men are here." Jade smiles as she shuts her locker door and leans against it.

I glance left and see him—baggy jeans hung on his hips, and his navy Polo hugs his tight, toned body.

I attempt to hurry and grab my books, but he's already beside me and putting his hat in my locker again.

I turn around and look up at him. His eyes are guarded, his jaw set. I wonder which Lucas I'm getting.

Narrowing my eyes, I whisper, "Don't you have your own locker?"

"Yeah, let's go there." He grabs my hand and, not wanting to cause a scene, I allow him to pull me behind him.

Standing at his locker, his grip on my hand unrelenting, he unlocks his door, steps to the side, and opens it.

Notes, letters ... freaking panties spill out of it and all over the flecked tiles on the floor.

"They get more creative every fucking day," he grumbles, kicking them away.

"Nice, Lucas, real nice." I kick away the pair of black thongs that land on my sneaker.

He slams his locker. "You think I like carrying my bookbag around? You think I like not using my locker because it's full of this shit?"

"Well, looks like there's room now."

He slams it shut as Mrs. Granger walks out of her English classroom and into the hall.

"You mind calling maintenance and asking them to clean this mess up?" Lucas asks.

"Oh my!" she gasps, hand to heart. "Of course." She turns and hurries into her classroom, repeating herself, "Of course,"

He takes my hand, and I'm so pissed that I don't yank it away.

At my classroom door, he leans down to kiss me, and I give him my cheek.

When I take my seat, I open my bag, and there's a note and a Polaroid of us. It was taken when he was pulling himself out of his pool, and I'm looking at him, blatantly taking all of him in, with that stupid smile on my face.

I look toward the door to see he's filling it, hands gripping the door jamb. Being that I'm at the desk closest to said door, he whispers, "That whole scene out there was embarrassing."

I know damn well he's not talking about the locker spill; he's talking about ... me.

I hold my hand to my heart, like Mrs. Granger just did.

"Allow me to apologize for embarrassing you." Then I turn completely away.

Out of the corner of my eye, I see him still standing there, expecting me to actually apologize. I can also see that he's blocking others from coming in. Normally, I would cave for those behind him, but not today.

After several seconds, he snaps, "Nice, Tessa, real nice."

* * *

I avoid him whenever I can, and it's not because I'm a total bitch. A bit bitchy? For sure. Yet, still, not even two weeks in and so much has happened, so much that I haven't allowed myself, nor have had the time, to wrap my brain, my thoughts, my freaking mind, the part not ruled by a physical attraction that is stronger than I ever imagined, around it. And yes, I like Lucas, and I know he's seen different sides of me. Hello, even the drunken, "bite my nips" side, but he did a literal three-sixty within two minutes yesterday, and now he's acting like a Neanderthal.

I eat lunch in the library, and when I open my backpack and see notes he's snuck in during some of our classes, I shove them to the bottom of my bag instead of reading them.

Walking out of the locker room for practice, we pass the football field. I avoid looking at him and get into a conversation about tomorrow's game and hair braiding tradition with Phoebe.

She looks past me for a second then back to me. "So, this is about the avoidance of the football star and not really the braiding, right?"

"I'm legitimately excited about braiding your hair for your first game and—"

"Okay, stop." She giggles and smacks at me. "I got you, T. Ross." She motions between us. "Just make sure you have my back on the field."

She throws her arm around me, and I'm reminded of the day we met, the fact that I was immediately drawn to being her friend, like a weird spark exchanged between two girls that I feel will withstand the test of time. I will make damn sure I don't get too wrapped up in all my teenage angst and family drama, both of which are new to me, to make her more a part of my life.

When we finish practice and pass by the football field, I see Lucas getting an ass-chewing from his coach.

At home, the fact that the phone isn't ringing bothers me a bit, even though yesterday I left it off the hook purposely, I still expected he would persist.

After finishing my homework and putting the Shepard's pie in the oven, I ask Jake and Kendall if they want to go to the playground at the state park for thirty minutes and am met with a resounding *yes*.

Hanging upside down, making silly faces at Kendall, I see Lucas standing two feet away and must look like a freak when I fall from the monkey bars.

He catches me ... of course he does, and I immediately snap, "Put me down."

He does.

"Kendall, will you go push Jake on the swing? I'll be over in a couple minutes."

When Kendall and Jake are out of earshot, I turn to face Lucas. "What are you doing here?"

"I needed to see you, tell you I'm sorry, again, or whatever else it is you need to hear to end this freeze out," Lucas whispers.

"Sorry for what exactly, Lucas? Is it for making me completely uncomfortable in front of your mother? For almost killing us in your car? For not letting me go when I asked you to? For tormenting me every time we're alone? Sorry for not answering me when I asked what's wrong? Sorry for what?"

"I don't know," he answers.

I shake my head. "Well, when you figure it out, let me know."

Then I walk away.

* * *

After saying goodnight to the kids, and still wanting to run down to the falls, I decide not to be an idiot, because it's dark, and going alone in the dark would be almost as bad as going with someone. I call it *my spot*, so everyone knows not to bother me there.

I walk into the bathroom and grab the first sweatshirt I see off the top of the laundry basket, pull it on, knowing it's *his*, that it wasn't washed after my five-mile hike and that it still smells like him.

I walk out through the living room and step out on the deck, sit in one of the chairs, and pull the sweatshirt up and over my knees. Inhaling his scent, I wonder if he'd consume so much of my mind, my feelings, if he wasn't so ridiculously hot. I mean, what if I dated just a regular boy, even a cute one? Would it be like this?

Jesus, what is wrong with me? If I keep on like this, will I be shoving panties in his locker like the rest of the girls?

After a few more minutes of shaming myself, the door opens and Alex steps out. "What are you doing out here?"

"Just sitting."

"What's up with you and Lucas?" He sits on the chair next to mine. "He played like shit at practice today, got yelled at by the coach."

"The coach yelled at him for having an off day?"

"Yep." He nods. "So, what's going on?"

"He makes my head spin. I act horribly around him. I'm confused, that's all," I confess.

"Do you think you're falling in love with him?"

"I don't know." I laugh at the thought. "I can't get enough of him, or I'm furious at him. There doesn't seem to be an in-between. It scares me."

"Have you told him that?"

"No."

"Well, I think you should." He stands and smiles. "Preferably before our game on Saturday." He sets the phone next to me. "This is making me crazy. Just answer when he calls."

"I left it off the hook last night."

"And I found it and turned it on. Still a business phone, Tessa, even without a cord."

As soon as he walks off, the cordless rings, and I force myself to wait until it has rung twice.

"Hello?"

"I'm sorry, Tessa, for all of it, not just one thing."

"Okay," I whisper.

"Are we okay then?" he asks.

"I don't know. This is crazy for me and—"

"We work things out better when we talk face to face, even better knee to knee. I want to come see you now, to talk, to—"

"I have a busy day tomorrow, and I need to stay focused. I want this to slow down. It's all moving crazy fast."

"I don't want it to, Tessa. I need you to—"

"And I need to slow down. If we're going to work, it needs to slow down."

"Goodnight, Tessa Ross."

"Goodnight, Lucas Links."

My chest is tight, my body tense, and tears are building behind my eyes, because his voice sounded ... tortured.

I hit the on button and dial his number. Unlike me, he answers on the first ring.

"Tessa?"

"I forgot to tell you sweet dreams."

"Yeah?"

"Yeah. So, goodnight, Lucas. Sweet dreams."

* * *

I get to school early because I need to see who wins the battle. The warriors on the left side of the battlefield, Team Lucas. The side who cracked last night at the tiniest bit of vulnerability he showed, and at the thought of hurting him, picked up the phone and dialed him immediately. On the right, Team Self-Respect, and a side of me that was more sensible and believed taking a break was a good idea and wanted to see if he would respect my request, which then the name could be changed to Team Tessa, and somehow, I believe that would level the battleground.

Team Self-Respect, now renamed Team Tessa, won, and that makes me happy and sad all at the same time.

Fourth period is our first class together today, and when I walk into class alone, it doesn't go unnoticed. The whispers began.

When he and Tommy walk in, he walks past me from behind and gives my ponytail a tug. "Looking good, Tessa Ross."

The whispers immediately quiet.

Phoebe giggles from her seat next to me. "I'm seriously going to start keeping a running list of all the passengers on the gossip train. I should make one column of haters and the other hopefuls."

The whispers then stop altogether.

"Have I told you yet that I love you?" I ask her.

Smiling, she shakes her head.

"Well, I do."

"Aw …"

The first note of today reads,

> *Good morning baby,*
> *You look gorgeous today.*
> *Lucas*

And I read it several times, over and over again.

I spend lunch in the library again, because if he can give me space when I ask for it, I need to be strong enough to stay away. That and I need to get my homework done and study for a test, and I won't be studying tonight, not after the game.

* * *

After school, as we walk out to load onto the bus, the football team is outside, and Lucas stands, arms across his chest, scowling. The look he is sporting hurts more than I wish to admit.

I jog up to him and watch his eyes turn from pine to fern.

"Wish me luck?"

He reaches out, grabs my hip, and pulls me into a hug. "Good luck, baby."

Before I fall into his warmth, his hug …. him, I step back and wave.

"Wish I could be there today, Tessa. Win, okay?" Alex yells.

"Of course." I laugh then head back to the bus.

I climb over Phoebe to get to the window and hold my hand against the glass as Lucas mouths, "*Thank you.*"

As afraid of my own feelings as I am, I can't help but feel like he is supposed to be mine … *for now.*

"You look like you feel better," Jade says.

"I feel better. Ready to braid Phoebe's hair and then kick ass."

* * *

When Coach V told Phoebe she was starting, she immediately lost all the pink in her cheeks. I understood, it being her first game and all, but Coach V starting her is because she has skill and heart.

She's now rocking French braids, one on each side, and two little pigtails. She was sure I wouldn't be able to do it. Little did she know I made poor Jake let me practice on his hair a couple years ago, so I can braid pretty much anything.

Now in the home team's locker room, Jade breaks out the blue and white ribbons to tie at the ends of our braids. Something catches her eye, though, and she drops the ribbon a good foot from my hand. I catch it before it hits the locker room floor.

"Hey, Katie." Jade waves.

I look to where she's waving and see the redhead, the same redhead who was a complete and total bitch at the last football game.

"Katie?" I ask, tying the ribbon to one of the two braids in Phoebe's hair.

Some girls from the opposing team begin whispering

and laughing mockingly toward us. Jade looks at them and rolls her eyes.

Kate raises her eyebrow, looks Jade up and down, turns, and then walks away.

"And how do you know her?" I ask.

"She's Tommy's ex. You met her on Saturday night. You may not remember her. Anyway, she was really nice, so either that was an act or she's just super competitive. I'm gonna go with an act ... final answer."

We all agree.

"Well, now we have to serve them girls in a bowl with a spoon." Phoebe, bless her heart, tries acting badass.

After we're all ribboned up, we head out to the field.

On the way, a group of girls approach us.

"Hey, are you two dating Lucas and Tommy?" a girl with more of a yellowish-blonde color hair asks.

"Yes. Why?" I ask.

"How long?" a different blonde, this one more on the strawberry-blonde, asks.

"A few weeks. But I'm not sure it's any of your business." I look her up and down as she does me.

"Been there." The first blonde smirks.

"Done that," the other chimes in.

"Three of us on the team have. Good luck."

The other rolls her eyes, and they all turn on their cleats and walk away.

"Why is it that skanky bitches want to tell people when they have been used up?" Phoebe yells at their backs.

When they don't reply, she shrugs and raises her stick, like a sword, and laughs. "Let's take it to the field."

* * *

Blue Love

Just my luck, I end up covering the yellowish-blonde, Blonde Number One.

"Has he shown you the trick with his tongue yet?" she asks me.

The ball is coming toward us, and I dart past her, running down the field, dodging players while dribbling the ball.

Kate is goalie, and well, she obviously sucks because I score without issue.

"Oh, apparently not." Blondie Number One brushes against me as she gets back to position. "Full of frustration, huh?"

Again, the ball comes in my direction, and as I'm ready to hit it, Blonde One purposely hip checks me. A whistle is blown, and she's given a green card by the umpire. Fortunately, I'm able to pass to Becca, who has possession and almost makes the second goal.

The rest of the period goes the same way—Becca and I have the ball most of the time, yet neither scores. Phoebe is playing middy and has managed to stop almost all the back shots from being received by the opposing team, and Jade is bored out of her mind in the goal.

The first period ends, one to zip.

As we take the field, Jade yells, "Tessa, look who's here to see us."

I turn and see two white hats coming our way. I give him a smile, and Lucas gives me a wink.

I watch as the three blondes look up at him, gushing, and now I'm going to be distracted.

"Head in the game, T. Ross," Phoebe yells, bringing me right back to focus.

Blonde Number One smiles as we wait for the whistle

to start the second period. "So, is he here to see you, or one of us?"

I ignore her and somehow manage to score another goal.

The next play starts. Blonde One has the ball, but I quickly close her down.

"Bitch," she yells.

"Good at it," I snap back, scooping the ball past her and hitting it to Phoebe.

"Madison," someone yells from the sidelines, and Blonde One turns to look. Now I have a name.

While she's distracted, I get the ball, and then she trips me with her stick and I fall hard, so hard that the wind is knocked out of me.

A whistle blows, and the game is stopped.

"Are you okay?" Phoebe asks, rushing toward me and holding out her hand to help me up.

Standing, I watch as the ump issues Madison a yellow card and sends her to the sin box.

"So worth it!" Madison yells.

"Tessa," Coach V calls me over, and the first step on my ankle, I cringe. "We need to fix that."

Panting, I sit on the bench. "Wrap it. I want to go back out there."

Coach shakes his head. "I think you should—"

"I'm good," I say, glaring at the bitch in the box, but she's looking toward Lucas, and he's looking at me.

Once my ankle is wrapped, I hop up, ignoring the pain, and smile at him as I take the field.

He shakes his head and adjusts his hat.

Once in position, I look up again at Lucas and see him watching me with disapproving, narrowed eyes. Looking away from him, I see Blonde Two running up to take

Blonde One's recently vacated position, and I can't help but laugh.

"What's so funny?"

"You and I paired up. Your coach raffling off this position?"

She glares at me.

Still laughing, I ask, "Are you as nasty as Blonde One?"

"Worse."

"Perfect." I beckon her with my hand and goad, "Bring it."

The whistle sounds, the ball is passed, and not by my team, but by the opposing team. I snag it right away.

Whack! Another stick to the ankle, and I am on the ground.

Two seconds later, I'm joined by Blonde Two because Phoebe absolutely had my back.

"You okay?" she asks, pulling me up.

"I will be." I nod, knowing damn well I'm going to hurt like hell when the adrenaline wears off, because Blonde Two hit me in the same fucking spot!

Phoebe is carded.

"So not worth it, Phoebe!" Jade yells down the field.

Phoebe holds up her card and laughs as she walks to the box to join Blonde Two. "I beg to differ."

I set up for my penalty shot. "This one's Jade's."

I hit it in the goal without issue, smiling, even though I am in some serious pain, as I walk away.

"T. Ross! Get in here!" Coach V yells.

When I see Blonde Three replacing her, I can't do anything but laugh.

"I've got this, Coach."

Standing in front of her, I ask, even though I already know the answer, "Are you as crazy as the other two?"

Blonde Three sneers.

"Don't hold back now, you hear?"

"Tessa," Lucas yells from the sidelines. "Enough! Get your ass in here."

I shake my head as I watch the ball coming toward me.

When Blonde Three swings, and not at the ball, I jump over her stick, clearing it and nab the ball.

Hustling down the field, I feel a stick to my back, and it fucking hurts, but I do not relent.

When the horn sounds, I throw my stick on the ground, set to go after her. When a sharp pain shoots up my leg, I fall to the ground and am so pissed at the cry I allow to escape.

Arms come around me and lift me up, strong arms ... Lucas's arms.

"Put me down, Lucas, please," I whisper. "I want to walk off the field."

Walking—*er*, limping—toward the bench, Coach V yells, "T. Ross, next time I tell you to come off the field, you better damn well listen to me."

"Yes, sir." I force a smile through the pain and sit on the bench. "But check out the score. We kicked their butts."

"Yeah, we did." He lifts my leg onto the bench. "That has got to hurt." He quickly grabs an icepack and sets it on my leg. "Let me see that back."

I glance up and notice Lucas, looking aggravated.

It's obvious that he doesn't like Coach V lifting my shirt.

"Seriously?" I shake my head, and he looks away, lower lip popping out in a pout.

"Ouch, ouch, ouch!" I suck in a breath through my teeth as Coach V touches what is probably a nasty bruise.

"Are you fucking kidding me!" Lucas sneers as he looks at my back. "Those bitches."

Blue Love

"Links, you mind your mouth, you got it?" Coach V points a finger at him.

"You sure know how to pick them, Lucas." I force a laugh.

"Those ex-girlfriends, Links?" Coach snaps.

"Sort of." He looks away.

"Any others we need to know about for the rest of the season?" Coach asks.

"Several, I'm sure. I've already met four of them, and they've all *touched* me in some way." I hold a hand over my heart mockingly.

"Links, are they all field hockey players?" Coach asks.

"I don't think so. They were mostly cheerleaders." Lucas scowls at the ground.

"They still should be. Clearly, they're not hockey players. I mean, again, look at that score."

"All right, Tessa." Coach V shakes his head. "I'm not going to kid you; this is going to hurt like crazy tomorrow. If it gets red and puffy, I want you to go to the emergency room. Links, can you see that Miss Ross gets to the bus without getting jumped by your fan club?"

"I'll drive her home," Lucas states.

"Not happening." Coach V walks away. "Get her to the bus."

I shrug. "The bus it is. I'm really not fond of your driving, anyway."

When I look up, I see a green storm of wild and angry brewing in his eyes.

"I'm so sorry this happened to you, Tessa. I can't believe they—"

"Lucas Links, you didn't hurt me; they did." I nod toward the three girls still sitting on the bench getting their asses chewed out by their coach, rightfully so. "I'm still pissed at you about the other day, but not about this." I reach up and grab his hand to get his attention. I nod to the bench, and he swings one leg over it and sits. "So, this will definitely not be for us; it'll be for them. Kiss me, please."

Lucas swings his other leg over, scoops me up, and cradles me in his arms. Then he kisses me sweetly.

I grab his face, tracing the tight muscles of his still clenched jaw, and kiss him harder. Tracing my tongue across the seams of his lips, I coax them open, and then I rub my tongue up and down his.

Cinnamon and spice. Absolutely delicious.

When I feel I need a breath, I pull my lips away and lay my forehead against his chest.

Cupping the back of my head, he places a gentle kiss to the top then runs his hand down my back.

I immediately wince, and his hand falls away.

"Baby, I'm sorry," he whispers as if he, too, is in pain.

When I feel a slight and knowing hardening beneath me, I ask in a joking manner, "Is that for them, too?"

Narrowing his eyes, he says, "Never again, Tessa. This is all for you." He chuckles darkly. "Sorry about the shit timing."

Feeling my eyes getting heavy and, even in pain, my core begins to heat.

Embarrassed by what now seems like my natural reaction to Lucas, I whisper, "I think I should get to the bus."

He looks down. "Can we wait a couple minutes? And maybe you should get off my lap. That may help the, uh, issue."

"Think of something disgusting. Maybe that will help?" I offer.

His lips twitch up as he pulls the brim of his hat down and chuckles. "You, Tessa, amuse me."

"Well, I hope that's a good thing."

Lucas sighs. "Please don't smile at me. That's not helping, either."

I slide off his lap and sit next to him on the bench to wait "it" out.

The three blondes start doing laps.

"Hey, Lucas," Blonde One calls out, "we're just trying to toughen her up for you. We know you like it rough."

"Shut up, Madison," he hisses at her as they pass.

"Blonde One is Madison. How long did you date her?" I ask.

"We didn't date. We just had sex."

"And you like it rough?" I whisper, truly wanting to know.

"Tessa, you can't say that right now." He gives me pleading eyes.

"Oh, sorry." I try not to smile.

The Three Bs are now coming around again, and Blonde Two licks her lips and says, "Hey, Linksy, you hungry?" When she asks this, she lifts her skirt up to mid-thigh, and I can't help but laugh.

Lucas looks at me like I've lost my mind. Then he looks at her and snaps, "Grow up, Lucy."

"Two is Lucy. Hmm ... and you like to—"

"No," he said in a monotone voice.

"Hey, Lucas," Blonde Three starts.

"Go fuck yourself, Carla," he says through clenched teeth.

"Oh, I know how that turns you on. Same cell number? I'll call you, and we can set up a time so you can watch me go ... well, you know."

"Number Three, the coward that hits from behind, is Carla?"

"I'm all set now. Let's get you to the bus."

Enjoying pissing off the Three Bs, a little too much, I

do not object at all when Lucas suggests he give me a piggyback ride. As we pass by them, as they continue running laps, I kiss his neck.

"That's for your fan club."

He laughs, and so do I.

"Links, come say hi before you leave," comes from a crowd of guys standing near our bus.

Looking over the crowd, I notice someone else watching Lucas and me, and this person is not a fan. It's my mother.

"Lucas, she'll be riding home with me."

"Shit," I grumble.

"Of course, Mrs. Ross," he says then follows her to her car.

Angry, I am so angry that she is here.

I drop my face into the crook of Lucas' neck and inhale before he sets me on my feet. One foot hurts too bad to even allow it to touch the ground.

"Sorry about this."

Mom bends down and looks at my ankle. "We're going to the ER."

"Mom, it's fine. Just take me home."

Ignoring my request, Lucas asks nervously, "Do you think it's bad?"

"I don't know. I just want to be sure," she replies in the form of a snap. Eyes narrowed, she then continues, "Lucas, why did they go after her like that?"

"Mom, could we leave, please?"

"I'm sorry, Mrs. Ross."

He looks at me. "I *am*, Tessa, very sorry."

"It was *not* your fault," I assure him loud enough so Mom gets the clarification that she clearly needs.

Mom opens the passenger door, and I quickly get in,

hoping to get Mom out of there before she can treat Lucas any worse than she just did.

Closing the door, I watch Lucas walk over to the boys standing by our bus.

Mom slides into the passenger seat and turns fully facing me, ready to lecture me, I'm sure, when I hear, "That your new piece of ass, Links?"

"Tessa is my girlfriend," Lucas snarls at him.

"How long have you been tapping that ass?" another asks.

"She's not like that, man," Lucas snaps.

"You got a virgin?" The guy laughs. "What the hell are you waiting for? Want me to break her in for you? She looks like she could be a lot of fun, and she definitely has stamina."

"Don't fucking talk about her like that." Lucas grabs him by the shirt and pushes him against the bus.

He put his hands up in the air. "Okay, man, okay …"

Tommy grabs Lucas's shirt and drags him back. "Can't pull that shit anymore. You have eyes watching you."

As they walk away, Lucy smacks his butt then smirks at me. Lucas keeps walking.

"Call me, Linksy," she says.

He doesn't look back.

"Is that what you want, Tessa?" Mom asks, voice full of disgust.

"Did you hear a word he said Mom? He's exactly what I want."

Chapter Twelve

TESSA

The twenty-minute ride from the field to Lake View Medical Center, neither Mom nor I say a word. I know she's angry, and so am I.

Before she even turns off the car, I open the door and get out. My ankle is now throbbing, and the bruise has turned into a nice shade of purple.

She hurries in front of me to get to the door, which makes no sense since it opens automatically. We bypass the front desk and walk straight through to the triage area.

"Have a seat. I'll be right back."

I sit and watch Mom walk up to one of her work friends, who types something into the computer. I'm sure it's my name, date of birth, reason for today's visit—all things I could answer by myself. And, at eighteen, I'm no baby, but she certainly has a way of making me feel like one.

When Mom returns, she is carrying a yellow bracelet. I hold up my wrist, and she puts it on me. Then she takes my vitals and types in the results, adding it to my chart.

Several friendly faces walk by, waving and saying hello. This, of course, is expected since Mom has worked here for three years now. When I see a wheelchair coming down the hall and Mike, the radiologist, pushing it, I smile as he approaches.

"What happened to you?" he asks, looking down at my ankle.

I shrug. "Field hockey game."

"And what position did you play? The ball?" he jokes.

I laugh. "No, forward, actually, and we won."

"By the looks of your ankle, that's a damn good thing."

"I had some good shots, played the whole game, and walked off the field after the clock ran out." I smile, pleased with myself.

"That's impressive. Now let's go see what we have going on."

After the x-rays have been taken, Mike wheels me to a triage room, where a phlebotomist is waiting.

"For an ankle injury?" I laugh.

The phlebotomist smiles as she takes five tubes out of her portable tray.

At least Mom isn't in the room, I think.

Once Vampira has drained me, she exits the room.

It doesn't take long for the door to open and the doctor to walk in, nose in my chart.

"You have a tiny fracture, a hairline fracture. It's so small, in fact, that most people would not have even caught it. The bruising on your ankle is pretty severe, but should heal quickly as long as you take it easy. I'm going to apply some salve to it and wrap it up tight."

He washes his hands then turns around. "It also says here that you would like to start birth control pills. We're going to need to do a vaginal exam and make sure everything is all right before I give you the prescription. The pill needs to be taken at the same time each day."

Maybe I'm a bit shocked, or maybe I misheard him, so I ask, "You're doing a vaginal exam?"

"No, Tessa, I wouldn't feel comfortable with that. A nurse practitioner will come in when we're finished up with your ankle. I'll come back after your exam and answer any questions you may have."

He looks extremely familiar, and even in the white coat, with a stethoscope draped around his neck, hair covered by a surgical cap, glasses covering his eyes, it takes but a second to realize who this man was.

"Is my mom on the pill?"

He sits on the stool at the end of the examination table, removes his glasses, and looks at me pointedly. "Tessa, that's nothing you and I will be discussing."

"You wanna discuss it with my father, her husband?"

"Tessa Anne Ross." Mom burst through the door. "That's enough!"

"What the hell is this? Just because I have a boyfriend, you're putting me on the pill? What if it's too late? What if he and I have been screwing for weeks now? Shit, you may be a grandma soon. Hey, Doc, what's it going to be like banging a grandma?" I slide off the table, pissed as tears fill my eyes.

"Maggie, things will be better if you stay outside. I can handle this." Doctor Feel Good opens the door, and Mom walks out, not giving a fuck how I feel ... how she's made

Blue Love

me feel. "She's trying to help you, Tessa. Most moms wouldn't think to do this, and many times it's too late."

"Well, I'm sure I'm not pregnant, because I swallow."

Holy shit, Tessa, what are you saying? What are you doing?

But rage overtakes rational thought, and I cannot stop, no matter how much I wish I could. God, how I wish I could.

"No need for condoms. He won't wear one, and he has been around."

He leans against the now closed door. "Your lab results show that there is no pregnancy." *Of course not, idiot! I haven't had sex yet.* "And you're STD free. The nurse practitioner will be in momentarily."

"Get. Out. Now."

"I need to tend to your ankle."

"You can fuck off!" I yell, and the first tear falls.

* * *

When the nurse practitioner comes in, she cleans up my ankle, applies salve, and wraps it.

"I need you to change into this robe, removing everything from the waist down. You can leave it open in the back. I'll give you a few minutes, okay?"

I need a few minutes—hell, I need an escape route—but I do as asked, while wiping angry tears from my face. "Yeah, sure."

When she returns, she tells me exactly what she's going to do. "Have a seat at the end of the table, lay back, and try to relax. I know it's not easy, but we'll do this quickly, get your prescriptions ready, and have you on your way."

Lying back on the table, I watch as she pulls out what looks like legs from the end of the examination table. I have no idea how I've never seen anything like this in the dozens of times I've been in an emergency room before. It looks like a robot, the Vagatron 5000.

"Go ahead and put your feet in the stirrups and try to relax your knees." I watch as she pulls on rubber gloves then takes some sort of headband off of the tray, puts it on, and flicks on a light.

Suddenly, I feel like my vagina is being haunted by a depraved hunter using a spotlight.

I also feel like I'm going to be sick.

Typical me, I try to make a joke to make a horrible situation less so. "I can assure you there are no deer in any place that you may need that spotlight to find and finish this exam."

She gives me a sad smile. "My husband is the hunter in the family. I've never even picked up a gun."

She holds up her hand and tells me, "I'm going to do an exam now."

Her fingers enter my vagina, my knees snap shut, and the tears build again.

"I know it's hard, but please relax your knees."

Relax? I think. *Relax!*

She pokes around inside of me, and I have never felt so disgusted in my life.

"Now a slight pressure on your bottom."

When her finger pushes in my ass, I jolt up.

"Tessa, sweetheart, we're almost finished. Please lie back."

I watch as she grabs something that resembles a claw. "You're going to feel a little bit of pressure."

Voice quivering, I tell her point blank, "That thing is not going in my ass."

"No, of course not. That part of the exam is over. I apologize if you didn't know—"

"Topics of premarital sex were strictly prohibited in the

Ross household," I say, digging my nails into and ripping the paper covering the table.

"I'm sorry to hear that. When you leave here, I'll give you my card. I'll write my home phone number on it. You can call me anytime."

Then I watch as she squirts some sort of lubricant on her fingers and rubs it against my opening.

"I'm going to take a sample, so again, slight pressure." She pushes the instrument inside of me.

I feel pressure, a pinch, and tears begin to fall down my cheeks.

After swabbing my vagina with a long Q-tip-looking object, she sets it into a petri dish.

"Tessa, we are almost done." Her voice is soft, and I can tell she feels horrible. I know she's strictly doing her job, but this is awful.

Next, I hear a *click* and the pressure is gone as the clamp is removed.

"You can sit up now, Tessa."

She hands me a tissue, pushes her stool back, and I sit up. She then folds the Vagatron's cold metal legs.

"Everything looks good, Tessa. The only issue is your uterus is slightly tipped, but that isn't a big deal, okay? Do you have any questions?"

"One." I sniff as I use the tissue to wipe away my tears.

"Ask me whenever you're ready," she says as she begins putting notes in my chart.

The lump I was hoping would go away grows bigger as I ask the burning question, "Am I still a virgin?"

She quickly stands up, walks beside me, grabs another tissue, and begins wiping my tears. Then she wraps an arm around my shoulders and says, "Of course you are. There is a thin layer of skin farther up in the vagina, still intact, and will be until you have sex or there is heavy manual stimulation."

I nod as I blow my nose.

"Tessa, I can sense that you and your mother are having issues. I am serious about you using my number. It's hard to get information that you need without open communication with your mom. Maggie is a good woman. I have known her for years. She's a good friend of mine, and she loves you. But if you can't talk to her, use my number. And whatever you ask, no matter the issue, it stays between you and me."

"If she loved me, she wouldn't have done this to me." My body shakes in a silent sob. "I don't want him back in here. Can't you just finish this up? I want to go home. I don't want her back in here, either. She can go get the car ... Can you tell her that, please?"

"Sure, Tessa. I'm going to leave so you can clean up." She sets the box of tissues next to me. "Inside."

I nod my understanding.

"I will be back with paperwork for you; your mom will have her own, okay? You may have some bleeding, so there's a pad if you want to use one."

After cleaning off the goop, I get dressed quickly then wait for her return.

She hands me information on STDs—*lots* of information—three packs of birth control pills, and a bunch of condoms. *And* she explains how to use them.

As promised, she hands me her card with her office information on the front and her personal number on the back. She gives me crutches to use for two weeks, which she explains will help me heal better—the less I put weight on it, the faster I'll heal. Then she tells me that Mom will be setting up my follow-up in two weeks.

Once I step down, tears fill my eyes.

"You're going to want to take those pain pills for the next couple days and use those crutches at all times."

***

Looking around the car, I realize that I left my bookbag on the bus.

"Dammit."

"Tessa, your mouth," Mom snaps.

With that, the three-minute freeze out, ignoring my mother's existence, thaws.

"My mouth, Mom? What about my vagina? How does it feel to sit outside a room, knowing someone is in there, raping me on a hospital bed?"

"It was time for you to have an exam, Tessa. It's routine that all women have once a year, once they're sexually active. And you better not speak like that again." Mom's voice is trembling, but I don't know nor care if it's out of anger or sorrow.

"Your boyfriend, Dr. Feel Good, and you make that decision together, Mom? Did you two have a lengthy conversation about my vagina?" I ask in the rudest manner possible.

"Tessa, that's enough." Her words and lip tremble.

"No, it's not! What the hell makes you think that any part of that was okay?" I scream.

"Your actions, Tessa. You're kissing that boy at the end of every game, and the way you sat on his lap, and he was holding you today, Tessa—that's what made it necessary!" she yells back.

"So, you get to decide who penetrates me first?" The tears pour out of me, now flooding down my face. "I hate you, Mom, and want you to know that you literally opened that box, so now it's game on!"

She says nothing, and neither do I ... until she starts toward her apartment.

"Not a chance. I want to go *home*. And remember, I am eighteen years old. Oh yeah, and freshly penetrated!"

* * *

The first thing I see is Jade standing at the window in the farmhouse, and I thank God for that.

I crutch my ass in so fast that I'm surprised I don't fall flat on my face, not that it would matter. It's basically the only part of my body uninjured at this point.

She meets me at the back door, and the first thing she says is, "Oh no, Tessa, are you okay?"

"I'm fine, but I want to tell the story only once, so can we go inside, please?" I ask, wiping my face with my sleeve to get rid of the tears.

I know Mom's following me into the house, and there's no way I'm going to stand for her staying here.

She opens a cupboard and grabs a glass of water. Then she opens the bottle of pills and dumps one in her hand. She walks over and hands them both to me. "Take this. It'll help with the pain."

I swallow back the pill, looking at Dad's back as he stands in front of the stove.

"Warming up your supper, kiddo."

"I'm not really hungry."

Mom then says, "Tessa has a small hairline fracture on her ankle bone. She will have to be seen in two weeks to see if she can be released for PE and field hockey. Her bruises are pretty severe, and she's going to hurt a lot more in the morning. She can have a pain pill every four to six hours, but it will make her drowsy. She should stay home from school tomorrow."

Blue Love

"I'll stay with her for a few hours," Jade offers.

"Jade, honey, you need to go to school. John, what is your schedule tomorrow? I have to work until three."

"I have a delivery in the morning. I'll be home by noon," Dad answers.

"Jade and then Dad it is," I say, closing my eyes.

"That's up to your father, Jade," Dad says, and then … "Is that all, Maggie?"

I open my eyes and see Dad's looking at her in a way I've never seen him look at her—angry.

"Yes. But I'm gonna say goodnight to my kids."

While Mom says goodnight to everyone then kisses my head before walking to the door, I push food around. When I glance up at her, I see tears falling down her face as she leaves.

Dazed, I watch her headlights disappear from sight, from out the window.

"How are you doing, girl? How you feeling?" Dad asks.

I don't answer.

"Besides the obvious, what's wrong?"

"Everything and nothing. I'm feeling loopy. I feel so dirty, I need a bath."

* * *

Jade draws me a bath and helps me unwrap my ankle. It's hideous, and even though the pill stopped the pain, it didn't stop the ache. It just made me not care about it all that much.

Kendall helps me get dressed, since Jade went home to get her overnight things.

Jake's a mess. He's either laughing at my inability to focus on a conversation, pissed off that someone hurt me, or telling me to be quiet so he can hear the TV.

Then, I'm out and, apparently, out for a while, because when I wake up, Alex has my feet on his lap, and Jade is back with her stuff, and everyone else is in bed.

"Lucas hasn't called, has he?" I try to sit up, but my head feels like a lead balloon, and instead of pushing forward, I lay back and laugh.

"Jesus, does he have this place bugged or what?" Alex laughs when Jade answers the phone.

"She's kind of stoned." She pauses. "I guess you could try?" She walks over and hands me the phone, then sits on the floor in front of the couch.

Speaking slowly, hoping not to slur, I answer, "Hello?"

"You okay?" He sounds mad.

"*Pfft*, fine as frog's hair."

I did not just use one of Aunt Josie's weird redneck terms while talking to Lucas freaking Links.

"What?" he asks with amusement in his voice.

"Uh-huh?"

He sighs. "Drunk then stoned, all in less than a week. What am I going to do with you, Tessa Ross?"

"I don't know how to answer that. Anything? Maybe more, but my eyes have invisible weights on them. Big, heavy weights, probably bigger than even you could lift. So, I'm going to …" My eyes close, and I can't open them. "It's dark in here."

"In where?" he asks.

"In my eyes."

"Okay," Alex laughs, taking the phone and handing it to Jade.

"Okay. Thanks for coming." I yawn. "Goodbye."

* * *

Blue Love

I wake up in severe pain and having to pee. The problem is that Jade's asleep right in front of me on the floor.

I try to get up but whimper when I set my foot on the floor.

"Hey, let me help," Jade says.

I hobble to the bathroom and drop my sleep shorts and undies.

"Gross," I grumble.

Jade wakes up to find me in the bathroom, and bleeding.

"Tessa, it's not your week," she says.

The fact that we know each other's cycles might be a bit odd, but it is what it is.

"Tessa?" Jade hugs me.

I didn't realize I'm crying until she hugs me, and then nothing holds back the emotional vomit as I tell her the whole story. I tell her about Dr. Feel Good, the Vagatron, the stirrups that didn't involve a pony ride, the vagina spotlight, the finger in the ass, the clamp in my vagina, and being put on the pill. Then I tell her how much I hate my mother for putting me through what felt a lot like someone touching me without permission, and on her say-so, and that I hate myself for feeling sorry for her when she walked out last night, in tears.

Jade begins to cry, too. "I'm so sorry, Tessa."

"Don't cry. It's stupid."

"No, it's *not* stupid."

"I need another bath."

"Okay." She steps back, and I look down.

"Can you grab me some clothes?" I ask as I completely take off my panties.

Opening the pill bottle, picking one out, she hands it to

me then fills a cup of water and hands me both. "Of course. What would you like?"

"Period panties, and one of Lucas's sweatshirts. I have a collection started," I call after her.

* * *

By the time I'm done bathing and dressed, I feel fabulous, because the drugs kicked in.

Hopping toward the living room, I yell to Jade, "I feel much better. No more tears. And thank you for forgetting my bra. The friction is—"

"Tessa, the boys!"

"The boys what?" I laugh as I round the corner.

And I nearly die when I see Lucas, Tommy, and Alex sitting in the living room with some sort of breakfast on the coffee table, but I don't, because I'm feeling the effects of the Tylenol 3.

Alex doesn't even try to make it less awkward as he asks, "What did Mom do to you, Tessa?"

"Alex …" I shake my head. "Not now."

Alex fists his hands at his sides.

I notice Lucas and Tommy looking at my ankle. Tommy looks shocked. Lucas looks pissed.

"It's not as bad as it looks." I hop to the couch. "Most people don't even know they have a fracture when it's this small, but the bruising looks bad. Hurts like hell, too, but I have really good pain meds."

Still radio silence in the room.

In my head, that's still a bit foggy, all I can think about is saying anything to make it go away.

"So, breakfast looks wonderful. How about we eat?"

"I'll get plates and napkins," Jade says as she rushes to the kitchen.

And now I'm alone with three males who just heard an awful lot about last night.

"It is too quiet. You guys should try one of those pills. They make you feel all sorts of funky."

And it stays that way as I force myself to eat half a bagel and drink some juice.

"The pills also make you tired. You guys should get to school." I lay down. "I'm going to fall out soon, anyway."

Tommy and Alex stand so fast that it makes me laugh. Can't blame them for wanting to get out of here.

"I'll hang here with Jade for a while. Unless Jade wants to get to school?"

"No, I'll stay. And Tessa, sit."

"Did you just say *Tessa sit?*" I snort a laugh. "I should kick your ass."

Jade laughs. "I'm not thinking you'll be kicking anything for a while."

"You're good for two weeks, but I will remember."

Tommy laughs. "Your blue eyes are almost black; you won't remember a damn thing."

I lift my legs, one at a time, to curl up on the couch. "Would you all get out of here and let me convalesce?"

"Convalesce?" Alex laughs.

"SAT prep." I yawn and hold up a thumb.

Lucas stands up from the love seat, walks over, and grabs a pillow, putting it behind me. He then sits at the other end of the couch and carefully pulls my legs down to rest on his lap, cringing when he sees the purple and yellow bruises that run from my knee to the top of my foot, up close and personal.

Jade cringes. "We need to wrap that."

"I'll be fine." Eyes heavy, I look down at Lucas. "Go to school."

"Go to sleep," he returns. Then he gently lifts my leg.

"I'm so sorry, baby." He then places featherlike kisses from my toe to my knee.

"Lucas, you didn't beat me with a hockey stick." I sigh. "And, by the way, there are other places that I'd like your lips."

"Tessa, go to sleep." He throws the Afghan over my face and laughs softly.

"You wanna tell me what happened before we head to school and get bombarded with questions?" Alex says as he walks from the bathroom.

"Jade, that's all you," I mumble.

Jade gave the play by play.

"Who the hell were these girls, Lucas? Ex-girlfriends?" Alex asks.

"Not girlfriends, per say; just girls I used to … well, you know," Lucas answers.

"So, four girls have gone after my sister because of you?"

"I think it's because they're freakin' crazy. It's not Lucas's fault," Jade snaps at Alex.

Alex stands quietly for a few moments before he asks, "Phoebe went after one of them?"

"Yep, she got carded," Jade said.

"Nice. I like Phoebe." Alex chuckles. "But question: did hockey become more dangerous than football?"

Alex and Tommy leave for school, but Lucas refuses to leave. Jade insists on staying for a couple more hours, too.

Eyes closed, I hear the screen door slam once, twice, three times, and I yawn. "Stupid door."

* * *

Blue Love

I wake up having to use the bathroom. When I sit up, I whimper, this time because my stomach is cramped.

I'm hunched over, grabbing my belly, when I feel Lucas grab my waist to steady me.

"Good morning, sleepy head," he whispers.

"Hi, Lucas."

After setting a glass on the coffee table with his other hand, he steers me back to the couch, squats beside me, and asks, "You okay, Tessa?"

"I'm fine, thank you. I do, however, need to go to the bathroom."

He helps me up, wraps his arm around my waist, and all but carries me to the bathroom door.

It shocks me when it opens and Jade smiles. "You look, um, better."

I sigh. "You're not very convincing."

"Avoid the mirror," she suggests, walking around me and out.

After using the bathroom and getting pissed because I'm still bleeding, I wash my hands. Then I brush my teeth and throw my still wet hair up in a messy bun on top of my head.

Using the crutches that Jade left by the door, I make my way out to the living room.

"I don't plan on taking any of those pills again until bedtime. I feel like a bum."

Lucas shakes his head and finishes cleaning up the coffee table, and I sit on the couch and put my leg up on the pillow that he's set on it. I grab the remote to turn on the TV. "You guys go to school. Dad will be here in a couple of hours, and I'm going to sit here and veg. I'll be fine."

"All right, I'll get your schoolwork and bring it to you after school," Jade says. "Do you need anything else?"

"Just one thing. Find out when we play them again."

Jade nods. "Will do. See you after practice."

Lucas sits next to me and pulls me gently into his side.

"Weird. I just heard her leave, but the door didn't—"

"Spring just needed to be reattached."

"You fixed the door?" I ask, eyes misting up.

"Wasn't a big deal."

It is. It's such a big deal, and he doesn't even know it.

"Thank you."

He wraps his arm around me a bit tighter.

"You can go now, Lucas. I'll be fine."

"I'm not leaving. As many times as you tell me it's not my fault, I know it is. I'm staying here."

"Okay, again, it's not."

"Tessa, there is a lot you don't know, and I want you to. I want you to know everything."

I grab his chin and turn his face toward me. "Tell me then, and look at me when you do."

"I've known the girls from yesterday for a long time. I have slept with them on and off for two years. They knew about each other, and even though they'd get jealous, they kept coming back ... until about six months ago."

"Why would you do that to them?"

"I'd get drunk, and one of the three was always around. When we had sex, it wasn't nice sex; it was rough, kinky, nasty, and with toys. We fucked, Tessa. We never made love. At one point, they decided that we should all sleep together. I thought it would be cool."

Oh my God.

"My mom was away one night, and they all came over with a bong. And, well, it was every man's fantasy."

I swallow hard and ask, "How often did this happen?"

"From the fall of sophomore year, I think. Yeah, my mom takes a break and goes to dry up before Christmas. Most of the time, her little trips are in the fall."

"Who do you stay with?"

"I stay by myself. I can handle it."

"Apparently not," I joke, and poorly.

"Tessa, I just told you that I had sex with the three girls who beat you black and blue with a hockey stick yesterday, and you're making jokes? I know this sounds cliché, but you really aren't like any other girl I've ever met."

I giggle.

He rolls his eyes. "And I'm not sure if that's a good thing or if you are totally and completely insane."

"Let's consider the girls you've *met*." I point to my ankle.

His lips curve up a bit, but he looks down. "I enjoy spending time with you, and I feel like, for the first time, I can be honest with someone. Hell, I've never wanted to, or actually could before. I swear that's why I fell in love with you."

"Why, Lucas Links, I think you should look at me when you're talking to me." I grab his face and turn it to look at me. "If you want to take it back, you can. Maybe you love me like a sister or a friend. It's okay."

"I wish I could," he said. "But I can't, Tessa. I don't think I will ever be able to. You're real, you're special, you're perfect, and"—he looks up at me—"I think I love you, Tessa Ross."

Resting my forehead against his, looking into his green eyes, I smile. "As much as I'm scared out of my mind, I think I'm in love with you, too." We gaze into each other's eyes. "Now, I want some lip action."

Smiling against my mouth, he kisses me softly, gently, unrushed, and he does it over and over again.

Then, against my lips, he whispers, "I don't think it. I know I love you."

"I love you, too."

He parts my lips with his tongue and pushes gently into my mouth, and it's as if he's kissing me for the first time.

Resting his forehead against mine, his hand on my cheek, thumb softly rubbing back and forth against my skin, he whispers, "Thank you."

"For what?"

He kisses my lips then says, "For loving me, anyway."

DELAYED GAME

Chapter Thirteen

TESSA

I don't heal as quickly as I thought, but regardless, the next three weeks, life is amazing. Every morning, Lucas meets me at my locker and walks me to first period class. We eat lunch together, and when he's at practice, I sit on the bench, watching my field hockey team become stronger. One Saturday, we took the kids to the zoo and out to lunch then had dinner at his house.

His mother seems to be doing well. He said he hasn't seen her drink in almost a month. She even attended football games and sat with me. Together, we watched him and cheered him on.

On Sundays, I went back to church. Kendall loves the stage, and Jake is even showing some interest in it.

After church, Lucas would join us for dinner. He always helped me clean up and do the dishes, and it normally ended in a water fight. After dinner, Dad and Alex would teach him to shoot. He's an awesome shot, and he will more than likely be hunting with them in November. We would occasionally go out to dinner with Jade and Tommy, too.

Even though I'm missing a big part of my life—Mom—my time with Lucas more than fills that void.

Sunday, when we get home, the phone rings, and I answer it, smiling.

"Lucas."

"Hey, baby, homecoming is Saturday, and I don't have a date. I've been so busy that I forgot to ask anyone. You free?"

"I don't know ... so many suitors. Let me see what I can do ... Hmmm, of course!"

Chuckling, he replies, "I left a present in your closet. Hope you like it."

I run upstairs, phone pressed to my cheek, and open the closet, where a beautiful, floor-length, light blue gown hangs from the door. Kendall is asleep in bed, so I do a silent happy dance as I sneak back out of our room.

"It's beautiful, thank you!"

"Thank you ... for loving me—"

"Anyway," I finish for him.

* * *

Today is my first game since my "ankle issue." It's at home, and it's against the Three B's. I'm nervous, but ready.

Sitting in Economics, I watch as Lucas, who now sits next to me in class, bounces his knee up and down.

I clear my throat, and he looks over and asks, "You nervous, Tessa?"

I point to his knee and joke, "Are you?"

He scowls. "I'm serious, Tessa."

"A bit, yeah. Of course. But—"

"Then don't play," he says, completely serious.

I roll my eyes. "What's the worst that can happen?"

He leans in close, looking far too serious, and says, "Tessa, I can't see them hurt you again when I know that it has everything to do with shit in my past."

"Just be there, Lucas. I'm not afraid of them. Just be there, and I'll be fine."

The bell rings.

We stand, and he takes my hand.

Once in the hall, now around more quiet whispers of onlookers, he kisses me. Hand gripping the back of my head, tongue spearing between my lips, his mouth covering mine, everything about this kiss is harder and more ... urgent.

"Get it, Links," comes from a male voice down the hall, and he steps back, glaring in the direction of the voice, looking like he wants to kill someone.

"Let's get to class." I grab his hand and pull him behind me.

* * *

At lunch, as I'm pushing my food around, Lucas takes my fork, loads it up with pasta, and says, "Open."

Not wanting him to worry, I laugh and open my mouth.

"Now bite it."

The way he says it is a miserable attempt, although also funny, to mimic what I said to him in the park.

He arches a brow, and I roll my eyes, sitting back and chewing. Then he loads the fork again.

"Need the carbs, baby. Open."

From behind me, I hear the annoying and unmistakable shrill voice of Sadi. "Good God, what now? Did they break her hands, too?"

Without thinking, nor caring, I push back in my seat and stand. "Walk with me, Sadi. If you don't, I'll drag your ass out of here."

"Tessa, let it go," Lucas says.

"I'm not afraid of you, bitch. Let's walk." Sadi storms out of the cafeteria.

"Locker room!" I yell at her.

Lucas grabs my hand, but I pull it away. "I got this."

"Tessa!" he yells, and I look back to see Alex and Ryan holding him back.

"Ignoring her shit hasn't done a damn thing. Let her go," Ryan insists.

"She gets hurt, and it's on you!" Lucas heads for the locker room.

"My sister's going to be fine," Alex growls.

Storming into the locker room, I come face to face with a seething Sadi.

"What the fuck is your problem with me?" I yell.

"Isn't it obvious, you whore?" Sadi yells back.

I lean against the lockers. "I guess it is, but tell me something. Is this making it any better for you? Does this help you get through your day?"

"Don't try to shrink me, Tessa. The minute you stop fucking him, he'll be crawling back to me. He always does!"

Blue Love

Shaking my head and rolling my eyes, I sigh. "Sadi, I haven't slept with him."

"Whatever. Now you're a lying whore." Her voice shakes but is much calmer. She looks visibly upset and confused.

I sit down on a bench and look at her. "No, Sadi, I'm not."

"So, is that your game? You're stringing him along so he pants after you like a little puppy?"

"I love him, and he loves me. It's not like that."

Everything about her hardens. "He loves you? What makes you think that, you delusional bitch?"

"Do you really want to know the answer to that question?"

"Among others," she says.

"Then ask away."

"Why do you think he loves you?" She looks at me with contempt.

"Because he tells me he does."

She shakes her head. "Have you even met his mother?"

I should not feel sorry for her, but it's hard not to. "You've seen me at games with her, Sadi."

"Has he told you about us?"

"That's not my business."

She looks around the room like she wants to escape then steps back and sits. "Do you know about the girls who beat your ass at the hockey game?"

I nod. "I do."

"Did he tell you he told me he loved me?" Sadi asks.

"Yes."

"Does he still?" she asks, tearing up.

"I know he cared after you jumped me in the parking lot, or he wouldn't have gotten you out of there."

"Does that bother you?"

"No. You share a past."

"We do." She squares her shoulders and looks at me. "I was pregnant. I had an abortion. I aborted our baby." Then she begins to cry.

I walk over and sit next to her. Then, without thinking of her as the torturous bitch she's been, seeing her now as the girl who Lucas once loved, I put an arm around her and pull her head against my shoulder.

"Don't you want to know why?" Sadi sniffs back tears.

"It's not any of my business. That's between the two of you and God."

"He slept with the girls who attacked you, and I wanted his game to be over. I couldn't handle it. I was scared, and I didn't want to have his baby and be connected to him forever. He hates me because of it, and I hate me, too." She starts to shake.

The story he told wasn't exactly the same, and a bit of unease begins to set in, but the words, "Thank you for loving me, anyway," makes it as okay as it can be.

"I can't imagine what it must have been like, to have to make that decision. I'm so sorry."

"I hate you. I hate you so much." She cries then whispers, "And I don't know why."

"I understand, and I don't know how. But I do know that it's hurting you to be so angry. You're stunning and young, and although I have yet to see it, I bet you're lovable."

She laughs silently as she wipes her eyes and pulls away. "How do you do it? How do you not give in to him?"

"He told me he loves me, and I love him. I want it to be right and have no regrets if it ends."

She smiles weakly. "Can I still hate you?"

"If you need to, I guess, but could you please stop trying to beat me up? That's getting annoying," I tease,

Blue Love

sort of, because she says nothing more, and I guess it is what it is.

The bell rings, and I stand. "Gotta get to class."

"Good luck tonight," Sadi yells from behind me as she follows me out the door.

I turn back. "Thanks, Sadi."

Outside the locker room, Jade, Becca, Phoebe, Tommy, and Lucas stand waiting. Down the hall a bit, I see Alex and Ryan, who both nod to me. I nod back, telling them, without words, that I am fine, and yes, they were right in assuming I'd deal with it and walk out unscathed.

Sadi walks up to Lucas. "I forgive you." Then she walks away.

To witness that forgiveness is kind of beautiful. I mean, beautiful if it wasn't Sadi and she wasn't saying those words to my boyfriend, who she shares a past with, and still both clearly have some sort of feelings toward each other.

Lucas grabs my hand and pulls me toward him. "Are you okay?"

"Yes," I reply.

"Are you pissed at me?" he asks.

I shake my head and whisper, "You left out the fact that you were with the three blondes before, you know?"

His face hardens. "You told her you knew?"

"No, she asked me if you told me what happened with the two of you. I told her it was none of my business. She got emotional and told me what she'd done. Then she told me why."

He steps back. "You hate me now?"

"I told you, and now her, that I was not involved with you then. That was your past. As long as it stays there, we're fine." I place my hand on his chest, and he tenses up. "I have no problem letting it go. But Lucas, you have to make yourself forgive her. She made a horrible decision on her own that was brought on by the pain you caused her. No, it wasn't right, but who are you to judge her?"

His lip curls. "So, I'm a piece of shit because of what she did?"

"No, Lucas, but you hurt her. Regardless of what she did, you need to take some ownership and forgive her, starting with saying you're sorry that your head was wherever the dark place it went to when this all went down."

He steps back. "Why do you think you get to tell me what to do? Who do you think you are?"

I look at him, confused at the sudden change, and then tell him, "The person who loves you, anyway."

He steps back then storms off.

I immediately feel ill. Like mouthwatering, I'm-going-to-throw-up kind of ill.

I turn and run back into the locker room.

"You okay, Tessa?" Jade asks, pulling my hair back as I vomit.

"No, Jade, I'm not." I throw up again.

* * *

Sitting on the bench, braiding Phoebe's hair, I tug at the ends. "It's grown so much in the past three weeks."

"Do you like it better like this or shorter?" she asks, reaching over her shoulder, holding a Saltine. I grab it with my mouth and nibble at the end while tying the bow at the end of one of her braids.

After finishing the cracker, I answer, "Your hair is full and has so many cool layers. It looks great either way."

Becca holds out a cup of juice with a straw, and I take a drink as I tie the second bow. "Thanks, Becs." I look back

Blue Love

at Phoebe, who is holding Jade's compact, looking at herself. "You're all set."

"You feeling better now?" Jade asks.

"Yeah, I'm good." And I am. Regardless of what happens on the field, with Lucas, or … Mom.

"Head in the game, Ross," Becca says.

"Attention ladies, this is your captain, Phoebe, speaking. It is going to be a rough flight, but we are in for a smooth landing. The penalty box is to your right." She points like an airline attendant would then points again. "And to your left, the bench where you can enjoy some cool, refreshing Blue Valley water, or a complimentary ice pack."

I can't help but burst out laughing.

"In case of emergency, please feel free to utilize the exit. But, above all, be sure to be alert and make every stroke count."

"I seriously love you." I laugh as we all grab our sticks.

"Love you, too, T. Ross," she whispers.

* * *

Passing the football field on our way to the hockey field, I glance over, but Lucas doesn't even turn around.

It should piss me off that he thinks the way he does of me. "*Who do you think you are?*"

"Go get 'em, Tessa!" Alex yells.

I look from Lucas to my three friends, who I know are counting on me.

"Head in the game, T. Ross." Becca smiles.

I nod and begin to pick up the pace, wanting to get the hell out of there so there is no more distraction.

After Coach V wraps my ankles—both of them, which may be overkill, but so are the new shin guards that Mom dropped off at the house—I lace up my cleats then head to the side of the field to stretch.

Out of the corner of my eye, I see the Three Bs coming onto our field and fight the urge to flip them off. Instead, I glare at them.

"Tessa, you're going to defend today," Coach V yells.

"Not a chance." I smile, focused on them.

"I'm the coach, T. Ross. You just got back, and you need to listen," he lectures me.

"You're also human and have a competitive nature. Would you want to be sitting in the back against a bunch of bitches that messed you up?"

He shakes his head. "Mouth, girl."

I don't reply.

He sighs heavily. "Fine, but the minute they start messing with you, you're going back, got it?"

"I prefer to sit in the box over the bench. I'll be fine."

I start where I always have, and B1, Madison, is right in front of me.

"Back so soon? Guess we didn't do that great of a job then, huh?"

"I'm not into the three on one thing. Actually, never been asked. Guess I'm good enough all by myself. So, right now, it's me and you, so give me all you got, girl."

"You little bitch," B1 sneers.

"You want to start name calling? I can think of a few for you, too."

The ball is passed while she's looking at me and has no clue it's coming toward us. I make the most of it and, in less than five seconds, I make my first goal.

After a team hug and congrats, I walk back over and smile at B1.

"Great shot, Tessa!"

I glance to the bleachers and see Lucas's mom. I can't even believe she's here, but she is.

Smiling, I give her a wave then look back at B1.

"You ready to play yet?"

"I came ready," she stews.

"Hey, you ever met Lucas's mom?" I ask. "I mean, been to the house when she was there?"

"Of course I've been there when she was home!" she snaps.

"Oh ... so I wonder which one of us she's here to see?" I nod to the bleachers, and the whistle blows. As she looks dumbstruck at Katie, I nab the ball and again score.

Back at the line, I laugh. "You falling asleep on me, B1?"

"B1?" She looks at me like I'm stupid.

"B stands for *blonde*, at first. I soon realized *bitch* was better suited. But hey, it's your choice. I really don't give a shit."

Madison drops her stick and lunges at me.

On the ground, in a pile, I quickly end up on top and hop up. "Is that all you got?"

The umpire red cards her immediately.

From across the field, Phoebe yells, "Don't you go stealing all the fun. I want to play, too."

I give her a thumbs-up then turn to face B2, and I can't help but laugh. I swear I can see steam coming from her ears.

"Hey, nice seeing you again." I stretch my arms, one after the other, across my body. "All better, thanks for asking."

B2 says nothing, so I do.

"Are you going to play nice today?"

B2 smiles. "Not on your life."

"That's what I thought, and that's why the cops came

today." The whistle blows, and I nod toward the bleachers, making her think my head is not in the game. B2 turns and looks while I dart out, grabbing the ball and head toward the goal.

Becca is open, so I pass it to her.

Back on the line, B2 bares her teeth. "Nice try, Ross. No cops!"

"Not yet. Try me." I glare at her then shake my head. "Did you see Lucas's mom?"

"What's she doing here?" she asks.

"She's here to watch me play, because her son loves me." *Or loved. Doesn't matter now. Head in the game and playing defense as well as offense.*

"He told you that?"

"Every day."

B2 swings the stick at my head. I duck, and the whistle blows.

"Red card, bitch. See yourself to the box."

Once she's gone, I take a deep breath and close my eyes. *Two down, one to go.*

I watch as Alex, Ryan, and Tommy walk toward the field, but no Lucas. After further inspection, I see him finally. He's in the distance, talking to … Sadi.

"And you thought you could change him?"

I turn around to see B3, eyes void of malice.

"That girl has been the only one he has turned me down for, and look, things haven't changed."

Defeated already, I ask, "Are you here to play, or are you gonna try to kick my ass again, too?"

"Looks like your ass just got kicked. Let's play."

The whistle blows, and we both go for the ball. Carla gets it first. I quickly snag it back and head down the field, only to have Carla nab it back and pass it down the field. Phoebe stops it and passes to Becca. Carla grabs it again.

Blue Love

I run after her, fighting for possession, but Carla shoots at the goal. Jade blocks it.

Carla takes it back and makes a goal.

Back at the line, I nod. "Good shot."

She nods off the field, toward Lucas, where Sadi is hugging him, and he stands, arms to his sides.

"You going to let it happen again?" she asks, raising her eyebrow.

She's talking about Sadi and Lucas, and not the goal. I prefer to focus on the game. I promised my team that my head was in it, so it will be.

"Not a chance," I say as the whistle blows.

Ball in front of me, I head down the field and hit it in. Tommy's ex doesn't even try to catch it.

High-fiving my teammates, I go back to the line.

"Good shot, Tessa Ross."

The whistle blows again, signaling half-time.

Carla grabs my elbow as I start off the field. "Hey, you going to be okay?"

"Yeah, I will be. How about you?"

"As long as I stay sober, there is nothing there. Just got caught up in a dirty game, that's all." She shrugs.

"Did you know him when you were"—I pause—"sober?"

"A little. We are all fucked up and have shitty family lives. You know, the broken family, kids falling in the cracks. We are 'emotionally disturbed,' as my shrink says." Carla smiles a bit.

"My parents split a month ago, so I guess I'm emotionally disturbed now, as well," I joke, and then we both laugh.

"Hey, Tessa, Carla," Lucas says from the sidelines.

"Hi, Lucas," Carla says. "How are you?"

"I'm well. Are you three still trying to kick my girlfriend's ass?"

"Well, she and I are good; the other two are red-carded."

"You okay, baby?" he asks.

I look away, not ready to deal with him.

"Oh, you're mad at me? About Sadi? You asked me to apologize to her, and I did."

"Holy shit." Carla laughs. "Lucas Links is in love."

Lucas nods, and his face starts changing color. He's ... blushing.

"I am." He grabs me and pulls me into him, kissing the top of my head then telling her, "Sobriety and Tessa have been good for me."

Sobriety?

"Well, Lucas, I'm happy for you. Truly, I am," Carla says sincerely. "It's a work in progress, but I'm getting there, too."

"I think you're my favorite ex so far," I tell her.

She laughs, and so do I, but it really wasn't a joke.

"See you in a few minutes, Ross, so I can kick your ass up and down this field," she jokes, I think, and then she walks away.

I look up at Lucas. "You're not mad at me?"

Lucas laughs. "I didn't say that. But maybe I directed it at the wrong person." He kisses me softly then steps back.

"Your mom's here."

"No shit?" He looks toward the bleachers. "You are my little ray of sunshine."

"I have to ..." I nod toward my team.

"Go. I'll go hang on the bleachers with Mom."

And just like that, I'm on cloud Lucas ... again.

The game ends 3-1.

* * *

Blue Love

After showering, I walk out and see Lucas standing next to his car ... smiling.

I run to him, jump into his arms, and kiss his entire face.

"Slow down, crazy girl." He laughs.

"I love you, Lucas. I was so scared you were pissed at me."

"Let's get something straight. I am pissed at you, or was. It hasn't sunk in yet, but I love you, anyway." He winks then kisses my head.

"You threw up after our fight?"

Embarrassed, I look down.

"Wow, Tessa, I have some effect on you, don't I?"

"Yeah, and it scares me."

He looks past me and stiffens.

I turn back and see B1 and B2 behind me.

"So, Lucas, you love this girl, huh?" B1 asks.

"Well, hello, Madison and Lucy," Lucas says calmly.

I groan. "It's like the movie *Scrooge*. So, we have four down and how many to go?"

He kisses the top of my head then steps back.

"Are you two here to apologize?" he asks the antagonists.

Alex walks up, and Lucas nods to Alex's truck. "You want to take Tessa?"

"Anywhere she wants to go." Alex pulls me away. When I try to wiggle free, he grabs me up.

"Oh, so that's what you're into now?" Lucy asks. "He's hot. I'll play with him, too."

Both girls laugh as they check out Alex.

"Nice ass," they call after him.

Phoebe starts off after them, but Alex grabs her around

the waist and carries us both to the back of the truck where his tailgate is already down, and he sets us on it.

Phoebe blushes. "Wow, you're strong."

Alex smirks. "And you're feisty."

She giggles, and even though I want to kick his and Lucas's ass right now, all I can think is, *Why didn't I think of that?* They're ... perfect for each other.

"Look at them. Aren't they cute?" Jade claps. "You have a date for homecoming, Alex?"

"Not yet," he says, still looking at Phoebe.

Jade smiles. "Ask her, then."

"Butt out, Jade." Alex's eyes never leave Phoebe's.

Phoebe looks confused then disappointed, but Alex never looks away from her.

And so, it begins, I think then focus on Lucas.

The two Bs stand in front of him, and his hands are deep in his pockets.

"He's her brother," Lucas says. "It's not like that."

"So, what is it like?" Lucy laughs.

"Yes, do tell," Madison purrs.

"I am sorry for whatever it was we were doing. It wasn't right of me to treat you all like that."

"Oh shit, Linksy, we're big girls. We loved it. Carla may be out, but there are still two of us that want to play." Lucy reaches for his waistband.

He moves away. "Knock it off. I'm sorry if I hurt you in any way. This is done. I have a girlfriend. I love her. And you two better leave her alone."

That's right, bitches.

"If we don't, will you spank us?" Madison asks.

"We are done here." Lucas walks away and toward me.

"See you soon," Madison calls after him.

"Not a chance," he yells back, staring at me.

Lucas walks up to the truck, grabs me, then pulls me

behind him. Looking around wildly, he then turns and looks the same way at me. He leans down and presses his forehead against mine, and if green eyes could catch fire, his just did.

A chill runs up my spine.

"I'm supposed to give Phoebe a ride home, Lucas."

He yells over toward our friends, "Alex, I want to take Tessa home; could you give Phoebe a ride?" Lucas reaches into his pocket and tosses his keys to me. "You drive, please, to my house."

He is acting off, so I don't argue. I hurry to his car, open the door, slide into the driver's side, and adjust the seat and mirrors as he climbs in the passenger seat, leans it all the way back, and crosses his arms over his chest.

"He's letting her drive," Lucy gasps.

Madison sighs. "Well, that's that."

***

Driving, I feel his eyes on me, and it's making me uncomfortable.

He grabs my hand closest to him and holds it over his chest. His heart is beating wildly under his incredibly chiseled chest as he tries to control his rapid breathing.

Suddenly, a deer jumps out in the road, and I swerve. "Shit!"

He darts up. "What was that?"

"A deer," I say, slowing down then blurting out the burning question, "Are you mad at me?"

"No, baby, I'm just frustrated right now." He removes his white hat and runs a hand through his hair that's gotten longer.

"Oh."

Frustrated about what? Sadi? The three Bs? What?

"Pull over up here. There's a turn around."

And now we're turning around.

I pull over, and he reaches toward the steering wheel, turning the key to shut off the car.

"Baby, I need to tell you what is going on with me right now, and I need you to listen. Can you do that for me?"

"Of course. I would do anything for you."

"Fuck, Tessa, that's not what I want to hear right now," he whines.

"I'm sorry, Lucas. I don't know what you want me to say."

"Tessa, you know how hard it is for an alcoholic or drug abuser to stop using?" he asks.

I look at my lap. "I've read about it."

He laughs out loud, and I know it's at me.

"To clean up, addicts have to stay away from their drug of choice, right?"

I nod.

"Now, imagine someone was trying to clean up in a bar or frat house, or … I don't know, anywhere that drug is available. It would be impossible. Tessa, my drug of choice is sex. And I feel like a fucking crackhead that has a pipe surgically implanted in his body."

Confused, I ask, "How is sex like a drug? I don't get it."

"Fuck, Tessa." He grabs my hand and places it on the crotch of his pants. "This is what I'm talking about."

I yank my hand back, and my heart … hurts. "You want them?"

"No, Tessa," Again, he laughs at me. "This didn't happen there. It happens as soon as I touch your hand, kiss your lips, inhale your sweet, flowery scent."

"Lavender." I scowl down at my lap, where my hands are clasped together, and I run my thumb up and down the back of one of them.

"You are killing me." He slams a fist on the dash in frustration, not anger.

"Okay." It's not like I haven't thought of this happening with him. In fact, I have … a lot.

I reach over and place my hand back on him, stroking him outside of his pants. Lucas groans and pushes against my hand … then pushes it away.

"Lucas, I—"

"As soon as that happens, things will change. I love you, Tessa. You make me want to be a better person. You make me want to love you in a way I never have loved. You have loved me better than anyone, not because you have to, but because it's who you are. I want to spend a very long time with you. I'm terrified that fucking will mess up everything good about us. I'm not willing to change what we have. And yeah, it—"

"So, you're never going to have sex with me?" I interrupt his super sweet declaration, annoyed that he thinks he's got all the control here.

He throws his head back in an angry and frustrated laugh.

"Lucas, now you need to listen. Sometimes, I feel like you're waiting for this to fail, and I will never feel what it's like to have what everyone else has—"

He punches the dash again, swings the door open, and then jumps out.

Just as pissed as him, I throw the door open and jump out, yelling my own frustration and anger at him. "Is this a game to you? Do you like to play with my head and make me feel like I'm less desirable than any one of the dirty dozen, Lucas? Do you think I –"

"What are you talking about, Tessa? I'm trying to be better for you. I'm not playing a game!"

"Am I an experiment? A new toy? I want you, too, and

sorry I don't know what it feels like to be an addict, but I want more with you so badly, and you keep acting like you don't want me. I'm confused. This is all new to me, and if it is going to work with us"—I stomp toward him—"it will work because of this." I hold my hand over my heart. "I'm guessing the bonus is ..." I stop and point toward his erection.

"I know you know that you think that way, and I wish that I had been brought up to feel that way. I want to change. And I know I am. Hell, I have looked four girls in the eyes today, knowing they are as fucked up as I am and told them I was sorry because it's the right thing to do, because in the short time I've known you, I believe you when you say that's needed."

"Okay," I whisper as tears fill my eyes.

"Okay what, Tessa?"

"I don't know!" I cry. "I don't know how to make you feel better. If we have sex, it'll get old for you? If we try to be friends, I think I'll die without knowing you love me the way I love you. I don't know what to say or do, okay, Lucas? All I know is, right now, I feel helpless and stupid, and my heart hurts and—"

He closes the distance between us and pulls me into a hug. The hug that always makes me feel loved.

"I would stay here forever with you if I knew that it would make you happy," I whisper, and my tears stop falling when reality hits, and it hits hard.

Stepping away from him, I look up into his confused eyes and no longer feel the same way about that hug.

"Lucas, I know that I love you, and I'm happy and feel loved when I'm with you, but what happened earlier at school, and just now ..." I grip my shirt above my chest. "It hurts. I'm willing to do whatever it takes to keep you happy, but it has to be forever, and I know right now you don't feel like it can work. So, I'll step back and give you the space you're trying to make. And maybe you'll miss me, and maybe you'll love me. And Lucas, I'm not going anywhere, but you have to figure out how you really feel."

He says nothing for several minutes, while a movie reel runs through my head.

"*Thank you for loving me, anyway.*"

"*You make me want to love you in a way I never have loved.*"

"*You have loved me better than anyone.*"

"I should get you home," he whispers, opening the passenger door.

We drive for a while, and my feelings start becoming moot, my heart numb.

I ask, "You okay?"

"I'm better as long as I have you."

Is that what you really want? is what I want to ask. Instead, I nod.

He takes my hand, holding it tight. Not bone-breaking tight, but tight enough that it feels like he's hanging on to me like I'm some sort of lifeline.

Wanting to believe we have a chance, I look over and ask, "Remember, at the game, when I told you to think of something unpleasant when you feel like you're going to, um, explode? You should do that."

He laughs. "Okay, I will."

"Got any ideas?"

"None yet."

"We'll work on that."

Nothing more is said the entire ride.

He walks me to the door, hugs me tight, and then kisses the top of my head. "Love you, Tessa Ross."

Throat now tight, I force a smile and look up. "I love you. See you in the morning. Drive safely. Call me when you get home."

When I walk inside, I see a sink full of dishes, bookbags on the floor, and hear the TV.

I grab the cordless phone off the charger and hold it as I walk through the kitchen and into the living room. Dad and the kids are all watching TV.

"Sorry we missed your game." Kendall yawns. "We were doing hay. Alex said you won."

"Sure did?' I smile and look around. "Where's Alex?"

Alex ... Phoebe. God, I hope that for both of them.

"At Ryan's," Jake answers. "One of the horses is having a baby."

"Cool." *Very cool.*

I do the dishes, make lunches for school, sweep and mop the floor. Then I head to the bathroom to brush my teeth and wash my face. All the while, I keep the cordless at arm's length. Then I throw in a load of laundry.

Resigned to the fact he isn't going to call, I begin to get ready for bed.

The phone rings.

"I'm home safely. I love you more now than yesterday, Tessa Ross," he says, sounding winded.

"I feel blessed having you in my life, Lucas Links, so I thought of something."

"I thought of something, too—losing you."

"That is so sweet. All I could think of was dead puppies."

"You make me laugh."

"I'm a very funny girl."

But I'm really not. Hell, I'm wondering if I even know who I am.

SURPRISE

Chapter Fourteen

TESSA

By Friday morning, I'm a mess. I have that feeling, the same one I had over the summer, the one of a pending storm.

I haven't been sleeping or eating much, and I miss Mom. But I know it's only because of everything going on with Lucas. Except for the occasional hello and goodbye, I haven't talked to her at all.

The past couple days, Lucas looks unhappy, and to see someone whose smile lights up the world and you desperately want to see happy that way, it makes me feel unworthy.

Jade breathes out the words, "Oh damn."

I look down the hall and see Lucas carrying a big

bouquet of yellow roses and white daisies. Tears immediately fill my eyes.

"Damn, Tessa, they were supposed to make you happy, not sad."

He wants me to be happy.

"I am happy." I hug him. "It's just that, two days ago, I was afraid I would lose you, and today, you're here with flowers. I love you. They're beautiful." Then I kiss him as if we're alone.

He pulls away first, closes his eyes, presses his forehead to mine, and whispers, "Dead puppies," over and over again.

Laughing as I bat away tears, I ask, "Did it work?"

"It did ... right up until I opened my eyes and saw you," Lucas whispers then pops a kiss to my cheek.

"Maybe I should blindfold you before we kiss."

His nose flares and eyes close.

"Oh, sorry, I wouldn't have guessed. Dead puppies?"

"A whole room full of them." He laughs.

* * *

"So"—Becca sits at the lunch table—"the big dance is tomorrow, and we were thinking mani-pedi's and a bit of waxing tonight, the four of us."

"Sounds great." I beam. Yes, I'm back to beaming. "After practice?"

"What sounds great?" Lucas sits next to me.

"The four of us going to get waxed." Phoebe laughs.

I look at Lucas. "You don't mind, do you?"

He closes his eyes.

"Dead puppies?" I whisper.

He laughs and nods.

"Wax does it for you?" I am seriously confused by this.

I mean, eyebrow waxing? What could possibly be sexual about ... Ohhh.

He arches a brow.

I look away. "We are going after practice to get mani-pedi's and *eyebrow waxing*."

"Right after?" Lucas asks.

"If we don't, we won't be home until midnight."

"Where are you going?" he asks.

"Probably Ithaca."

"Can I drive you?"

"I think I'll ride with the girls. It would be silly for you to drive me."

"I want to," he says firmly.

"Are you upset about this?"

"No, it just means I won't see you tonight."

"But I will have pretty feet and nails for the dance on Saturday."

"I like them the way they are." He sticks out his lower lip purposely.

"I want to be beautiful for you."

He scowls. "If it gets any better, then you better bring a basket of those puppies with you."

I laugh. "Why don't you, Tommy, and Alex go to dinner? I'll call you and let you know where we are and when we should be done, and maybe we can hook up after?"

"Or maybe I will go home and pout," Lucas says.

"If you do, take a picture. Incredibly adorable." I kiss his nose.

His brows shoot up. "Did you just call me fucking adorable?"

* * *

After school, we pile into Becca's car and drive to Ithaca with the radio cranked and singing at the top of our lungs. We talk and laugh as we get pampered.

I choose French tips, so it looks like I actually have nails. Jade goes red, Phoebe hot pink, and Becca light pink. Then we get our eyebrows waxed, and I brave a bikini wax, something I regret right away.

After, I find a payphone and call Lucas.

"Hey, baby, what are you doing?"

"Hanging at home."

"Are you still going to meet us for dinner?"

"Nah, I'll see you at the game tomorrow."

"Lucas, are you—"

"Tessa, chill. I'm tired. No big deal."

"Yeah. Sure. See you tomorrow."

He hangs up, and I feel sick … again.

I turn to look at the girls, and Jade's smile falls as soon as she sees my face.

"What's going on?" Jade asks.

"Lucas isn't coming out." I force a smile. "Doesn't mean we can't."

"Alex isn't, either." Phoebe smiles adorably. Alex asked her to homecoming, which has been the highlight of my week.

Jade hops out of the car. "Then it's just us girls. I'll call Tommy and let him know."

"Don't, Jade." I shake my head. "You don't want him to get mad at you."

"Mad at me?" She laughs. "He'll completely understand."

And he does. He tells her to have a good time, and he doesn't hang up on her, either. He tells her that he loves her.

Blue Love

After dinner, Jade says, "Let's grab something for your boo-boo-face boyfriend at McDonalds and drop it off. Make out for a few minutes, we'll wait in the car, and then everything will be fine."

"Sounds like a good idea, right?" Phoebe asks.

"Yeah, actually, it does," I agree.

* * *

"Next right, and then his house is the Colonial on the top of the hill." I smile as we get closer to his place and pull into the driveway. "I'll run in and be right back."

Becca pulls in, and I jump out. I run to the side and walk through the gate.

He's in the hot tub, shirtless, and head laying back. For a second, I think he's asleep, but even with the sun setting in the distance and shining in my eyes, I see a smile spread across his insanely handsome face.

Smiling back, I hold up the bag. "Hey, I wanted to see you, so I brought you …"

My mouth drops open, and I drop the bag when he groans, hisses, and a blonde head rises from the bubbling water.

When she tries to kiss him, he opens his eyes and yells, "Dammit, Sadi!" and jerks his head to the side.

His eyes widen when he sees me.

Move, just move, I scream, but no words come out, and I remain frozen.

When he yells out, "Fuck, Tessa!" I am able to turn and run.

"Bye, Tessa," Sadi calls after me, and I hear a splash.

Fighting with the gate latch, Lucas grabs me with wet hands and turns me around. I smell alcohol on his breath.

"I didn't fuck her, Tessa. Don't be mad."

"I'm not mad, Lucas. I'm broken." I try to turn before tears fall, but he pulls me toward him and tries to hug me. "Get your hands off of me before I scream."

He shakes his head, and the pain in his eyes hurts me worse than my own.

The first tear falls and, of course, it's for him.

"You are so much better than this." I try to pull away, and he tightens his grip. "You need to let go of me *now*!"

"Tessa, you okay?" I hear Jade just beyond the gate.

"Now Lucas. Let go of me. Now." Another tear falls, and he wipes it away. "Don't. I'm not one of those weak, needy, sick bitches you seem to thrive off of. I want you to hear me now, Lucas Links. I will never chase you like those—"

The gate opens, and I hear Jade gasp.

I hold up a finger, telling her to give me a minute, and finish. "—like those whores. I will never chase you. This is over. Take your filthy hands off me *now*!"

"Tessa, I know you hate me right now, but I love you, baby," Lucas pleads.

"I don't want that kind of love." I swallow back the tears, and they burn like lava. "I was devastated when I met you, and I'm a little bit broken right now, but not that kind of broken. If you ever thought you loved me, I'm telling you that you lied to yourself, and to me. Now, you *will* leave me alone." I turn and walk toward Jade.

Sadi yells from behind me, "Buh-bye, farm trash."

Jade starts toward her, but I grab her arm and whisper, "Don't. I need you now, and this is done."

I look up to see Phoebe and Becca standing just beyond the gate, their faces telling me that they heard everything.

We drive home in complete silence, and not one more tear spills.

"I need a minute," I say as Becca puts the car in park.

"Of course. Mind if I go in and use the bathroom?" Becca asks.

"Me, too?" Phoebe asks.

"Of course."

A few minutes later, Alex walks out, and I can tell he knows.

I open the door and get out. Jade follows me.

He grabs me and pulls me into a hug.

I whisper, "Alex, I'm not going to fall apart."

"No, you aren't. We Rosses are strong."

* * *

The first thing I do when I walk into the house is grab a garbage bag from the pantry then head upstairs, where I fill it with everything he has ever given me. I set it by the door, kiss Kendall, and then lay down in her bed.

Minutes later, Jade climbs in behind me and hugs me.

"You're going to be fine," Jade whispers.

"I am, but what a waste of a bikini wax." Then the realization hits. "I have to sing the 'National Anthem' tomorrow at the game. Do you think they'll be pissed if I blow it off?"

"No. But you won't." Jade hugs me tighter.

Homecoming

Chapter Fifteen

TESSA

I walk onto the field just before the homecoming game starts.

"Thank God, you're here, Tessa. You're on in five minutes." Cody, the announcer, sighs his relief. Then he hurries me off to the center of the field to do a mic check. A few seconds later, the music starts. I look up in the stands, find Kendall and Jake, and smile. Then I look to the sky as I sing.

Relief washes over me as I hit each note, and when the crowd cheers and claps, relief washes over me that it's done.

"Thank you," I say into the microphone.

As I walk off, Toby Green, homecoming king and star

quarterback from two years ago, who also works on the farm every summer, touches my shoulder. "You have an amazing voice, Tessa Ross. And can I just say ... wow." He looks me up and down. "You are gorgeous."

"And you're just as handsome as ever." I force a smile and, yes, flirt, which is totally out of character for me, but Sadi Black has not stopped smirking at me, and fuck her if she thinks I'm anything like her. Like I ever will be.

"Do you have a date for tonight's dance?"

"Actually, I don't. Why do you ask?"

"That's criminal." Ever the character, Toby drops to one knee, takes my hand, and kisses it. "Tessa Ross, can I escort you to the dance tonight?"

"You'll have to ask Alex. He's over on the bench."

"Stay here." He stands and winks. "I'll be right back."

I watch him—well, Lucas's reaction to him—as he asks Alex if he can take me to the dance.

Jade comes up beside me. "Toby Green, Tessa? He's hot!"

I shrug. "And right now, he's asking Alex, who happens to be standing next to Lucas, if he can escort me to homecoming."

We watch as Toby runs across the field to me. Then he grabs me up and swings me around in a circle before setting me back on my feet and kisses my cheek. "He said I could take you as long as I was a gentleman."

"Great. We can meet here at eight."

"No, Miss Ross. I'll pick you up at seven thirty." Toby nods toward the field. "I have to go announce homecoming court. See you around."

Cody announces Toby, and the entire field erupts in applause. He's kind of a hometown legend and the first to be accepted into Annapolis Naval Academy. But more than all that, he's genuinely a nice guy. If you asked anyone what they thought of Toby, not one person would have a bad thing to say about him.

The first person he calls out is Lucas, and my heart slowly sinks. It plummets when he stares directly at me as he walks onto the field. And then, when he mouths, "*I love you*," I hurt for him. I hurt because he clearly has no idea what love is. Not that I'm an expert, but the kind of love I want involves two people. Two.

I shake my head as Toby calls the last boy, Alex.

I tear my eyes from Lucas and search for my brother, who looks completely taken aback, not having expected, like some of the others have.

I smile at him, and he shrugs.

A moment later, Jade's name is called, and then ... mine?

I look at Alex, and he laughs, apparently reading the shock on my face.

Standing on the field, Lucas makes his way to me and positions himself next to me as we stand for pictures. I look at the crowd, and in it I see at least three men with clipboards. *College scouts*.

"Yes, I do love you, Tessa. Don't give up on me. I fucked up, but I have—"

"Good luck today, Lucas." I force myself to smile.

He stares at me intently, looking for something he's not going to get, and then, shoulders slumped, head hung down low, he walks back to the bench.

"What was that about?" Jade asks.

"I want him to be okay." I shrug. "Head in the game, you know."

The game starts, and I sit with the girls. Toby comes to sit with us.

He puts his arm around my shoulders. "So, that QB out there, was he your date?"

I nod.

"Did he hurt you?"

"First"—*love*—"crush thing, you know."

"Did he cheat?" Toby asks.

"Yeah," I whisper.

"We're going to have a lot of fun tonight making him wish he never messed with Tessa Ross. Make him jealous. But, for now, I'm going to sit down there so we win this game. Then you'll see I'm a much better option ... when you're ready."

Shocked, I swing my glance to him.

He winks. "By the way, what are you wearing?"

The blue dress, but not anymore. What can I do besides laugh? So, I do. Then I tell Toby, "I have no idea."

* * *

The Saints won the game. As much as I wanted to run from the field and get to the falls, I held my head high as I walked past the snickering Sadi and her group of friends and out to Alex.

"You played amazing." I hug him.

When I step back, Lucas is standing next to me, arms crossed, head down, peering up at me through black lashes, eyes pained.

"Could you come with me, please?" I ask him.

"Yeah, yes, of course, anywhere." His voice is full of hope, which again, hurts me.

He follows me to Jade's car. I open the door and pull the bag, filled with the things Lucas has given me, out from the back seat and hold it out. "These are yours."

Lucas steps back, looking wounded. "Those were gifts, baby."

"I don't want them."

Lucas grabs my hands. "Tessa, what can I do to fix this?"

"Can you turn back time?" I ask, sadness for him dwindling and anger beginning to brew.

He shakes his head.

"Then nothing, Lucas."

"I won't accept that."

"Then you never knew me. I'm not the do-over kind of girl. I'm not like them." My throat begins to burn, and tears immediately fill my eyes.

"I know that, Tessa. And I know I broke you, and I'll do anything to put you back together."

I feel my face contort, anger near boiling point. "I'm not Humpty Dumpty!"

"Fuck, Tessa, I wish I was like you. But everything about you makes me want to be better, and no one has ever made me feel that way. Please, baby, just let me explain," Lucas pleads.

"I went for a pedicure and came to see you because I knew something was wrong. I walked in to see a girl who attacked me, a girl who you profess to despise, with her mouth full of you. I will never be that person for you or anyone else. Even though it was only six weeks, I did love you, Lucas. I would have done anything for you. You thought so little of me that, out of all the people in the world, you chose to fuck her," I spit.

"I did not fuck her, Tessa—"

"Okay, Lucas, you fucked her mouth, the same mouth that spewed disgusting comments about the person you profess to love. Do you know how wrong that is? Do you?"

"I do." He looks away, but not before I see his eyes misting over.

No, no, no, I scold myself as my heart begins racing, and

my hands wish to comfort him. I don' t want to see him cry.

"Don't." I shake my head. "Please don't."

"What can I do, Tessa? Just tell me what I can do?" And a tear falls.

I reach up and wipe it away. I can't bring myself to remove my hand from his face. I swipe my thumb over his lips, and he pulls me into a hug.

"I have never cried over a girl," he whispers in my ear. "I have never loved another, not truly loved them. I've never wanted someone the way I want you, Tessa. I didn't take you even when you offered yourself to me on a silver platter. I'm trying, baby. You deserve a better me, and I'll prove that I can be that person for you, even if it takes me forever. And I don't fail. I love you."

It almost sickens me how desperately I want to believe him, to kiss him. How I want him in every way that I have for weeks ... but what he just said is just words.

He pulls away before I do, further making me feel pathetic, and gently kisses my forehead.

"Be better for you, not me, Lucas."

"I will, and then it's you and me forever." Again, he sounds hopeful. "See you tonight."

"Lucas," I call after him, and he looks back. "I'm going with someone."

He scowls slightly. "I know, but I also know you'll be okay. You're not like me."

***

"This is perfect." Jade holds up a chocolate brown, halter-style dress. "The open back is amazing."

She turns the hanger, so I can see it.

"It's great, Jade." I look at her and smile. "You look stunning."

Jade is wearing red with a lot of sparkle, of course, and high heels. Her hair is done and swept half up, and she's wearing gold hoop earrings and a necklace. She looks amazing. With her, that was effortless.

"Hair and makeup time." She smiles like she does every day. If you didn't know Jade, you'd think it was kind of heartless, but knowing her like I do, I know that smile is the opposite. She's all heart and wants everyone to be happy, and she once told me that everyone who is living and breathing should smile simply because of that.

She works her magic, and when I look in the mirror, I almost don't recognize myself.

"Thank you, Jade." I smile at my reflection then hers. "You're stunning, Jade Ross, as usual. Tommy is a lucky boy."

A knock at the door has us walking into the kitchen. Jade opens the door then steps back, smiling from ear to ear as Tommy steps in, wearing a black suit and his hair is a little more styled than usual. He looks amazing.

The way he looks at Jade is absolutely priceless. His eyes sparkle, and he looks at her with awe in his blue eyes, and she looks at him exactly the same.

I'm happy for her, truly, yet it also hurts a little bit.

"Go." I laugh, shooing them to the door.

"See you at the dance, Tessa. We'll wait for you so we can walk in together."

Alex walks into the kitchen, attempting to make sense of his tie. "You look amazing."

I walk over, bat his hand away, and start to fix his tie. "And Phoebe is a lucky girl to have arm candy like you tonight."

Alex frowns. "What did he do to you?"

"Nothing physical, Alex. I'll be fine. First crush." I step back and look at his tie. "That's all. And I want you to be his friend."

"Tessa—"

"No, Alex, he needs people like you in his life, and I cannot be that person right now, but you can. You and Dad have made plans for shooting and hunting and—"

"That's not fair to you."

"He could have had anything he wanted from me, Alex, and he didn't even—"

His eyes smash shut. "Okay."

"And Jade's boyfriend is his best friend, he's your friend, teammate, and—"

"Yeah, I said okay."

He opens his eyes, and I give him a smile.

He hugs me again. "Toby's a good man."

I push him away. "Go get our girl."

"Our girl?" He laughs.

"Yeah, Phoebe is one of my favorite people, so—"

"One of mine, too."

"Good, because if you hurt her—"

"Oh no, if she hurts me, you still have to be her friend," he cuts me off.

"I said, if you hurt her."

He rolls his eyes. "Good to know what side you're on."

"Oh, I'm definitely on yours. Have you seen how the single girls in our school, and those around us, act?"

"Yeah, Tessa, which is why I've remained single."

"Until Phoebe."

He nervously messes with his tie. "Yeah. I guess."

* * *

Looking out the window, toward the back field, I want nothing more than to tear this dress off, put my hair in a ponytail, and run, but backward, rewinding the past few months, restarting my senior year, and remember who I am ... or who I was. I am forever changed.

When I see a navy blue Jeep Wrangler pull in, I inhale a deep breath, grab my Polaroid so that I can get pictures of Jade and Tommy, Phoebe and Alex, and Becca and—I don't remember his name, because I've been a shit friend —like she took all those pictures of me and Lucas. Something tells me none of them will ever throw their Polaroids into the garbage, wanting to forget that, deep down, so deep down, in fact, that I didn't ever want to admit it, that I wished he would have been my first and forever. The fact that Alex burned the burnable portion of the trash that night was a sign. We were just a thing. Maybe a catalyst to helping Jade find Tommy, and Phoebe to come out of her shell, and Alex to take notice. And there it is ... and that was that.

I walk out onto the porch, feeling like a weight has lifted off my shoulders, and smile as Toby climbs the porch stairs.

His eyes lit up, and it hits me that Toby Green truly is extremely handsome and has a smile that feels like a hug. "Tessa, you look stunning."

"Well, thank you. You look amazing, Mr. Green."

He holds his arm out, and I slide mine through his. Then we walk down the porch stairs.

When I reach for the door, he beats me to it and opens it.

"Thank you, sir."

"Where's your dad?" he asks.

"He's in the shop."

"Can we go say hi?"

"Of course."

After we pull around back, Dad walks out of the shop, wiping his hands on a grease rag. He walks up to the driver's side.

"Hey, Toby, how are things?" He holds his hand out, and they shake.

"They're great. I'm off for the long weekend, and then back to Annapolis. I wanted you to know Tessa is in great hands tonight, John."

"I have no worries." Dad pats him on the back.

"Can you take a picture of us?" Toby grabs my camera and hands it to Dad.

We step out of the vehicle.

"In front of the barn?" Toby asks.

"Sure."

Dad takes several shots. Some are silly, and some are a little more of the typical posed photos. When we're done, Toby opens the door for me, I get in, and then we head out.

"You're going to be okay, Tessa." He squeezes my hand. "That boy is going to regret messing with my date. Are you ready to put on a show?"

I smile. "I'm ready to have a good night with friends."

"And you will."

* * *

Toby jumps out and runs around the Jeep to open the door for me and help me out. As I hook my arm through his, a little red convertible parks a few feet away. A tall, leggy brunette gets out of the car, and then the passenger door opens and out steps Lucas, dressed in a black suit and wearing aviators.

I look away quickly and smile up at Toby.

"Quarterback?" Toby whispers.

I nod.

He winks. "Show time."

He slides his hand around me and places it low on my back, which, because of the dress, seems to be open. I follow suit, wrapping my arm around his waist, beneath his suit coat, and although I've hugged Toby before, I never realized how thick and strong his back is. He then kisses the top of my head, and all of this happens while we walk by Lucas and his date.

When we're far enough away, I whisper, "I think you chose the wrong profession, Green. You should have been an actor."

"Are you kidding me? And miss this? Besides, I'm only half-acting." He winks. "The rest is real. I'm going to show you what it's like to be treated like a princess, and someday, when you're older, hopefully we can try it out for real."

I have no idea how to respond to that, and when he opens the door and says, "After you, princess," I don't have to.

Jade, who is waiting for us, looks over my head and narrows her eyes.

"Don't, Jade," I whisper, shaking my head.

"Hello, Tessa. Hey, Tommy," Lucas booms from behind us as he walks in. "Tommy, you remember Marie?"

"Hello, Marie." Tommy gives her a tight smile then gives Lucas a look, as if to say, *what the hell?*

"Tessa, this is Marie," Lucas says.

Toby reaches out his hand to Lucas. "Hey, I'm Toby, Tessa's date and future husband."

"Oh, really?" Lucas laughs haughtily.

"I've known Tessa for years. She's grown into a stunning young woman, don't you think?" Toby asks.

"Yes, she is," Lucas says. "Young being the operative word, Toby, right?" He deliberately doesn't wait for the answer to the question. "And this is Marie. I've known her for years, too." He leans in and whispers into my ear, "Number one."

I can smell alcohol on his breath.

I glare at him for two reasons now and, in anger, hiss, "We both brought our number ones. Yours is already used up, mine will break me in soon enough."

"You two need a minute?" Toby asks me.

My face starts to burn at the thought of him possibly hearing me, and I take his hand. "Nope, we're done here."

"Good, because I don't like to share." Toby drops my hand and places his hand on my back, caressing my bare skin before resting low, really low on my back. He leans in and whispers, "You okay with this?"

I reach around him and bravely pat his ass. "You better plan on stepping it up, Green."

"My pleasure."

As we round the corner, he turns around and … kisses me. It's soft, and sweet, and it's honestly exactly what I need. When he starts to pull back, I take his face in my hands and kiss him back.

"Get a fucking room," I hear Lucas hiss when he turns the corner.

I ignore him and keep looking at Toby. "That was nice."

I see Tommy grip Lucas's shoulder. "Keep walking, Links."

"Yes, it was," Toby says.

"I'm sorry. This must be weird for you." I feel my already heated face full-on blushing.

"I asked you to the dance before I knew all this, Tessa. Regardless, you're hurting, and I'm here, and don't think for a second that I'm not enjoying myself. I've watched you for years grow into what you are today. I'll be damned if I will let some punk screw with that perfect heart of yours. And that future husband stuff, file that under things to do after college." He winks at me, making my face catch fire. "You kiss like an angel." He then takes my hand, and we walk down the decorated corridor and into the gymnasium together.

Walking under the balloon arch, we enter the gym that is decorated with blue and white streamers and fabrics covering the walls, canopying the ceiling, and twinkling white lights softly illuminating the gym and transforming it into something that was supposed to be special.

Toby gives my hand a squeeze, and I squeeze back.

I look across the empty dance floor at the cafeteria tables that were moved in for this occasion, covered with white linens and blue and white carnations, in vases, as centerpieces.

Jade and Tommy are sitting with Marie and Lucas. Alex, Phoebe, Becca, and Joshua—her date—sit at the table beside theirs. Both tables have two extra seats.

Jade nods to them, and I silently thank her for giving up prime seating for me.

"You ready, angel?"

I nod and step closer to him.

Toby pulls out a chair for me, and I set my camera on the table before sitting down.

"You two look stunning," I tell Phoebe and Becca.

Phoebe is in a hot pink, sleeveless dress that comes to just above her knees. Becca is wearing a pale pink A-line dress.

Becca stands. "We should do pictures."

"Sounds like a plan." Phoebe stands next.

Toby hasn't even sat down yet. I look up. "Sorry."

"This is your night; don't be sorry," he says, placing his hand on the small of my back, and then we head to stand in line.

I am acutely aware that, behind Jade and Tommy, Lucas and Marie are standing in line, too. Toby pulls me closer to him, as if he senses it.

Phoebe suggested that us girls take a picture together first. So, the four of us stand in front of the white backdrop, with balloons on each side of it, while the professional photographer takes our photos. We do silly poses, which would have been fun, had it not felt forced.

Walking away so Alex and Phoebe can get their pictures done, Lucas grabs my arm. "We need to talk."

"Let go of my arm." When he does, I ask, "What do we need to talk about?"

"You okay, Tessa?" Toby asks.

Looking at Lucas, I nod.

Lucas's eyes are hard and angry when he says, "You're not wearing a bra."

The dress is backless, and wearing a bra wasn't necessary, but him talking to me like *that* pisses me off, so I tell him, "I know. It's very freeing."

His nostrils flare. "Do you have a coat?"

Okay, so that may have not been the best way to deal with a drunk Lucas.

I shake my head. "Lucas, what do you want?"

"For you to forgive me," he states.

I clip out, "I have. Let it be."

"If you hadn't left me for them—your friends—this wouldn't be happening."

Pissed, I lean in and whisper, "I got a bikini wax when I was there, too." Then I step back. "That was supposed to be for you."

His mouth gapes, and I see Marie shift her weight, which isn't much, from one foot to the next.

Fuck this.

"That pain won't be wasted tonight. Now, you have fun with Marie." Then I walk away.

"You okay?" Jade asks.

"Never been better. I told him I wasn't wasting the wax. Now, where's my date?"

* * *

While dancing with my friends and having a good time, I'm also painfully aware that Lucas stands on the edge of the dance floor, with an obviously bored Marie by his side.

I'm also not so painfully aware that Sadi is aware, and it helps me not worry so much about what his mother would think of me when she arrives, which I should not be worried about at all.

When the music stops, Toby, who is standing with Alex and Josh, walks to the mic, right before I spot Mom and Dad joining the parents grouped together on the outskirts of the makeshift dance floor.

"Good evening, ladies and gentlemen, it's an honor to be here to pass the crown on"—he chuckles and holds up two fingers—"for the second year in a row. Last year's king and queen, Allen and Samantha, weren't able to make it due to being somewhere across the country, working with the Peace Corp and doing good things around the globe, so this year, you get me again."

Laughter and applause comes from all around me.

"So, let's do this, shall we?"

After the court is called, four of us remained. Either Lucas or Alex will be crowned the Blue Valley Saints King, and either myself—which is a shock, because it should be, hands down, Jade—or Sadi—which is a disgrace—will be crowned homecoming queen.

"Ladies first." Toby smiles as he's handed an envelope.

Sadi whisper-hisses, "Gonna take your crown like I took your man."

I roll my eyes. "Neither mean shit to me, Sadi. Enjoy."

"And your queen … my date, Tessa Ross." Toby smiles. "Come up here, angel."

I look at Sadi and, yes, it's bitchy, but I love the shocked expression on her face, and I can't help but smirk.

Standing next to Toby, he crowns me and gives me a quick kiss on the nose. "Stay up here and help me crown the king." Then he hands me the king's crown.

When he opens the envelope, he chuckles. "And your king, Lucas Links."

Lucas walks toward me, tall, shoulders squared, and confident as hell, but his eyes appear desolate. He stands in front of me, bows his head down, and I place the crown on his head.

"Congratulations, Lucas. Now smile so your mom can take your picture."

He smiles that dazzling Lucas smile, but it doesn't hit his eyes as he pulls me to his side. "Smile Queenie."

After the cameras flash, I try to step away, but Lucas tightens his grip on my waist.

"Lucas, please let go."

"Never." Lucas turns and looks at me, his eyes burning into mine. Then, before I can get too pissed—hell, even before I have time to pull my eyes from his—he lets go.

Toby's voice comes across the microphone. "Will the king, queen, and court please step to the floor for your dance."

Lucas takes my hand, and as we pass the DJ, he stops

for a split-second and says something to him. Then he pulls me to the dance floor and the music begins.

"Eternal Flame."

"This isn't over, Tessa. I love you, and I know you feel the same."

The song, the sadness in his eyes, the fact that he truly seems to believe what he says is right and true, makes my heart begin beating faster inside my chest.

Out of the corner of my eye, I see Toby watching me, and instead of appearing jealous, he looks completely at ease.

On the dance floor, Lucas grips my hips possessively then slides one hand up my back. Scowling, I look from Toby to Lucas, who is not looking at me. He's glowering at Toby as he pulls my head to his chest and kisses the top of it.

"Stop it," I whisper.

"For the camera, Tessa Ross."

I look around for his mom and can't find her. I look up at Lucas, confused.

Why isn't she here for him?

* * *

The rest of the night, I hide behind the Polaroid, making sure to get plenty of pictures of Jade and Tommy, Phoebe and Alex, and Becca and Joshua. Each time I glance in Lucas's direction, he's watching me intently.

"Hey," Alex says from behind me. "Thinking a bunch of us should go to camp after this."

"I concur." I nod.

"Should I invite—"

"You can, but I'm thinking he already has plans."

With Marie.
Everyone agrees.

* * *

Toby didn't plan on coming, saying it should be a Blue Valley senior class thing. I strongly disagreed.

We stop at the farm to get changed, and Alex has already given Dad a heads-up and gotten his approval.

I change into jeans and a long-sleeved, black Pearl Jam tee and dump out my duffle to pack up some socks, sweatpants, and a sweatshirt or two in case one of my friends forgot how cold it gets, even by the fire.

Zipping up my bag, I see a note in the pile of books I dumped out. Apparently, I'm a masochist today, because I pick it up and read:

I wish it was me taking you tonight. I wish I could let you see what I know is there, deep underneath the black in my heart.
Day 1 without Tessa Ross hurts my heart.
LYA,
Lucas

I hate that I still feel so much for him, even with what he'd done with Sadi, and the fact he brought Marie—*his number one*—to homecoming.

To clear my head, I look out the bedroom window toward the falls as I sling my backpack over my shoulder. Under the light, I notice that, in this drama going on in my life, I haven't even noticed that the leaves are changing color.

My great-aunt Anne once told me that "Once you love, you never stop; it just changes." Yes, it was about a cat that died, but still, I suppose it's true in all things.

***

Walking out the back door, under the driveway lights, which is basically a streetlight, I watch as Toby, now in jeans, is in the process of putting on a sweatshirt. He's jacked and beautiful. Fuller and broader than Lucas.

Pulling on the sweatshirt that says "*NAVY*" in yellow letters, he smiles, clearly seeing the expression on my face.

"Damn, Toby. My fake date is fine."

"And the Future Mrs. Green is hot as hell, and a queen to boot." He opens the door. "Let's get to getting."

Climbing in, I laugh. "Let's."

Toby reaches in the back, grabs a cowboy hat, and sets it on my head. "Trade the tiara for the country girl crown?"

I laugh. "Hell yes."

***

When we pull off Harvest Road and hit the dirt path, Toby sighs. "This place is one of my favorites."

"Mine, too.

"After-parties on John Deere Lane always were my favorite."

"Wait—what?"

"All through high school, your dad has always let us guys, who worked for him, come up here after dances. Kind of a nonverbal agreement to show up when deer camp opened and do our part to help out. True sense of community." He laughs. "But yeah, *party on John Deere Lane.*"

"For your information, it's Doe Camp when the girls

Blue Love

and I are here."

Throwing his head back, he laughs. "Then so it is, angel, then so it is."

Toby parks by the pond and jumps out before hustling around to open my door.

He turns so his back is to me. "Jump on."

On his back, he walks toward the wood pile already set up. I assume Dad must have come up here and done it when Alex spoke to him about the after-party.

I notice headlights cresting the hill as Toby and I make quick work of starting the fire. Obviously, he's done this a few times.

When it's started, he pulls an Adirondack chair up closer to the fire. He sits and pulls me onto his lap, wraps his arm around me, and kisses the top of my head. All part of the act, I'm sure.

"Relax and enjoy, Tessa."

Alex, Phoebe, Jade, Tommy, Lucas, and a few others see this as they walk toward us. I look for Marie but don't see her.

Mike and Ronnie, two football players, carry a cooler and set it down close to us. "Anyone want a beer?"

"I do," I answer, and Mike tosses me one. I completely avoid looking at Alex.

Toby laughs. "Your dad would have your fine, little ass, girl."

"And he would have yours if he heard you say that." I laugh as I pop the tab.

As soon as it touches my lips, I regret it. *Beer is even worse than wine.* But Maggie and John didn't raise a quitter.

"Alex, you want one?" Mike asks.

"No, one of us has to be responsible," Alex quips.

"Not it." I raise my beer, and everyone laughs. Well, not everyone. My close friends and Lucas certainly don't.

255

"Links?" Mike asks.

"No, I'm good," Lucas answers.

I finish the beer.

After a bit, I start to get chilly. Goosebumps cover my arms, and Toby seems to notice.

He whispers in my ear, "Check this out."

He lifts me off his lap and stands up. "Angel, you cold?"

"Why, yes, I am," I try not to laugh, or drool, as he pulls his sweatshirt over his head. The tee shirt under it rises to indecent levels and, good God, he has an amazing chest.

He then steps forward. "Arms up."

I do, and he puts the sweatshirt over my head, asking, "Better, angel?"

"Not quite yet." I laugh nervously as I notice everyone looking at us. And Lucas? He's fuming.

"I'll be right back." Toby kisses my cheek then hurries toward the pond. I assume to his Jeep.

As soon as he's out of earshot, Jade says, "Holy shit, Tessa, he's freakin' hot, but he always was."

Everyone except Tommy and Lucas laugh out loud.

"And he loves Jesus," Becca adds.

"He's nice." I shrug.

"Understatement of the century." Phoebe laughs. "He's perfect for you. Already family."

"You are, too." I wink.

"But is there a spark?" Jade asks.

I nod. "And he kisses like—"

"Like what?" Toby asks.

Startled, I jump and whirl around. Toby plants a kiss to my lips.

"Just like that." I smile and step back.

He sits in our chair, and yes, I guess it's ours.

Needing a drink, I glance back at Mike. "Can I get another?"

"Hell yes." Mike laughs.

When I turn to go to the cooler, I notice Lucas is in a chair behind it. When I open it, Lucas closes it with his foot.

"Excuse me." I roll my eyes.

"You've had enough," he whisper-hisses.

I push his foot off and grab not one but three beers, and then I slam the cooler shut and return to Toby.

He pats his lap and, as I sit, he chuckles, "Thirsty, angel?"

Glaring at Lucas, who is glaring at me from across the fire, I answer, "Yes."

Toby then throws a blanket around the front of us while I toss back another beer, this time without stopping, and then another.

"Slow down, angel."

"No." I look over my shoulder at him. "Shouldn't you be kissing me?"

He turns me in his lap and whispers in my ear while lifting the blanket, shielding us from the onlookers. "I understand you're going through some things—I'm here for you—but I want no regrets and no awkward moments after tonight. I'm not rebound material, Tessa. I'm a keeper, and you, angel, deserve to be kept. One more kiss for me, not him." His kiss is soft and given with sincerity, and it's my favorite Toby kiss. "How was that?"

"Beautiful."

"Do you need more, or can we take this at our pace?" he asks with more sincerity in his eyes than I've ever seen.

"No, Toby, I can wait."

Toby uncovers our faces, pulls my head to his chest, and I close my eyes.

Fire

Chapter Sixteen

LUCAS

If there is a hell on earth, it resides in the same place that felt like heaven just weeks ago and, this was it. Hell is watching Tessa as she falls asleep in the arms of another man while trying to keep my cool. The same cool I promised Tommy I would keep, and Tommy then promised Alex Ross I could handle.

Being that few people in my life have mattered, like Tommy, I am intent on not breaking said promise.

"We're out of beer," Mark announces.

"There are two over here. She doesn't need them." Toby Green strokes her hair and does so while looking at me, giving me a slight shake of his head.

Fuck you, I think, but don't say, because that would not be keeping cool.

I know this asshole cares for her, but it doesn't make any of this situation, one I have managed to get myself into, any easier.

I broke her, she told me so, and now Toby is going to fix her.

Because I don't know how.

I stand up and walk to Tommy. "Hey, man, I'm going to go down to the cabin and crash. You staying here?"

"Yeah. Alex is, too." Tommy stands, and we do our handshake, which amounts to half-handshake, half-high-five, followed by a one-armed hug slash shoulder bump.

"All right, see you in the morning," I say, avoiding Jade's glare by bending over and picking up some discarded cans as I walk away.

"How can you talk to him?" Jade asks.

"Pretty girl, he's my friend. I've known him all my life, and I love him like a brother," Tommy replies in a way I know damn well I'm fucking up his happy, too.

"Okay," she says as I grab another can and glance back to see her kiss him. Then I hear him make a noise that I sure as hell don't need to hear and her whisper, "Four and a half more months there, hot stuff."

"It's going to kill me. Do you have any clue how amazing you looked tonight? Now? Every day?" Tommy asks.

Jade laughs and answers with the kind of confidence a woman should have with her man. "Yes, I do."

I toss the empties into a cooler, look once again at sleeping Tessa, and then hike down the path toward "Doe Camp."

Once inside, I climb into the loft and attempt to force myself to sleep.

Minutes later, the door of the cabin creaks open, and I peer through the slats down through the railing and watch as Toby carries Tessa into the cabin, lays her down on the pull-out sofa bed, and kisses her cheek.

"Sleep, angel. I'll be back."

After Toby leaves, and knowing how soundly she sleeps when she's fucked up, I climb down the ladder from the loft, sit beside her, and watch her sleep.

Toby's right; she is an angel.

I carefully rub soft circles on the back of her hand, and the anger I feel inside, at myself, turns to regret. Her skin is so soft; her lips full and beautiful, fucking kissable; and her damn hair, all tousled and messy. I push away a soft, stray strand off her face and desperately wish I could hold her, but I'm not that fucked up ... am I?

I bend down and brush my lips across hers, and she exhales. I kiss her lips lightly. Weak, I then gently suck on her lower lip, not caring what's right or wrong at this moment. I don't even care if, in her sleep, she thinks I'm Toby. That's how desperate I am to touch her again, and the fact that she's asleep makes it possible.

At least this way she can't show with angry eyes, or tell with angry words, just how much she now despises me.

Then, in her sleep, she whispers, "Lucas, I love you," as a tear rolls down her face.

At this moment, I don't give a damn how desperate a move this was. It is not only worth it but gives me ... hope. I kiss away her tear.

I told Tommy that she deserves a better man, and I vowed to become that, no matter the time it took. With all my heart, I know I can. More importantly, I know I would never give up trying to be that for her.

I hear footsteps approaching from just outside and

quickly move to the ladder and climb up to the loft where I lay like a thief in the dark.

Through the wooden railing, I watch silently as Toby lays in bed next to Tessa, holding her in his arms.

I listen as Tessa mumbles something incoherently, and he asks, "Sorry, Tessa, did I wake you?"

She jerks a bit and turns her head in his direction. "No, I had a dream."

"Wasn't about me, was it?" Toby asks, pushing away that same strand of hair.

Hell no, it wasn't, I want to scream.

"No, it wasn't," she admits.

"Tessa, what happened?"

"It's complicated. Very, very complicated."

Understatement of the year, I think.

"Do you want to share?"

Who the fuck is this guy? GI Joe or Oprah?

"I don't know. I feel weird telling you about my issues with Lucas," Tessa admits.

"Tessa, this is me. You and I have known each other forever. Don't start acting different with me because we kissed. I won't let things be weird. As I've said, I saw what was going on as soon as I asked you to the dance and quickly figured out why you had no date."

"What gave it away? I mean, at first?"

"You sending me to ask Alex permission should have been my first clue. The Tessa I know and love doesn't ask permission for anything. But that didn't give it away. It was the quarterback. When I asked Alex, he sneered '*no, you can't*' at me through clenched teeth." He chuckles.

"Seriously?" She laughs.

What did you expect, Tessa? You set me up!

"So, did you have …?" Toby starts to ask.

"Toby! You're really going to ask me that?" she interrupts.

"Why not?" he asks.

Because it's none of your fucking business, dick.

"No. But I did get drunk and come onto him. He didn't do anything." Tessa sighs. "Toby, why do you think he didn't?"

"He cares about you, Tessa. Just seems like the kind of guy who doesn't know how to show it. Maybe he's afraid. Maybe he's a virgin."

Maybe you're a douchebag, I want to scream.

Tessa laughs. "He's not. I was going to be unlucky number thirteen," she whispers the number.

"Damn." Toby chuckles.

Tessa tells him about Sadi, and the *Three Bs*, as she calls them, and about the many times she offered herself to me. She tells him about the good things, too, and that she loves me and that I said those words to her, too. But she doesn't tell him the more personal stuff. Not about the abortion or the drunken mother or absent father. She holds my secrets safe. Then she tells him about the day she stopped at my place and how she froze, and that she never thought it was possible to be numb and still feel the pain she felt since that night. It crushes me. She tells him about Marie being number one, and what she said about Toby being her number one. They laugh at that. But it, too, hurts like hell to hear.

"You are going to get through this, Tessa, and I'm going to help you," Toby tells her then asks, "You know how you felt when you kissed me tonight? And not the ones that were part of the scandal."

Fuck, I can't hear this shit. I need to get out of here.

"Yes," she says softly.

"What did it feel like?"

"Like it was enough, like it wasn't rushed, like it would be there whenever I wanted it," Tessa says, and my ego bursts like a balloon and flies out of control.

"Okay, and what about with him?" he asks.

If my cool wasn't on the line, I'd throw myself over the railing and risk an injury right now.

"I couldn't get enough," she says, "and I wanted more."

Okay, much fucking better. I link my hands behind my neck and get comfortable.

"Tess, you know me, right? You know that, if I tell you something, it's the truth. You know, if I promise you the moon, I'm going to do whatever it takes to get it for you. I'm safe and comfortable. I'm not going to hurt you and, in your heart, you know that, even though we've never had a conversation like this, even though we never had feelings like this for one another before, right?"

"I guess. But I did have a crush on you the summers you helped with hay." Tessa sighs.

Just fucking great.

"And I've already told you that I know your heart and love it. So, with the quarterback, it's not like that. You are so eager to please him—"

"All right, Toby, I get it. I don't know him. I haven't formed a relationship with him based on trust and friendship, right?" She begins to cry, and I have to force myself again not to jump. "It was starting, I was starting to trust him with my heart, Toby, I really was, and then I don't know what happened. I don't know why he would cheat. I truly would hate to think it was over a bikini wax and mani-pedi."

He chuckles. "Do you talk to him as freely as that?"

"What do you mean?"

"Bikini wax?"

"No, he didn't know that until I told him today. I told him I wasn't going to go through that pain for nothing and sort of alluded to the fact that—"

"I get it, but you can't talk like that to someone without driving him crazy."

"Why doesn't it bother you?"

"It's all about self-control. If I want a relationship with you someday, I know I need to pace this. I need to let you grow a bit more into the woman I know you're going to become. If I check out the new do, I'm not thinking that pace would remain, so let's not talk about that." He pauses and chuckles uncomfortably. I know that sound—dick is thinking with his dick. "We should go to sleep, please."

"Oh," she tells him, "you should think about dead puppies. Are you a virgin?"

Toby laughs and, although it's funny, I refuse to. "No, Tessa."

"So, how many women have you been with?"

"Four."

"Oh." She sounds surprised. "Is four a lot?"

"More than it should be."

"So, twelve is like way too many?"

"Different paths, Tessa. Don't judge; just try to understand. Everyone has their own journey to walk. But, for you, Tessa, two is too many, got it?"

She yawns. "Uh-huh."

Minus the four women and his lips on my girl, this guy should be wearing sandals and walking on water, I think.

"What are you doing tomorrow?"

"Children's choir practice and running are all that I have planned." She yawns again.

"I have family to visit, but after that, can I take you on a real date? One with no pressure or expectations?"

"I would love that."

Blue Love

Scratch that, he's still a dick.

She rests against him, and they fall asleep while I lay high above them, feeling like I may get sick.

* * *

I watch as Tessa, who always wakes up earlier than anyone else, walks out to the back porch. She stretches and yawns, looking at the sky. The sun is shining, and there isn't a cloud in the sky. She walks to the outhouse then washes her hands in the creek and squats beside it, watching the water run. She hugs her knees, closes her eyes, and takes a deep breath, allowing the fresh, crisp fall air to fill her lungs.

I know I should stay put, give her the chance to have her alone time, but right now is probably the only time I get her alone and have any hope of her listening.

I step from one stone to the next, crossing the creek, and she stands, watching me.

"Good morning, Tessa." I shove my hands in my pockets, because I have no idea what else to do with them.

"Good morning. Did you stay last night?" she asks, looking around, confused.

"I did."

"Where did you sleep?"

"In the loft." I watch her reaction and expect a glare. She surprises me with an eye roll.

She crosses her arms. "Did Marie stay?"

"Of course not, Tessa. You know I wouldn't bring her here."

"Do I?"

"Tessa—"

"No big deal. You should have. Opportunity missed. I

guess that's too bad. I mean, the connection you two share must be wonderful."

"How was your date?"

She does glare now and, sick but true, it's hot. "You should know; you were on it with me."

I lock eyes with her. "Yeah, all the kissing was awesome to watch."

"Oh, I'm so sorry. Maybe you can go with me tonight so you can watch me give him a blow job, Lucas." She tries real hard to sound strong but, her voice quivers. "Maybe I can see if he will kick your ass after I screw him."

"Good morning, Tessa. Hello, Lucas," GI Jock Itch interrupts as he walks toward us.

"Could we have a minute, please?" I ask through my fucking teeth.

"Tessa, is that all right with you?" Toby asks.

"Sure." She shrugs, eyes still locked with mine.

Toby walks away.

"I'm sorry, and I wish you would let me explain the situation you walked into the other night," I whisper.

"Um, well, sure, let's hear it," she says.

"I was stoned and drunk, and—"

"Why?" she interrupts.

"It was a rough afternoon," I say with zero expression.

"Because I went to get my nails done?" she asks. "Because I wasn't there to Lucas sit?"

Pissed, I point out, "It's not at all about you."

"No, it's not, but you hurt me, and you won't have the opportunity to do it again. I'm done here." She begins to walk away.

Fuck, fuck, fuck. Redirect.

"Stop, Tessa, please. Just one more thing, and I won't say another word."

She turns and raises her little nose in the air, in what I

suppose is an attempt to appear to look down at me. Cute, and if shit wasn't already sideways, I'd point out I tower over her, so unless I get her a step ladder, it's really ineffective.

Instead, I stick my tail between my legs, because I have to make this right, and ask, "Can you be my friend for a while? I have some things to work through, and I don't want you to not be in my life. So, can we try to be friends? Please?"

She hugs herself and looks from one eye to another a few times. If last night's GI Leno wasn't proof enough that she's confused, the way she looks now would erase all doubt I have to go easy and do this right.

I take a few cautious steps toward her then grab her shoulders nice and gently, watching her lip quiver. Then, when I know she's not going to pull away, I hug her. She sinks right in, and I am reminded how perfectly she fits with me and how perfectly I fit with her. She fists my shirt and rests her forehead against my chest.

"I know I don't deserve you, Tessa, but please don't count me out. I have never needed someone's love as much as I need yours. Be my friend. If that's all you can give, I'll take it. But I need you to know that I love you, and someday, with some work, you'll never doubt that again." I press my lips to the top of her hair and inhale. Then I kiss her quickly before untangling our arms and releasing her.

I wait until I watch her take in a breath and let go of my shirt. Then she looks up at me, turns, and walks toward ... him, and then I watch them walk away.

Tommy comes out of the cabin and waves for me to come to him.

I follow him to his car and get in. We sit in silence until we get to the road.

"How are you doing, man?" Tommy looks over at me.

"Fine."

"Answer a question?"

"Sure."

"Why did you bring Marie to the dance?" he asks.

"I needed to see her, and I didn't have a date."

"You want Tessa back?"

"Yes, very much."

"Want some advice?" Tommy asks, and I nod. "Stop bringing your crazy exes around."

I chuckle. "Wasn't like that."

"Then, what are you doing, Lucas? Because I'm confused."

"I'm getting better, Tommy, for her," I say. "And for me."

Tommy nods. "I'm so glad you finally feel you're worth it. So, what are you doing today and tonight?"

"Laundry and cleaning today. Not sure about tonight. Any plans?"

"Going to Jade's to meet the family after church. Wanna come?" Tommy asks.

"No, thanks. You have fun with that." I smirk, knowing how nervous he is about meeting her dad. He says he can't hide how much he wants Jade.

"Go to church with me?"

"Sure. What time?" The car swerves, and I grab the wheel. "Watch the road."

"Sorry, man. But, just so we're clear, you did just say you'd come to church with me, right?" Tommy seems shocked.

"Yes, buddy, I did."

"Wow, I think you love her."

"I do, Tommy, I do," I say. "I just wish it wasn't so hard."

"If anyone can win a girl over, it's you. Just give it time."

"Tommy, the road, please," I insist then laugh and point out, "This is why I always drive."

The rest of the ride is silent, except for the music playing on the radio.

Tommy pulls into my driveway and puts the car in park. "Okay, church at—"

"Nine-thirty?" I ask, getting out of the car.

"Sunday school starts at nine, man."

"Tommy, you haven't been to Sunday school in a year. Don't push it." I laugh as I shut the door then head inside.

I grab a notebook out of the junk drawer and a pen to write down my thoughts because, when this is over, I want her to know how I felt each step of the way. Then she will realize she wasn't the only one hurt by the unfortunate events that led to our "break." She would know there wasn't a day that passed when I didn't think of her.

I held you today at the same time I let you go. I trust in what I feel for the first time. You'll be part of me forever. I'm forever changed because of you.

Day 2 without Tessa Ross sucks, but I can make it, right?

LYA,
Lucas

GOODBYES

Chapter Seventeen

TESSA

Looking at myself in the mirror, I really hope I'm not too underdressed. I have no idea where we're going, so jeans would have to do. These ones are my favorite, and I stepped it up by leaving the long sleeve tees in their drawer and opting for a white blouse and a denim jacket. I also threw on one of Molly's scarves to give it a splash of color to brighten up my Plain Jane outfit. I straightened my hair and even applied a swipe of mascara and lip gloss. Jade would be proud.

One more quick look in the mirror, and then I head out to the kitchen.

As soon as I round the corner, Toby is walking in and, thankfully, is also wearing jeans. He's also wearing a

Blue Love

sweater that fits him like a glove. He's so handsome with his dark brown hair cut short and his blue green eyes always smiling. He's also a good four inches taller than me. He's six-foot and in amazing shape.

"Hey, Tessa, how was church?"

"Great. How was your morning?"

Walking to me, he answers, "Crazy, busy, and much better now." He hugs me tight, and his hugs are like a favorite sweatshirt. "You ready to go?"

The kids run into the house, yelling his name. He scoops up Kendall, and Jake jumps on his back as he twirls them around in a circle.

After he sets Kendall down and Jake slides off his back, he grabs a video tape off the counter and hands it to them. "You have got to watch this. It's a classic!"

They have already seen *Star Wars* half a dozen times, but none of us mention it.

The kids politely smile, and he looks at me. "They've seen it, haven't they?"

"A few times. But it was nice of you to think of them."

"We'll watch it every day!" Jake cheers.

"Where are you two going?" Kendall asks, looking at him all dreamy-eyed.

He looks at me and asks, "Lunch and a movie sound okay?"

"It sounds perfect."

* * *

Holding hands, we drive to Ithaca Commons, where we sit outside at a small café while talking about his plans when he graduates from Annapolis Naval Academy in two years.

"What will your job be?"

"I am going to be an MD," Toby says, taking a bite of his lunch.

"So, you'll be a medical doctor?"

"Hopefully," Toby says, laughing as he wipes his mouth then mine.

"Sorry." I blush. "Will you move a lot?"

"Probably every four years."

"Won't you miss your family?"

"Of course I will. I do, however, get thirty days of leave a year. Four weeks off a year, and I get to travel and help people, and the majority of the major military hospitals are on the East Coast, so it will be just a short plane trip or a long drive home." He sits back. "Does that bother you?"

"No, I think it's wonderful. It would just be hard, that's all."

"What would be hard?" he asks. "Being away from family."

"Yes, I guess."

"That's what some people do, Tessa. But the big picture is pretty awesome. I'll retire in my forties. If I am married by the time I am twenty-seven and the wonderful woman I marry wants children, we can raise them while traveling and seeing the world, if we choose. By the time our perfect little monsters are heading into their teens, we can drag them, kicking and screaming, back here. I can either work or coach their sports team. Ya know, be present. The sacrifices I make today will be huge rewards tomorrow."

* * *

Heading to the mall, we continue talking about our goals and dreams, and even about the possibility of a future with us. I admit fully and totally that Toby makes me smile and there isn't a moment when I'm with him that isn't enjoyable. I love the way he allows me to feel desirable and innocent. As with Lucas, I felt like I wanted everything right now. It's nice with Toby. But the fact Lucas is ever present, and the fact I still see the sadness in his eyes, as if they are etched in my mind, makes it feel wrong to still want something with Toby, yet I do.

Hand in hand, we walk through the mall, deciding to go grab some ice cream. That's when I see Lucas standing at the head of the line ... with yet another brunette.

As if he senses my happiness and is hell-bent on destroying it, he turns, and our eyes meet.

Ice cream in hand, the happy couple walks past us, but Lucas stops next to me and whispers, "Jill, number two."

Fuming, I pretend he's not even here and look up at Toby, who chuckles and shakes his head.

"What?"

"You'll figure it out."

Figure what out? I wonder but don't ask, because Lucas Links is not going to ruin another moment of my freaking life.

We order ice cream and decide to skip the movie and instead sit and talk.

I'm home by two.

He walks me to the door and kisses my cheek. "Thank you for a great weekend."

"No, thank you. You have been amazing and have opened my eyes. When will I see you again?" rushes out in a flurry.

He smiles.

"Oh, I'm sorry."

"You are so beautiful," he says, staring into my eyes. "I'm going to be back in a few hours to shoot with John and Alex. Will you be here?"

I nod. "Yes."

"See you then, Tessa." He steps back, toward the door, still smiling as he reaches behind him and opens it.

Then he leaves.

* * *

I wake up to Toby sitting across from me, smiling. "Tired, angel?"

"I guess I was." I sit up. "I will be right out. You go ahead."

When I walk out into the barn, I immediately see Lucas. *What the hell is he doing here?*

Okay, Tessa, forgiveness. Just heard an hour sermon on it at church.

Tommy sits next to him, and Lucas whispers something to him.

Dad calls me, and I look away from them.

"Hey, Tessa, these boys don't believe you can shoot. Will you prove me right?"

"Sure. Let me grab my bow." I head to the small room that holds basically an arsenal that Dad and Alex have collected over the years and grab my bow.

When I walk back out, I notice a shit-ass grin on Lucas's face.

"Hey, Lucas, why don't you run in the house and grab an apple to put on your head?" I joke … sort of.

"I don't think that's a really good idea." He smiles in such a relaxed way that I think maybe we actually can be friends.

Blue Love

Standing in front of the target—a plastic deer set up in front of hay bales—I whisper, "Sorry fake Bambi," as I load the arrow, draw back the bow, and hit a bull's-eye.

I turn and look at Dad, who nods proudly, and then I ask, "Anyone else want to try?"

Alex is first, and he does well. Tommy's a tad bit off but does hit the target. Toby is just outside the bull's-eye.

"Lucas, you want to try?" Alex asks.

Wearing a white hat, a fitted Henley, and jeans that sit on his hips, looking as perfect as ever, he pushes up off the stool, a piece of straw hanging out his lips, and turns the white hat backward. "Sure, I'll give it a try."

Sweet Jesus, I think and immediately look away. Unfortunately, my eyes meet Jade's as she walks in, fashionably late, and she sees it immediately.

She scowls and mouths, "*Fucking white hat boys*," and we both start to laugh.

He walks up to me. "Never done this before, and I was always taught to ask the best for advice. You wanna help me out?"

"Sure." I shrug, as if it's no big deal, but it ends up being a much bigger deal than I thought. I have to help him with everything, including his stance. And, at one point, I swear I hear him take a deep breath in.

I turn, look over my shoulder, and whisper, "Did you just smell me?"

He grins and shakes his head.

I narrow my eyes. "Friends don't sniff friends, unless you're a dog sniffing another dog's ass. I'm not a dog, you got it?"

Lucas grins. "Tessa, are we friends now?"

I roll my eyes. "Yes, Lucas."

"Thank you. I think I got this."

Without concentrating one bit, he pulls back and

shoots. His arrow kisses mine dead center. "Huh, look at that."

"Beginners luck. Do it again."

He does.

I laugh. "You've totally shot before, faker."

He shakes his head, grin playing on his lips.

"Then do it again."

And he does ... four more times.

What can I do but laugh?

"Let's get the guns out," Dad suggests.

We shoot for three hours straight.

"Tessa, you're going hunting with us this year, right?" Dad jokes.

"Not in a million years. I've told you; give me a bunch of disgusting people, twelve maybe thirteen, I'll shoot them before I'll shoot a defenseless animal."

"Wow, Tessa." Toby chuckles. "Wouldn't want to get on your bad side."

I smile at him. "Please don't."

* * *

Toby and I stay behind when everyone else leaves to lock up.

"When do you have to leave?"

"My flight leaves from Ithaca tomorrow at six. I need to be there at five," Toby answers.

"Can I drive you?"

"I would love that. What time do you get out of practice?" Toby asks.

"Four."

"All right then, I'll meet you at the school, like, four-fifteen?"

"Sounds like a plan." I nod.

"We could make it a date. It would be our third." Toby winks.

I could love you, I think as he takes my hand.

"Can I hug you?"

He tugs my hand, pulling me into him. "You don't have to ask, angel."

After just enough time ticks by, he kisses the top of my head.

I look up at him and wonder if he's ever going to kiss me again, because he hasn't at all today.

I won't let it happen again. I want to know before he leaves if I could feel the same desire with Toby that I felt with Lucas. So, I push up on my toes and kiss him. He kisses me back gently, but when I attempt to deepen it, by way of my tongue, he pulls away.

Mortified, I start to step back, but he grabs my hand. "Don't be angry at me. I'm in no hurry. I don't want you to be, either."

I look away.

"Tessa ... don't be like that."

"Sorry."

He pulls me toward the door then steps out as he tells me, "No, Tessa, not like that, either. I want to kiss you. Things need to be clear in your head, though."

I don't say anything. I just follow him to the back door of the house. He opens it for me, but he doesn't let go of my hand.

"Tessa, you need to know that I find you irresistible. Every part of me wants to hold you and kiss you. I gotta listen to my heart, though, and it's screaming *not yet*."

I nod and, for some reason, I understand. "Okay."

He kisses the top of my head then nods to the door. "See you tomorrow."

When I walk in, I tell Dad, "I'm taking Toby to the airport after practice."

He looks up briefly from the paperwork strewn on the table. "Okay."

I kiss the top of his head then head into the living room and see Kendall and Jake on the couch.

"*Louis and Clark* is starting." Jake says to me, his eyes glued to the TV.

"Let me go get my PJs on, and I'll be back."

I run up the stairs, taking them two at a time. Once in my room, I start to open the top dresser drawer and see a note sitting on top of it.

Your skills amaze me, my new friend. The only time my mind wandered out of friendship lane was when you said, "Do it again." Day 3 without Tessa Ross was a little better. I didn't make her cry;
that's a start
LYA,
Lucas

I hold the note to my chest and smile. Then ... I scold myself.

* * *

The girls and I are eating lunch in the cafeteria when the boys walk in.

Tommy sits down, but Lucas turns around and starts to walk away.

"Sit with us." I point to the empty seat across the table.
"You sure?"
"We are friends now, right?"
He takes a seat across from me.

"So, at church yesterday, the sermon was on forgiveness," Jade says, smiling, knowing this is where my head is.

"I'm not sure I remember what ours was. Do you, Lucas?" Tommy asks.

"Forbidden fruit," Lucas answers and rolls his eyes at me.

Mouth full of milk, I grab a napkin and let the milk fly into that instead of across the table at him, laughing and choking at the same time.

"Tessa, are you okay?" Phoebe asks, deeply concerned as she pats my back.

"I'm fine." I laugh, looking at Lucas, who is full-on grinning.

"Well," Becca says, "he certainly does give us the message we need when we need it."

To that, he and I both laugh even harder.

"Well, isn't this nice?" Sadi's voice hisses from behind me. "Did we kiss and make up?"

Rage, I feel rage as I whirl around in my seat and look at her. "Oh hey, Sadi. Good news. I was so impressed with your scuba technique that I decided to just go for it. We fucked all weekend."

"Whore," Sadi spats then walks away.

"Good at it," I yell at her back.

"Tessa!" Becca snaps. "What happened to forgiveness?"

I stand up. "I forgave the bitch. She blew my boyfriend."

* * *

Crying at my locker in Make-Out Hall is also not a place I saw myself senior year, yet here I fucking am.

I hate this about me—the crying when I'm angry. And, right now, I am beyond angry.

Knowing hands land on my shoulders and turn me. As soon as he sees my eyes, he says sorrowfully, "I am so fucking sorry, baby." When he attempts to hug me, I shove him back.

He holds up his hands and shakes his head. "How am I supposed to react when you're crying?"

"I'd suggest you stay the fuck away." I point to myself. "This is not me being sad; this is rage."

He steps forward and leans down so we're eye to eye. I turn my head, not wanting to feel what I feel because of the way he's looking at me, as if to show me he, too, feels like I do.

"Tessa, don't cry." He wipes my fallen tears, and I jump back as if his touch was electric. "Please, Tessa, look at me."

I look at him with angry, narrowed eyes.

"I'm so sorry."

"I can't do this, Lucas. I want to, but it hurts." I slap away the remaining tears.

"You said we were friends, and I'll take it, but I still love you."

I see enormous blonde hair out of the corner of my eye and grab his face, kissing him. Pissed he's not even trying, I kiss him harder. Then I hear a growl escape against my mouth.

He opens his mouth, and I plunge my tongue in deeply, licking him, tasting him. He grabs my hair and pulls it back, now hovering over me, taking control of the kiss. When I start to pull away, he reaches down and grips the back of my leg, pressing his enormous body against mine, making me feel how hard he is. I whimper as his lips press kisses down my neck.

"Lucas," I whimper.

He moves back to my lips, grinding his hips against me as he now runs his hands up the back of my legs, under my skirt, and grab my ass.

Fire blazing at my core, he crashes his mouth over mine again, kissing me, tasting me, as he presses against me harder, grinding faster, licking deeper, against my locker.

I am on fire, burning with desire, as he dry fucks me against the brick wall.

Gasping for air, hoping to breathe in some semblance of control, I tear my mouth away from his as a pulse quickens between my legs in a way I have not experienced, causing my desire to reach an all-time high.

I run my hand down his hard abdomen, and then lower. He pushes his erection into my hand and hisses loudly in my ear.

What am I doing? What have I done? I scream inside my head.

"I can't do friends, Lucas, when all I want to do is that." I rub down his hard length then pull my hand away. "And I can't do that again because it hurts so badly."

I start to slide under his arm, but he grips the sides of my face.

He narrows his eyes as he says, "I'm going to put you back together, Tessa." He strokes my hair so gently as he looks me over like he's trying to memorize me. "I broke you, and I'm working on fixing you."

Angry again at myself and him, I push his hands away. "How are you going to do that when you're out at the mall with your next ... fu ... partner?"

"She was an ex, Tessa. I need to fix myself before I can fix you." He rubs up my sides slowly, and my back arches. "Do not stop being my friend, regardless of where this journey ends. I can never lose you, do you understand? Never." He kisses my forehead then wraps me in his arms, and I swear I feel his strong body tremble.

"I'm taking Toby to the airport after practice," I whisper.

"Tell him I said good riddance. I mean, goodbye. And when you're with him, remember it was my dick rubbing against you, giving you your first mini O and making you want more, not his."

I bite my lip, thinking about how good he felt and wondering if, in fact, I did have a "mini orgasm," and if that was a mini, what on earth would a life-sized one feel like?

"You two done?" Sadi interrupts.

"Never." His eyes never leave mine.

"Wow, kind of like us, huh, Lucas?" Sadi hisses.

I start to move, but he holds me still, eyes never leaving mine as he says, "Nothing like us, Sadi. I told you that all summer and the other night. Now walk the fuck away before I make good on my promise."

His promise?

"Fuck you, Lucas!" Sadi storms away.

The bell rings, and he steps back before the halls fill with students leaving classrooms.

"Friends, Tessa?"

"We'll see."

* * *

Toby is waiting for me in the parking lot after practice.

"Hey, angel." He smiles as I walk up to his Jeep. "We can take the Jeep if you'll do me a favor."

"Sure." I nod, not really paying full attention because I

just walked past Lucas in his white hat, standing with Tommy and looking at me.

Toby opens the door for me, and I drop my backpack on the floor before buckling up.

Sliding into the driver's seat, he asks, "Can you drive this back to your place and park it out back? Your dad said it was okay. You can drive it anytime you want. And, by that, I mean, drive it all the damn time."

"Are you for real?" I ask, and he nods. "My dad will not allow that."

"Already said he was okay with it. And Tessa, this isn't a ring. Hell, Links can ride shotgun, and I wouldn't care."

"Um ... he won't be."

Laughing, he cranks up the radio and peels out to the song "She Don't Know She's Beautiful" by Sammy Kershaw blasting.

I know I need to tell him about what happened today, and I need to do it soon, but it feels a bit too soon when Toby pulls into a parking lot by the lake, parks and hops out. He grabs a cooler out of the back then opens my door, takes my hand, and walks us over to sit on the ground.

"Let's chat." He opens up the cooler and pulls out some wrapped sandwiches, handing me one. "How was your day?"

I word vomit everything, from Sadi in the lunchroom, to the kiss, but definitely leaving out the mini O thing, which I'm not even sure is real, or if it is, if it really happened.

He sits behind me, stretches his legs out, and pulls me back against his chest.

"Tessa, you'll get through this. Just go slow. Promise me you'll go slow."

"I will. And I know this is none of my business, but do you date when you're in Annapolis?"

He laughs. "No, Tessa, and I wouldn't want to. I told you; I have a past and have learned from it. I have goals. I have a focus and know exactly what I want. I want you to be able to figure things out, too. You're young, angel."

"I'm sorry."

"Don't you dare be. John and I had a long chat about you today, and he wants you to experience life before you settle down. He doesn't want you to go through what your mom and he are dealing with right now."

"He said that?" I gasp.

"Yeah, he did."

* * *

As we walk into the airport, I feel a weird sadness, blanketed in selfishness and guilt, surround me, yet I still ask, "Can I kiss you goodbye?"

"Yeah, and I'll say yes if you drive the Jeep, no matter where your head is."

Tearing up, I nod.

He holds my face and gently kisses my lips, and then I walk him to his gate.

"See you soon, angel."

"See you soon, Toby."

He kisses my head, turns, and then walks down the hall.

I sit and wait as his plane takes off.

Not wanting to go home yet, I decide to go to the mall and use some of my birthday money.

* * *

Blue Love

I park outside the Country Seat entry and walk in. Unsure of what I'm looking for I just walk.

As I pass the food court, I roll my freaking eyes when I see Lucas standing with yet a different girl, this one with short, chin-length brown hair. She's cute. Maybe he could dry hump her like he did me this afternoon. Not that I'm one to judge, because I am straight-up the hoe of all the senior high school virgins.

The girl is smiling and looking up at him. She hugs him, and he hugs her back, but it's not a long, lingering, dry-hump-against-the-wall kind of hug.

When his head turns, I know I'm busted, and then he smiles at me.

"Is that her, Lucas?" The girl claps.

"It is." He nods.

She skips toward me, pulling an amused Lucas behind her, and I am forced to stand there. "Hi, I'm Amy, and I take it you're Tessa?"

I nod and watch as Lucas pushes his hands in his pockets.

"Wow, Lucas, she's beautiful."

I force a smile. "Nice to meet you, Amy."

"So, I'm one of his sexes." She laughs.

You have got to be kidding me, I think.

"What number was I, Lucas?"

He holds up three fingers.

She looks back at me. "I think it's amazing what he's doing. I can see why he's hot for you, Tessa. Good luck, you two. I have to go meet my fiancé. Wedding in six weeks. Much to do!" She basically tackle-hugs me before walking away.

Lucas chuckles. "Hello, Tessa."

"What was that?"

"That was number three ... Amy," Lucas says.

I act like it's no big deal. "Oh, your third ... what did she call it?"

"Sexes." Lucas rolls his eyes. "I guess that sounds better than saying ex-fuck. I never dated her."

"Oh."

"Come eat with me. I'm starving." He grabs my hand.

I pull mine away. "I already ate."

"Will you sit with me while I eat?" He holds his hands up. "It's a very public place, friend."

Not wanting to feel any lamer than I already do after the friend comment, I shrug. "Sure, but I have to leave soon."

"You aren't buying anything? What are you doing all the way out here, then?" he asks.

I try not to act pissed that he doesn't even remember, but it does sting a bit.

"Oh, GI Joe." He laughs then whispers close to my ear as we walk toward the Chinese takeout place, "So, how did that go? Did you tell him you kissed me today?"

I nod.

"How did he take it?"

I lift my chin. "Like a man."

He points to a table. "Mind grabbing that free table before it gets snagged?"

I do as he asks and sit uncomfortably while he orders Chinese.

He sets the tray on the table then takes one of the sodas and places it in front of me.

I notice chopsticks on his tray and laugh.

"What?" Lucas asks.

I point to the chopsticks. "You know how to use those things?"

"You don't?" He looks seriously shocked.

"No, I mastered the fork, and then the knife, and from there, life was good."

He laughs. "Well, I'm going to teach you, then."

I watch as he opens his, and then he opens the others and tries to hand them to me.

"No, thank you." I sit back as far as I can.

"Not up for debate." He stands up and walks behind me. "You hold them like this."

I cave and make an attempt.

"Awesome, now try it for real."

With my hand in his, he shows me the mechanics of eating with sticks. When I get it, he finally lets go.

With the sticks in my hand, I pick up a piece of broccoli, and I hear him inhale, breathing me in. He then kisses the top of my head and says, "Good job, baby."

Before I have time to scold him, he skates around the table and sits. "Now try the noodles."

I pick one up without issue, and as I try to put it in my mouth, it slips between the sticks and lands on my chest.

"Lucky noodle." He smiles. "Do you need me to get it for you?"

Tossing the sticks down, I grab it and set it on the table. Then I open a wet wipe and spit clean my shirt. The entire time, he's staring at me.

When I finish, I raise an eyebrow and say, "Dead puppies, my friend."

He laughs, and it's the good kind of laugh. The kind of laugh that—

"Lucas Links," comes from behind me, and I look back as two redheads approach the table.

Lucas shoves some food in his mouth, waves, chews, and swallows before saying, "Hello, Tina. Hello, Tammy."

"What's up, Linksy?" The one he nodded to when he said Tina smiles as she ogles him.

He stands up. "This is Tessa, the girl I'm out of my mind in love with."

Oh ... My ... God.

"Oh, so that's why you haven't replied to my calls?" She blatantly looks down at the crotch of his pants and bites her lower lip.

"Yeah, about that. I'm sorry that I treated you that way. It's disrespectful, and I can promise that it won't happen again. I hope you two can find someone who makes you very happy. You both deserve that. I'm sorry if I hurt either of you in any way."

"Either of us?" Tammy asks. She looks at the other girl. "You had sex with him? You knew I was sleeping with him! You're my sister, for crying out loud!"

"You didn't have dibs or anything," Tina snaps.

"You were dating, Rigs!" Tammy yells.

"Not the whole time," she comes back with.

I stand and look at Lucas. "Can we go?"

"Yep. Goodbye, ladies." Lucas picks up his tray, leans in so his shoulder hits mine, and says, "Seven and eight."

"Sisters, Lucas?" I quip.

"Yeah, I was drunk and didn't realize they were sisters at the time." He's trying his best not to smile.

I smack him. "You really are awful." Then I promptly turn away so he doesn't see me smile.

After depositing his trash and tray, he catches up to me, grabs my shoulders, and says, "I'm sorry. I'm going to be better, Tessa. I promise."

Laughing, I ask, "What were you thinking? These partners of yours may be nice to look at, but how could you stand to hear them talk? All but two I have met are freaks, Lucas."

"Stop laughing at me." Lucas pouts. "In my defense, I didn't really talk to any of them."

We both laugh.

"So, that's nine, Tessa. Only three more to go."

"Are the rest as dreadful?" I ask, walking in no general direction at all, just to get out from the face-to-face position I now find myself in.

Reality finally hits three steps from the point where he told me. *Only three more to go.*

Lucas is seeking forgiveness.

I don't know why, when he had done what he did after doing something similar with Sadi, that it makes me happy, but then I quickly realize I'm not happy for me. I'm happy for Lucas. Truly.

As we walk past the pet shop, a puppy makes a break for it. I squat down, and he runs right at me, and I swoop him up. He begins feverishly licking my face, and I can do nothing but drop to my ass and laugh.

"You're so damn pretty all the time, but Tessa Ross, there is not a damn thing I have ever seen in my life that is more beautiful than your smile."

I feel my throat and eyes heating up and whisper, "Lucas, don't."

He squats down and gives the puppy a scratch behind the ear. "I know, baby, I know."

The clerk runs, gasping when she sees the little escapee. "Thank God."

I push myself up off the floor, and when the clerk reaches for him, he growls.

"Can I carry him in?" I ask.

With Lucas beside me, I play with the little guy over the plexiglass wall he's caged in as he relentlessly tries to jump back out.

"You like him almost as much as he likes you, don't you?" Lucas asks.

"We had a dog like him for twelve years. His name was

Hans, after Han Solo. Alex named him. He died at the end of last spring."

"You should get him, Tessa. Look at him; he wants you to come take him. *Get me out of the pen, Tessa. I need you to save me*," Lucas says in his best puppy voice.

"My dad would kill me." I smile at the puppy. "But the kids would love it."

Without asking permission, I reach in and pick him up. He immediately nuzzles into my neck and nibbles on my ear.

I Eskimo-kiss his wet, black nose then set him back down. He barks as I walk away, yet I forge forward.

Walking past Victoria Secret, Lucas grabs my hand and tries pulling me in. I easily pull away and keep moving forward, both of us laughing.

I decide to stop at Gap, wanting to buy a couple pairs of dress pants. Lucas buys some long-sleeved Polos, and I grab Jake and Kendall a new sweatshirt and some socks. They are both hell on socks.

It's not uncomfortable shopping with him. It's actually nice, too nice. So nice that I take an extra-long time in the changing room, expecting Lucas to leave.

When I come out, he's sitting with my backpack, which I forgot I left with him. *Obviously the reason he didn't leave.*

I nod to the County Seat entrance. "I need to get going."

He shrugs. "I get it. Let me walk you out."

It's not until I see the Jeep that I remember how big of a deal it may look like to Lucas.

"He gave you his Jeep?" Lucas asks, shocked, narrowing his eyes.

"No, but I can drive it whenever I want. I'm probably going to just park it behind the shop."

"We should take it for a spin. Go parking in it."

"I wouldn't do that to him, or with *my friend*."

"Only at school?" Lucas asks with a bit of bite behind his question.

Deserved.

"That was a mistake—"

"No, baby, it wasn't."

"Lucas—"

"Can I hug my friend goodnight and not talk about this shit? It's been a good hour, Tessa Ross. Let's leave it at that, okay?"

I hug him goodnight, and it feels so damn good, so right ... but I know better.

* * *

Once the kids are in bed, I dig into my backpack to grab my Lit book and see a note.

She kissed me! And I didn't want to sneak her in the locker room and bend her over the bench (until now, as my wildly filthy mind is racing), but rubbing against her almost made me cum in my pants. And then, at the mall, she dropped a noodle on her chest and, well, all the dead puppies in the world could not have stopped my mind from racing then.
Day 4 without Tessa Ross ... Well, it wasn't all that bad. I can fix this. And I will
LYA,
Lucas

FALLING

Chapter Eighteen

TESSA

I wake to the strangest dream, one that feels incredibly real.

I get out of bed and look at the clock. It's only four thirty in the morning. A full hour before I need to be up.

When I hear the same sound from my dream, I swear I'm losing my mind, but I hurry down the stairs, anyway, where I hear it again!

When I slide across the floor and into the kitchen, I see Alex looking around, confused, and I realize I am not hearing things.

The sound is really yipping, and it's coming from the mudroom.

Blue Love

We both run to the door, and Alex grabs the lock, turns it, and opens the door. I slip out.

My face basically slits in half when I see the huge metal cage surrounding the fluffy yellow lab, and when he sees me, his tail wagging like mad, he starts barking like crazy.

"Oh no, buddy. You need to *shh* ..." I say, making quick work of opening the door.

As soon as I grab him, he stops barking and immediately starts lapping at my face. He then nuzzles into my hair and nibbles on my ear.

Apparently, all his puppy energy is now gone as he then promptly falls asleep.

Beside the cage is a fifty-pound bag of puppy food and dozens of cans of wet food. Next to it is a navy-blue leash and matching collar with a silver engraved name tag. I smile as I look at the name "*CHEWY*."

"What is this all about?" Alex asks, opening a bin and pulling out shot records and other paperwork, a packet of flea and tick ointment, and several chew toys. Under the bin, is a large pillow that the puppy, Chewy, might someday grow into. Next to that is a food and water dish.

"Lucas."

"You cleaned house today." Alex yawns. "A Jeep and a puppy. What the heck do they see in you?"

"What the hell is that thing, Tessa?" Dad asks as he steps into the mudroom, running a tired hand through his hair.

Chewy decides to wake up from his puppy coma and growl at him.

"A puppy, Dad. His name is Chewy." I give him a puppy-sized squeeze. "He's a gift."

"And who do we have to thank for that?" Dad scowls at Chewy, who is again nibbling at my ear.

"I don't know. There wasn't a note." I shoot Alex a

look, begging for him to keep the secret.

"I'm going back to bed." Dad yawns.

"Can we keep him? Please, Dad?" I beg.

"As long as you take care of him." He yawns again. "We still have that invisible fence collar from Hans, right?"

I nod.

"All right, then."

Alex hands me an envelope with my name on it then scratches Chewy under his chin. "I'm going back to bed."

Holding Chewy like a baby over my shoulder, I open the sealed envelope

He was still whining in agony when I walked back into the mall to grab food since our dinner was interrupted. He missed you. I understand how he feels. He may be a mess at first, but with your guidance and love, he will be okay
LYA,
Lucas

Snuggled up on the couch with Chewy I desperately want to call Lucas and thank him, but then Dad would know. I want to wake the kids, but also want to hog all the puppy snuggles until they wake up.

I snuggle him for half an hour then decide to get up and get ready.

Before laying Chewy on my pile of clothes that need to go in the wash, I hold him up close to my face and try to get a picture with my Polaroid.

By the grace of God, it works.

By the time the kids get up, I am ready for school, my bag is packed with both school stuff and for the game tonight.

And when they come down the stairs, they freak out, in a good way.

* * *

Our first class together I slide him the picture, on the back I'd written

I don't know how to thank you, my friend.
Tessa

"I have a few ideas," he chuckles under his breath, and I smack him.

"Relax. I worked them all out in the shower."

Oh. My. God.

He then whispers, "Thank you for that, by the way."

* * *

At lunchtime, Lucas sits across from me, and we stare at each other the entire time. His focus on my eyes is fierce.

"Did either of you hear the bell?" Jade asks.

Both of us laugh and stand. As I pass by Lucas, he grabs my hand as if it was second nature. When I stiffen, he notices.

He lifts my hand and kisses it before letting go. He then lifts his chin. "See you later, Tessa."

God, I hope so.

* * *

We're ahead by three at the end of the third quarter when I hear a puppy barking and look across the field to see Lucas carrying Chewy up the bleachers. After he sits, he raises Chewy's puppy paw and gives me a wave. I laugh and wave back.

"Lucas got a puppy?" Phoebe asks.

"No, Lucas got me a puppy," I whisper. "His name is Chewy."

I don't look at Phoebe's reaction. I'm sure she's disappointed. If she was still falling for a guy after what went down with him and me, meaning Sadi, I would be disappointed in her.

I keep my head in the game and don't allow myself to look over until the game ends in a score of seven to three. When I do, he's surrounded by girls all gushing over him and Chewy. Lucas is smiling as he sets him down, and Chewy's little puppy paws run as fast as they can to me.

I bend down, pick him up, and give him puppy-sized hugs as he gives me puppy kisses.

I laugh then laugh harder when I see Lucas walking over and half the swarm of Bs buzzing around him follow.

"Links, is that your baby?" the goalie from the other team asks as she reaches over and pets Chewy. "Got to be. He's a handsome little guy."

He lifts his chin to her. "Hey, Julie, he's actually Tessa's puppy. Tessa, this is Julie."

"Nice to meet you, Julie," I say as I try to stop Chewy's tongue that has slipped into my mouth twice now.

"You, too," she says coldly then turns and faces him.

"So, Lucas, you free tonight? I've missed you."

Lucas clears his throat. "Actually, I have been meaning to get a hold of you."

Unbelievable. I laugh inside as I walk away.

I introduce Chewy to the team as Lucas says his apology to one of the dirty dozen.

I feel a tug on my braid and look over my shoulder.

"Number six." He then bends down and kisses the top of my sweaty head.

"How did that taste?" I laugh because *ew*.

"Like more." He kisses my head again.

What the hell? I think. "S'mores?"

"Yeah, s'mores." He chuckles.

Getting all swept up in Lucas and knowing where that will lead, I know I need distance.

"Can you keep him while I go shower?"

Lucas takes a deep breath and sets his jaw. "Of course, he's way more distracting than a basket of dead ones."

Shower.

After a cold shower, which was brutal, but hey, I've heard it helps chill one's libido, and Lucas alone sparks it up enough, but Lucas with Chewy, it makes me think seriously stupid thoughts.

Walking out, I see Lucas throwing a toy for Chewy in the field, and Chewy running after it. But he certainly hasn't mastered the art of bringing it back.

I hurry out and watch as he sniffs around the field and chooses his spot to pee.

"Aw … he's got to go potty. Good boy, Chewy."

"You get he's pissing on your starting position?"

"Oh my God, he is." I laugh.

"He's marking his territory, baby." Lucas shakes his head.

"Great game, Tessa Ross," Maxwell, one of the soccer players, says as he walks by, seriously looking me up and down.

"Thanks, Maxwell." I nod then quickly look back to Chewy but catch Lucas scowling at Maxwell.

"Tessa?" Lucas arches a brow.

"Yes?" I arch mine back.

"How offended would you be if I pissed on your leg and marked you as mine?"

I smack at him.

Smiling, he then asks, "Was John angry?"

"Actually, no, he was great about it. We still have an invisible fence from Hans so that helps."

"That's cool, so Chewy will be an outside dog?" Lucas asks, concern etched in his eyes.

"With Hans, when we were outside, he was, too. The invisible fence kept him safe. He slept inside with us every night, but if he wanted to go out, and we were preoccupied, he was safe to go out alone for a bit. When we weren't home, he was inside. Chewy has to be trained on the boundaries, and we have to know he's ready. It'll be a while before he's out without anyone supervising," I explain, hoping to reassure him.

"Okay, good." He looks relieved.

"Do you want to keep him for a few hours?"

"Like joint custody?" He shakes his head. "Tessa, he's yours. He chose you."

"Would you like to come up for dinner then?"

He smiles. "I wouldn't want to impose."

"Do I need to beg?"

"Oh God, please don't." He looks down at his dick.

Oh my. "Dead pu—"

He puts his hand over my mouth. "Not in front of Chewy."

I narrow my eyes and bite his hand. His eyes roll back, and then he closes them on a groan.

I laugh. "You're sadistic."

"You have no idea," he moans.

My heart begins racing, and my brain then catches up. What the hell am I thinking? With what happened with Sadi just a few days ago, here I am, having these thoughts again.

"Okay, no dinner then?"

"I would love to, but right now, Tessa, I think I should go home," he says sadly.

"Then, why do you look upset?"

"I've just had a rough few days."

"Yeah, me, too," I mumble as I grab Chewy's leash.

"Before you run off, I just wanted to let you know that I'm going away for a few days."

I look up, and he looks down.

"Oh. Why?" I mentally kick my own ass for asking. "I'm sorry. I meant to say *have fun*." I look down, and he laughs. "Well, I don't know what I should say."

"What do you want to say, Tessa?" Lucas asks.

"Are you okay? Is your family all right? Where are you going? Are you going alone? Do you want to have sex before you go so you won't want anyone else? Probably all the creepy, crazy, jealous girlfriend things boys hate, and I'm not even your girlfriend."

What the fuck is wrong with me!

A smile, a very genuine smile, begins to grow on his perfect face. "I'm driving down to New Jersey to see my dad for a couple days. It's been a while. I loved that you asked if I was okay first. That's not what a creepy, crazy, jealous girlfriend would ask." Lucas laughs. "I am doing no one else. Well, no one at all, actually. But there's this girl I love, anyway." He steps forward, grabs my hip with one hand, and Chewy's leash with the other, and hugs me.

"Aw ... how cute ... you two had a puppy." Sadi walks by and flips us off.

"Fucking hate that bitch," he grumbles.

"When will you leave?" I ask, wishing I was strong enough to step back.

"As soon as I leave you." He kisses the top of my head. "Be back for school Friday morning so I can still play in the game."

"Please drive safely and call me when you get there."

Visitation

Chapter Twenty

LUCAS

I walk into the house and stand in the kitchen for a few minutes. My bag is already packed and sitting by the door. I walk through the house and make sure everything is locked up tightly, grab my phone charger, and then turn off the light.

I walk out and slide into my car, start it, and pull out of the driveway, trying to mentally prepare myself for the dreaded five-hour drive, trying to look at the bright side—at least one of my obligatory nights will be without the drama that always ensues when my father, Landon, is in a new relationship.

I reach up and turn on the radio, and the Bangles are singing our song, "When I See You Smile." I will take that as a good sign.

* * *

Five hours later, I'm mentally prepared for what I am about to deal with. Brick by brick, I built the wall protectively over my heart and engaged the shield around my soul. By the time I pull into the driveway of Dad's lake house, I'm exhausted.

The motion lights come on, lighting up the entire driveway, and I blink away the sting as I look at the house and see Dad and a new blonde, who is way too young for him, walk out onto the porch. *Here we go*, I think as I kill the engine and step out of my car.

Before I even say hello, Dad is introducing his newest conquest.

"Lucas, this stunning woman is Mandi, with an I."

Of course, with an I.

"And Mandi, this is Lucas, star quarterback, honors student, and my devastatingly handsome son."

She smiles. "Nice to meet you, Lucas. You're almost as cute as your daddy."

"You alone, Lucas?" Dad asks, looking past me and at my car.

I nod.

"Losing your touch, boy?"

I roll my eyes. "Dad, can we discuss this later?"

"Just odd. You always bring something to keep you warm." He winks and laughs as we walk in the house.

I walk into the kitchen and set my bag down. Then I put my phone on the island and sit in one of the leather stools lined up in front of the counter. "Dad, can we talk alone for a minute?"

"Mandi is privy to everything in my life. Talk freely,

son." He turns away from me and smiles back at Mandi, with an I. "Hey, sexy, would you grab us a couple beers out of the fridge?"

"Sure, Landon," she says, smiling.

"Dad, I need to talk to you alone."

Mandi sets two beers on the granite countertop. "Landon, I'm a little tired. I'm going to head up to bed. You two talk." Mandi smiles. "Very nice to meet you, Lucas."

I force myself to be polite. "You, too."

"What's going on, Lucas?"

"Mom's in the hospital. She had a relapse last Friday. I want to get her into rehab, and I need your help," I say, fully prepared for what comes next.

"The psych ward again? What the fuck is wrong with her?" Dad asks. "That bitch has never been able to keep it together for more than six months."

"Don't talk about my mother that way."

My phone rings, and I quickly silence it.

He grabs my phone and looks at the screen. "Tessa Ross? How long have you been doing her?"

"I haven't *done* Tessa." I grab my phone and put it in my pocket. "It's not like that with her. So, are you going to help Mom or not?"

"Why should I? I've paid for the house, I pay all the bills, and you have a credit card with no restrictions." He takes a long pull off his beer. "What more should I be obligated to do for her?"

"For her, Dad? You've been divorced since I was three. You try to make her feel worthless. Jesus Christ, Dad, you put the house in my name even before I turned eighteen. You broke your legal agreement. You're obligated, even though you don't fucking get it," I snap.

"Drink your beer, son. You need to relax. And watch your tone; I'm your father."

"My father who is giving his eighteen-year-old son a beer to relax. My father who wants to know why I didn't bring a piece of ass with me and who wants Flavor of the Month to be present for our conversation. My father who has known I've stayed alone since I was fourteen while my mother dries up and that's a fucking walk in the park because, since I was old enough to remember, I've been cleaning up her vomit, and you don't give a—"

"That's enough, Lucas," he cuts me off. "You cannot blame me for your mother's problems. It's not my fault she's an alcoholic!"

"How many of your ex-wives aren't alcoholics, Dad?"

"That's not my fault." He puffs out his chest.

"Well, ask yourself what the common denominator between them is." I stand and grab my bag to head upstairs.

Once behind closed doors, I pick up my phone to call Tessa back.

When she answers, I simply say, "Here."

"Okay," she whispers.

"Sweet dreams, Tessa Ross."

"You, too, Lucas."

Lying in bed, I wonder if she read my letter today and hope she realizes how much she truly means to me, hoping I got it right.

She's more precious to me every day. Her innocence and heart are pure and perfect. I want to be her soft place to land when she feels like falling. I dream of making her as happy as she makes me.
Day 5 without Tessa Ross makes me realize I have to become the man she deserves. To love and take care of her always,
LYA,
Lucas

***

When I wake up, Dad is gone. I grab a pair of shorts and lace up my sneakers. Then I pull out my phone and call Tessa's house. The answering machine picks up, but I don't leave a message. I toss my phone on the bed to head out for a run.

As I'm running, I see Leah outside her parents' house, where I first met her last year. She sees me, squints to be sure it's me, and then waves frantically. I slow down and stop in front of her, smiling and holding up a finger while I attempt to catch my breath. She laughs, smiles back, and pushes her hair behind her ear. I turn and bend, putting my hands on my knees to get my breath steady.

When I've got it under control, I turn and ask, "Hey, you remember me?"

"Of course I do, Lucas." She smiles.

"I'm going through something, and, well … I fell in love, and she made me realize how wrong I've been to act like I did—the whole sleeping around thing. So, I'm sorry, Leah."

"She must be something special."

"I hope you've found someone who treats you better than I did."

"I haven't. I've been waiting to see you again."

"I'm sorry. Please forgive me." I pull my shirt up to wipe the sweat from my face.

She eye-fucks my abs. "Forgiven."

I shake her hand, content that I've made amends, and then finish my run.

***

Getting out of the shower, I hear Dad call up, "Anyone home?"

"I'll be down in a minute," I answer as I dry off.

As soon as I come down, Dad nods toward the kitchen. "Let's eat lunch, Lucas." He then looks at his watch. "Your sisters will be here at two. I have a sitter coming to watch them while I'm at a meeting with possible investors. I'd like you to join me."

I decide it's best I give in to some of his request, hoping he coughs up the money to pay for Mom's rehab.

We agree that I'll meet him at four, and when he leaves, I allow myself to get excited to see my sisters. Tessa is close to her family, even in the midst of a divorce, and I want that, too. I just hope it's not too late.

At one thirty, as I finish washing my car in the driveway, Audrianna pulls in with Alexandra and Ally. I smile as I watch the little beauties, with big green eyes and caramel hair, dressed in matching pink dresses and white shoes, climb out of her car. Their hair is in pigtails with ribbons tied perfectly around them, bouncing with each step. They favor Audri more, but they also carry similar traits to me and Dad.

"Hello, Audri," I say, winding up the hose and smiling at the girls. "They are beautiful."

"How are you, Lucas? Ally and Alexandra, this is your big brother, Lucas. Do you remember him, girls?" Audrianna asks.

They both nod their heads and smile shyly.

I hang the hose and walk over to squat down to eye level with them. "I'm going to hang out with you guys for a few hours before I have to go meet Dad for one of his meetings. What would you like to do?"

Audri answers her ringing phone. "Hello ... Oh, okay

... I'll see what I can do ... No, I understand ... See you soon. Dammit," she mumbles under her breath as she hangs up.

"Ashley," she calls to her sister, who I didn't realize was with her, "we have a problem."

"Is that your aunt?" I ask the girls.

"Yes." They giggle in unison.

"Good, I need to talk to her. Audri, do you mind?" I nod toward the car.

"You're asking permission?" Audri asks.

"Look, what went on between us was a long time ago. But yeah, I guess I am."

"She's happy, Lucas," Audri cautions.

"Good. I am, too" I nod to the car again. "Is it all right?"

"Go ahead." Audri looks at her watch.

I walk to the car and open the door. "Hey, Ash, you look amazing. Can we take a walk?"

Ashley's eyes widen. "Lucas ... I don't think that's a good idea." She looks toward the girls. "I am ... seeing someone."

"Me, too, Ash." I wink. "I just want to apologize for some things."

"Okay then," Ashley says hesitantly.

I always liked her. Well, her ass was what drew me to her. She has an apple of an ass and never said no to anything I wanted to do to her, or it. But that's not the only reason she's probably the only one I truly liked. It was because she was so chill, and yeah, she hated my dad, too.

We only walk a few feet away, and then I give my normal spiel, but I ask that she and I remain in contact for the girls.

She hugs me. "You deserve to be happy, Lucas."

"So do you, Ash." I hug her back.

"We're good, right?" she asks.

"Yeah." I give her another squeeze then step back.

When we walk back over, Ash gets in the car, and I start toward the girls, who are sitting on the porch, but Audri stops me.

"I overheard you say you were seeing someone. Are you being good to her?"

"I'm trying. She just …" I can't help but smile. "I don't know. She's just different than the other girls back home."

Audrianna smiles with her eyes. "It is so nice to see you happy, Lucas. I don't think I have ever seen you like this."

"I know. Things are changing." I look back to my sisters. "I'd really like to get to know them and be a brother to them."

Tears fill her eyes. "I should have fought harder for him to pay attention to you. I wish I hadn't been so wrapped up in our drama and helped—"

"Not your fault."

She wipes away a tear. "Well, it may be late in the game to tell you this, but I now see how hard you work and how strong you are to get where you're going in life. I'm so proud of you, Lucas. Your successes are completely your own."

I nod because I'm not sure what to say. This is all new to me.

"And the girl? I hope she deserves you."

"She deserves better, but I'm working on being that for her."

"Don't sell yourself short." She smiles and looks toward the car at Ash. "We're going to have to change our plans. The sitter is going to be about an hour late." She waves for the girls to come.

"No way. I got this. We can have fun together, can't we, girls?" I swoop them up and spin them in a circle.

"Oh no, Lucas, you don't have to," Audri says, looking a bit nervous.

"Please, Mommy," the girls ask in unison.

"Audri, I promise they will be fine. I won't break them."

"He'll be okay," Ash says.

Audrianna reluctantly agrees, and then she and Ashley take off.

"Wanna see the treehouse?" They ask, and before I answer, they grab my hands and drag me to the backyard.

"Wow, this is so cool," I say, climbing up behind them, thankful it's low to the ground. Otherwise, I'd probably worry they'd fall. Note to self: I am going to be a shit father. They'll be wrapped in bubble wrap.

We play Princess for an hour, and I'm thankful they want me to be the prince, and it's pretty awesome that they both want me to marry them.

"Okay, but only because it's pretend. When you grow up, its only one prince for each of you. And he better be really good to you, because if he isn't, do you know what'll happen?" I ask in a low grumble.

Their eyes widen.

I throw my hands in the air, making giant claws. "Your brother will turn into a dragon and gobble them up." I pull them into my arms and pretend to chew on their ears.

I hear a laugh and look behind me.

"Totally adorable." Leah holds up a camera. "May I?"

Confused and hoping this isn't some fucked-up ex lay issue, I ask, "What's up, Leah?"

"She's here to watch us, but she doesn't have to. Now we have you!" Alexandra hugs me tighter.

I point to her camera. "Take lots. And I want copies."

The next couple hours are a riot. Honestly, I think this is the only time I've played like a real kid. Kind of makes me sick that I used to be jealous of what they had with Dad, because they obviously have much the same—an absent father. Never again will I feel like that. They're family, my family, and straight-up, it feels real damn good.

After changing, I give them hugs. "I have to meet Dad for a couple hours, and then I will be back. Are you spending the night?"

"We don't spend the night, silly." Ally laughs.

"Well, maybe tonight you can. Should we call your mom and ask?"

"Yay!" They both clapped.

Leah gives me Adrianna's phone number, and I call to ask. She's reluctant but agrees that it's all right if Leah stays, as well. Leah's cool with it.

When I tell the girls, they flip.

On my way to meet Dad, I call Tessa, and she answers this time.

"Baby," I say, laughing. "I've had the best day I've ever had here." Then I tell her all about the girls and checking two more names off the list of exes. She's happy for me; I can hear it in her voice. "I'm rambling. Tell me about your day."

Tessa tells me she spent the evening with Chewy, training him on his invisible fencing system. That Chewy hates the beeping noise he heard when he got too close to his fenceless boundaries, but she's sure he's going to be a quick learner.

We say goodbye and hang up as I pull into the country club.

* * *

After the meeting, I'm happy that he doesn't freak out about the girls staying over, but I'm annoyed that I had to leave my car at the country club, because Dad kept buying drinks, and his new investors seemed to like the fact that I drank with him. John Ross wouldn't be impressed. I couldn't say shit because I needed to keep the peace, and it was well worth it.

* * *

When we walk in, the girls run to me, and I pick them up and spin them around, because I love the sound of them giggling and they love the spinning. The issue I didn't realize is I'm a bit tipsy, so the spinning comes to a sudden halt.

"Okay, girls, hot tub time?"

They race around and get changed then meet me on the back deck, where we all jump in the custom-made, twelve-person tub that overlooks the lake. Dad joins us.

"Hey, Leah, could you grab my camera and take a picture of us?"

"Of course." She smiles.

Dad looks at the girls then me. "They have really taken to you, Lucas."

"They're great, Dad. They really never spend the night?"

"I'm a very busy man," Dad reminds me.

Of course you are.

After about twenty minutes, I climb out. "All right, little princesses, time to get ready for bed. It's getting late. Leah, could you wash the chlorine off them and get them in their PJs?"

"No." Ally stomps her foot. "We want to stay with you!"

"Okay, why don't we all sleep in my room, pillows and blankets on the floor? It'll be like we're camping," I suggest.

The girls jump up and down, splashing as they clap their hands.

I shower, wash my face and brush my teeth, throw on some pajama pants, and then I flop on my bed and call Tessa.

"Hello?" she answers quietly.

I decide to recite the note I would have normally written to her. "Day six without Tessa Ross has been enlightening. From her, I have been able to see what family is supposed to be. I have two sisters, who are amazing, and we are going to *camp out* on my floor tonight. Without her light shining through me, I would have never been able to or have the desire to see how precious love is. LYA, Lucas."

She sniffs and replies as if she has written it, too. "I hope you have a great time. I miss you. And, BTW, you made me cry … Love … your friend … Tessa."

"I'm sorry, Tessa. That wasn't my intention."

"Happy tears, Lucas. Thank you. Go have fun with your sisters."

"I'll call you later. Or tomorrow?"

"Whenever you want to call, I'll be here."

* * *

"Hey, Lucas, the girls got carried away with the water. Do you have a shirt I can wear?" Leah asks, soaked to the skin.

I hop off the bed, grab one from my dresser, and toss it

to her as the girls run in, dive onto my bed, and start jumping.

Laughing, I ask, "Hey, can I jump, too?"

Leah stands on my bed with a camera and takes a bunch of pictures of us jumping and laughing as she tries not to fall.

I catch Dad leaning against the doorjamb, smiling.

When he sees me looking, he pushes off and says, "I think it's bedtime, you four."

"Go give Dad a hug, girls," I whisper to the girls, and they jump off the bed and run to him.

In minutes, I have them tucked in on the floor, otherwise known as Camp Links.

They insist on me sleeping between them, and they also ask me to say prayers with them.

It's been years, but I remember the words. "Now I lay me down to sleep, I pray the Lord our souls to keep, as the angels watch us through the night and keep us in their blessed sight. God bless Mommy, Daddy, Aunt Ashley, Ally, Alex, and Lucas. This we ask in Jesus' name, Amen."

"Aw ... thanks." I laugh.

Ally yawns. "We say it with Mommy and Aunt Ashley every night."

"That's cool. Real cool."

* * *

I wake up a little bit tipsy still, having to piss, and when I come out and tuck the girls in tighter and grab my pillow, I put it at the foot of my bed so I can hear them better if they wake.

I lay down, phone in hand in case she calls me, close my eyes, and think about Tessa. *One more sleep, and I will be able to explain everything.*

I'm having a hot as fuck dream when I realize it's not a dream at all.

The girl is grinding on me, kissing me, doesn't taste like cool mint, and her lips aren't Tessa's.

"I want you, Lucas. Take me again."

"Oh God, Leah! No, no, no," I whisper as I push her off me.

"We've already done it once. You seemed to really like it. Let's do it again." Leah bends to kiss me again.

I move, and my phone clatters on the floor.

"Shit, Leah," I whisper. "The girls are sleeping right there, and I already told you I was sorry about the first time. I was different then."

Leah stands up. "Sorry, I just thought …" She begins to tear up.

"Leah …" I sigh. "Okay, just …let's forget this happened, okay? Just go back to bed."

She quickly leaves my room, and I lay there, thinking how close I came to fucking up. About what could have just happened and how it would have ruined everything I've been trying to accomplish over the past few days.

* * *

Tessa

I wake up on the couch after having a dream about Lucas, and my mouth is dry, possibly because of all the kissing in said dream.

When I walk into the kitchen, I see the answering

machine flashing red, alerting me of a message. Worried I missed a call from Lucas, I press play.

"I want you, Lucas. Take me again," a woman's voice says.

"Oh God, Leah! No, no, no," Lucas whisper.

"We've already done it once. You seemed to really like it. Let's do it again," the woman says.

"Shit, Leah, the girls are sleeping right there," Lucas replies and then the message ends.

I play it again and feel the blood drain from my face as I slide down on the floor and begin to cry.

Oh no, you don't, Tessa Ross. That's enough. He's a player.

I grab the phone, ready to call him then stop, head a mess, and feeling like a total idiot. Then, possibly losing my fucking mind, I begin to laugh.

"I am officially done. I'm such an idiot, and he's such an ass. I am officially done. Two months is nothing. I'll be fine." A tear falls, and I wipe it away. "No more."

* * *

LUCAS

I wake up to two giggling girls staring at me. "Well, good morning, my gorgeous, intelligent princesses. How did you sleep?"

"It was wonderful, my prince." Alexandra grins.

Ally giggles. "I felt a pea under my mattress."

"Well, we mustn't have that," I fake pissed.

I swoop them up and set them on my bed. Then I set out to destroy Camp Links in search of the pea. "I've found the culprit, my lady. I shall banish it from the kingdom." Laughing at myself, I hurry to the bathroom and flush the toilet. Then I walk out and inform them, "Pea belongs in the potty."

The girls laugh hysterically.

* * *

After breakfast, Audrianna comes to pick them up.

"No, Mommy, we want to stay with Lucas," they plead.

"Well, my fair maidens, I must return to my kingdom far away. I have dragons to slay on Friday night." I bow.

"We want to watch."

"Then I shall send the royal father a video reel."

Dad is standing in the doorway of the kitchen, obviously amused by the interaction between us, and he looks at Audri. "Well, ya know, I'm considering driving up tomorrow to see Lucas, um ... slay the dragons. Maybe you three can come with me?"

Audrianna blushes. "I'm not sure that's a good idea."

"Lucas, could you take the girls to get their things?" Dad asks, looking at Audri.

I hurry the girls up the stairs then stand and listen to their conversation from the hallway.

"Audri, we can go together, as a family. No pressure, but he seems to really enjoy them. I have never seen him happier, and they clearly adore him. I know that it would be too much for me to ask to take them alone, but will you go with us?"

"Landon, this is for the kids, all three of them, do you understand?"

"Sure."

"And what about your girlfriend?"

"I think this is more important right now. She will have to deal with it or not. It's really not a big deal to me."

Smiling, I hurry up and help the girls, and then we all hurry back down.

"Okay, the princesses are ready," I say, carrying one of the girls under each arm.

"Well, my fair ladies," Dad says, "your mother and I have decided we're all going to watch Lucas slay the dragons tomorrow."

They clap as they wiggle out of my arms and run to Dad.

"Mommy, too?" Ally asks as she jumps in his arms.

"Yes, Mommy, too," he says, eyes on Audri.

While Dad helps them to the car, I call Tessa and leave a message.

"I'm leaving in about an hour. Should be home at around one. I'm going to come in so that I can make practice and see you. Guess what? My dad, sisters, and their mom will be coming to the game tomorrow night. The girls can't wait to meet you, and please excuse anything my father may say. Most of my bad habits of the past come from him. See you soon, Tessa Ross. LYA."

From the doorway, Dad clears his throat and holds out a check. "Here's a check for your mother's rehab. The conditions are as follows: first, you come here one weekend a month. I want to see you, and your sisters would obviously like that, too. Second, your mother stays in treatment for three months. I want her to recover for good this time."

"Thanks, Dad." I nod, fighting back emotions. "See you tomorrow."

When I start to walk out, he pulls me in for a hug, and I can't remember how long it's been since we hugged. I'm pretty damn sure this is the first time it actually felt unforced.

NO MORE.

Chapter Twenty One

TESSA

Since hearing the message, and obsessively listening to it before pulling the tape out of the recorder and shoving it in a place that no one else in my family would ever hear it, I've gone down a rabbit hole of self-shame. I mean, who still wants the guy who had Scuba Sadi popping out of the fucking water days ago and now Leah? The guy who's been going to his "sexes" and apologizing to make things better for us? To fix himself for me?

I mean, I got to hand it to him, he did go all the way to New Jersey to have sex with someone to keep up the charade. I guess, like Vegas, "What Happens in Jersey stays in Jersey," unless you're so stupid you send a message to the girl you're trying to dupe with all this "change for you" bullshit.

So damn stupid, part of me still wants that change to happen.

So, here I sit, at lunch, knowing he's going to be coming back today, hoping it's after lunch, because I must keep my shit together, because he has a *big game*. One that Tommy and Alex keep talking about more scouts coming to.

Apparently, no one is answering prayers today because, as I look up, here he comes.

"Hey, baby." He wraps his arms around me from behind, kisses my cheek, and then sits next to me.

I am so angry that I seriously want to not only cry but punch him in the face. He's been playing me since day one, and I am so tired of his game. I mean, why me? Not that I would wish him on anyone else, but why?

Heart beating against my chest, I can't even remember what my well-thought-out revenge plan was. How pathetic am I that him just being close makes me feel better than I did when he was away? Pathetic. Totally fucking pathetic.

"You okay, Tessa?" he asks.

Afraid of what may come out of my mouth, I simply nod.

Smiling and excited, he leans in and whispers, "So, tomorrow some colleges are sending recruiters here to check us out. My dad talked to the head coach from Syracuse personally. Isn't that cool? I'd be close to you and at a great school."

I want to tell him I already know, and that he's so lucky I'm dumb enough to give a shit ... about the team, so I'm not saying what I really not only want to say but need to say. And suddenly, I feel the bad kind of butterflies in my stomach now.

"Tessa, what's going on?"

I point to my throat.

"You lost your voice?" he jokes.

"No. Just sore," I whisper, but the truth is I'm afraid that, if I talk, I'll cry.

When he touches my forehead, I tense up. "You aren't warm."

I look down when I feel my eyes narrow, and my blood boil.

"Baby, are you okay?"

The bell rings.

I stand so fast that I nearly knock the chair over. "See ya." Then I dart out the door.

Where the hell is Aretha Franklin's voice in my head when I need her? R.E.S.P.E.C.T is needed, and not just from him, but from my own damn self.

When I walk into class, I sit, concentrating on inhaling and exhaling, praying that I don't break down. A moment later, Jade sits next to me.

"You have been acting weird all day. But what was that about?"

If I told her the truth, she would either tell Tommy, kick Lucas's ass, or both. Neither can happen, not now, anyway.

"I'm just feeling off. I'll be fine."

* * *

Field hockey practice ends with me being exhausted, which was the point. I ran back to the school in record time and quickly hurried into the locker room to change, opting out on taking a shower until I get home, to avoid the football team. Knowing how pumped they are about the scouts, and knowing that not only Lucas, but Tommy, has aspirations for playing football in college, and that Alex is excited to have something more than straight A's to add to his college resume, I don't want my mood to be a burden. Also knowing Lucas's father and sisters are coming, and regardless of what he's done, I know he deserves this. After the game and his family visit, I can finally be done with this.

I hurry to the truck and look around for Jade. She said she'd be out here after saying goodbye to Tommy, and Alex is always the first out, yet here I stand, waiting for them, overwhelmed and feeling like I could begin crying at any moment.

One more day, I whisper to myself, trying to hold it together. *One more day.*

I climb in the truck, pull my knees up, and hide my face in them.

"Tessa, what the hell is going on with you?" Lucas's voice startles me. "Are you sick? Do you need to see a doctor, baby?" He opens the door and reaches in to touch my forehead.

"Don't." I jerk my head away.

"Okay, Tessa, sorry." He looks confused but also concerned. "I need to know what is wrong."

You are what's wrong. You and your games.

"I have my period and don't feel well," I lie, hoping the menstrual cycle will have him running for the hills.

"Oh, okay." He doesn't run; he leans in and whispers, "Do you get like this usually? I mean, is this normal?"

I glare at him. "No."

He holds his hand against his chest, over where a heart would lie, if he actually had one. "Okay."

"Lucas, come up for dinner. Tessa put a roast in the crockpot big enough to feed an army," Alex offers as he walks toward the truck.

Blue Love

Are you kidding me?

"Sounds good," Lucas says. "You all right with that, Tessa?"

"I'm probably just going to bed anyway, but you're more than welcome, *bud*," I say through clenched teeth.

He looks amused as hell at that, and then he shakes his head. "Ride with me?"

"I would rather not move."

"All right." He smiles as he closes the door then walks to his car.

"Tessa, what's going on with you?" Alex asks.

"I have my period," I tell him, knowing damn well it freaks him out.

Alex cringes. "Gross."

* * *

We pull in the driveway, and I all but throw myself out of the truck before it's even in park and hurry to the house.

Chewy bounds up to me and pounces. I quickly swoop him up in my arms and snuggle him, whispering, "Missed you, boy."

When Lucas and Alex walk in, Chewy sees him and goes crazy.

"Daddy's home, huh, boy." Lucas holds his hands out, winking at me as Chewy squirms in my arms.

"Traitor," I whisper as I hand him over before heading over and checking on dinner.

I open the lid and shove a fork in it.

"Is it done yet?" Jake calls from the mudroom. "I'm starving."

I look back and see them all wrapped in towels and

cringe when Kendall asks, "Did you tell Lucas about the hot tub?"

"I forgot."

"That's cool." Lucas reaches over and messes up Kendall's hair.

Unable to stop myself, I say, "Yeah, Lucas likes hot tubs, don't you?"

When I look back, he looks hurt, and the fact I did that hurting gives me zero pleasure.

"Wash up; dinner's ready," I announce.

I grab plates out of the cupboard and scoop roast, potatoes, carrots, onions, and celery onto each plate.

"Sorry, baby," he whispers. "We do need to talk about that sometime soon, okay?"

"Spare me the details, please." I walk around him and set Kendall's and Jake's plates on the table.

* * *

After pushing the food around on my plate and deciding there is no way I can eat because the lump in my throat, the one that's holding back all the tears and emotions, is in the way.

"Please excuse me," I say, standing up, putting my plate on the counter, and then heading to the living room.

When I lay on the couch, I hear Dad whisper, "What's wrong with Tessa?"

"She has her period," Alex grumbles.

"Does she always act like this when that happens?" Lucas whispers, and I want so badly to kick him in the nuts.

"No," Alex and Dad say at the same time.

When I hear them all begin to push away from the table, all I can think about is Lucas leaving and being able to finally crawl in a corner and cry, which is exactly what I need to do to wash away some of this horrible day. But he doesn't. Lucas offers to help clean up.

I listen as he, Kendall, and Jake wash dishes, and they go on and on about Chewy and his progress with training.

"Well, I would love to help him with that when football season is over," Lucas offers.

Why, why, why?

To make it even worse, instead of leaving, he says he's going to come and say goodbye to me.

I roll to my side, facing the back of the couch, and promptly pretend to sleep.

He sits beside me and kisses my cheek. "Goodnight, baby. I love you," he whispers in my ear before standing and leaving the room.

I listen as he says goodnight to everyone, including Chewy, and then he leaves.

When I roll over, I hear the crunching of paper. I sit up and look around.

He left another note.

Day 7 without Tessa Ross has been odd. I don't understand woman things, but I'm here anytime you need me. Just like you have been for me.
LYA,
Lucas

Tears flood my eyes, and I hurry to the bathroom to cry in the shower.

When I walk back out, Dad asks, "You okay?"

"Yeah, Dad." I give him a kiss on the head. "You?"

"Your brothers and sister are loving the hot tub, but you haven't spent a second in the thing."

"When field hockey's done, I will."

The phone rings, and Dad chuckles as grabs the newspaper and opens it. "Might as well grab that."

"Can you?" I ask.

"Avoiding Lucas," he mumbles as he grabs the phone and answers it. "Ross family, John speaking." He pauses. "Yep, she's right here." He hands me the phone, and I give him the stink eye. He replies by rolling his.

"Hello?" I whisper.

"Hello, angel. I had a minute between study sessions and was thinking about you."

"Toby," I whisper as I walk to the front door and step outside.

"How are things?"

"Things are all right. I miss you. When will you be home again?"

"Thanksgiving, and not soon enough. Just a short stay."

"*Ugh*, I can't wait to see you." *And I seriously can't.*

"Sorry, angel."

"Not your fault. I'm proud of you. You're a good man, Toby Green."

"Feels good to hear you say that, Miss Ross."

"Green!" I hear someone call his name in the background.

"Thanks, angel. I love hearing your voice, but duty calls."

"Chat later, then?"

"Of course. Night, angel."

* * *

Tossing and turning in bed, I can't help but compare the two of them *again*. Lucas makes me lose my mind. Hell, I don't even know who I am half the time. I feel like the world is spinning faster and faster whenever I'm around him.

Toby stops the spinning, grounds me, and I can truly tell him anything. It blows my mind that he didn't seem surprised when I told him about the kiss in the hallway, and even more so that he seems to understand Lucas and appears to feel compassion for him in a way.

It's three in the morning when I finally fall asleep, and before I do, I turn off the alarm and leave a note for Alex that I'll be going into school late, due to … my period.

*　*　*

I decided to avoid lunch and most of my classes with Lucas by going in super late.

Opening my locker to grab my books, a note drops out.

Very worried about you, baby. I need to know you're okay.
LYA,
Lucas

Yeah, I'm freaking great, I mumble flippantly.

Arms snake around my waist from behind, and I feel like I want to vomit.

"I know you don't feel well, but I need a hug or a kiss. I'm a ball of nerves right now. I want SU to choose me so I can stay close to you."

Selfish ass, I think, but I lean into his hug just the same.

Turning me, he says, "Tommy, too, for Jade, ya know." He then wraps his arms tighter around me and kisses my forehead, and my world starts spinning faster, but I don't want to enjoy it. No, I want to drop to my knees and beg for it to stop. But I allow him to lift my chin, and then he lightly kisses my lips before pulling me into a tighter hug and burying his face into my neck, like this is perfectly normal.

It's not, and neither is the fact that I allow it. In fact, I hug him back, knowing this is the last time I will ever allow it again. The last time I will feel his arms around me, holding me, making my heart beat so fast, so hard, that it feels like it may explode. Now I know for certain that it's not beating because of the love I think I felt for him; it's beating because it's trying to escape so it doesn't get broken.

I pull back and give him a kiss, and he immediately relaxes, the total opposite of what I feel. And then I kiss him again, hoping to leave him wanting more so that I'm not alone in the misery.

His tongue slices through mine, and he gently begins exploring my mouth. I don't reciprocate. I don't want to remember how he tastes.

Little voices come from behind me, screeching, "There he is!"

Lucas smiles as he breaks our kiss. "Time to meet the family."

Before I can react, he turns around, squats down, and opens his arms as two beautiful little girls jump in his arms. Then he stands and spins them in a circle, both giggling as he tells them, "I missed you two." He sets them on their feet.

"Lucas, is this your princess?" one of them asks.

"One of the three." He winks.

Or four or thirteen.

I manage to hold in my thoughts and smile. "Hello, Ally and Alexandra. I'm Tessa."

Lucas kindly points to them as I say their names.

"She's beautiful," Alexandra tells Lucas.

"And you both are, too. And very sweet."

"Where's the doggy that's always with you?" Ally asks.

"What?" I laugh.

"I showed them the picture of you and Chewy when I was in Jersey." Lucas winks. "Chewy's at Tessa's house. He doesn't go to school yet. He's too young."

God, he looks so different. Younger, innocent even.

"Tessa, this is my father, Landon, and my stepmother, Audrianna," he says.

Lucas's father looks like I imagine Lucas will in twenty years—handsome and tall with dark, clean-cut hair and amazing green eyes. And Audrianna is beautiful, as well, with gray eyes and straight blonde hair.

I wave. "Pleasure to meet you."

His father looks me up and down, making me feel like I'm being judged at the county fair.

Audri, however, steps forward and hugs me. "It's wonderful to meet you, Tessa. It's nice to put a face to the name of the girl who has made Lucas so happy."

"Thank you."

"She's beautiful, Lucas." Landon nods his approval. "Good job, son. Would you like to join us for dinner before the game, Tessa?"

"No, thank you," I whisper.

Landon looks at me as if he's annoyed.

Lucas steps in. "Tessa hasn't been feeling well for the past couple days. She just got done with hockey practice. She should probably go home and rest before the game. You are coming to the game right, baby?"

Big girl pants, I remind myself.

"I wouldn't miss it for the world."

"She's not pregnant, is she, Lucas?" Landon asks bluntly.

My jaw nearly hits the ground.

"Dad," Lucas sneers, "quite the opposite."

Holy shit! Did he just tell his father I have my period?

"Okay, we have managed to make Tessa uncomfortable in less than five minutes. Let's get in the car and wait for Lucas." Audrianna hugs me again and whispers in my ear, "I am so sorry for that. He can be such an ass."

I whisper back, "No need to apologize."

"I want you to know that Lucas loves you, and I see him finally. He hasn't had the best role model, so again, thank you." Audrianna kisses my cheek before turning and taking the girls' hands.

"Well, hello, Landon, Audrianna, girls," Sadi says as she approaches. "I see you've met the farm girl. No offense, Tessa."

"None taken, Sadi." I roll my eyes.

"Sadi, you look beautiful." Landon literally beams.

"And you, Mr. Links, are hot as hell, as always." Sadi laughs.

I catch Lucas looking at Audrianna, his eyes narrowed.

Audrianna shakes her head. "Let's go, girls."

"She isn't a princess, Tessa," Ally whispers, and a laugh bursts from my lips.

I lean down and whisper, "She's a nasty, old troll."

Both girls laugh then hug me.

"Will you bring the doggy tonight?" Ally sweetly asks.

"I don't know. He may be very busy doing doggy stuff, but I will certainly ask him."

"Don't be long, Lucas. Girls, let's go. Nice to meet you, Tessa." Landon turns and walks toward the car.

"Sorry about that, baby." Lucas hugs me. "The girls love you almost as much as I do."

I don't reply.

"I hope you feel better soon. Can we get together after the game?"

"Maybe, if you win." I force a smile at him.

"She smiles, thank God." Lucas kisses me sweetly as his father honks the horn, breaking up the kiss.

"See you tonight." He reaches into his bag, grabs his away Jersey, then hands it to me. "Will you wear this tonight?"

I want to scream, *hell no*.

"Sure, Lucas, anything for you."

He kisses me again before walking away, backward, smiling at me.

Chest tightening, I clench his jersey in my hand and remind myself, *Just one more night, one more game, and then I can stop pretending*.

* * *

When I return home, I call the pet store and get a breakdown of each item that Lucas bought for Chewy so that I can pay him back. I have enough money from my birthday to pay him fully.

I decide not to disappoint Lucas's sisters and bring Chewy with me. I also bring a lawn chair, therefore avoiding the bleachers and using Chewy as an excuse. Kendall and Jake sit with me.

It doesn't matter where we sit when we watch the game, it's absolutely amazing. Another shutout by the Saints, and they end their regular season undefeated.

Jake grabs Chewy's leash and heads for the field at the end of the game. Kendall and I follow. When Jake drops the leash, and the little fuzz ball takes off through the crowd, all three of us chase after him.

When we find him, he's pulling at Lucas's laces, his sisters already on the ground, going crazy over him.

"Sorry about that." I squat down by them and take his leash, giving him enough slack to still act a fool. "I think he was excited to meet you both. I told him all about the two pretty princesses."

As they play with him, I watch a man in SU apparel approach them.

"That was an awesome game, boys." He shakes Alex's, Tommy's, and Lucas's hands. "How long have you three played together?"

"Tommy and I played together all through high school. Our schools merged, and we started playing with Alex this fall. Alex, this is your first year playing, right?" Lucas asks.

Alex nods.

"Unbelievable, right?" Lucas asks the scout.

"None of you play like high school students. You men, all three of you, were amazing out there." He then looks directly at Lucas. "How are your grades?"

Again, Lucas speaks, "All National Honor Society, but Alex is first in our class as of right now ... until I beat him." He winks at Alex.

"Amazing, so do you also play basketball?" he asks, and all three nod their heads. "Don't go getting injured. You'll be hearing from me soon." He shakes Lucas's hand firmly.

I give Alex a hug, and he spins me around. "We did good, right?"

"Good?" I laugh. "Understatement of senior year."

When he sets me down, I see Mom and Dad next to Lucas's family.

"Alex, is it?" Landon asks. "You did great. How do you know Tessa?"

"She's my sister, sir," Alex answers.

"Oh, okay." Landon looks relieved, and it hits me. He thought Alex and I were ... gross.

"Thank you for getting him here." Alex nods to the SU recruiter walking away.

"No problem." Landon smiles.

Lucas is staring at me, so I lean over. "Good game, rock star."

He snatches me up and kisses me softly but firmly.

"My parents," I remind him.

"Oh, sorry, Tessa." Lucas puts me down but takes my hand.

"Dad, Audrianna, this is John and Maggie Ross, Tessa and Alex's parents. This is Kendall and Jake, but her sister Molly isn't here. They're Tessa's family. This is my father, Landon; stepmother, Audrianna; and these two are Princesses Ally and Alexandra."

Lucas's sisters smile and curtsy. "How do you do?"

"Very well, thank you." Kendall curtsies back and giggles.

While our families chat, Lucas pulls me aside.

His eyes drop to my chest, as I knew they would, and then back to my eyes. "What are you doing tonight?"

"Not that."

"Tessa, you're not wearing a bra." He pulls me into him. "And damn you feel good." He runs lazy lines up and down my back, his body against mine. He feels so good against me, too good. I'm going to miss this so much.

Take it while you can, I think, *and leave him wanting more.*

I wrap my arms around him, close my eyes, and hold tight. Lucas kisses me on the head and sighs contentedly.

I look up and lick my lips, beckoning him to kiss me. He doesn't disappoint. Lost in a soft, sweet kiss, I hear my mother clear her throat and step back.

I turn around and all of them are looking at us. Audrianna is smiling. Landon has a shit-ass grin on his face. My parents, unimpressed.

"Tessa, you're staying with me tonight, correct?" Mom asks, and I nod. "The kids, the dog, and I will be waiting in the car. Nice to meet you all." She nods to Lucas's family, turns, and walks away.

I look at Lucas and smile. His head is down, and he's looking up at her through dark lashes, trying not to laugh. He seriously is so damn beautiful, and he'll remember I'm not all that bad, either.

I remove the hair tie from the back of his Jersey.

"You have another one of these besides the one you have on?" I ask, hoping I sound sexy.

Eyes darkening, he nods.

"You should give them to your little princesses. Armor for what lies ahead in the years to come, from all the boys who may try to break their hearts."

I lift the shirt over my head slowly, seeing his eyes widen as he stares at my erect nipples. His mouth opens slightly, and he licks his lips.

"Be good to them. Family is always there, Lucas. Teach them that, okay?" I whisper then kiss his cheek and step back. "Do you think your dad will be as impressed with these as he seemed to be with Sadi?"

"Tessa ..." His voice, deep and husky. "Baby, you are gorgeous, and he's just an ass."

I brush my lips against his. "Teach him how not to be. Show him your heart, Lucas. I have to go." I grab a sweatshirt out of my bag and pull it over my head before turning toward his family. "Nice seeing you all, I have to go."

I walk over to grab the chair and the other things that I left sitting there when Chewy took off. It's then that I see the envelope with the money and the letter I meant to give to Lucas. "Dammit."

"Tessa, let me help you," Lucas says as he rolls up the blanket. He spots the letter sitting on the chair with his name on it. "For me?"

"Yes, but open it tomorrow after they leave, okay? Promise?"

"I promise." He grins as he bags up the folding chair, swings it over his shoulder, and then grabs the bag full of blankets and chew toys, carrying them to the car while holding my hand.

"See you tomorrow," Lucas says as I slide into Mom's car and shut the door.

I nod then look at Mom. "Please go."

I feel the first tear fall *again*.

Once at Mom's tiny apartment, I head straight for the small room and crash on the bottom bunk. Then I cry quietly with Chewy curled up beside me, and Mom and the kids graciously leave me alone to do just that.

CAMPING

Chapter Twenty Two

LUCAS

It feels weird but good that Dad, Audri, and the girls are staying with me, and the girls are delighted to be able to swim in the heated pool, while Dad is busy on the computer inside, working.

Looking between the girls and Dad through the closed French doors, I am startled when Audrianna sits down beside me at the outdoor dining area.

She smiles. "Sorry if I—"

"No, don't be. Just not used to all this, you know?"

She knows that, by all this, I mean her, Dad, and my sisters being here. It's the first time Dad has stepped foot in the place.

"Your home is very nice." She smiles almost sadly at me.

I sit back in my chair, remove my hat, run my hand through my hair, and nod. "Yeah."

"Have you ever considered moving to New Jersey with your father and allowing—"

"No."

"I'm sorry, Lucas."

"Don't be. Not your problem." I shrug.

"Lucas, I should—"

Not wanting to talk about Mom, I interrupt, "Does Leah watch the girls a lot?"

"Only once a week when they see your dad. Why?" Audrianna asks.

I tell her about last year at the lake party when I met her and about my recent apology. Then I tell her all about what had happened Wednesday night.

"No way!" she gasps in shock. Then she whispers, "And you turned her down, Lucas?"

Rolling my eyes, I nod, and we both laugh.

"Well, maybe there is a God. Lucas, the boy with the raging hormones, has grown up." She winks. "Could you teach your dad that trick?"

Dad walks out as we're laughing and asks, "What's so amusing?"

"Nothing," we answer at the same time.

After patting me on the back, Audrianna takes the girls inside and gets them ready for bed so they can "camp" in my room. I surprise them by grabbing the tent from the garage and setting it up for them.

I read them two princess stories, and then, as Tessa suggested, I give them each one of my jerseys and tell them the jersey is a magical shield against evil princes. The three of us sit in the small tent, smiling, as Audri takes a million pictures with the same camera she snapped hundreds of photos with all day and promises to give me copies.

Chapter Twenty Three

TESSA

Waking up after silently crying myself to sleep, I find the light still on. I reach over to grab a packet of tissues from my bag. Reaching in, I feel a note.

I pull the note out, knowing it's from him. Then I walk out into the kitchen and stand in front of the trash can, fighting the internal battle, knowing I need to throw it away and also knowing I'm going to losing the battle. I unfold the paper and read the hastily written note:

Day 8 without Tessa Ross has been interesting. The whole meeting the family thing was different. Obviously, my sisters love you, and that makes me happy. Audri adores you and has threatened me not to screw up with you. And also, thanks to the gifts God gave you up front (the

girls, baby), I think you may have won my dad over. Regardless of all the amazing events of today, it is you I find myself still in awe of.
BTW, no pressure, but you could start your pills Sunday?
LYA,
Lucas

Note to chest, I swear I feel my heart ripping apart, and bile rises in my throat, because how pathetic am I that I believe ... or want to believe, he truly feels this way?

"Tessa."

I jump as I look over my shoulder at Mom holding out her cell. "For you."

I turn and take the phone from her. "Hello?"

"Hey, baby, you're not easy to get a hold of." Lucas chuckles.

"Is something wrong?" I ask, because why else would he be calling.

"No, the opposite actually. Things are great."

Not buying it, I ask, "How is your mom doing? Is she okay with your dad and everyone staying there?"

"She's away," he clips then clears his throat. His voice is soft again when he says, "Just wanted to have you carve out some time for tomorrow. We need to talk."

"I'm spending tomorrow with Mom and the kids, then tomorrow night is girls' night." The bad kind of butterflies begin causing chaos inside my belly. "I don't feel well."

"Ba—"

"I will talk to you tomorrow at some point. Great game today, and please enjoy your family."

Stomach turning, throat burning, eyes filling, head spinning, and heart breaking, I hang up. It makes me physically ill how Lucas can say the things he does to me after doing all the things he's done behind my back. And the emotional mind fuck is even worse. I care for him, deeply and truly. I care that he's okay, and he seems to be. He seems happier than he has since the day we met.

I want him to be happy.

But then, the hot tub, the recording ... *I matter, too.*

Tomorrow, this ends, and it ends with me.

Chewy sits on my foot and licks my hand. I pat his head then scratch behind his ear. "You need to go potty, boy?"

He heads to the door and pulls his leash. *The leash Lucas bought for him.*

And tomorrow, I buy a new leash.

"Let's go."

* * *

Walking back in the apartment, I am even more sick to my stomach because Chewy loves Lucas, and I fear he bought him for me to keep that connection.

I bend down to unhook his collar, and Mom clears her throat.

I look up, and she smiles sadly and says, "Tessa, please know you can talk to me about anything. Whatever it is that's going on, I want to help you through it."

The floodgates open, tears fall, and Mom just hugs me, which of course makes me cry harder, because I need her right now, too.

"It's just a mess, Mom. He says all the right things, and he has changed. He loves those little girls, and he says he loves me. I feel like his heart has changed."

Sobbing in my mom's arms, while Chewy sits on my feet, I tell her about the girls he made things right with and about the voice message, and she begins crying, too.

Using her thumbs to wipe away my tears, she asks, "Tessa, have you and he—"

"No, Mom, we haven't, and I'm so glad I didn't. But I'm not going to lie; the night I saw you at dinner, I got wasted in the restaurant while I watched Dr. Feel Good rub your hand."

"Oh, Tessa, do not cheapen—"

"I was a mess, Mom," I defend myself. "I was watching my mother with another man." I step back and ask her, "Have you slept with him?"

"Of course not, Tessa," she whispers. "Dating him is bad enough. I feel horrible. It's just that your father and I …" She stops. "We'll talk about that someday. For now, it's about you. I'm so sorry you have been hurt. And I'm proud of you." She takes my hand and pulls me behind her into the tiny living room. "Sit."

I do.

"Let me tell you all the reasons you deserve better than what he's offering."

I fall asleep, head in her lap, while she pets my hair, comforting me, or maybe it's to comfort him, like when I pet Chewy.

THE BIG MEET

Chapter Twenty Four

LUCAS

In the morning, Alexandra, Ally, and I wake up and head to the pool. The girls still can't get over the fact it's cold outside and warm in the water.

I get out as they dive for toys in the shallow end. Drying off, I watch through the open French doors as Audri walks into the kitchen and I hear Dad say, "Good Morning, Audri. You look beautiful, as always."

"I feel great. The first time in almost four years that I have slept for eight hours straight. As if this day couldn't get any stranger, I walk out here and see you in front of a stove. Who knew you could cook?"

His lips curve up. "You were always so damn sweet until ..." He shakes his head. "I miss you, Audri."

"Oh no, you don't," she whispers, and I jump back as

she walks toward the door. "I am going out to take some pictures. When breakfast is done, will you bring it out?"

"Oh, I'm bringing it, Audri." Dad chuckles.

Audri walks outside and takes several deep breaths, looking to be trying to shake off her shock. I can't help but chuckle as I watch her attempt to compose herself. Then she begins taking photos.

After several minutes, Dad "brings" out breakfast—waffles with whipped cream—and the girls hop out and dry off. Audrianna hands them each a robe to keep warm.

"I brought it." Dad winks as he pushes in Audri's chair.

She looks at me, and I can't help but laugh as I pull my hat down. Her lips tip up as she giggles.

"What's so funny?" Ally asks.

Dad sits down next to her and answers, "I brought it."

We all bust up laughing and, for the first time in forever, I seriously believe life may be getting better.

* * *

As Audrianna and I clean up the mess in my room, Dad helps the girls brush their hair after their shower for the very first time.

I whisper, "Some advice?"

Audrianna nods.

"He *thinks* he brought it."

We both laugh.

"Make him work for it. I know he loves you; I can see it. Make him earn it."

"I don't know, Lucas. I can't fall apart again, not like last time. The girls are older now, and I have to worry about them, and now I think I have you, too. So, I'm not sure."

"Whatever you do, Audri, I want to be part of their

Blue Love

lives. I want family. Thank you for bringing them into my life."

We hear the girls coming down the hall, and they streak into my room, laughing. Dad looks shocked as he rushes in, two towels in hand, and he's soaked. He tosses Audri a towel and each one of them quickly grab a girl and wrap them up.

"You two," Audri says, guiding them back out, "need to get your bottoms covered. Back to the bathroom. Now."

Once the bathroom door shuts, I zip their bags and ask, "What are you thinking, Dad?"

"I'm thinking I screwed up." He smiles.

"Then fix it and give her time."

"My son giving me better advice on women than my father gave me? How did that happen?"

"Tessa, Dad. It was Tessa."

Ticking Boxes

Chapter Twenty Five

TESSA

Unable to eat, I push my scrambled eggs around on my plate. I am dreading the conversation I know I have to have with Lucas, but I know it has to happen today, because I can't pretend that everything's okay at school.

"Get showered. We're going shopping." Mom grabs my plate and empties it in the garbage.

Already showered, Kendall and Jake immediately jump up and head toward the bedroom as Mom's phone rings and she answers it.

I watch her face drop, and her eyebrows knit together.

"Just a minute please, Lucas. Let me see if she's available."

I stand up, hold one hand over my queasy belly and the

other hand out for the phone thinking, *No time like the present*.

"Hey," I whisper as I walk into the bedroom.

"Morning, baby. Got time to squeeze me in this morning?"

"We're going shopping." I tell him, instead of just telling him this is done.

"You're seriously killing me, Tessa Ross."

"Look, I don't—"

"I know how important family is, thanks to you."

Unable to hold back my emotions, I say what needs to be said, "I love the way you are with them, and I know they love you. Your stepmother is very sweet. And you are a rock star on the field, Lucas Links."

"Thank, bab—"

"I'm not finished." My voice breaks.

"You okay, Tessa?"

I clear my throat. "I don't know how to say this, because it's not like we are dating, but we need a break. I have been holding this together for two days for you because, regardless of what has happened, I need you to be okay. I ask—no, beg—you to be okay."

"I'm good, but you're freaking me the fuck out. What is going on? I thought things were going well, but I'm very confused, baby, especially after being reimbursed for Chewy. He was a gift. Is this a female thing?"

I huff, "I don't even have my period. Just let it go."

Pissed, he retorts, "Fuck that, Tessa! I have changed for you. What kind of games are you playing with me now? The Tessa I fell head up my ass in love with would not be so cold. Is it GI Joe? Come on, baby; give me something."

"It has nothing to do with Toby, and everything to do with the voice message on my family's answering machine."

"What the hell are you talking about?"

God, I want to shake him. No, slap him.

"You really wanna do this to me? Make me say her name? The girl who you screwed in Jersey, and then had a come-to-Jesus moment—"

"I did no such—"

"Shut. Up."

"Tessa, this is—"

"Over. That's what this is. I've held this crap in for three days now. The name Leah ring a bell? I was kind enough to make sure to not stress or worry you so you could get through your game and your family being here. I even kissed you, for crying out loud, *for you*, even though it tore me apart knowing what you did. Because, Lucas, I do care, but I need you to give me the same respect I have given you. I am begging you. Let me heal. In case you don't remember, eight days ago, I found Sadi in your hot tub, and now Leah? That's two. I won't give you three."

"Tessa, you need to shut up and listen—"

"Don't call my mom's phone again." I hang up and bat away the tears. Then I walk out, hand the phone to Mom, and finish getting ready.

After a good cry in the shower, first about Lucas, and then about how freaking tiny the shower is, and how quickly the hot water runs out, I use mom's phone again to ask Jade to get the girls together for a girls-only night at the farm. Then we go shopping.

* * *

"Have fun with the girls tonight. Call me if you need anything." Mom gives me an extra squeeze before I get out of the car with Chewy.

"I will." I squeeze her back before sliding out, and then

I lean in through the back window to tell Kendall and Jake, "See you two tomorrow. Love you."

Walking in the house, I feel a tinge of guilt for not telling Mom, who I somehow feel a different kind of closeness that I've never felt before, that Alex and Dad are on a delivery and won't be back until at the earliest two or three in the morning, but I need to push reset on this year, attempt to make some semblance of the mess it is, and possibly enjoy all that we—Jade, Becca, and I—always dreamed it would be.

I know it will not be the same as we imagined. It's already changed. Homecoming queen? That should never have been me. It should have been Jade or even Becca. That aside, the other changes did not happen because Lucas came here; the changes happened before he even came to Blue Valley.

Chewy finishes eating the food he abandoned yesterday when we were walking out the door to go to the game and I asked the question that makes his ears perk up, "Wanna go for a ride?" and then heads straight to his doggy bed.

Squatting down beside him, I scratch behind his ear. "Neither of us got much sleep it seems, huh?"

I hear someone pulling into the driveway and stand up. Chewy, however, does not.

Looking out the window, I see Jade jump out of Uncle Jack's truck, slam the door behind her, kicking stones as pushes up her sleeves and stomps toward the house.

As soon as she walks in, she demands, "Tell me what that idiot did now."

So, I do, and I do it holding back tears, because she said, "He gets no more of those, okay, Tessa? You are going to be fine. I'm here, and we're going to be okay."

When Becca and Phoebe arrive, Jade fills them in on the audio recording.

"Road trip?" Phoebe asks, and we all laugh. "I'm not joking. I wanna kick his ass."

I walk over to the cupboard, open it, and grab a bottle of Dad's whiskey. Holding it up, I say, "No, but Becca, you'll have to excuse me because I'm going to drink my face off tonight."

"Tessa, that's not a good idea," Becca says.

"I think it is," Jade says as I twist off the cap and take a drink. "Whatever Tessa needs. Bonus, we have the house to ourselves, a hot tub, and music."

"Yeah, let's rock this joint!" Phoebe yells.

They all laugh, and I grab a bottle of wine.

"On the menu tonight is whiskey and wine, ladies."

UNANSWERED

Chapter Twenty Six

LUCAS

I wake and the anxiety hasn't dulled, so I take another hit and wait for the chill to kick in. It doesn't. And realization hits that I'm not going to let this go until Monday. I shower, brush my teeth, and throw on some clothes. Then I decide *fuck it* and take a couple more hits for courage before shoving Mom's pipe under my sink. Then I jet.

Heartbeat heavy, but slow against my chest, I anticipate how this is going to go down. Telling her the truth is going to suck, but knowing how hurt she is sucks worse. And if I wasn't so chill, I'd be all fucked up, overthinking what I'm doing. Letting people in, past the façade, is never easy, but neither is caring about someone enough to chance the embarrassment. Which is why it doesn't happen. But, with her, there is no other way. I want her. Hell, I love her, and I know it, because I've never felt it in my entire life.

I need things to move forward, and I need to take it at a pace set for a marathon, not a fucking sprint.

I reach down to grab my bottle of water when my wheel jerks and my tires hit stone. Then everything around me turns in a circle. Not gonna lie; it's kind of cool at first. It's guardrails, trees, lights … pain, and then it's black.

* * *

"Son. Son, wake up. Open your eyes."

I wake to a pounding head, metal scraping, and old man Whitman wrenching open the door.

"Just sit back, Lucas. The ambulance will be here soon."

When they arrive, I'm already standing outside my car.

"Get him on a stretcher," Sadi's cousin, Jeremy, says to his partner.

"You tell her anything about this, and my father's lawyers will have your license."

He nods, and I'm guessing by the look on his face that he's pissing a little.

At the hospital, after my vitals are taken, and a CAT scan of my head is done, the sheriff walks in the room and administers a breathalyzer. I pass. Of course I pass. I'm just hoping they don't ask me to piss in a cup.

"You're Lucas Links, the QB who's been in the papers?"

"Yeah, that's me." I smile big, knowing that it may be lost on a male, but hey, you never know.

"You have someone to call?" the sheriff asks.

"I can get a ride, yeah."

"An adult, Mr. Links." He looks up from his clipboard. "One I can lay eyes on and speak to."

"Can you give me a minute?" I ask, pulling my phone

out of the plastic bag that they have my clothes and belongings in.

He nods and walks out into the hallway.

Tommy is my first call. I know before I even ask that his parents are not going to let me stay with them, but I try, anyway. He suggests I call Alex and tells me that he's on his way.

"Really no sense in it, man. I'm fine."

"You and I, we're brothers. We're ride or die."

"Piss poor choice of wording, wouldn't you say?" I chuckle. "And seriously, don't bother. I don't want your parents being pissed off at you because of me."

"Screw them. I'll be eighteen soon. I'm coming. Call Alex."

I call Alex.

Alex and John are ten minutes away and arrive before Tommy.

My eyes are closed, and the pain pills are in full effect when I hear John Ross ask, "He okay?"

I open my eyes. "I'm fine. Car's not so good."

"John." The sheriff holds out his hand and shakes his then Alex's hand. "Mr. Links was in a bit of an accident and has a concussion; he needs an adult to take him home."

"We can do that." John nods.

"You sure you're all right, son?"

"Yes, sir." I sit up, grab my ball cap, and put it on.

"Well, not exactly. He passed the breathalyzer, but I'm not convinced. However, when I talked to the judge, he said he would rather not come in and deal with this on a Saturday night. He also said he wants the Saints to kick a little ass at sectionals, and from all the talk, Mr. Links is a crucial part of the team."

"He is," Alex states.

The sheriff continues. "Our problem lies here; his mother is up at Tully, in rehab for the foreseeable future, and Judge Jones says Mr. Links has to have supervision until he's nineteen. You willing to take him on, John?"

"Yes, I am," John agrees to the terms of my sentence.

I would personally thank Judge Jones, but it seems he's not really in it for me, but rather the season and a win. I take that off my list of shit to do. And then there's Tessa. She's not going to be real receptive to the idea ... at first.

"He can stay with us."

"Mr. Ross, I appreciate it, but your daughter is probably going to be severely pissed off if—"

"Never mind Tessa," he cuts me off. "I'll deal with it. Let's go."

The sheriff agrees then adds, "And you bring Blue Valley a championship."

Tommy appears in the doorway. "That's a guarantee."

* * *

Following behind Alex and John, Tommy and I pull into the driveway of the farm, and Tommy asks, "You good?"

"I'm exchanging my freedom for a chance to right some wrongs, Tommy. I'm not just good; I'm a fucking superhero." I laugh. "Or a villain. Time will te—what the hell?"

"Holy shit." Tommy barks out a laugh as we watch Chewy run to the farmhouse with something hanging out of his mouth, tail just a-wagging.

I'm about to go all angry fur daddy when I see who my boy is running from.

"Fuuuccckkk." I jack my hat down when I see four naked bodies, and there is only one my eyes lock on, the one leading the pack, Tessa Ross. She's mostly legs, killer tits, and then there's that tiny peach that's utterly delicious-looking.

As quick as they appeared out of the darkness, they disappear inside.

I chuckle. "Gonna be an interesting night."

A sharp rap on the window has me jumping to attention, and the voice following that sharp sound reminds me there's a new sheriff in Links Land.

"You boys forget what you saw, you hear me?" John barks.

I see Alex behind him, sucking in his lips, biting back a laugh, as I open the door to Tommy's parents' SUV and nod. "Yes sir." Then I look down at my feet as I follow John and Alex into the house.

Inside, I see two empty bottles of wine and half a bottle of whiskey on the kitchen table.

John shakes his head and yells, "Tessa Ross, get your ass dressed and get down here *now*! The rest of you, too!"

I sit my ass down between Tommy and Alex at the Ross's kitchen table. Not one of us dare say a world; me because I know damn well I'm probably going to bust up laughing as John slams a cupboard and pours himself a cup of coffee from his thermos.

I hear feet pounding down the stairs, and then all four girls appear in the kitchen, this time dressed in PJs.

"What the hell is he doing here?" Tessa looks at me and slams her hands on her hips.

"Tessa, sit your ass down and keep your mouth shut," John snaps.

"No! Why are you home, and why is he here?" She stomps her foot like a toddler throwing a tantrum, and not a teenage girl who was just busted drinking and running naked through the backyard.

Tommy is the first to break, and then I can no longer fight my grin as she throws me a pissed off glare.

"Tessa, you are to sit *now*!" John yells as he slams his hand on the worn wooden table. "I am going to talk, and after that, you have a lot of explaining to do, so I certainly won't start sassing me, young lady."

Tessa scowls and sits as far away from me as she possibly can without leaving the room, which happens to be on Jade's lap, which also makes me silently laugh.

"Jade, should I call my brother?" John asks.

"No, Uncle John, please don't," Jade whispers her plea.

"First of all, Lucas will be staying with us for a while, possibly for three months until his mother is out of rehab."

Rehab. I sigh and close my eyes, wishing I had been given the chance to tell Tessa about Mom, but understanding John may not know that she wasn't aware, and even if he had, in light of the situation, he might not have even given it thought.

John lays down the law. "He's been in an accident and was released with conditions; one of them being that he has supervision. Tessa will have to deal with it. I've already given my word."

"I don't think that's a good idea, Daddy." Tessa sneers at me. "I might kill him in his sleep."

To that, I can't hold it in. I laugh, and so do Tommy and Alex.

John raises his voice. "You were both fine at the game. What the hell has changed?" He looks between us. "You know what? Never mind. Who the hell knows what tomorrow will bring? Lucas will sleep—"

"Speaking of sleep, what kind of sleeping arrangements will we have? Because, trust me, Daddy; you shouldn't want him under the same roof as me." She glares at me.

Blue Love

"Tessa, shut up," Alex warns her.

"No!" Tessa yells at her brother.

John then yells, "Tessa, enough!"

"No." She starts to cry.

A million times over, I'd rather see her pissed, because it hurts to see her cry. "Tessa, don't cry—"

"Shut up, Lucas! Just shut up!"

"Both of you, knock it off. You need to make a phone call to your dad, Lucas. I will have some explaining to do with Maggie in the morning."

I stand up, thankful for the opportunity to get the hell out of the room. "I'll make that phone call."

Outside, I dial Audrianna.

"Hey, Audrianna, this is Lucas. You still with Dad?"

"I am. Is everything okay?" she asks.

"Yeah, but I kind of need a favor."

"Of course, what is it?"

"I kind of got in an accident tonight and—"

"Oh my God, are you okay?"

"I'm fine. I already went to the hospital and got checked out. Tessa's father came and picked me up. Apparently, the sheriff and the judge are both football fans, so I got out of a lot of trouble."

"Were you drinking?"

"No, it wasn't alcohol." I sigh. "Hit Mom's pipe."

"Lucas, your sisters—"

"Won't happen again."

"You need to promise me that you don't do that again. Ever," Audri says with such a motherly tone that it makes me smile.

"I promise. Do you think you could have Dad call his insurance agent in the morning?"

"Of course," she says kindly.

"Another favor?"

"Lucas ..." she sighs.

"Could you call Tessa in an hour?" I rattle off her number. "Let her know what I told you about Leah. She's calling it quits on us and needs the truth. I will explain ... tomorrow?"

"Of course. We'll talk in the morning."

When I walk back in, John points to the empty chair, and I sit.

He then looks at Tessa. "Now, what the hell are you four thinking tonight?"

"Well, I thought I was in love with that boy over there. I forgot his name, but the one right there," she slurs, pointing and scowling. "And the night I saw Mom at dinner, I got drunk on our date. It wasn't the stomach bug. I was a bad girl—"

"Tessa, enough," Alex cuts her off.

"Lucas, is that true?" John asks.

"Yes, sir, but I got her home to Alex." I give Tessa a look, basically asking her *what the hell are you doing?*

"Tessa, is that true?" John asks.

"Yes, but there's more, Dad. I kiss him a lot, and I like it," she says obnoxiously.

John looks at her in confusion, and I sit back in the chair and pull my hat down.

"And when I wanted to go out with my friends, he was pissed, and we brought him dinner, and Sadi's head popped out of the water because she was giving him a blow job," Tessa snarls at me.

"Is that true, Lucas?" John asks me, and I wish I could disappear.

Instead, I head down Truth Road. "Yes, sir. The night I came home and found my mom on the floor, I called the ambulance. Sadi's cousin, Jeremy, is an EMT, and he must have called her after. They took Mom to the hospital.

When I came home, I smoked a bit of pot and sat in the hot tub. I woke up to your daughter's voice and Sadi coming up from out of the water."

"None of that shit goes on in my house."

"I understand, sir."

John scrubs a hand over his face. "Seeing your mom like that must have been rough, Lucas—I am sorry—but that's no reason for you to be dipping your toe in addiction waters. Pot's a steppingstone."

I feel blue eyes burning into the side of my head as I nod to John.

I look at her, and she puts her nose in the air. "Oh, and he went to his dad's house and had sex with Leah when he told me he loved me."

Tessa, quit while you're ahead, I think, feeling sorry for her, and I try not to laugh.

Seeing this, she snaps at me, "It's not funny, asshole."

"Tessa, watch your mouth. Lucas, this is my daughter. Is what she said true?" John asks.

"No, sir. I had sex with Leah a year or so ago. She now happens to be my sisters' babysitter when they are at our fathers'. Audri insisted she stay since it was the first overnight they had with my father since he and Audri spilt. I fell asleep, thinking of Tessa, and woke up to someone kissing me. I stopped it as soon as I realized it wasn't Tessa. Apparently, my phone dropped and redialed the last number I called."

John then looks at Tessa. "Do you have any other questions you need answered?"

"Yes! Were you drunk or high?" Tessa snaps.

"I had a few drinks with my dad at the country club, and he drove us home." I shrug. "That's probably why it took me a few minutes to wake up."

"Well, maybe you have a problem with alcohol," Tessa huffs, and it's followed by a hiccup.

Everyone laughs, and she buries her face in Jade's shoulder, and Jade purses her lips together, trying not to laugh as she rubs her back, comforting her.

John sighs his annoyance at the entire situation then says, "Lucas, I think you've turned away more than I've had in a year."

"Dad, that's not funny" Tessa yells at him.

"You're right; it's not funny in the least," he grumbles then looks at all of us. "No nonsense under this roof, do you understand?"

"Yes, sir," I answer.

"Girls, why are you drinking?" John asks but sounds like he regrets it.

"'Cause Tessa was sad and wanted to, Uncle John," Jade says, and Tessa glares up at her. "And we wanted to mark it off our senior year bucket list. We stayed here. No one drove. We won't do it again."

"Why were you in the hot tub, naked?" John asks, definitely regretting that he has to address that, and we boys burst out laughing. He sighs, "Boys, enough."

"Mr. Ross, nudity isn't really that bad unless it's for sex that's not between husband and wife," Becca tries to explain.

"Really, Rebecca?" John asks.

"Jade had a point earlier; we weren't born with clothes on," Becca whispers her defense.

"Alex, I'm done with this for tonight. Can you make sure everyone stays clothed and doesn't drink?" John asks as he walks out of the room.

"Yeah," Alex says, and he finally looks at Phoebe, whose face has been buried in her hands since he walked out. "Phoebe, just so you know, we can still see you."

Blue Love

She whispers, "No, you can't."

Tessa stands and leaves the room, and I watch as she walks away.

Tommy whispers, "Let's keep this party going. What's next on that list, Jade Ross? A rated-R movie?"

We all laugh, including Jade, as we follow Alex into the living room where there is an oversized couch, two love seats, an old wooden rocker, and a recliner.

Phoebe and Alex take the loveseat, Tommy and Jade the other, and I sit on the couch.

Tessa walks out of the bathroom, arms crossed, and looks around. Her eyes meet her brother's, and he shakes his head in disappointment. This is a little bit more than wrong, since his girl, who was also running bare ass through the farmyard, is all curled up next to him, but as the newest resident here at Ross Farms, I keep that to myself, but make a promise that I'm going to get Alex to trade his tea for a shit at least once before graduation.

I pat the spot next to me, and she walks over, shakes her head, and sits on the floor in front of the couch instead.

"Fuck that," I mumble as I scoop her up and set her next to me.

Looking at me, a million questions dance in differing shades of blue, yet she doesn't ask one.

"Are we okay?" I ask.

Her bottom lip pops out. "You're a freakin' hero, and I'm a whore."

I laugh. "I think we know better than that. Where's your phone?"

"In the kitchen, on the counter. Why?" she asks but avoids looking at me.

"Audri is going to call you just in case you don't believe

the Leah thing. She knows about it. And I want to tell you that Audri likes you a lot."

This should make her happy, yet she still looks incredibly upset, and then our boy, Chewy, takes this time to bring in a bathing suit and drop it on my lap. When Tessa snatches it up, I know it's hers.

I scratch behind his ear. "That's my boy."

Everyone laughs. Tessa? She pulls her feet up on the couch and buries her face in her knees.

"You believe me, don't you?"

"Yes," she says into her knees. "I just feel like an ass, and I am loa-ded."

"I would have thought the same thing, Tessa. I just wish you'd asked me."

"Why didn't you tell me about your mom?" she asks, now resting the side of her head on her knees, looking at me.

"I didn't want you to pity me. I wanted you to love me for me, not because you feel like I'm some sort of cause."

She sits up. "We all have things that we could do without in our lives, right, guys?"

Jade raises her hand. "I do. My mom is a junky, too."

"I was almost raped by two different foster kids," Becca blurts out.

None of us say a word. Speechless.

"My dad shot my mom, and then himself, in front of me." Phoebe laughs, and now Becca's secret isn't the most shocking. "*Ding, ding*! I win, right?" She looks down and whispers, "Please don't tell anyone. It's rather embarrassing."

Alex pulls her closer and tucks her under his arm.

"My family is a mess right now, and I'm no better," Tessa breaks the silence.

Everyone looks at Tommy, and I about die when he announces, "I have a huge penis."

Everyone busts up laughing.

Jade looks at him then around the room. Her glance then shifts to the crotch of his pants, and then swings up to him, blushing. A sly smile starts creeping across Tommy's face, and then he winks at her. She shakes her head back and forth and rolls her eyes like she doesn't believe him.

"He's not joking, Jade. He's unbelievably well-endowed." I chuckle.

"How do you guys know? You hang out naked together? Gross." As soon as Tessa says that, she palms her face like she just remembered that she herself, just moments ago, was in a similar situation.

"This coming from the streaker." I throw my arm around her. "I bet it was your idea."

"It was," the girls all say at once.

"I love your curiosity," I whisper in her ear.

"I love you," Tessa says even lower than a whisper, as if it were just a thought.

I cup her chin, lean in, and kiss her.

"No hands, man," Alex reminds me.

I raise them up, lips still on hers, and she pulls back, eyes blinking and looking confused.

Chewy whines, and Tessa quickly stands to take him out. Then she holds her hand out for me. "Come with me."

"Be good. I promised Dad," Alex reminds us.

"Maybe they don't want to be," Phoebe says, looking at Alex. "Maybe I don't want to be."

She kisses him, and he takes her face between his hands, breaks the kiss, and whispers, "We're not running a race, Phoebe." He kisses her forehead. "There's no rush." He then kisses her nose. "None at all."

Buzzed Beginnings

Chapter Twenty Seven

TESSA

Thankful for Phoebe's distraction, I pull Lucas outside and watch as Chewy runs to his favorite spot to pee. Then I look back at Lucas.

"Tell me it's true that Sadi and Leah were—"

"Every word I said in there was true."

"Tell me that you—"

"Tell you that I love you?"

I nod, wanting desperately for it to be true.

He grabs my face and looks me dead in the eyes. "I never stopped telling you I love you. Not for one day, Tessa, not one."

Flinging my arms around his shoulders, I kiss him. Then he moves his hands to my ass, and I jump up, wrapping my legs around him, and I kiss him deeper. It feels like the first time in forever that my heart isn't breaking as I do.

He presses his lips hard against mine, tongue kissing me back. Then he sits, with me straddling his lap. Body humming, I whimper at the feeling of my most heated parts connecting against him like this.

He rips his lips from me, turns his hat backward, presses his forehead to mine and, in a deep, rough voice, says, "We need to communicate."

I grab his face, and with my lips back against his, I tell him everything I'm feeling right this second. "I missed your lips, your arms, your eyes. I want you, Lucas. How's that for communication?" Then I kiss him hard, unable to control myself anymore. I push my tongue into his hot, sweet mouth and, within seconds, I feel him hardening beneath me.

I reach behind me and pull my pajama top over my head.

Looking down at me, he groans. "You are fucking gorgeous, baby."

Leaning in, I nip his lip then kiss every inch of his face, moving to his neck and chest. He hisses, and I look up at him. He looks as if he's angry, so I kiss his lips again.

Lifting me up and off him, he tells me, "Tessa, baby, no drunk sex with you, and definitely not here."

"You have something against picnic tables?" I huff.

"That's twice I have seen that move tonight. I kind of like it."

"What move?"

"The foot stomp."

I didn't even realize I did that once, let alone twice.

I roll my eyes, and he grabs my face, running his thumb across my lower lip, and closing his. When he opens them, he smiles, and it's a sweet kind of smile. And, although I'm not thinking sweet things, I'll take it.

He takes my hands and asks, "Tessa Ross, will you be my girlfriend?"

"Lucas Links, promise to never shatter me again? Like, no more drinking, or smoking, or—"

"Or taking even half a sleeping pill and hit the peace pipe so I can try to forget that I walked in the house and found my mom passed out and almost drowning in her own vomit?"

I hug him. "I'm so sorry. I wish you had told me and—"

"Kind of hard to talk to you when you're—"

"I hate her. I hate Sadi so fucking much." I step back and ask, "How's your mom now?"

"She had a fucking needle in her arm this time—"

"I love you, Lucas. I'm so sorry. Just please talk to me, okay? Third time will not be a charm." Tears don't just pool in my eyes; they flowed freely.

"It won't happen again," he promises.

"Then yes, I'm yours as long as you want me."

"Forever, baby?"

It's definitely not the right time to think of Toby, but I do just the same.

"What's wrong, Tessa?" he asks, rubbing his fingers slowly up and down my side.

"Toby," I whisper.

"He's a good guy." Lucas nods and takes my hands.

When he laughs, I realize I must look shocked.

"I'm not stupid." He reaches down and grabs my shirt, pulling it over my head.

"I just feel awful. He has never done anything but show me kindness. And then there's you."

"Me?" he sighs exaggeratedly.

"Well, Lucas, you really didn't do anything either, except not tell me what's going on."

"Couldn't do that when you weren't talking to me, and I wasn't ready to talk."

"I'm such a bitch. You sure you want me to be—"

"Yeah, I want you." He laughs.

"What's so funny?"

"You're drunk, Tessa, and you're kind of funny."

"You're stoned, so probably everything is funny."

Both of us are laughing as he pulls me in for a hug.

Face in the crook of his neck, I inhale his scent and sigh, "What is my dad thinking, letting you stay here?"

"I don't know, but I am grateful. Just think, you get to do my laundry and cook for me."

"You wish." I push him away.

"No, really, it'll be like being married but without the sex." Lucas smiles sarcastically.

"By the sound of my dad tonight, it's exactly like being married."

We both crack up, and I climb on his lap and hug him tight. "I love you, Lucas Links."

He lifts my chin. "No more Toby. I won't share you."

"He's my friend, though, Lucas. I can't just—"

"I don't get the whole friends with the opposite sex thing—it pisses me off—but I want to understand. Let me ask you a few questions. Does he get to do this?" He lightly runs his fingertip across my pebbled nipples.

I shake my head.

"These are mine, right, baby?" He bows his head and nips at one then the other over my shirt.

My back arches, and I push into him. "Yes."

"Let me clarify, baby; whose are these?" He rolls one then the other between his teeth.

"Yours, Lucas. They're yours."

"Perfect. I really love them." He runs his hand up my back then wraps it around my hair and kisses me hard and urgently as he skates his other hand up my leg and under my pajama shorts and begins rubbing my inner thigh.

Heat burns so hot inside me that it begins to liquify between my legs.

When his fingertips rub the damp silk there, he asks. "Baby, whose is this?"

I rock against his touch. "Mine … ours … yours, Lucas. I'm yours."

"Your panties are damp, baby." He pulls his hand out from between my legs and sucks on his finger then pushes them right under them again. "Not wet enough. You're drunk, and I'm high … I promised no drunk sex with you, but I could still make you come, fucking you with my finger. Would you like that?" He rubs between my legs, over my panties harder, causing me to moan and whimper. "Whose is this, baby? Whose hot little pussy is this?"

"Yours, Lucas. Only yours." I reach between his legs and rub my hand up and down his hard, bulging erection. "And this is mine."

"Someday soon, it's going to be all yours." He dips his finger underneath my panties, and the burn, the heat, the electricity pulses between my legs. "This is mine, too. I am claiming it right now." He rubs across my clit, and I cry out against his neck. "Shh … baby, keep quiet. I want to play right here for a while."

He continues to rub circles around and across my clit as I rock into his touch and feel something … something … something … "Oh Go—"

Lucas covers my mouth, and I swear on everything I want to bite him, until I hear my brother's voice. "Tessa, you out here?"

I inhale then exhale a frustrated breath before replying, "Be there in a minute."

"I love you, baby," Lucas whispers as he kisses me softly then lifts me off his lap and sets me on my feet. "Walk in front of me, please."

"Okay," I whisper as I nuzzle into his neck again.

"Fuck, I can't wait to be buried inside of you."

I push up on my toes and kiss him sweetly. "We have to go in."

"I know. Stay in front of me to hide the surprise you caused in my pants."

Smiling, I do just that as I look around for Chewy. "Come on, boy."

Inside, we sit quietly and pretend to watch Dr. Quinn, but neither of us are paying attention at all.

Chapter Twenty Eight

TESSA

I hear him before he walks into the kitchen, mumbling, "What the hell was I thinking?"

I take in a deep breath and try not to act like I'm ashamed of myself for last night, but I am. "Good morning, Daddy."

He's not even looking at me when he says, "Tessa, you have church today. Actually, all of you do. Wake them up. Everyone needs to get ready."

I move to stand in front of him so he sees me. "Daddy, I am sorry."

"Oh no, Tessa Ross, that look's not going to work."

I step to him and hug him.

"Okay, that may help."

Smiling, I step back and grab the spoon. "I'm making breakfast."

"Fine," he huffs. "Just don't do it again!"

Everyone sleeping in the living room, where we all crashed last night, starts to laugh, and he grumbles.

When they all walk in, each of them says, "Good morning."

"You all think you got one over on the old man last night. Let me tell you that none of you did." He points to Lucas. "You pull that shit again, driving while under whatever influence you were under, and my daughter will not ride with you again while I'm alive."

"Yes, sir." Lucas nods.

"You girls drank here. I'd rather that then in a field somewhere and driving home, but that doesn't mean you have my permission." He steps toward the door. "And for the love of God, all of you keep your damn clothes on! You eat, and we all go to church. God knows we could all use a little Jesus."

When he walks out, we all laugh.

* * *

After church, Lucas and I head to his house to grab some of his things. And, although I've been with him more than twelve hours, the butterflies begin to flutter their wings inside my belly. As much as I like this kind of flutter, I'm not sure I like the nerves that come with being with him alone. And I know this is because of the feelings and the desire that sparks inside of me when we are.

I put the truck in park then turn off the engine.

"Come help me?" he asks.

"Sure," I say as I open the door.

Before I take a step, he has my hand and is all but

dragging me behind him. It isn't until we're in his room that he lets go.

He walks into his closet and asks, "Why were you looking at me so weirdly at church?"

"Did it make you uncomfortable?"

"Kind of. What's going on?"

"I don't know. Things are just ... different."

Lucas peeks out of his closet and looks at me, confused.

"Two days ago, I was a wreck, and so were you, and I didn't even see it. Now you're living with us and—"

"You okay with that?"

"I don't know. It should be weird, don't you think?"

He turns and walks into his closet. "A little bit, especially because I think everything you do is hot, even the foot stomping thing last night—"

"Twice," we say at the same time.

He looks out of the closet, and I am once again mesmerized by how seriously stunning he is, and those eyes that, when not covered by a hat, or guarded by what I now know is a pain in which no one but maybe Tommy seems to know about, are without their shield and full of a happiness, ease, and confidence that makes him even hotter.

He seems to notice that I see him, truly see him, and it makes him nervous. I know this because he runs his hand through his hair, as if looking for that hat, to shield his eyes.

Not wanting him to hide behind the shield, and also not wanting to overwhelm him, I turn and give him some privacy.

"You going to miss this big bed? This house? I mean, my house isn't like this."

"Are *you* going to miss this big bed?" Lucas asks, wrapping his arm around me and flattening his hand over my lower belly. Then he turns me to face him.

When we kiss, it's different. Not in a bad way, but softer, gentler, and maybe a bit more playful.

I smile against his lips, and he pulls back. "Are you laughing?"

"I wasn't, but now—"

"You're being—"

"Sorry, it just feels different. You kiss me differently now."

"How so?"

"It's sweeter."

His scowl deepens, and he pulls me closer. "Was last night sweet?"

I feel my face burn and shake off the thought of last night. "Not like that. It's … You're … like, less guarded, or you're not in a hurry. Maybe that's what you want now?"

He picks me up and tosses me onto the bed. Crawling up beside me, he narrows his eyes, his nostrils flare, and the muscles in his jaw pop.

Goofy smile creeping up on my face, I scoot back. "It's not like you're in a rush, or like you want to tear off my clothes and bend me over the bed right now. It's like you can enjoy it, and … well … I don't know." Flustered, I flop back then roll over, hiding my now burning face in his comforter.

"Tessa, I absolutely want to tear your clothes off and bend you over the bed. And make no mistake, the shit I'm gonna do to your hot as hell bod isn't sweet, and it'll only be gentle the first time, because you're gonna need that. Maybe it's you. Maybe you're less guarded, maybe you trust me a little more. You're more relaxed. Maybe you finally believe me when I say I love you." He kisses the back of my neck.

I turn to look at him, and his cell phone rings.

He digs in his pocket, pulls it out, flips it open, and

then pushes off the bed as he answers. "What's up?" He listens for a moment then says, "Yeah, almost done. See you in a few."

He hangs up, grabs my ankle and, in one swift move, he somehow flips me to my back and pulls me toward the edge of the bed. All of the insanely sexy physical feelings caused by that move dance with what he just moments ago said, and my heart beats against my chest, anticipation making my head spin.

"Your mom will be at your place in an hour. Alex says we need to be there."

Just two words—*your mom*—drenches every feeling of desire inside of me.

"Great."

A smirk plays on his beautiful lips as he turns and walks toward his closet.

I push up on my elbows and watch him. Okay, I watch his ass. He seriously has the best ass.

"So, you know how Jade and Tommy have their six-month rule?"

Lucas laughs. "Yeah, I hear his countdown almost daily."

"I think we should pick a date. That way, there's no pressure, but we know it's going to happen."

"Okay." He chuckles. "How about tomorrow?"

Grinning, I say, "Tomorrow, it is."

He peeks put of his closet, eyes wide.

"No, seriously. Let's pick a date."

"How do you just pick a date, Tessa? How will that be at all romantic or spontaneous? You know, the stuff you girls like."

"Better get going. My mom will be at the house soon." I start to stand, and he rushes the bed, pulls me up, and into him.

"What's an acceptable amount of time, Tessa Ross?" he asks, trying not to smile.

Scowling, I look away. "I don't know."

He pushes my hair away from my face and over my ear, and totally serious, he asks, "Do you need a date?"

I look away and nod once. "Yes, actually. I think I do."

He grabs my face and tilts it so I have to look at him. "What are you thinking? Honestly, I want to know."

"Well, lots of things. Like maybe I need to know because I'm concerned you won't be able to wait that long for me," I say. "Or that you actually don't want me."

"How can you think I don't want you?" Lucas asks.

"I don't know." I shrug. "Maybe because I've offered it up on a silver platter, as you said, and you turned me down."

"You were drunk, baby. I don't want you to hate me," Lucas whispers.

"What if I said I want you now?"

"I would kiss you like this." He gently takes my face again and kisses my cheek then moves down my neck and up to my ear. He sucks my earlobe for just a second then moves down my neck again, across my collarbone, and up the other side of my face to my ear. "And then I would lay you down on my bed," Lucas whispers, stepping forward so the back of my legs hit the bed. He runs his hands down my face, my neck, my sides, and he grabs my ass firmly but gently and lifts me, putting me in the center of his bed. Then he again crawls up from the end of the bed, reaches over his head, and pulls his shirt off.

Nothing could drown the desire stirring inside me as a shirtless Lucas, now straddling my legs, leans down and kisses me softly on the cheek and whispers, "Your shirt would be next," as he takes one thick finger and traces from my lower lip, down my throat, between my breasts, down my belly, that cages the butterfly fury, and runs it under the waistband of my jeans.

I don't want him to stop, but I know, God how I know, that if this moves any further, we'll be late.

I grab his hand, stopping it from moving any lower. "Lucas, my mom."

"And then I would hear that," he grumbles and rolls off of me and to his side. "Yeah, we need to pick a date. This is going to kill me."

Laughing, we both slide off opposite sides of the bed, and Lucas walks to his closet to grab his bag.

* * *

Once on the road, I reach over to grab Lucas's hand.

"Baby, my dick is stone, my balls blue, and you touching me right now isn't going to help things to change by the time we get to the farm."

So, we ride in silence.

Cresting the hill, I see Mom's car.

"Things relaxed, or should I pass and circle around?"

"Your mom's car flattened my proverbial tire. We're good."

Pulling into the driveway, I ask, "Any ideas of when we should, you know?"

"I have a question first."

"What's that?" I ask, parking behind the barn.

"I think we have the kissing thing down pat, wouldn't you say? It's two months today. Last night, we played. My finger actually toyed with your clit." Lucas wags his brows.

"Ew … that's a gross word."

"Say it," Lucas eggs me on. "Say clit, baby."

"I will not." I try and fail to keep a straight face as he whispers clit over and over.

"We were fucked up. We start over now." He lets out a frustrated breath. "Two weeks kissing."

"I really like kissing you."

His voice huskier now as he looks at me, he says, "Me, too, baby, but there are other things that I want to do to you. Other places I wanna kiss you."

My heart begins to beat faster. "What and where?"

"Your tits, baby. They are the most perfect I have ever seen."

"Sorry, that can't happen. I already offered, and you turned them down. They're kind of mad at you."

"Please tell them I'm sorry." Lucas grins.

I lift my shirt, exposing my new light blue, lacey front clasp bra. "Tell them yourself."

"Tessa," he growls.

"Don't talk to me; talk to them."

He reaches over, and I slap his hand away. "You better apologize to them first. They are not those kind of girls."

"I'm very sorry, sorrier than you can imagine, that I didn't take you up on your offer at the lake. You're lovely, and I want nothing more than to touch you right now, skin on skin, nothing between my hands, my mouth, and you. May I?"

Giggling, I pull my shirt down. "They accept your apology but want you to wait until Friday."

"I'll take that." He sits back in his seat and exhales.

* * *

Mom's upstairs when we walk into the living room, and she yells down to us, "Tessa, Lucas, come up here, please."

"Good luck," Alex says, clearly annoyed.

Mom is screwing something into the bedroom door when we walk upstairs.

"These are door alarms," she says. "At night, John will turn them on, and in the morning, he will turn them off."

Lucas nods. "Okay, Mrs. Ross."

I cross my arms. "What if we have to pee in the middle of the night?"

"Well, the alarm will go off, honey. That's kind of the point." Smiling tightly, she opens the door then closes it. The alarm goes off then silences. "See? No big deal, right, Lucas?"

"No big deal, Mrs. Ross," he agrees.

"Tessa, your dad filled me in on the details—all of them." Mom seriously glares at me. "Lucas, I am sorry about everything you've gone through, I truly am, but please remember that Tessa is my daughter, and she means the world to me."

"Yes, ma'am, I will."

"All right, then. Tessa, you'll come with me on Wednesday nights, understand?" she asks.

After crying on her lap, and seeing her as she once was again, she deserves my respect, so I give it to her. "Yes."

"I'll see you then." She hugs me ... and I hug her back.

* * *

After she walks down the stairs, I realize I didn't thank her, so I hurry down the stairs.

Alex, standing by the archway, holds up his hand to stop me. Then he holds his finger over his lips to tell me to be quiet. So, we stand and eavesdrop, as we have a million times in our lives.

"Do you know what you're doing?" Mom asks Dad.

"Do any of us, Maggie?" Dad's voice is pained.

I peek around the corner when Dad says, "'Maggie," and I see him grab her and hug her, and she hugs him back.

A few moments pass, and then she looks up at him. "See you Wednesday."

She steps back and wipes at what I assume are tears then heads to the door.

I try to will Dad to stop her, but he doesn't.

He stands at the sink and watches her leave through the window.

* * *

I walk back up the stairs, fleeing the angst that is our family, to the greatest distraction I've ever had, maybe even greater than music, and lean in the room, where Lucas is hanging clothes on a portable rack that Mom and Dad must have set up when they set up the cot.

I walk in and start pulling clothes from his bag.

I shake my head when I see it's a pair of black boxers.

Lucas looks over his shoulder at me, and I toss them across the hall into my room.

"What are you doing?" Lucas asks as he hangs a gray Henley.

"New pajamas." I grin then whisper, "I'm going to be in your pants tonight."

"What did you say?" he asks, laughing.

"Do I really need to repeat myself?" I glance down at his groin and lick my dry lips.

"Please, don't," Lucas pleads.

"Fun killer," I joke as I turn and reach back into his bag and pull out his white hat. I step up to him and put it on his head. "The first time I saw you, this was on your head. You look so hot in white hats."

"I thought I was an arrogant ass?"

"You were, sometimes still are, but you've always been a lot of fun to look at."

I reach in and grab his cologne—Drakkar—take it to my room, and spray my bed. Lucas follows me in and flops on my bed. "This is where you sleep every night, huh?"

I nod as I straddle him like he did me.

His eyes widen, and he whispers, "I promised your father no hands."

I grind against him, as he did me a while ago, and he grabs my hips. I bat them away.

"No hands, Mr. Links."

He puts his hands in the air and stands up, giving me no choice but to hold on. When I feel him hardening against me, I smile.

"Down, girl … please."

I slide down his body, all the way to my knees.

He steps over me and whispers, "You're killing me, Tessa."

I follow him across the hall and grab his waist. "You said *down girl*. I was going down."

He takes my hands and slides them up his abs, kisses them, and groans. "It's going to be a long three months if I'm fighting this every day."

He turns and kisses the top of my head, and I see a pained look in his eyes.

"Does it hurt?"

He looks at me and shakes his head. "Kind of."

"Well, how? What's it feel like?"

He looks up, amused, but when he looks down at me, he tells me straight. "Like … pressure and no explosion."

"What does the explosion feel like?" I grin.

"Well, for me, it's kind of like when you have to pee really bad and you have to hold it for a long time. That's the pressure. And then when you finally go the bathroom, that feeling times twenty. Not sure what it feels like for a girl, though." He runs his hand through his hair. "But I'm sure you'll let me know"

"Deal. So, next Friday, you get these." I point to my chest. "And I get that." I point to his erection.

"Tessa, are you two done up there?" Dad yells up.

"For now." I shrug.

Lucas closes his eyes and shakes his head from side to side.

And something in his amusement reminds me I'm seriously out of my league.

"What's going on in that pretty head of yours now?" Lucas asks.

Without thinking, I tell him, "I'm dirty when I'm around you."

He looks wounded.

"I'm sorry, Lucas. I didn't mean to hurt you. I just feel like I'm ready to burst, like I can't get enough, like I could eat you up over and over again. I'm scared that when we do it, it'll be great. I mean, really great." I take his hand. "But then what? The chase is over; we've had sex. I'm scared of that, Lucas."

He hugs me. "What happens after, Tessa, is love. You told me that, and I know it will be true with you. I love you, I want you forever, and I don't want to share you with anyone. I want to make you smile for the rest of our lives. So, love is what happens, just a deeper version of what we have now."

My head spins as I smile against his chest. Lucas Links, a boy with a past, with the dirty dozen, who grew up without guidance, is the sweetest boy I have ever, or will ever, meet.

"You know, Tessa, I'm scared, too," he whispers against

my head. "I've been with lots of girls, and even thought I was in love once, but it was nothing like what I have with you. I've never felt this way, ever, about anyone, not even my parents. You want what's best for me. You've even hidden your hurt to allow me to shine. And I am scared shitless that you're going to hurt me, too. But I won't let that happen to us. I won't ever give you a reason to doubt how I feel."

I look up at him and see nothing but the truth in his green eyes. At this moment, I can say one hundred percent that I trust him with my heart.

"I'm sorry, Lucas. I will never doubt that again." I reach up and cup his cheek. "Not ever."

* * *

The hunting crew began pulling in for the normal Sunday target practice as I pull a covered casserole dish from the cupboard then preheat the oven. I look over my shoulder and see Lucas leaning against the doorjamb.

Pushing off, he asks, "Can I help?"

"Nope, go shoot. I'll be out when dinner is in the oven."

"That's my girl." Lucas grins. "Cooking me dinner; that's so hot." He kisses my cheek and asks, "You sure?"

"Go!" I laugh.

When he leaves, I push up my sleeves and get to work.

I pull the roast from the fridge and run it under water, hoping to thaw it faster and loosen the wrapping. Then I grab potatoes, peel and cube them; and slice onions, celery, and carrots. I rinse the roast again, put it in the casserole dish, season it, add the vegetables, and then top them all with garlic before putting it in the oven.

Twenty-minute prep. Ninety minutes to perfection.

I wash my hands then go to switch laundry.

Looking out the back window, I watch as Kendall and Jake play with Chewy. I also see that the lawn has gotten overgrown. There won't be many more days that mowing will be possible. It also happens to be one of my favorite thinking chores, a place where I am totally alone with my thoughts.

After throwing on one of Lucas's sweatshirts, I head out to the shop then check the gas. I top it off then jump on the big green machine.

Kendall and Jake take Chewy in, because the fool loves to chase the lawnmower, and then they run out to the barn to hang out with the guys.

In a little over an hour, the lawn is mowed, and I have had my fill of the smell of fresh cut grass. I park the mower then head inside. It smells pretty amazing in here, too.

I pull the casserole out of the oven and set it on top of the stove, trying to think of the last time that I wasn't a ball of nerves with worry. It's been months.

Mom and I are finally getting along, and Lucas is here.

I smile, thinking how I woke up in his arms this morning, and then we went to church together. Then I smile bigger thinking of the realization that I had upstairs as we unpacked his bag.

Sure, things would be great if Mom and Dad were back together, and maybe if I read things right when I saw their exchange earlier, it may happen. But, right now, life is good.

I turn and see Lucas leaning against the counter, smiling at me.

"What are you thinking?"

"Guess."

"Is it about me?" he asks, walking toward me.

Always.

"You are very full of yourself, aren't you?"

"Just hopeful, I guess. You didn't answer my question." He hugs me.

"Yes, it was about you."

"Good. Can I help with anything?" he asks as he steps back.

I turn and open the cupboard to grab the plates to set the table. "Nope. I want to take care of you tonight."

And I do, very much so. I'm sure it's been so long that someone has done that for him, if ever. He truly deserves it.

Lucas pulls himself up onto the counter and watches me set the table.

Then I open the casserole dish and check the temperature again.

"Done?" he asks.

"Yeah." I toss the oven mitt onto the counter then head to the bathroom to grab a hair tie.

When I come back out, I walk over to him and hit play on the boom box. Pearl Jam is on.

I walk back to the stove, grab a knife from the butcher block, and then I begin cutting up the roast.

"Thing's falling apart," Lucas says, setting his chin on my shoulder.

I grab a piece, blow on it, then hold it up for him. He closes his mouth around my fingers and sucks gently.

I hook my finger and turn my head to kiss his cheek.

My body begins vibrating as he caresses my finger with his tongue. Then he releases it and turns me as "Black" begins.

"Dance with me?"

I link my fingers behind his neck, and he grabs my hips as we dance.

When the song ends, I step back. "Gotta get this cut up."

As soon as I begin, Dad, Alex, Kendall, and Jake walk into the house.

"Tessa, you mowed that lawn and made dinner?" Dad asks, and I nod. "Feeling guilty about something?"

I give him apologetic eyes for what I've done these past few months and for what I know I will do in the future.

***

After dinner, I sit on the counter and take a million pictures as Lucas and Alex do the dishes.

"What's the deal?" Alex asks.

"I'm pretty sure no one will believe it when I tell them that two of the football players taking Blue Valley to the championships do dishes at home."

Lucas shakes his head, and Alex rolls his eyes. Then I point out that they missed a few spots.

As I'm distracting them, Kendall and Jake are busy sneaking clean dishes from the cupboards and setting them with the dirty dishes so they had more to wash.

Alex eventually catches on and grabs the sprayer, soaking us all.

After I change, I come back out and again sit on the counter, taking more pictures of them soaking up the water on the floor. Then it's business as usual for a Sunday night —Kendall and Jake shower and get dressed for bed, and I iron clothes for the next day.

Alex brings his down, and I iron them, as well, but when Lucas sits at the table with his, and I reach out to grab them, he surprises me.

"No, Tessa. I've done it myself for years. I got it."

I take them, anyway. "I want to."

***

After my shower, I put on Lucas's black boxer briefs under my nightgown. Then I put on a black, knee-length robe, knowing Dad will prefer that to just the nightgown.

When I walk out, Lucas isn't sitting on the couch, but when I go to get a drink, I see through the window. He's outside, on the phone.

He smiles as he hangs up and walks back in.

I'm sure I look at him with concern, because he says, "Dad, and all is well."

"Good." I smile then grab my Physics book off the counter. "Do you have homework?"

"No, but I should probably do some studying. I need to try to beat your brother out of his valedictorian spot." Lucas winks.

"Good luck with that." I laugh as I head into the living room and sit on the couch.

He sits down on the other side. I catch him looking at my thigh. He clearly sees his boxers.

"Nice, huh? Surprisingly comfortable. I like them."

"I like you in them," he whispers then grabs a pillow from the back of the couch, sets it on his lap, and clenches his teeth.

I can't help but laugh.

He shakes his head and whispers, "Killing. Me."

***

I wake to him taking my book off my lap. "Hey, baby, it's time to go to bed."

"Okay." I stretch and get up.

He walks me into my room and kisses me as we stand

in front of my bed. Then he presses his forehead against mine, looking into my eyes, and unties my robe. He slips it off my shoulders, lifts my nightgown, and smiles at the boxer briefs. Then he kisses me again.

"Damn," he whispers before walking backward out the door.

I hear him walk down the stairs and clear his throat. "Mr. Ross, I'm going to bed now. Thank you for all this."

"Lucas, we all need help now and then. You're a good kid; it's not a problem. Now get up there so I can set those alarms or Maggie will have my hide."

A New Day

Chapter Twenty Nine

TESSA

Opening the door, I expect the alarm to go off. When it doesn't, I suspect Dad has already tuned it off.

I hurry down the stairs, grab the crockpot from the pantry, set it on the counter, and then plug it in. Then I pull the pork roast from the fridge, unwrap it, and rinse it. I pour a little bit of vegetable oil in the bottom of the crockpot, then some apple cider vinegar and chicken broth in a bowl and stir it up. I drop the roast in the crockpot, dump two bottles of barbecue sauce on top, and then dump the mixing bowl of ingredients in. Placing the top on the crockpot, I finally set the temperature to low.

"And dinner is done." I smile as I walk to the sink to

wash it out and clean it then hit the shower before anyone else wakes up and gets there first.

***

When I step out of the shower, I realize I forgot to grab a towel. After wringing out my hair, I step out and carefully walk across the tile to the clean clothes basket of towels *and* ... I slip.

More accurately, I slip as Lucas walks in, and he catches me. Of course he catches me.

"Forget to lock the door, baby?" he asks, completely unaware that his big old hand is on my boob. "I'm not looking."

"No, but I guess we don't have to wait till Friday," I whisper, looking down.

"Fuuuck," he hisses. "Christ, Tessa." Yet, he's not moving.

I reach out with my foot and grab a towel with my toes, dragging it over before grabbing it and covering myself.

He still doesn't move.

"Good morning, Lucas."

He slowly opens one eye and starts to pull his hand away. I place my hand over his and hold it there.

"Good morning, Tessa."

Eyes glued to his, I move my hand, causing his to move, and he slowly caresses my breast as he kisses me softly, over and over again.

When I hear movement coming from above me, I step away when they begin to come down the stairs and Lucas heads to the door.

"I'll go out. You stay." I grab my robe and throw it on, then kiss him quickly.

The entire time I dress, my heart is beating a mile a minute, thinking about how amazing his hand felt on me.

Lucas and I pass each other on the stairs, not even making eye contact.

I head to the kitchen and pull down some glasses before setting them on the table and hurrying to the fridge, where I grab the orange juice and fill all five.

I grab a dozen eggs and breakfast sausage. Then I grab the milk, turn on the stove, and place two pans on the burners. I empty two boxes of sausage into one cast iron pan, scramble up the eggs with some milk, spray the pan with oil and, while I wait for it to heat, I grab bread and pop four slices in the toaster. Then I pull plates out from the cupboard and set the table.

Lucas walks in, looking so damn hot, freshly showered, and asks, "Do you ever relax and let anyone else help you out around here?"

I point the spatula at a chair. "Have a seat, Mr. Links. I told you that I want to take care of you."

"And what if I wanna take care of you?"

"Oh, you will." I giggle as I turn back to the frying pan.

And just as it seems it will always be, Kendall and Jake bound into the kitchen.

"I'm starving," Jake says, sitting down.

I laugh because Jake is always starving. "Good morning, Jake. Good morning, Kendall."

Kendall walks over and hugs me. "I'll do toast."

"Sounds good."

After we eat, I pack lunches, and just in time, too.

"The bus," Kendall yells as she runs out.

"Have a good day," I yell to them.

"Gotta stop at the store and grab some gum," Alex says as he stands. "You two ready?"

"Shit, what about Jade?" I ask.
"Tommy's got her."

* * *

I hurry to Jade in the parking lot, and we walk in together. The boys aren't far behind.

Lucas walks with Tommy to his locker and doesn't even bother going to his. I don't blame him since I have now witnessed the letters that fall out of it a couple times now, and I see how pissed he gets.

"So, how's married life?" Jade asks.

"Just like Dad said." I laugh, and so does she.

From behind, I hear, "Hello again, Tessa." Lucas grabs my hand, turns me, and pulls me in for a kiss.

After the kiss, I step back and smile. "Hello again to you, too." I look around and see how people are looking at me, and I don't like it. I'm sure they're confused. Hell, I would be, too.

"Baby?"

I turn back to Lucas. "I want to kind of keep it quiet that you're living with us. Is that okay?"

"Sure, but why?" Lucas asks.

Sadi walks by and hisses, "Whore."

"That's why."

Lucas shrugs. "If that's what you want, okay. But maybe it would shut her up."

"I seriously doubt that."

"Sorry, Tessa."

I lean in and give him one more kiss before we head to class.

* * *

The next two days fly by—school, practice, home, and kissing whenever we can. We are never far from each other, and every time I look at him, he's looking at me.

I don't have to wonder if he loves me; he shows me and tells me he does all the time, and I give him the same.

On Wednesday, I stay with Mom, and we honestly have a nice time. We go out to dinner, just the two of us, for the first time ever, and talk about school, hockey, and Lucas. I avoid any talk of Doctor Feel Good, not wanting to know about that part of Mom's life.

We also talk about the upcoming week. On Saturday, my team is going to sectionals, and Alex and Lucas have a game the same day. Mom plans on coming to my game, and Dad will take Kendall and Jake to Alex's. Friday is the only day that is left wide open.

And when I'm about to go to bed, Mom's phone rings.

She holds it out. "I'm sure it's for you."

When I take it, she stands. "I'm going to shower."

I nod to her and answer, "Hello?"

"Hope everything is going all right, baby. I miss you." He chuckles. "Okay, so I miss your cooking."

"Ha, ha, ha, silly boy. Is that how it's going to be after just three days? I'm not sure this is going to work. All your expectations are exhausting."

"Tessa, you know I was joking, right?" he asks, completely serious.

"Thus, the silly boy."

"I miss you."

"I miss you, too," I whisper.

"Sweet dreams, baby."

* * *

Blue Love

Thursday morning, I ride the bus to school, something I haven't done since Alex got his license, but like I told Alex, it would be silly for them to pick me up.

I sit with one of the girls from my team, a sophomore named Katrina.

"Are you dating Lucas Links still?" she asks.

"Yes." I nod.

"Everyone from our old school was in awe of him. He's pretty good-looking, but the way he treated girls sucked," Katrina says, "He's different with you. I think he really likes you."

"I think he does, too."

We chat about the upcoming game, which is definitely a better conversation than I anticipated after she led with Lucas.

When the bus pulls to a stop, Lucas is standing there with a sign that has my name on it, like he's a chauffeur waiting for me.

"Okay, I *seriously* think he likes you." She laughs as we step off the bus.

"Good morning, Tessa Ross."

"Good morning."

"May I take your bag, ma'am?" Lucas asks seriously.

I laugh, toss my bag at him, and raise my nose in the air as I walk past him. "Of course you can, but do keep up."

He grabs my hand, turns me around, and sees me grinning.

"You snubbing me?" Lucas asks before kissing me.

I kiss him back with a little tongue then slowly pull away. "Never. You taste too good."

"S'mores?" Lucas asks.

"Absolutely." I kiss him again.

Coach V walks by and clears his throat loudly. We laugh and walk into school, hand in hand.

* * *

Lucas is standing against a black SUV when I walk out of school after practice.

"What's going on?" I ask, looking at a brand-new and obviously expensive vehicle.

"Dad decided to trade my car in for this one. Nice, huh?"

"Yeah, I'd say so." I shake my head disapprovingly.

He opens the passenger door for me and takes my bag. "You don't like it?"

"No, it's awesome, but if I got high and wrecked a car, my butt would be walking." I slide in.

Laughing, he walks around and opens the driver's door. He tosses my bag in the back then slides in. "Yes, stellar parenting—rewarding me for bad behavior. No wonder I'm a screw-up."

I reach over and squeeze his hand. "Don't talk about yourself like that. Let's take it for a spin."

It has four-wheel drive, a moon roof, and three row seating; the first two with captain's chairs. It's brand new and fully loaded. When he got it, he said there was a bow on the steering wheel with a note that read, *"Thank you, son."*

"Do you think he's thanking me for getting all smoked-up and driving?" Lucas laughs.

"No, I think he may finally be seeing the real you. You deserve this." My eyes heat up and, typical me—well, Tessa the senior—I change the tone of the conversation. "Hey, do the seats recline all the way?"

"I like the way you think, baby. Let's get out of here and find out." Lucas starts the SUV and peels out.

I play with the radio and stop when I hear the song "When I See You Smile." I grab his hand and sing to him as he drives.

"Sober and singing to me?" He grins as he raises my hand and kisses it.

I decide to take the spotlight off my singing by finding out if these seats do actually recline.

They do!

Then I take his hand, kiss it, and place it on my breast, smiling as I watch Lucas now become … uncomfortable. His nostrils flare, and his jaw twitches as he keeps his eyes on the road, and one hand on my boob.

In no time, he pulls over on a dirt road that leads to one of Dad's fields, and my heart begins racing even faster than it already was, and that's seriously fast. He parks the car, leans over the console, and kisses me, and not soft, but hard. With his other hand, he grips the back of my head and pulls me up, kissing me deeper. I moan as he plunges his tongue into my mouth, enjoying the sensations caused by our physical connection. The way he makes me feel is amazing.

Breasts heavy, aching for more pressure, I arch my back, pressing into him, and he squeezes my nipples, causing me to burn harder, causing my breaths to become more difficult to catch.

Lucas pulls back and watches my face as he rolls my nipples between his finger and his thumb. He watches my face for my reaction to his touch, and I whimper his name and open my mouth, begging for his kiss.

"Baby, you are fucking gorgeous," he groans.

I close my eyes and bite down hard on my lower lip as I feel his breath against my cheek before he kisses it.

And then … his phone rings.

"You have got to be fucking kidding me," he growls as he sits up.

My eyes flutter open, and I watch as he adjusts his erection and flips open his phone. "This is Lucas."

I can't help but giggle at the way he answers—all businesslike.

I wait as he listens to whoever is on the other end of the call.

"We are on our way. Thanks, Alex." He closes the phone, ending the call, and looks at me. "We okay, baby?"

"We're perfect. But it's still not Friday." I giggle.

"I love you, Tessa."

"Love you, too." I sigh as I pull down my shirt and adjust the seat.

Smiling, he puts the car in gear, turns around, and pulls out onto the road.

"Are the girls still mad at me?"

I nod once. "Yes."

"Really?"

"They're upset because you stopped."

I swear his voice squeaks when he says, "I had, too."

I laugh as his face begins to turn red. "Lucas Links, are you embarrassed?"

"Yeah, and what the hell is up with that?"

* * *

Pulling into the farmhouse, holding hands, we see Dad and the kids standing out by the fire pit, grilling dinner. Lucas parks his brand-new SUV, hops out, runs to the passenger side, and opens the door for me.

Dad yells over, "Lucas, that yours?"

Blue Love

"Yes, Dad, it's punishment for his reckless behavior," I quip, answering for Lucas.

Dad looks at us, and then back at Lucas disapprovingly.

"I know it's not right. Your daughter graciously pointed that out to me." Lucas gives a weak smile.

"Glad to hear she listens." Dad nods.

"She doesn't just listen; she teaches me," Lucas says.

I head inside to get washed up for dinner.

When dinner is finished and the kids are all set for the next day, I head out to sit on the porch and put on my headphones. I'm set to perform for my voice class in two weeks and have not practiced. We had to choose a song from a Broadway play. I picked a song from Dream Girls—"Hard to Say Goodbye, My Love."

I softly sing through the audition song a few times softly, because repetition is the way I learn.

Completely focused, I only look up when I hear Lucas chuckle. I look over my shoulder and see him sitting on the steps with a book in his hand.

"What's so funny?"

"That song, that's never going to happen to us. We will make it. I promise you that."

My heart warms, and I think to myself how lucky I am to have someone like him.

Standing, I set down my sheet music, walk over, and sit behind him, wrapping my arms around him.

"Oh hey, baby. I didn't see you there," he jokes, and I squeeze him tighter. "You're distracting. Can't you see I am trying to get some studying in?"

I rub my hands up his hard abs and chest and kiss the back of his neck as his head falls to the side and rests on his shoulder. I lick his neck then give it a nip.

"Tessa, you need to stop."

"I can't wait until next Friday," I whisper in his ear then lick his neck again below the same spot. I grab one of his hands and bring it to my mouth, gently sucking on his finger. I bravely reach down and begin to rub his thigh, waiting to feel him harden and lengthen under his pants. When he does, I begin to stroke him.

He hisses, "Fuck, baby."

I move my hand faster, and his head falls back, resting beside mine. He exhales against my cheek before kissing it as his mouth then falls open and he lets out a groan. I love the way he sounds when I touch him. It makes me burn with want to touch him even more.

I rub my hand up his abs then down, pushing it between his hot hard and heated skin, in the waistband of his jeans. I wrap my hand around his hard, velvety-feeling erection and, as if I have done it a million times, I begin to stroke him.

"Oh God, baby," he groans. "Please don't stop. I'm so fucking close."

I feel him jerk in my hand and hot liquid spills over my fingers. He holds his breath for a few moments then slowly releases it with a groan.

I pull my hand out, rubbing the sticky liquid against his skin and stand, telling him, "Good thing you have a book to carry in front of you."

Stepping around him, I look down and see his eyes are heavy and filled with lust. I wink and begin to walk away, feeling victorious.

"You caused a mess." Lucas closes his eyes and smiles. "I like this game, but before it's over, I assure you I'll be the one who wins."

I watch as he stands with a book in front of him, steps to me, and kisses my cheek.

"Go in ahead of me and give me a minute to calm the chaos you caused."

* * *

I am sitting on the couch, reading, when he comes out of the bathroom from his shower. I can't help but grin, and he gives me a wink.

He sits next to me and kisses my hand. Kendall and Jake come in and squish between us, and then Chewy takes it upon himself to jump on me. I give him a scratch behind his ears as he sits on the floor by my feet.

"Who wants popcorn?" I ask as I pet Chewy.

Kendall and Jake both say, "I do!"

I head out to the kitchen, grab the air fryer from the cupboard, and set to popping. When it's finished, I bring a bowl into each of the kids first, then come back out and grab one for Alex, Dad, and Lucas.

I toss pieces of popcorn to the kids, and they try to catch them in their mouths yet fail. Then they throw some to Lucas, Alex, and even Dad.

"You are all terrible at this." I laugh.

"You think you're any better?" Lucas asks.

"Bring it on," I joke.

When he does, I catch the very first piece, and then both Jake and Kendall toss me pieces, trying to make me miss. I make sure I don't.

After all the popcorn is gone, most of it on the floor, I am deemed the champion.

After the mess is cleaned and the dishes are done, Jake and Kendall head to bed, Alex walks into the kitchen to call Phoebe, and Dad walks outside to use his cell phone.

Lucas takes this opportunity to whisper, "You're pretty good with your mouth, Tessa. First, the whole finger trick, and then the popcorn was nice." He smiles as he rubs his thumb across my lower lip.

I bite lightly on his thumb. "Next Friday, you and I will find out how good I really can be."

* * *

The next morning, I make ham and eggs, and then I make lunches.

"Did you like taking the bus yesterday, Tessa?" Jake asks.

"Nope. It's still stinky and smelly, just like I remembered."

"Yeah, it sucks," Kendall says.

"Watch your mouth, Kendall," I say, trying not to laugh.

"How about, two days a week, you ride with us?" Lucas asks.

The three of us look at him, all pretty shocked.

"Are you serious?" Jake asks.

"Why not?" Lucas shrugs.

"Can we today?" Kendall asks excitedly.

"You'll have to ask your sister." Lucas winks.

"Do you know they have to be there twenty minutes before us?" I ask.

He smiles and wags his brows. "Uh-huh."

Oh, I think and can't help but grin. "Well then, okay."

* * *

When Lucas and I walk in from school, Mom, Dad, and Jake are sitting at the table. I notice immediately that Jake has a black eye.

I drop my bag and ask, "What happened, Jake?"

Blue Love

"Jake was suspended for the day—he got in a fight," Mom answers.

"A fight ... What? How did that happen?" I ask.

"Joel Black punched me in the eye, because I told him that Lucas lived with us and he was your boyfriend." Jake rolls his eyes.

"Why would someone punch you for that?"

"Joel is Sadi's younger brother," Lucas says quietly. "I'm sorry, Jake."

"Did you punch him back?" I snap.

"Yep, that's why I got suspended." Jake smiles.

I hug him really tightly. "Good job, buddy."

"Tessa, that's not appropriate," Mom corrects me.

"Then it's going to be really inappropriate when I kick his sister's—"

"Tessa," Dad warns.

I grab Jake's face and raise my eyebrow. "It won't happen again without major consequences, I promise." I kiss his head.

"I'm so sorry," Lucas tells Jake again.

Jake smiles. "I'm not. Now Sarah thinks I'm cool."

"Mr. and Mrs. Ross, Tessa, I'm sorry."

"It's not your fault, son," Dad says.

Blood boiling, I stand up and walk outside.

On my way out, I hear Mom tell Lucas, "You might want to go calm her down. You've never met Tessa the Terrible, have you?"

* * *

Five. I start the countdown as my feet pound against the cracked sidewalk, the kind of crack I want to give Sadi fucking Black—a permanent one.

I round the lilac tree, no longer flowering, and hit the

driveway.

I run even faster now, eyes on the field beyond the shop.

Four. I inhale deeply as I run between the bare fields, feet pounding against the hard, uneven, rutted dirt driveway.

Faster.

Three. I push myself harder as I approach the bare cornfield.

"Two," I pant as my feet hit the overgrown grass.

"Tessa Ross!" Lucas yells from somewhere behind me, and I slow down. "Wait up."

"Try to catch me, Links."

I turn back around and run as fast as I can, but he quickly catches up.

"Give me a challenge, Ross." Lucas smiles as he turns and runs backward ahead of me, mockingly.

"First one to the trees wins." I fly past him.

"You ready to get your fine ass kicked?" He passes me again.

"Hey Links, I'm no cheerleader. I can beat you. Check this out." When he turns, I slow down, pull my shirt up, and toss it on the ground, leaving me in just my sports bra.

"Not fair, Ross." Clearly sidetracked, he stumbles.

I points to my shirt and yell, "You better get it, or I will tell my daddy that you took it off me."

When he does, I pass him and yell over my shoulder, "See ya at the trees, Links."

I run as fast as I can, and when I'm almost there, he grabs me around the waist, slowing me down and moving in front of me. I wrap my arms and legs around him as he walks us to the edge of the woods and sets me down. Then he softly falls on top of me. We both start laughing as we try to catch our breaths.

He rolls to his back and looks up at the sky. Then he turns to his side and looks at me.

"I won," I say, smirking.

He smiles as he leans in and kisses my cheek, my neck, and begins moving down. And then we hear a tractor.

"Shit." I laugh. "My shirt!"

Lucas gets up, hurries to it, and then holds it up, saying, "Say please or I'll tell your daddy what a naughty girl he has, Tessa the Terrible."

"Forget it then." I stand.

"Dammit, Tessa. Here." He laughs and throws my shirt at me as Alex gets closer.

"You better stand in front of me and block the view."

He does. "You, Tessa Ross—"

"Won." I smile. "And, by the way, you haven't seen Tessa the Terrible yet." I kiss his cheek.

"No, but Tessa the Tease … that's another story." He smacks my ass.

My jaw drops, and I scold him, "Lucas!"

"Sorry, baby, did I hurt you?" he asks with true concern.

I wag my eyebrows then wink.

"Tessa." His voice is gravel. "Killing. Me."

We walk toward Alex, and he begins to lower the bucket. "Mom sent me down to see if you were both still alive. Wanna lift?"

We both hop in.

Lucas looks back and yells over the loud sound of the tractor, "Alex, what are you doing tonight?"

"Not sure. Why?"

"How about you, Phoebe, Tommy, Jade, Tessa, and I go out to dinner? We can all ride in the new SUV. It'll be an early night—big game tomorrow for all of us." He squeezes my hand.

"Sounds good. I'll call and ask."

"Cool with you, TT?" Lucas smiles.

I smile back. "Can I pick the spot?"

"Of course." Lucas links his pinky with mine as Alex begins driving faster.

"Good, you get to meet my aunt tonight." I grin then look back at Alex and yell, "Hey, Alex, we're going to go to The Spot."

"You sure he's ready for that?" Alex laughs.

* * *

When we pull into The Spot, Lucas asks, "Your aunt works here?"

"She sure does." Jade chuckles.

"I thought you said she owns it?" Tommy asks.

"That, too," Jade says, grabbing her purse off the floor.

I watch Lucas as we walk into the rundown bar and make our way through the dining area.

The decor is definitely rustic, the tables all picnic tables surrounding a makeshift dance floor. As we walk by each table, almost everyone says hello.

We sit down, and I hear Josie say, "Hey there, babies."

I watch as Lucas takes her in. Like her bar, she's also a little bit rough, but beautiful just the same.

She gives Alex, Jade, and myself all hugs and says, "You haven't been to see me in almost three months. The last time I saw you two girls was when I took you to the concert. You still love Pearl Jam, or have you moved on?" she asks while looking over Tommy and Lucas.

"We definitely still love Pearl Jam." I tell her with a laugh.

"We're sorry, Aunt Josie." Jade smiles. "Been a little busy. This is Tommy. Tommy, this is my aunt, Josie."

Josie looks him up and down and says "All right, boy, stand."

Tommy stands.

She looks him up and down. "Nice. Now turn around and let me get a look at that butt."

Laughing, Tommy turns around.

"You on the pill yet, Jade?"

Tommy looks shocked but, being that we are used to Aunt Josie's bluntness, Jade just smiles and answers, "No, not yet."

"You can have a seat now, Tommy. You're a doll." She then looks at Alex and asks, "Now, who is this pretty little thing?"

Alex smiles. "This is Phoebe."

"Very nice to meet you, Phoebe. Be good to him; he's a keeper." Josie gives her a hug.

Blushing, Phoebe smiles. "I think so, too."

Aunt Josie turns to me, smiling as bright as the moon, and shakes her head. "Tessa, Tessa, Tessa, who might this be?"

Before I have a chance to say anything, Lucas smiles that dazzling smile, stands up, waves his hand in front of himself, turns around so she can get a good look at his ass, and then looks over his shoulder and says, "I'm Lucas, the lucky one Tessa said yes to." He then does one more full three hundred and sixty degree turn and laughs. "Pretty nice, huh?"

Oh. My. God. He did not just say that.

"Hell yes!" She laughs.

"Now you?" he says, making a circle with his hand and causing Aunt Josie to blush. I swear to God that's the first time that has ever happened.

"You coming up to help out during deer season, and then when the snow starts falling, girls?" Josie asks us.

"I don't know," I answer honestly

"I will," Lucas offers.

"What kind of experience do you have?" Josie asks smugly. "Oh hell, who am I kidding? You wear a tight tee-shirt and jeans, you're hired. Can you wash dishes?"

Lucas smiles. "Yep."

I can't help but laugh again. "All right, I'm in, but we are both playing a sport right now."

"That's fine. We can work around it." Josie nods. "Jade?"

Jade smiles. "I'm a little busy right now. I'll check my schedule."

"Kind of a lame crowd tonight, and no one is singing along. Go get them started and dinners on me." Josie winks at me.

"Dinner is always on you." I laugh as I stand. "All right. Any requests?"

"Joplin, baby!" She twists up her bar rag and snaps my butt before I have a chance to get away.

Grabbing the cordless mic, I stand in front of a nearly full dining room and wait for the music to start. When Joplin begins, so do I, but I'm focused on the crowd, not Lucas, because I don't want to feel anxious or nervous about doing something I've always loved without giving it a second thought. By the end of the song, though, I find myself singing to him and watch as he sings along, smiling.

At the end of the song, I start to set the microphone back in the stands when Karaoke Joe asks, "One more, Tessa?"

"Sure," I agree. "Pick one for me, will you?"

I can't help but laugh when Shania Twain's "Any Man of Mine" begins. It seems only natural to sing the song to Lucas.

I shake off my nerves, grab a chair, and set it beside

me. I then curl my finger, calling Lucas to the stage.

He has no problem coming up and sitting, and I have no problem singing and dancing around him.

When the song ends, I'm surprised when Lucas stands, walks over to Joe, and whispers something in his ear.

As I walk off stage and toward the table, I hear Lucas say, "Tessa Ross, care to join me?"

"You sure about this?"

"Hell no, but I'm going to try." He turns his hat backward as the old song "Don't go Breaking My Heart" starts.

Every bit of the nerves I had dissipates when he begins. The boy can sing ... Of course he can. I'm pretty certain there isn't anything he can't do.

When the song ends, he twirls me in a circle, and we finish with a kiss, the sweet kind.

The crowd begins clapping, hooting, and howling; the loudest obviously coming from our table.

When we get back to the table, prime rib and chicken parmesan are waiting on plates, family-style, in the middle of the table.

Before I have time to sit down, Aunt Josie links her arm through mine and pulls me aside.

"He's beautiful, Tessa, talented, and the way he looks at you ... swoon."

"He isn't alone, Aunt Josie. I am head over heels in love with him."

"Be careful, baby girl. I don't want to see you knocked up before you graduate." Josie winks.

I look around to make sure no one heard her before I admit on a laugh. "We haven't had sex. And by the way, why aren't you having this talk with Jade?"

"Has she?" Josie asks.

"No."

"He's living with you, right?" Josie asks.

"Yep."

She chuckles. "That's why I am talking with you and not her."

Before I have a chance to sit down, Phoebe and Jade grab me and pull me back up to the stage.

I am shocked when Phoebe is the one to request the song, grab the mic, and begins singing Joan Jett's "I love Rock and Roll."

When we finish, I hug Phoebe and tell her, "You can sing, girl."

"Pretty good?" Phoebe asks.

"Damn good." I laugh.

"We're goddamn rock stars!" Phoebe throws a victorious fist in the air.

* * *

When Alex, Lucas, and I return from dinner, Dad is in the recliner. "Josie called and said she gave Lucas a job?"

I laugh. "Yep."

"What's so funny?" Dad asks.

"Lucas has never had a job in a kitchen. She didn't care, because she thinks he's cute."

Dad rolls his eyes and nods to Lucas. "You'll do fine. Just be careful—she's a cougar."

"I'll be careful." Lucas chuckles.

"You kids need to get to bed. Big games tomorrow." Dad stands then walks out to the kitchen.

"I had a lot of fun tonight." Lucas gives me a peck on the cheek.

"So did I. It was fun. I don't know why I was surprised that you can sing, but we'll have to make sure to do that again."

KNOCKED DOWN

Chapter Thirty

LUCAS

She looked cute as hell, and sexy, too. Never thought that was possible until her, but right in front of me, with pigtails braided, is five-foot-eight of legs, tits, a tight little ass, the kindest, most telling eyes ... I smile. I swear to God above that I'd do anything, including possibly joining a circus, because Tessa Ross is in her blue and white warmup gear, headphones on, dancing and singing as she cooks breakfast for five, as she does every morning. This, in and of itself, makes me love her even more.

She turns and sees me standing there and doesn't even act startled like she has for the past several days. She just pulls the headphones off her ears, sets it on her shoulders, and smiles.

"How the hell is it that you look so damn hot all the time?" I kiss her. "Good morning, baby."

"I made breakfast."

"I love you," I whisper then kiss her cheek again.

Laughing, she says, "You better."

She smiles as if I'm laughing, and it's cute, but down deep, I sometimes wonder if she knows just how much. I love her so much that sometimes it almost hurts. Never in a million years would I have thought it possible. I suppose I should have known. Movies, books, songs, poems have all been written on the very subject of love, but it wasn't until her that I actually got it. I hope—no pray—that she loves me even half as much as I do her, because then I have no doubt that she will be mine, and I'll be hers forever.

"You wanna listen to—"

"You saying my name over and over again?" I interrupt her.

"Head in the game, Lucas." She giggles as she walks over to the boom box sitting on the counter and turns on the radio.

"The Billboard top 100?"

"Don't tell Jade, but I've been slacking. It's kind of our thing. We listen every week, write down the songs that we love the most, and discuss them later." Her face turns red, and she shakes her head, pigtails bouncing about. "Must sound lame to someone like you, huh?"

"Not at all. Music just sounds better now, I guess. I never had a reason to pay attention before." Now I feel my face burning. It's kind of embarrassing to admit something like that. "Let's dance."

I grab her hips and pull her tight against me, just the way I like her—close.

Smiling that beautiful smile up at me, she puts her

hands on my shoulders. "You know there's no song playing right now, right?"

"*On the charts for four weeks in a row, climbing from number sixty-five to number forty-nine, 'Linger' by The Cranberries.*"

We both smile.

"Sing to me, baby?"

She begins, *"If you, if you could return. Don't let it burn. Don't let it fade. I'm sure I'm not being rude. But it's just your attitude. It's tearing me apart. It's ruining every day."*

"The fuck?" I force a laugh. "This song sucks."

She laughs and keeps singing, and even though the song is not like the one we danced to at the beginning, the one that makes me think of her every time it comes on, "Eternal Flame," I don't give a shit, because she's singing in that sweet voice, while her hands are on me, smiling up at me like I'm something more than a good fuck or someone who gives her clout.

When the song ends, she starts to pull away.

"Tessa—"

She wiggles out of my arms. "I'm going to burn the bacon."

I grab the plates from the cupboard as I watch her shake that ass as she stands at the stove, singing softly to every song that comes on.

"Want me to grab your book?" her little sister, who is seriously sweet, asks.

I mess up her hair. "Book?"

"She writes down her favorites every week," Kendall explains.

"Don't spill all my weirdo secrets," Tessa warns with a smile.

After I set the table, with Kendall's help and guidance, she runs to the other room. I swear that girl can't just chill, either. Chewy starts whining, so I take him out, and we play fetch for a long damn time. Works for me, though; a nice slow warmup for the day to come.

When I walk inside, I see Tessa and Kendall dancing to "Come Baby Come" and I can't help but laugh.

Kendall stops dancing. I assume she thinks I'm laughing at her, which is a hell of a lot better than the fact that I have all intentions in the fold of making Tessa do just that tonight.

"Go grab the book, Kendall. This songs gotta make a list."

She looks at Tess, who is fighting a grin. "You want me, too?"

"Yeah," she says, not looking away.

Kendall jets, and I turn my hat backward and make my way to her, and then we dance.

"Damn boy, can you suck at just one thing?"

"Not in my nature." I turn her around then pull her back against me, and she laughs as she grinds her tiny little ass with the obvious intention of making me hard.

When we hear feet tapping down the stairs, we both step away, and yeah, I sit my ass down so my semi is under the table, making a note to myself that wearing sweats sans boxers is a bad idea.

John walks in, Jake and Alex following behind him, and shakes his head when he sees Tessa dancing. Then, just like every meal at the Ross home, chaos ensues.

Not going to lie and say it wasn't jarring the first couple days I was here—hell, it still is—but now it's in the best possible way.

By the end of breakfast, we've all written in Tessa's notebook.

When John, Kendall, and Jake leave to head to town to

go to the parts store, and Alex hits the shower, Tessa and I finish cleaning up.

"Glad you're finally allowing me to help." I smile at her as I dry off a dish.

"You're not a guest anymore; been here a week now. You're officially part of the family." She grins. "Lucas Ross."

I hip-check her. "Love your last name, baby, but you need to know you'll be the one changing yours."

She looks at me and gives me that face, the cute one when she's trying not to smile, and her face starts to pinken. "We'll see about that."

"You're gonna wanna be one of those women who hyphenates her name, there will be consequences."

"You don't scare me, Lucas Links-Ross."

You scare the hell out of me, I think. But I push past that and grab her, pretending like I'm going to pick her up and throw her over my shoulder.

She wiggles away and laughs. "Let's focus on today, yeah?"

"Today's in the bag. I'm focusing on the after-party, the private celebration."

She washes a plate, ignoring the comment. "I don't like not being there to see you kick ass."

"I wish I could watch you do the same," I say, putting a plate in the cupboard.

She glances at me out of the corner of her beautiful blue eyes. "I'll give you a prize when you get home, if you win."

"But it's not Friday."

"It's been Friday for two days."

I nod. "Okay, if you win, I'll let you."

She smacks me. "Gee, thanks."

Laughing, I tell her, "You win, you'll get two. I owe you one."

"That look doesn't freak me out anymore. It kind of excites me," she whispers.

I step behind her, push her braid aside, kiss her neck, and then I grab her ass firmly. "You haven't seen excited yet." I reach around and flatten a hand on her flat belly then begin to lower it.

"Shower's free," Alex yells as he heads upstairs.

Tessa stops my hand from traveling any further. Then she grabs it and pulls me behind her through the dining room, living room, and into the bathroom. She shuts and locks the door behind us.

"Tessa, what are you doing, baby?"

She steps in front of me and hooks her thumbs under the waistband of my sweats.

"Damn, baby," I say as I lean in to kiss her.

She leans back and starts to go down to her knees.

"Tessa, where's my uniform?" Alex calls, and I quickly grab my sweats before my dick slips out of its cage.

"I'll bring it up in a second," she yells then tries to smack my hand away.

"Can't wait for what's to come, baby, but tonight's cool."

She scowls at me, stands, and then turns away.

"What's wrong, baby? Are you mad?"

"Yes, at myself. This is crazy. I don't think I'll stop next time we are alone. It's all or nothing, Lucas."

"It doesn't have to be that way. I can calm down. Sorry, Tessa."

"Don't be sorry. I want you more than anything I have ever wanted. I need you. I can't even kiss you anymore without wanting more. I feel like I'm losing it." She grips the counter. "Seriously, what is wrong with me?"

"I know exactly what's wrong with you." I turn her around, lift her up, sit her on the counter, then lift her shirt and unclasp her bra. I love the fact it's a front clasp. In less than a second, one of her girls is in my mouth.

"Oh God, Lucas," she whispers as I suck her pebbled nipple into my mouth, swirl my tongue around it, then bite down, all while inhaling her sweet scent. She grabs my hair and arches her back, pushing against my mouth as I cup her other tit, set on making her come.

And she does, more beautifully than I imagined.

Helping her sort herself, she looks at me and shakes her head. "I'm not sure—"

"Then don't." I adjust my cock.

"Tessa!" Alex yells from upstairs.

"She's coming." I wink at her, and she laughs as we leave the bathroom.

Filling her water bottle at the sink, we watch as Maggie pulls in, and she whispers, "Thank you."

"The pleasure was mine."

"How does that work?" Tessa asks, confused.

"You'll see tonight. We're winning this game."

I walk her out to Maggie's car and hug her. "Good luck, baby."

"You, too. I love you," Tessa says sweetly. She's a hell of a lot more relaxed, as I knew she would be after that evil sexual tension was relieved.

"You better." I laugh.

* * *

Tessa wasn't the only one relaxed after my mouth's intro to the girls. Apparently, I'd been holding back some tension, as well, because my arm was loose and on fire for the whole game. Alex, Ryan, Tommy, and I couldn't do a damn thing wrong in the field if we tried.

Needless to say, we won.

Last year, after each game, when I looked in the stands and there was no one there for me, it took a bit of my love for the game away. Today, even though my blood isn't sitting there, cheering me on, the Ross family is, and so is the head coach from SU, Coach Brown.

Direct eye contact was made, and he tipped his hat to me. No words needed to be spoken; I knew what this meant. I did, however, discreetly nod to Tommy, because there was no one else I'd want to take the field at SU with than him. Coach Brown lifted his chin, and it gave me a touch of hope.

Tommy deserved it just as much as I did. No one defends me like he does, on or off the field. Without him over the past three years, I wouldn't be who I am. Without Tessa, I wouldn't be who I am becoming.

I've never been the kind to pray to someone who never seemed to know I existed, but right now, I look up and whisper, "Thank you."

Tommy nudges me and nods to the far end of the field, where a bunch of men in many assortments of collegiate gear stand with clipboards.

"Wherever we play, we do it together," I assure him, and I mean it, too.

He holds up his fist. "You and me, man."

I tap it. "Always."

Tommy groans, "Don't look now, but the wicked witch of the—"

"Lucas, we need to talk," comes from behind me.

I don't bother looking back as I simply tell her, "No, we don't."

"I'm three months late!" she yells.

I freeze and quickly do the math in my head.

No, no, no, I think as my reality comes crashing down on me, *this can't be right.*

I glance to my side and see Tommy doing the same as I just did. Even though I'm better at math and normally take pride in that, I pray I'm wrong.

When he closes his eyes, bile begins to burn my throat.

I look behind me and see Alex hang his head.

"Did you hear me, Lucas?" Sadi asks, now standing in front of me.

When I say nothing, she reaches into her bag and pulls out a pregnancy test and what appears to be a bill from a doctor's visit. I look them over as she holds them, not wanting to touch them because, for some reason, that would make what I already know is real even more so.

My stomach sours, threatening to push the vomit up my throat. My eyes burn, threatening tears. I shake my head. "We'll talk later."

"When?" she demands.

"I'm not sure."

"Are you really living with her?" Sadi yells as I head to the tree line.

I stop then turn, pointing my finger at her, and sternly say, "Yes, Sadi. And you better leave her the *fuck* alone. Got it?"

"Yes," she says quietly then walks toward the parking lot.

I walk past the guys and into the woods behind the field. My legs give out, and I fall to my knees, taking in deep breaths and releasing them slowly, hoping like hell that I don't cry.

When my chest tightens, I hold my hand over it, trying to calm myself down, but it's not working. I'm having a hard time breathing or even expelling air. I feel dizzy and even more sick to my stomach now. Too many feelings that remind me of when I was younger.

I was six years old when the school nurse called and asked why I was not at school. I told her that mommy had fallen. Within minutes, the ambulance was at our home, along with a white car that had an official-looking seal on the door. They took my mom, and then the woman in the white car helped me pack a bag and took me.

This feels the same— this pain is the same inability to breathe.

I look up and see Tommy and Alex standing just beyond the tree line, giving me space. I know that they already know what's going on, but I don't think that I could possibly face them right now. Hell, I'm not sure if I ever would be able to face them again.

When I see John walking up to Tommy, and then stops to talk to him, I close my eyes and try to call on God, who I never speak to and never will again, to prove to me that He is there, to make this pain stop. I'd sell my soul if, when I open my eyes, it was all just a bad dream.

When I open my eyes and John is squatting beside me, I know that not even the devil wants my cursed soul.

Something breaks inside of me, and I scream out into the air. That's something I've never done. I've always managed to keep it all inside. I could now, I could manage my pain, but deep down, I know the worst is yet to come, the worst will be when I have to tell Tessa.

John wraps his arm around my shoulder and pulls me into a hug. "Son, you'll get through this. We'll help you."

I shake my head, and he helps me stand.

"The girls just pulled in. Give me your keys and let's get you out of here."

Wiping my face, we walk out of the woods and toward my SUV. Out of the corner of my eye, I see Tessa exiting the bus as Tommy opens the back door. I slide in, and he closes it behind me. Then he walks around the vehicle and slides in next to me.

"We've been through worse; we will get through this." Tommy wraps an arm around me and the first tear falls.

BAD THINGS

Chapter Thirty One

TESSA

I run off the bus as I watch Dad and Tommy swarm around Lucas, worry that he's been hurt. Then I spy Alex quickly and ask, "Is everything okay?"

Alex won't even look at me as he simply says, "Where is Jade? We need to go."

"Alex, you're scaring me." My eyes burn with tears as I yell, "Jade!"

Jade turns and runs toward me. "Tessa, what is it?"

"I don't know. He won't tell me." I look at Alex, whose eyes show deep concern.

The butterflies begin to swarm, and not the good kind.

"Phoebe." Alex looks at her then whispers, "Can you ride with Becca? I'll call you later."

"Of course," Phoebe answers.

I watch as Alex kisses her forehead then slides in the truck. Jade and I hop in.

The ride home is quiet. Alex, who always has to have the radio on, doesn't even bother with it.

When we pull onto the farm's driveway, Tommy rushes outside.

Jade and I slide out of the truck, and Jade asks, "What's going on, Tommy?"

And that's when we hear yelling from the house.

I stand frozen, listening to my father say his name. "Lucas, you aren't going anywhere. Put your bag down, son." He's trying to move out? "I gave my word to the sheriff, and you certainly don't need to be going anywhere right now."

"No disrespect, sir, but I can't stay here. I can't bear to see the disappointment in her eyes. Not again." His voice cracks.

"You have no clue how strong that girl is. Right now, you need people, and you have us. Now go get your ass in the shower and let me talk to her. I'll help you get through this," Dad orders.

We all head into the house, and I hear what I know to be Lucas running down the stairs. As much as I want to go to him, something is stopping me. I've never felt so afraid in my life, yet I also know that he needs me, that he needs us ... and that I love him.

The bathroom door shuts a moment later, and then everyone looks at me.

Dad walks into the kitchen, takes my hand, and leads me back outside. Standing on the deck, he looks at me sternly, the kind of look that proceeds a serious conversation.

"Daddy, what happened? Is it his mom? His dad? His

sisters?"

"No, baby girl, they are all just the same." Dad's eyes soften, and I swear I see pity them. "After the game, the blonde, Sadi, I believe, asked to speak to him. She said that she was three months late."

"She's lying, Dad," I say with conviction.

"She handed him proof stating otherwise—a pregnancy test. Honey, Lucas looked at it and walked into the woods behind the school and broke down."

The bad kind of butterflies still their movements, and as if my body is protecting itself, I begin to feel numb. "Are you sure?"

Dad nods firmly. "Yes, and he's in a very bad place right now. Can you try to keep it together for him?"

"Of course, Dad. I love him." At the use of the word *love*, my voice breaks. "I love him so much."

He pulls me into his arms. "I know this is rough, but he has over two months left here. Can you do that? Because, if not, you need to tell me, and I'll find a suitable—"

"He has to stay."

"Okay then." He nods. "Let's get inside."

When I walk into the living room, I see Lucas sitting on the couch, arms crossed over his chest, his white hat pulled down low, covering his eyes as he sits next to Tommy.

Tommy stands, gives me a hug, and whispers in my ear, "You going to be okay?"

"Of course I am, and so is Lucas."

I walk over and sit on the couch next to Lucas. "How was your game?"

"Seriously? That's what you are going to say to me right now?"

"Yep." I take his hat and turn it around backward. He looks up at me through those beautiful, long, black lashes

—he's heartbroken—and then looks down. "So, how was the game, Lucas?"

He laughs uncomfortably. "It was great. Lots of recruiters, and we won. How was yours?"

"Good. We won, too." I swallow hard then ask the burning question, "What happened after, Lucas?"

He turns his hat around and pulls it down, hiding his hurt. I watch as he takes in several short breaths, and then a tear falls, and now my heart, my heart that belongs to him, breaks, too.

I brush his tears away, take his hands, and kiss the back of each one of them. "You're going to be fine."

"How are you going to be, Tessa? Huh?"

I feel the first of many tears fall and answer, "I'm going to be fine."

He looks up at me and takes me in his arms. Neither one of us even tries to hide the tears.

Nose buried in my hair, he whispers, "I am so sorry, Tessa."

"I'm pretty sure this wasn't planned."

He shakes his head.

"Okay, then we need to come up with a plan for you."

He lets out a breath and takes my face in his hands, eyebrows furrowed, and says, "God, I love you."

"I love you, Lucas. I'll help you figure this out, okay? We'll figure it out together." I wrap my arms around his neck, take a really deep breath, then slowly exhale. "We've got this, Lucas Links."

Less than a second later, Lucas's phone rings, and he holds it up.

"Are you going to answer it?"

"I don't want to."

"It could be your mom," I whisper.

He flips open his phone and holds it to his ear. "This is Lucas."

As soon as I hear her voice, I want to take the phone and smash it. When I hear her taunting tone, in which she uses with him, I want to smash *her*.

"I said we need to talk."

"What do we need to talk about?" His voice shakes in anger.

"Our child." The way she says *child* feels like she's taunting him.

He looks at me, and I whisper, "Do you need a minute?"

He covers the phone and says, "I have nothing to say to her."

I whisper, "I'm sure you have questions, Lucas. Ask them."

He fires them off.

"How far along are you?"

"Well, let's see … we had sex a week before school started, so you do the math."

"Two and a half months?"

"Ding-ding," she says snidely.

"What are you going to do?" he asks.

"What do you want me to do?"

He balls his hand into a fist. "Well, it didn't matter last time, so why the fuck are you even asking me this time?" He doesn't even take a breath before he sneers, "By the way, I personally took you to get on the pill; what the fuck happened with that?"

"Should have used a rubber. Guess the pill is not one hundred percent, just like they said. And Lucas, I plan on keeping it."

His face turns red. "What do you want from me?"

"For you to be a man. Basically, the opposite of your father."

"Fuck you, bitch."

I shake my head, and he covers the phone again. I whisper, "Don't lower yourself to her level, Lucas. You are so much better than that."

He exhales a breath before saying, "Okay, you're going to need to spell it out for me."

"First, you need to get off the farm and the farm girl. I don't need to be stressed out right now."

His entire body stiffens.

I reach over and take his hand, gently squeezing it, and he looks up at me, eyes hard, jaw tense.

"I have to be here for three months; that is out of my control. As far as Tessa goes, I told you on the field. If you need me to repeat myself, here it goes: you are to leave her the fuck alone."

"Lucas," I whisper and shake my head.

"As long as you don't lay down with the dog, then I won't do anything to her."

Lucas sits up straight. "You also need to tell your brother to keep his hands off of Jake Ross."

"Jake started it," Sadi snarls.

By the look on Lucas's his face, I can tell he has had it. "Time to grow up, Sadi. You're going to be a mommy in less than seven months."

Sadi huffs, "As if you know anything about parenting."

He's not the only one who has had enough.

I reach out my hand and whisper, "Lucas, give me your phone."

He shakes his head and sits back, crossing his free arm over his abdomen.

Again, I whisper, "Then tell her name calling does

nothing. If we are going to parent a child together that needs to stop, and it needs to stop now."

He repeats what I said, verbatim.

"Fine, I want you to be part of this pregnancy. And when your mom gets home, I want to move in so that we can work on things. You need to get a job, because you'll be taking care of us, not your daddy."

His face is red, veins bulging in his forearms as he clenches his fists.

I whisper, "Tell her—"

"Lots of demands," he cuts me off. "My head is spinning. We'll talk more later."

"Yes, we will. Now and forever, this bond can't be broken. It's me and you, Lucas Links. Figure your shit out." Sadi ends the call.

He closes his phone. "I can't ask you to be part of this, Tessa. I love you too much for this to be your life."

"I hate to point out the obvious, but I make my own decisions. It isn't up to you." I scowl.

His eyes fill with tears as he asks, "Can I please kiss you?"

The way he says it is not said in a way that reassures me that things will get better, but I will not deny him. I take his face in my hands and kiss him gently. Then I slowly pull away.

"I'm sorry, Tessa."

I need to get out of here, so I say, "Don't be. Let's go for a ride." I stand and ask loudly, "Anyone want pizza?"

I reach out my hand, and he takes it. I pull him up, and then we walk out to the kitchen.

I know everyone was listening to us, but it's not because they're being nosy; it's because they love him just like I do.

Jade looks at me sadly, and I shake my head once. She

nods in understanding then answers, "Um, sure, let's get pizza."

I grab Lucas's keys off the counter, hold my hand out for Lucas, and announce, "We'll be back in thirty minutes." I look at Lucas and tell him, "I'm driving."

* * *

Behind the wheel of his SUV, I drive toward town, and the numbness begins wearing off. Anger is what I feel now. Anger, sadness, and loss hit me all at once, and my hands begin to shake as tears fill my eyes. Part of me wants nothing more than to make love to Lucas right here, right now so that I can experience that ultimate closeness that comes when two people truly love each other. I quickly pull off a side road, throw the vehicle in park, and look out the window.

How is it possible that I am parked in the very same place that Lucas and Tommy dropped us off that first time I rode with him?

As tears threaten to fall, I turn off the vehicle, throw open the door, and step out. I walk around the front of the vehicle, and my knees begin to shake, just as my hands are. It's the kind of shaking you feel when you are so cold that your teeth chatter, but instead of my teeth chattering, my knees go weak, and as I fall to them, my tears join in.

I hear the passenger door slam and gravel crunch beneath his sneakers as he runs to me, squatting down. He pulls me into his arms.

Crying harder than I ever think I have cried, I say, "You should have left me here and never looked back." I throw my arms around his neck, and he engulfs me in his big, strong arms, and we are knee to knee once again.

"Baby, I am so sorry." His voice breaks. "I am so fucking sorry."

I cry, and he cries … until no more tears fall. Then he pulls me up, arms still around me, walks me to the passenger side, opens the door, and I get in.

* * *

I sit in the vehicle while Lucas walks into the pizza shop to grab our order. A car pulls up beside us and parks. I don't bother looking. I really don't want anyone to see me. Perhaps I should invest in a white hat so that I, too, can cover my eyes when the pain becomes too unbearable.

It isn't until I hear her voice that I look up.

"Did you tell the farm girl the good news?" Sadi sneers.

I unbuckle my seat belt, throw open the door, and jump out. I begin running toward her and, as dumb as she is, she hops back in her car and locks the door. Lucas grabs me and pulls me away.

"Tessa, please don't," he whispers as he drags me back to the vehicle.

"I fucking hate her!" I scream and point to her as he opens the door and plops me in. "I fucking hate you!"

I didn't think it was possible for any more tears to fall, but they sure do.

I watch as Lucas grabs the pizzas off the hood of the vehicle, where he put them when he grabbed me and dragged me away before I broke that bitch's windshield. He then opens the rear driver's side door and sets them on the seat before he gets in.

Before he shuts his door, though, he yells at her, "Does that answer your question, Sadi?"

I see her smile in a way an evil villain would smile. "You better figure it out, Lucas. My child won't be around trash like that." She then glares at me. "Hey, farm girl, you may have gotten the crown, but I got the boy"—she places her hand over her belly—"forever!"

Lucas has to grab my arm and pull me away from the door as she starts her car, backs out, and leaves.

I pull my arm from him, pull my knees up on the seat, curling into the tiniest ball I possibly can, and sob.

When he parks in front of the barn, he gets out, walks around the vehicle, and opens my door.

"I'm so sorry, Lucas, I am so sorry. I just need a minute."

* * *

LUCAS

No part of me wants to give her a minute. Hell, I don't even want to give her a second, period. I just want to make this all go away. Instead, I walk around the vehicle, open the door behind the driver's door, grab the pizzas, and tell her, "Whatever you need, baby, just know I love you."

When she begins to shake, I know she's crying again, and I regret my words immediately, but I feel them to the bone. Hell, even deeper.

I have to be strong for her, no matter the pain I am feeling. I have no idea how I can even begin to make this up to her, but I swear I will die trying. I will do whatever it takes to make her smile again, no matter the consequences to me.

When I walk to the back door, it opens, and Jade asks, "How are you?"

I shake my head and shrug as I walk in through the mud room, to the kitchen, and set the pizzas on the table.

I can't let her stay out there. She shouldn't be alone in this. Her people are here, *as they always are*. So, I walk back outside, open the door, and lift her out of the seat.

"Lucas, I don't—"

"You aren't going to be alone. I won't allow it."

She doesn't fight it; she allows me to carry her in, and she clings to me as I do.

I walk past everyone in the kitchen and straight to the couch. I sit down, still holding her on my lap, and I don't let go. After a few minutes, or hours, maybe even days—fuck if I know time right now, all I know is pain, and the pain that I'm causing her—Jade comes in and sits next to us.

"What can I do to help?"

"Get her through this," I whisper.

"What about you?" Jade asks.

"I'll do what she wants." I kiss her head. "I think we both know what she's going to expect, no matter what the cost to her. So, again, Jade, you're going to need to get her through this."

"I will, Lucas, I promise."

"Thank you."

Tessa sleeps on my lap for over two hours, but it's not nearly enough time. It never will be with her.

Finally, she opens her eyes, lifts her head from my shoulder, and looks up at me. "I'm sorry."

"Please don't be, baby," I whisper to her.

"I wanted to kick her ass."

I smile. "Trust me; I know that feeling."

She doesn't smile; she begins to cry again, wrapping her arms tighter around me. "I love you, Lucas."

"I will always love you, Tessa." My eyes begin to burn. "Do you understand that? Always."

She's holding her breath and looks in pain as she forces herself to exhale.

It's crushing me. It's killing her. I should have known better than to believe that a girl like her would be untainted by a boy like me. Selfish, that's what I am, and I don't give a fuck right now. I kiss her, anyway.

She kisses me back, and then she pulls away, slides off my lap, and goes into the bathroom.

I look at Jade and nod to the door. "She needs you."

Behind the closed door, I can hear her muffled cry as she whispers, "I lost him, Jade."

"Tessa, I don't think so. He loves you," Jade attempts to soothe her.

I stand up and walk to the door, ever the masochist, and listen.

"We've done stuff, Jade. God, I was so close to sleeping with him. Can you imagine—"

"But you didn't have sex?"

"No, but other things."

"Oh, really. And how was that?" Jade asks.

"Wonderful. It made me feel closer to him, if possible ... love him even more. But I just can't do anything again. I have to let him do what he feels he needs to do, without complicating things any further."

"But, what do you want him to do, Tessa?"

I hear the shower start as she says, "The right thing."

I can't listen anymore. I walk over, sit on the couch, and try to think of what the girl I love thinks the right thing to do in this messed-up situation is.

After several minutes, she walks out, fresh from the

shower, and she's wearing one of my sweatshirts and a pair of shorts.

I pat my lap. "Come here, baby."

She sits on my lap, and I cover her with a blanket then hold her for a moment before kissing her and telling her, "I should go shower. Will you be here when I get back?"

"I'll be here, Lucas, always."

I have cried in the shower a few times in my life. It seems like the best place to do it. But it doesn't soothe the pain this time. I have not been able to come up with a solution, which is abnormal.

After I dress, I walk out and sit next to her, and she's holding a mug that reads, "*Ross Farms.*"

"There's a cup on the table for you. It's chamomile, supposed to be calming."

I pick up the cup and take a sip of the hot tea that I know damn well won't soothe the ache inside of me, but I absolutely appreciate the gesture.

"Dad and Alex went to get groceries." She sets her mug down. "Tommy and Jade left when you were in the shower. He said call him when you need him."

"Thank you."

"Is there anything you'd like to do? Talk about?"

Take that sweatshirt off and show you every move I have so you'll never forget me. So you'll never stop wanting me. Because I know damn well that you'll stop loving me soon. How could you not? is what I think. Instead, I ask, "Can I ask you some questions?"

She takes a sip of tea, peering over her mug at me, and gives me a slight nod.

"Do you think we can keep doing this, Tessa? Continue falling in love?" I scrub a hand over my face, trying to hide the vision of her before me as her eyes mist over. "Do you think you're going to be okay with me telling her to do this alone?"

She sets down her mug and sits crisscross, pulling the blanket over her lap. "I suppose not."

"Why?"

"Because I know who you are"—she reaches over and touches my chest—"in here, and I wouldn't want it to be any other way."

It fucking hurts to hear those words, but I didn't expect anything less, not from her.

"I know, Tessa, and that's why this is killing me. You love who you know I can be. And if I don't live up to that, you won't. So, either way, I'm going to lose you eventually."

She takes my hand and squeezes it. "I don't want to lose you, Lucas, and I am so afraid. The whole thing today … I wanted to kill her."

"I know. I'm sorry." I look down. "I want to be a good man, Tessa. I want to grow into the man you know is in here, but now I'm so confused. What do I do? What do you want me to do? Please, baby, just tell me."

"The right thing," she whispers.

"I don't love her. I never could. I love you, and that will never change." I grab her face, rub my thumb across her perfect lips, and ask, "Do you understand that, Tessa?"

"Yes," she says, tears burning in her eyes again. I can do nothing but hug her.

"I love you, Lucas." After a long embrace, she pulls away from me. "Will you still be my friend?"

"Will you want that?"

"I don't know, but I'll try." Her voice cracks.

"I will, too."

We fall asleep on the couch, just the way we should—in each other's arms.

***

TESSA

I wake up and walk outside to the deck, where I sit and look at the stars. Hands folded in prayer, I close my eyes and talk to God for the first time in too long.

"I'm so sorry for the way I have been acting." I begin to cry. "I know I've made mistakes, and I have to pay for them. I will, Lord, and I think I already am. I just ask that You please take care of Lucas. He's a good person with a kind heart, and I would have behaved worse if it weren't for him seeing something in me that I had forgotten. Please forgive my sins, and please God, he has to be okay. Please help him through this."

"Tessa?"

I look up and see Lucas standing at the door.

"Come back, baby. It's cold." He reaches out for my hand.

I wipe away tears as I stand, reach out, and take it. Then we walk inside together, and he sits on the couch then lays back, and I lay beside him, resting my head on his chest.

Never in my life have I been more comfortable than I am right now. Close to him is where I always want to be.

He holds me tightly, petting my head like Mom does to help me fall asleep.

Dad's voice wakes me, and when I open my eyes, I realize the sun is now up. I haven't slept this long for quite some time.

"Tessa, Lucas, time to get up and get ready for church."

I sit up and look at Lucas as he opens his sleepy eyes. I touch the side of his face and smile softly at him.

"Good morning, Lucas," I whisper.

"Good morning, Tessa," he whispers back.

All Over But the Crying

Chapter Thirty Two

LUCAS

Sitting in the Ross family pew, I watch as Tessa sings a song. I believe it's called "Blessings." I sure as hell hope, maybe even pray, that she has them in abundance. After me, she deserves them all.

At the end of the song, I see a tear fall from her eyes, and it takes every bit of strength inside of me not to get up and run to her, to wipe it away. Not just the tear, but all the pain I'm causing her.

Phoebe reaches over and grabs my hand, squeezes it, and doesn't let go.

When the song is finished, Jade reaches over, hugs Tessa, and wipes away the tear.

Phoebe whispers, "I know it doesn't feel like it now, and

it may not feel like it for some time, but I promise things will get better."

Unable to focus on anything else but her for the rest of the time the choir sings, I sit still as stone, a feeling I am not unfamiliar with.

When the sermon begins, I feel as if I'm being mocked by God. Lust is the topic, and up until I met Tessa Ross, I had known only that. In every Sunday school class that I have attended with Tommy, in the many years that I've known him, the teachings have always been of forgiveness. I would love to ask God how it was that, when I finally asked for it, I was not given it, but instead, I lost what was most important to me.

I see that Tessa is also struggling with today's lesson, but I also see that each blow that she has given, she takes with grace. There is no doubt that, after me, something good will come.

I close my eyes and ask God that He continue taking whatever He needs from me, as long as she doesn't have to deal with another heartbreak, being the selfish ass that I am. I also ask that He continue allowing us to be friends, unless the cause of such a thing would be devastating to her.

Jade smiles at her and wipes her tear. "You did great."

* * *

After church, Tessa, is quiet. We eat lunch, as we always do with her entire family, including Maggie, who hugs me before she leaves. It's almost embarrassing that she knows what a fuck-up I am.

Tessa sets to cleaning, and I decided to help John and his brother move some hay around. When I go back inside, she's already making dinner.

"Do you need any help?"

"Nope, all set. I think I'm gonna go for a walk." She closes the refrigerator and avoids looking at me.

"Want some company?"

"No, thanks. I have him." She pats Chewy then grabs his leash. She then removes his invisible fence collar and replaces it with the one that I bought her.

"Looks like he needs to size up."

"Yeah." She scratches behind his ear. "Time for change, my buddy."

At her words, my heart sinks lower, if that's at all possible, and I am rendered speechless. All I can do is watch her walk out the door with Chewy by her side.

It doesn't take but a minute of me standing here like a fool, trying to give her space, and all I can think about is the fact that she'll have all the space she needs soon enough. But, right now, whether she likes it or not, I know she needs me.

I watch her walk down the driveway, toward the field, before I start following her.

When I get to the barn, Alex steps out. "Word to the wise—you lucked out before. She doesn't like being followed down there."

"Her personal heaven, Lucas," John says. "Enter at your own risk."

"Thanks, man, but I can't let her do this alone."

I stay back as far as I can, giving her space, giving her time. When she begins walking into the woods, I follow.

I stand at the edge of the woods and watch as she walks down the path that leads to the water. Through the trees, I watch as she sits down. Then I hear say, "She's hateful and mean. No child deserves that. Lucas doesn't deserve this. God, please, please, please, help him give his child a good life."

I don't know how many times someone's heart can possibly break, but mine is being put to the test. I stand and wait as she hugs Chewy.

A lot of time passes, the sun is beginning to set now, when she finally stands up, hand full of rocks, and begins skipping stones. When her hand is empty, she starts the hike back up the hill. Stepping out of the woods, she sees me.

"Alex warned me not to come down here. They said it's your heaven. So, I waited here."

"Good move on your part. I may have kicked your butt, Links."

The use of the name *Links*, the way she says it, the way she smiles, I feel like I'm looking at a different person.

"Something is different with you." I search her eyes for an answer to the question inside my head. "You okay?"

She nods. "I suppose ... And you'll be, too."

"How are you so sure?"

"Because I decided I would be; now you have to do the same thing," Tessa gives me a soft smile. "Will you? Please?"

"If that's what you want." I nod.

"More than you know."

I grab her hand, and she freezes.

"Tessa, are you okay?"

"I'll be fine." She looks down at our hands. "But please, Lucas"—she swallows hard—"I can't ... I can't touch you."

"I'm sorry," I say, and not as if I understand. "But we are friends, right, Tessa?"

"Always." She starts to walk.

"So, friends hug, right?"

"Sure." She smiles sadly.

"Can I hug you? I mean, sometime?"

"Someday, just not right now," she whispers.

I can see in her eyes that the questions I'm asking are hurting her, but I am so confused at the metamorphosis she seems to be making before my eyes.

Normally, when I feel pain, there is always a way to make it better, but I know, as sure as I know the sun is setting, that she needs a break from me, and I need a break from seeing her pain.

Ever the selfish bastard, I tell her, "I need you now, Tessa."

"I need you, too, Lucas. And I'm right here. We ... Just, please, let this heal a bit first."

"Okay, baby."

She turns to me. "Thank you."

* * *

Stomach in knots still, since Tessa asked for space between us, when I need the complete opposite, I walk out and do the Sunday night thing— shoot with the guys. It's all pretty normal ... in unusual circumstances, but Tessa doesn't join us. In fact, when we come back inside, she has already gone to bed.

"John, I'm sorry, but I can't do this to her. I can't be here and see her hurting."

"Son, you don't have a choice."

Knowing that he's telling the truth, and also knowing it must kill him to see his daughter like this, too, but needing a break, I tell him, "All right then. I need to run home and grab some clothes and a couple books."

"Sure, just hurry back and drive carefully."

* * *

When I walk into my house, I feel the urge to break down. Hell I would even like to break things. But I know that will do nothing, so I find the quickest escape upstairs in my room, in a drawer, hidden behind my socks, instead.

I pull out my trusty bowl, confiscated from my mother's stash, and hit it a few times. Apparently, I hit it a few too many because, when I wake up, still high, I have a naked, familiar form lying beside me.

"I saw your car and decided to stop by. I know things are rough right now, but we both have needs."

Mouthful of cotton, I manage to mumble out, "Sadi ... get out."

"What? Are you afraid you'll get me pregnant?" she asks, and I glare at her. "It's been almost three months since I've had sex. I have needs, Lucas. You put out, or I will find someone else to poke this baby of yours in the head."

I push up off of the bed and stumble back against my dresser.

Sadi raises her knees and flattens her feet on my bed, allowing her legs to fall apart. "Tell me you haven't missed this, Lucas." She begins rubbing herself and spreading her legs wider.

I close my eyes and look away, not wanting to fall victim to my inner demon that knows all-too-well that sex is just sex, but that also, for a moment, it takes away all the pain. Then she moans, "Come here, Lucas. Fill me, please. I'm so wet, so hot."

I force myself to walk away and hear the bed creak then feet pattering on the hardwood floor. I grip the side of my bathroom doorway when she wraps her arms around me, pushes her hand down my track pants, and begins stroking me. She then ducks under my arm, stands in front of me, hand wrapped around my dick, and pushes down my pants.

"You wanna waste this, Lucas? You're hard for me." Sadi drops to her knees, licking her lips, and then rubs her tongue flat against my cock from root to tip. Unable to pull away, I close my eyes, not fighting her as she deep throats me and gags.

Stroking me harder and faster, as her tongue wets every inch of me, I do nothing to stop it.

"See? Feels good, doesn't it?" Sadi purrs.

"Either suck my cock or get the fuck out," I sneer. Rage is at a boiling point as I look down at her.

A victorious, malicious smile forms on her lips as she maneuvers me so my ass is against the wall. Knowing I will not win, knowing this is my fate—Tessa even said so herself in not so many words—I grab the back of her head and thrust fully into her mouth.

As saliva drips from the sides of her mouth, down her cheeks, I fuck her face hard, without giving a damn how she feels. In fact, I hope it's at least uncomfortable, because I know nothing in my life will ever be the same. I owe her no kindness, not after what she has done. But I know both of our beds have been made, and I'll be damned if we don't both have to sleep in the same messy bed we've made, apparently for the rest of our lives.

If she had not ended her last pregnancy, I would never have met Tessa Ross. Karma. I would not have known, and we would have been in the same damn position we are right now, except she would have gotten off, too.

She abruptly sits back on her heels and looks up at me.

"That's all you got, Sadi?"

"Are you gonna come?" She wipes the saliva from her chin.

I laugh, grab my erection, and stroke myself. "I don't need you to get me off, Sadi. My hand works just fine. It has for months."

"I'm not some farm girl, Lucas. I don't need flowers or have some fucking fantasy that you are going to love me. We both know love doesn't mean a thing. It ends, it's ugly, and the only thing either one of us truly needs is to get off once in a while." She stands, flattens her hands against the wall, and bends over in front of me. Then she looks over her shoulder at me and demands, "Fuck me and I'll leave so you can go back and wipe away the tears you would have caused her when she got tired of playing second string to your ego."

I grab the back of her hair, and my cock, and line it up before slamming into her. "This what you wanted, Sadi?"

"Fuck yes, Lucas!" she screams out as I bang her and she presses her hand against the wall, taking every bit that I give her. "Oh fuck, yes! Fuck me harder."

I hammer into her until she screams out her orgasm, all the while knowing that Tessa would never sound like that. She would never demand I fuck her harder, because we would have been perfect together.

I close my eyes and pull Tessa's beautiful face up into my memory, imagining how she would look at me, the sounds she would make for me, the way she would touch me back, the way I would never stop touching her, and then I come hard thinking of another girl while I am fucking someone I never wanted to fuck again.

Disgusted with myself, I pull out abruptly and turn away from her, needing the distance, only to be slapped in the face with my own reflection, my own mistake, staring back at me.

I can see Sadi's reflection, as well, and her evil smile as she says, "I've missed us."

I walk to the shower, turning on only the hot water. Then I step out of my pants and pull off my shirt. Stepping in, I allow the scalding hot water to rush over me as I scrub myself frantically, attempting to wash away my latest mistake.

Towel around my waist, I step out and into my room and see her. Lips curled, I tell her, "That never should have happened. I'm better than this now."

"That's just who you are, Lucas. But I seriously hope you'll be better than this for our child. But, even if you don't, I know me and this baby will be fine. You'll pay for the rest of your life for a mistake. Like father like son."

"Don't fucking come here again."

"I don't think that's going to happen. Me, you, and a baby, Lucas." She rubs her belly before pulling her shirt on. "See you at school tomorrow."

When she leaves, I get dressed then throw some things in my bag.

I pull my phone off the dresser, sit down, and call my dad. I tell him about the pregnancy and brace for him to lose his cool, but when he doesn't, I am struck dumb.

"You're still staying with the Rosses?" Landon asks.

"Yes."

"Do they know?"

"Yes, and John insisted I stay, anyway."

"How's Tessa taking it?"

My throat begins to burn, and I clear the lump from it before answering, "She's amazing, Dad. Strongest person I've ever met. We are going to try to be friends. And I certainly don't deserve that."

"Don't sell yourself short, son. You're pretty damn strong," Dad says with conviction.

I hear a woman's voice calling him. It's familiar, but I still ask. *Like father like son.* "Who's that, Dad?"

"Audrianna. She and the girls are here for the day," he says with a smile in his voice.

"Taking it slow, Dad?" I force a laugh.

"Yes, very. She's pretty insistent on it. We're actually going to counseling tomorrow."

"Good. Well, I have to get back before John wonders what happened to me. I'll see you Friday night at the State Championship, right?"

"Yes. Hopefully, all four of us will be there."

"Good. I want to see the girls. Goodnight, Dad."

"Goodnight, Lucas. I love you."

I don't remember the last time he said that to me, but I'll take it.

"I love you, too, Dad."

* * *

When I walk down the Ross's stairs in the morning and make my way into the kitchen, Tessa, as usual, is there, making breakfast. A quick sweep of the room, and I notice everyone's clothes have been ironed, lunches have been packed, and everything is business as usual. What's not usual is the fact that she's avoiding looking at me, even though I saw her spine stiffen when I walked in. She knows I'm in the room.

"Good morning, Tessa."

"Good morning, Lucas." She smiles, the kind that doesn't reach her eyes.

I did that to her.

"Did you sleep well?"

"I did. And you?" she asks, flipping a pancake.

I hate that our conversation is forced, but I continue on the path. "Yep. State Finals tomorrow, right?"

"Yes," Tessa answers, and I am painfully aware that she's trying to keep it together.

"You nervous?" I ask.

She shakes her head.

I know she's not nervous. She's Tessa, the girl who takes each situation in stride.

Selfishly, I ask, "Is it all right if I come?"

"Sure, that would be great."

"Good. Are you going to Alex's game?"

"Yes, Lucas, and to yours."

"Can I hug you yet?"

She looks down as she walks toward me. "Yes."

I reach out and grab her, pulling her closer. As if it's natural, she wraps her arms around my neck and kisses my cheek.

I lean down and brush my lips across hers, and tears immediately well in her eyes.

"Tessa, don't cry. Baby, please … I'm sorry," I say as I wipe them away.

She steps back, quickly turns, and then she walks to the bathroom. I follow, open the door, and walk in.

"Tessa, please. God, I am so fucking stupid, so selfish."

She takes a deep breath and allows me to wipe away the rest of the tears. "You can't kiss me, Lucas, okay?"

Pain resonating in my chest, anger at myself worrying my head, I say, "I won't … I won't do it again. I'm so sorry."

* * *

When we pull into the school, we both get out of the vehicle, and Alex follows.

Sadi pulls up beside us and parks.

I see Tessa's lips curl, and Alex sees it, too. He wraps his arm around her and guides her toward school.

I look at Sadi and glare.

"What? No kiss?"

I ignore her, but she continues.

"Did you tell her that you and I had sex last night?"

I reach out and grab her arm, squeezing. "You better keep your mouth shut. She and I are through. But you need to know I love her, and not a damn thing you do will stop that. I'm working through some stuff here, hoping that I can be a good father and we can parent together, and all Tessa is doing is being my friend. I promised her I would try." I lower my voice to an angry whisper. "Last night was a big blurry mistake. Leave her alone and thank God she made me promise to try with you."

Sadi yanks her arm away. "Fine, as long as you don't keep fucking her."

"It was never like that with her, Sadi. It was all here." I hold my hand over my heart and look at her, hoping she sees the truth in my words. "Don't you get it? *I love her.*"

"You loved me once, too, and before this baby is born, you will again." With that, Sadi storms away.

* * *

When I open my locker, my stomach sours as letters, panties, and even bras spill out onto the hallway floor. Tessa walks by and sees it then looks away as if I wasn't even there.

We stayed away from each other all day in school, which isn't easy when you share classes together, lunch, and study hall. And when she came out for practice, she didn't even look at the football field. It fucking hurt. But, at this point, my own pain means little. In my lifetime, I've grown used to it. But her pain ... her pain is harsher than any I've experienced.

Walking into the Ross home after school, I hear Alex tell Tessa, "I started the hot tub for you. Phoebe said you may need it. She said you went real hard at practice today."

"Thanks, Alex. Dinner's in the oven. Maybe after that, I will go out. You gonna come, too?"

As I walk into the house, Alex nods to her.

She looks at me and asks, "How are you, Lucas?"

"Good." I hang my backpack up beside the door. "Anything I can do to help?" My gut instinct causes me to wrap my arm around her, pull her into me, and kiss the side of her head.

"Lips off, Links," she forces herself to joke and playfully pushes me away.

"Sorry, baby," I whisper, but she doesn't reply.

The kitchen timer goes off, and she jumps up to get dinner out of the oven. I know she's just putting much-needed distance between us.

"We okay?"

She nods once.

"What's for dinner?"

"Chicken shit."

"Excuse me?"

Alex laughs as he walks back into the kitchen. "Look at it, man. Looks just like it."

John, Kendall, and Jake all walk in from outside.

John asks, "You kids hitting the hot tub after dinner?"

"Yes, Phoebe said Tessa overdid it today," Alex says.

John squeezes her shoulder before walking over to wash his hands.

I hate what I am making this family feel. A family already struggling.

Blue Love

* * *

After dinner is cleaned up, I watch as Tessa runs upstairs. Even in a one-piece swimsuit that shows little skin, she's the most beautiful thing I've ever seen or touched. When she returns, she has a towel wrapped around her.

"You going in?" Alex asks me.

"Are you?"

"Yep."

"Okay, then," I say as I stand up then make my way upstairs to change.

When we walk out to the hot tub, Tessa is already in, her back to us, ears covered in headphones. She has a towel partially over her face and is singing along to 2Pac's "I Get Around." My lips twitch at listening to her rap. Then Alex climbs in and she jumps, pulling the towel off her head.

"Hey, Alex." She laughs ... until she sees me. Then she does a sweep of my body, and a part of me that even I'd like to slap right now takes great pride in how she's checking me out.

Then she asks, "You getting in or do you need an invitation?"

I get in.

We sit quietly, Tessa keeping her eyes closed, me feeling like a perve watching the swell of her tits rise and fall, wanting to make her come again, because she deserves to have someone give her every joy in the world. And now I feel like a dick because, until her, I didn't understand that there was something better than getting off, that there was a place where lust met its superior—love—and made everything better.

Busted, I think as she opens her eyes and sees me creeping. Then she quickly closes them again.

"Alex!" John yells. "Phone's for you!"

Alex stands up. "Phoebe."

"Tell her I said hey," Tessa says as he gets out.

And now we're alone.

Once he's inside, I move over and take his vacated spot next to her, and take her hand.

She sighs.

"Sorry, baby, but this is awful. I miss you."

Eyes still closed, she asks, "How can you miss me, Lucas? I'm right here."

"This may come as a shock, but I miss the talking."

She opens her eyes and looks at me. "If you let go of my hand, I may be able to actually relax."

I lift her hand, kiss the back of it, and then let go.

She rolls her eyes. "So, what shall we talk about, my friend." She emphasizes *friend*.

"Where were you all day?" I ask.

"Avoiding conflict, avoiding seeing you, basically avoiding a breakdown. This morning was awful." She laughs but sadly.

"I'm sorry." *For more than you can even imagine.*

She looks between my eyes and sees that I am visibly upset, even though she doesn't know, and never can, about the mistake I made. "It's going to take some getting used to."

"I am so pissed that I didn't meet you before all that happened."

"Things happen for a reason." She nods with conviction, as if she's talking herself into believing what she just said. Then she whispers, "Can we talk about something else, please?"

"Sure, what can we talk about, baby?" I instinctively grab her hand.

She smiles. "How about what is acceptable between friends when they are of the opposite sex?"

"Okay, that'll be interesting. I have to be honest with you; I have never had a female friend."

She smiles genuinely then gifts me with a giggle. "Why does that not surprise me?"

"Let me have the rules."

"Let's start with appropriate touch. Hugging; a quick hug when you're excited or happy, and a longer one when someone needs comfort. Kisses; a quick one like the ones you give me on the head are sweet and show that you're there and being supportive. A kiss on the cheek in a situation like a death or congratulations, but never on the mouth. Hand holding is for support, but not an everyday thing."

"Well, what about when someone seems sad? What should I do when you look sad, baby?"

She ignores my question. "Now, let's talk about nicknames. Baby is for people who love each other as more than friends, and FYI, I used to love it, but it kind of stings now. So maybe use a last name or something fun."

"How about TT?"

She splashes me.

"Tessa the Terrible, Tessa the Temptress, Tessa the Terrific ..." I look down at the girls. "Tessa with the Terrific, Tasty T—"

"What are you guys talking about?" Alex asks, returning to the hot tub.

"Male and female friendship appropriateness." Tessa laughs. "Any advice?"

"Respect," Alex states.

"All right then, that's a lot to comprehend. I'll try."

Tessa stands up, a glimmer of lust in her eyes as I look her over. "It's a deal. Goodnight."

* * *

I wake from a dead sleep to the sound of Tessa screaming. I grab the magnet that I planned to use to disarm the alarm in the future and run to her room.

I watch as she tosses and turns, whimpering, crying, and I slide my arms under her and lift her up. Then I sit back on her bed and hold her.

"Tessa, baby, are you okay?" I ask as I kiss the top of her head over and over again, freaking out inside at the sounds she's making.

Tessa shakes her head as she wraps her arms around my neck. She then begins to shake, and I grab her blanket and pull it up around her while rocking her back and forth in whispering hushes.

In a voice rough from sleep, Tessa whispers, "Lucas, kiss me. Please kiss me."

I do as she asks. I kiss her. I start with her lips then her neck, and then I pull away.

The moon is shining through her window, reflecting the tears in her beautiful blue eyes.

"You look so beautiful. Even crying, nothing compares. Did you have a bad dream, baby?"

Her eyes flutter shut and, in a hushed voice, she tells me, "There was an accident with four people, and people died. I don't know who, but I know I loved them. Lucas, you have to promise me you'll be careful, please?" She then opens her eyes, and I nod my head. "No, say it. Promise me you'll be careful."

"I promise, Tessa, but it was just a dream, okay?"

"Please stay with me tonight," Tessa asks.

"Tessa, you really don't want that. You're just upset right now, baby."

Arms around my neck, she pulls me down and kisses me. It's full, it's deep, and it's full of just as much passion, maybe even more, than she's ever had for me.

Pulling away, she says, "I love you, Lucas. Please, be careful. Please, I love you." She kisses me again then pulls away. "Do you hear me?"

"Yes, baby, but—"

"Then why didn't you answer me?" She starts to tear up again.

"You didn't give me a chance, Tessa. I promise I will be careful."

"Good." She rests her head against my chest again and wraps her arms around me.

Within seconds, she's asleep.

* * *

I wake to her still wrapped around me and look down as her eyes open. She looks shocked.

"Good morning, baby."

"How did you get in here?" she whispers, looking over at Kendall, who is the soundest sleeper possibly in the entire world.

"A magnet. You had a bad dream. We can talk about it later. I need to sneak out of here before your dad or Alex wake up. I love you, Tessa Ross." I bend down to kiss her, and her eyes widen. I bypass her lips, the intended target, and kiss the top of her head.

On The Field

Chapter Thirty Three

TESSA

Heart beating against my chest, I walk into the arena and look around at the full bleachers. Thousands of people are here to watch tonight's game.

We run drills and practice plays, warming up. I'd rather be busy on the field than alone with my thoughts, wondering what the hell happened last night, what kind of dream did I even have. All I know is that Lucas cares enough that he held me all night long. Oh, and that I'm thankful Dad, Alex, Jake, and Kendall, who was sleeping in the same room, were none the wiser.

After warmups, when we walk off the field, I look up in the bleachers and see my parents, Molly, Kendall, and Jake walk in and take their seats. Then I see Alex, Ryan,

Blue Love

Tommy, and Lucas following behind. My heart skips a beat when Lucas flashes me his signature smile and gives me a wink.

I know that I should not still be feeling this way for him. And I know I have to get over it soon, but deep down, I have hope that maybe, just maybe, there is still a chance for us. If all I can have with him is a friendship, I'll take that, too.

"All right, Lady Saints, bring it in." Coach V blows his whistle and motions for us to huddle.

Once on the field, nothing else matters, I play hard. Honestly, I play harder than I ever have, because the dream of playing this game, the championships, was on Jade's and my bucket list for senior year, and I'll be damned if we lose.

We are two goals behind, going into the second half, and I am exhausted, but I've been through harder things than a freaking field hockey game.

Somehow, I manage to get the ball on the first play and make a goal. Now we are only one down.

In the fourth quarter, I get hit in the head with a stick, knocking me down. I quickly jump up then feel more than sweat trickling down my forehead. I reach up and pat the spot that hurts the most, then look at my fingers and see blood.

As the officials card the girl who hit me, I run off the field, straight to the first-aid kit, making sure my back is to Coach V as I quickly clean myself up. As I'm putting on a Band-Aid, Coach V turns me around.

"Ross, don't even think about it," Coach V tries to stop me from putting the Band-Aid over my head. "You aren't going back on that field with a gash on your forehead."

I stomp my foot. "This is my last game, Coach, and I am *not* sitting the bench. We're one behind, and I know I can get another goal to tie it up. Then we go into overtime and—"

"You see this shirt, Ross? You see the word *Coach* on it?"

I scowl at him.

"Yours doesn't say that, now does it? Sit your ass down and let me look at that head."

When the crowd erupts in applause, I look at the field and see Phoebe powering toward the goal. She swings and hits the ball, making her first goal of the game and tying us up.

"I want on the field, Coach V," I demand.

"Looks like you're going to need some stitches, so you have one of two choices, neither being the field. It's the bench or an ambulance."

The next play, Becca passes the ball back to Phoebe, who takes it in again, right before the whistle blows, ending our game.

I stand up, clapping, hooting, and howling, and then ... I throw up.

Once my stomach is empty, I do as Coach V suggests and sit my ass on the bench. I watch as Mom makes her way down the bleachers toward the field and see Lucas right behind her.

I push myself up and run to the field to celebrate with my team, where I throw up again.

Before I know what's going on, Lucas scoops me up in his arm, and I hear Mom tell Coach V that they're taking me to the hospital, that she was sure I had a concussion.

Lucas drives, and Mom rides with us. I sit in the passenger seat with the bag in case I throw up again.

At the hospital, we're seen quickly, and I receive three stitches in my hairline. Mom was right; I have a concussion. She wants me to come back to her house, but I insist on going back to the farm, wanting to sleep in my own bed. She doesn't fight me.

When we drop her off, she asks that Lucas makes sure to wake me up every couple hours, and if I throw up again, to make sure John is aware and to call her immediately. She also says, if I'm hard to wake up, he should call the ambulance, and she gives him the number. Lucas agrees to all those things, and I'm honestly pretty shocked she allows it.

Once we're alone, I give him a weak smile and say, "We won."

"You kicked ass, baby. But seriously, you need to chill. Never seen a girl play as rough as you do." He reaches out and takes my hand, giving it a squeeze. Then he reaches in front of me and opens the glove box, pulls out a little black box, and hands it to me.

"Open it and read the back."

Inside the black box is a silver necklace with two hockey sticks crossing one another, and on the back, it's engraved. "*LYA, Lucas*."

"It's beautiful." I squeeze his hand now, and he pulls it up and gives it a kiss. I tell him, "Thank you."

"Before you get freaked out, it's just a friendly gesture. I do love you, Tessa, even if we can only be what we are … for now."

My heart does what it always does when he's around, but it also hurt, shrinking with the realization that this is all we can be, and my aching head wonders what he means by *for now*.

Is it wrong to hope that maybe, just maybe, someday I can kiss him again?

After we get home, I lay on the couch in the living room, and Lucas insists on sleeping in the chair. He tells Dad that he promised Maggie he would.

I fall asleep but wake up when Lucas snuggles up to me on the couch.

"This is what a friend would do, Tessa, and I promised your mom I'd keep an eye on you."

Every three hours, an alarm clock that he had brought down from his room goes off, and every three hours, he gives me a soft kiss on the lips.

Each time he does, I whisper, "I'm still alive."

* * *

By Wednesday, I'm no longer avoiding the lunchroom, my friends, or Lucas. I shouldn't be surprised when Sadi walks by and makes a snide comment to me. I am surprised at my ever-growing maturity in the fact that I don't give it right back to her. Instead, I ignore it.

Lucas seems impressed, which makes me happy.

I find myself touching the necklace that lays against my collarbone to make sure it's still there. Friendship or otherwise, it's still a token of love. A love that, as quickly as it began, is being threatened.

It is said that you never forget your first, and I understand the context means the first person who you've slept with, but the words ... the words are what matters. My first love is, and always will be, Lucas Links, and it will never fully go away.

After lunch, my head hurts pretty badly, so I go to the nurse and ask to lay down. Of course she allows it. I sleep until the last bell.

* * *

Walking up to my locker, Jade looks at me with concern. "Are you feeling okay?"

"A little sore."

"We're going to stay and watch the guy's practice. Do you feel up to it?" Jade asks.

"No, I am pretty sure Crazy would get a little anxious. Besides, I'm going to run to the mall."

I head to the guys' locker room and yell in, "Hey, Alex Ross, I need the keys to run some errands."

Lucas walks out in black shorts, drying his hair then his chest.

He showers before practice? I wonder.

"Take mine, TT." He hands me his keys.

"You sure?"

"What are friends for? Just pick me up after practice."

"Thanks."

"Whatcha looking at?"

I roll my eyes because he damn well knows what I'm looking at and start to turn around, but he grabs my arm, stopping me.

I feel his breath against my neck when he whispers, "You like what you see, baby, don't look away."

I turn, dead set on reminding him of the rules of friendship, when he pops his pecs and winks.

I roll my eyes. "Oh please. All that"—I gesture to his chest and huff—"is awful."

He chuckles. "Uh-huh."

I stomp my foot and walk away.

Once in the parking lot, I get a little nervous about driving a brand-new vehicle until I see Sadi glaring at me. Then I lift my chin and march my ass to the driver's side, thinking, *Fuck you, bitch.*

I head to the mall where I use all my leftover birthday

gift cards and money I've been saving. I buy some new undies and bras at Victoria Secret. Then I go to the jewelers and purchase two sliver chains; one for Alex and one for Lucas. I also buy helmet charms and have them engraved. Lucas's is "*LYA*," and Alex's is "*BLESSED*."

* * *

When I pull into the school parking lot, I do so as Lucas walks out of the building. I pull up, and he jumps in as I watch Sadi, who is sitting in her little sports car, throw the door open. Me? I hit the gas.

Lucas smirks, knowing exactly why I did that, and asks, "Want to go get Chinese?"

I nod. "Yep."

I pull over in front of China Wok, hop out, and run in to grab the order he placed while I drove.

While waiting, I watch out the window and see him on the phone. He's pissed. Like, really pissed. I don't think I've ever seen him so pissed. Then he hangs up and starts to look toward the window, and I duck out of the way so he doesn't see me.

Food in hand, I walk out and hop in, seeing him grinning as he looks in my damn bags.

"Boy shorts, Tessa? That is so hot. With matching bras front clasps, no less." Lucas smiles. "Someone was feeling some sort of way, huh?"

Embarrassed, I quickly change the subject. "Who were you fighting with on the phone?"

"Her."

"Oh yes, *her*," I say, making a terrified face. "Sometimes, I forget."

He shakes his head and pulls his hat down. "Those are the times you smile."

"Not happy that I took your vehicle, huh?"

"No, happy isn't the word I would use to describe it, but it's none of her business," Lucas says, trying to convince us both that everything has truly changed.

I reach over and squeeze his hand. "It's going to be okay, Lucas. You've got this."

He takes a deep breath as he links his fingers with mine, and I hold his hand the entire way home.

Because friends do that.

* * *

I wake up crying from a dream, an accident, a horrible accident again, and Lucas comes in and holds me again, kisses me again, and calms me … again.

I also wake up in his arms again.

I easily slide out of bed but spend a lot of time just watching him sleep, knowing that, between me and everything crazy going on around him, he has more than likely lost more sleep than I can imagine.

I quickly pull my nightshirt off, put on my black bra, and throw on a light blue, ribbed turtleneck. Then I step out of a pair of undies and step into black lacey boy shorts.

It surprises me how much I love the feeling of being desired and hope that, with sexy underclothes, I can feel that way without the touching.

"That's one heck of a sight to wake up to," Lucas whispers, startling me.

I quickly bend down and grab the jean skirt that I chose to wear today. Yes, a skirt. It may not be my norm, but the jean part is. I figure it'll help me work my way to a skirt that's not denim someday.

"That's just as good." The bed squeaks as he stands up.

"Sorry, I didn't want to wake you. I don't think I've let you get much sleep lately," I tell him.

"Please, don't apologize. I wish I could wake up to that every day of my life, friend."

His hair is messy, and his perfectly ripped upper body is bare.

Me, too, I think as I pull him in for a friendly *thank you* hug.

"Oh," I gasp when I feel his erection against me. "You had better go ... I don't know ... take care of that before anyone wakes up." Then I rush him out the door and close it behind him.

Within minutes, I hear Dad head up the stairs to turn off my alarm.

"Oops," Dad mumbles beyond the door. "Must have forgotten to turn it on."

"Tessa," Kendall whispers.

"I'm sorry. Did I wake you?" I whisper as I hurry toward her bed.

"Yes. If he's going to come in here every night, maybe you should wear more pajamas."

"I'm so sorry, Kendall. It won't happen again."

"It's okay. I won't tell. He makes you stop crying. He's not doing anything wrong. But you need to wear more pajamas, okay?"

"Okay, Kendall." I lean down and push her hair away from her face. "Go back to sleep. You have another hour."

When I walk out, Lucas is waiting in the hallway.

"Thank you," I whisper as he pulls me in and gives me an erection-free hug.

Lips against the top of my head, he whispers, "I wouldn't want to be anywhere else."

Then we walk downstairs and part ways. He heads to the bathroom, and I head to the kitchen to throw in the

Blue Love

cinnamon rolls that Kendall and I mixed up to refrigerate overnight.

Once I've cut them up and put them in the oven, Lucas walks out and asks, "Can I hug you?"

Smiling, I hug him. "I think, after the game Friday night, we should invite some people up to camp." Alex walks into the kitchen, and I step back. "What do you think about camp Friday night, Alex?"

"Sounds like a plan," Alex says on a yawn.

After we all stuff ourselves with cinnamon rolls, we head to school.

* * *

Jade, Phoebe, and I ride with my parents and siblings to the game. And, due to traffic, we get there minutes before the game starts. I look out at the field as we make our way to our seats and notice that every player on the other team is big, like Alex, Ryan, Lucas, and Tommy big, and the rest of our team ... is so not. Like our teams' stars, they look like college athletes.

Once at our seats, I shove two fingers in my mouth and whistle. Alex looks up, and I wave. Then I watch as he elbows Lucas, who blows out an obvious breath then smiles.

Kendall smiles softly. "Looks like he was waiting on you."

I wrap my arm around her. "Us. They were waiting on us. We're all family."

I then blow a kiss, and Kendall giggles.

"Was that for our *family*?"

I mess up her hair and laugh. "It sure was."

I hear my name from the direction we just came and glance over.

Lucas's sisters come running toward me.

I open my arms and hug them. "Hello, princesses."

As they begin asking me about Chewy, I interrupt, "Your brother is looking up here at you two."

He waves, and they yell his name and wave back. Then they take off their coats, exposing jerseys that say, "*Team Links.*" Totally adorable.

"How are you doing, Tessa?" Audri asks, hugging me.

"I'm good. How are you?"

"I'm actually kind of wonderful." She smiles. "Thanks to you, I think Lucas gave me some great advice, so thank you."

Landon walks over, his arms full of snacks and little pom poms for the girls. "Hello, Tessa." He looks at me and scowls, "What happened to your head?"

I shrug. "Championship field hockey game."

"Did you win?"

"Yes."

"Way to go," Landon says, patting me on the shoulder. "Lucas and Audrianna tell me that you were pretty pissed off at my son the last time we met. I would have never known. Tell me, why did you act like nothing was bothering you?"

"I wanted him to win, and apparently, I'm a good actress."

He looks me up and down, in a different way now, then asks, "Are you acting now, with everything that has come to light?"

"No, Mr. Links. I know your son is a great guy, and forgive me if I sound, well, my age, but I love him and want what's best for him, regardless of what is happening. We're friends, and I hope we always will be."

"That isn't typical of your age, Tessa … Thank you."

Landon shocks me by leaning forward and hugging me, arms full.

* * *

The game started as expected—fiercely. Lucas was sacked for the first time all season. The opposing team obviously spent a lot of time on watching their tapes and knew the Saints were big on passing and blocked almost every chance Lucas had to do so. At the end of the first quarter, Lucas threw a forty-yard pass to Tommy, and he made the first touchdown of the game. He held up his J, and Jade smiled.

By halftime, they were tied. Landon got up and walked toward a row of what looked like college scouts and shook their hands, playing what I assume is the game anyone whose high school son is being scouted should play.

Me? My stomach is in knots with worry about him. Alex, Tommy, and Ryan can only do so much to protect him.

"You okay?" Mom asks.

"Give me a helmet and pads, and I'd feel better," I admit.

Audrianna grips my shoulder from behind and gives it a squeeze.

The beginning of the second half, Lucas passes the ball at the fifty-yard line and another first occurs—an interception.

I cringe. "Shit."

"Mouth, Tessa Ross," Mom scolds as Lucas pivots and runs after number 72, leaving the rest of both teams in his dust.

At the ten, Lucas tackles him, and the ball is loose. Lucas recovers it.

The whole Blue Valley side of the bleachers erupts in cheers. No one sits back down until the quarter changes. The rest of the game is Watkins against Lucas.

"I think I love Tommy, too," I yell over the crowd to Jade, because Tommy is like a fucking animal, throwing down everyone who tries to sack him, and Alex ... well, Alex catches a pass and makes a touchdown, tying the game in the last minute.

"Lot of game left." Landon claps. "Lot of game."

Ryan makes a killer play, intercepting the ball and running it back to the five.

On our feet, we watch as Lucas pulls his arm back to pass to Alex and gets tagged by an opposing player, spins in a circle, but before falling, he tosses the ball to Ryan, who dives over two of Watkins' players and into the end-zone.

The stadium erupts again, and Jade grabs me and Phoebe, pulling us toward the stairs. Screaming and laughing, we run down and rush the field with the rest of the Blue Valley's fans.

I run to Alex first then stop when I realize Phoebe should be the first to him.

I look around and see Lucas pushing through his gaggle of groupies and hurrying toward me. I meet him halfway, and as he lifts me, I wrap my arms around him.

"You are seriously amazing. Great game, rock star."

He smashes his lips against mine, and I can't help but smile against them while I wiggle out of his arms.

Smiling at each other, both like idiots, I see his dad walk up behind him and grip his shoulder.

I nod, and Lucas turns, and then he and his father hug.

"You played your best game today, son. I'm so proud of you."

"Feels like I played my first." Lucas laughs. "Gonna feel like it tomorrow when this adrenaline wears off, too."

Then the nails on the chalkboard, the cold bucket of water, the worst thing you could imagine at the worst possible time, shows up. She pushes up on her toes and kisses his cheek. "Great job, Lucas."

"Thanks," he says, looking right through her and toward his team.

He looks at Landon, who has the best poker face in the world, and I want to kiss him because, this time, I can tell he's here for his son, because he doesn't even acknowledge Sadi.

Landon nods, and Lucas looks in that direction. His sisters and Audri are coming for him, all smiling as they shake pom poms.

I bet Sadi wishes she brought hers ... bitch.

Number 72 from the other team runs up, smiling. "Good game, guys."

He looks at me. "Your boyfriend kicked my ass out there today, Ross."

"He's not her boyfriend," Sadi says loudly.

He smiles, winks, and looks me up and down. "Good to know. See you in two weeks, Tess."

"So, did you tell her yet?" Sadi asks Lucas.

I answer for him, so he doesn't have to deal with her shit right now when he should be celebrating. "Sadi, of course he told me. We are friends, remember?"

"So, he told you we had sex when he was living at your house?" Sadi sneers at me.

I turn and walk away before I lose my shit and punch a lying pregnant bitch.

* * *

As I get closer to my family, I see number 72 standing with them and find it odd until I see a man I recognize with him.

"Hey, Tessa, do you remember this guy?" Dad asks.

I give 72 an apologetic look. "No, sorry, I don't."

"His dad comes up every year for a week and hunts with us. He's joining him this year, too," Dad announces.

I nod to him. "Cool."

He puts his arm around my shoulder. "Tess, you're breaking my heart. How could you forget me?" He laughs. "We used to shoot bow together."

Gasping, I turn and look at him. "Benji?"

He grins. "You ready for me?"

"I used to kick your butt. I hope you've gotten better."

"We'll see." He steps back and looks me over. "Damn, you've changed."

I roll my eyes.

"No boyfriend, Ross?" Ben asks.

"Nope."

"Great. Then you're going to have to let me take you out some night," Ben says. "As in a date."

"I guess it all depends on how well you shoot. I certainly couldn't go out with someone whose butt I can kick." I lift my nose in the air. "And you're going to have to redeem yourself after that play."

We both laugh, and then he pulls me into a one-armed hug.

Lucas walks toward us, eyes all masked up.

I nod toward Ben. "Lucas, this is Ben."

Ben unwraps his arm from me and holds out his hand. Lucas reluctantly shakes it.

"Hey, Lucas, this one didn't remember me. Our fathers went to college together. They hunt together every year,

Blue Love

and Tess here"—Ben puts his arm back around me—"used to kick my ass when we shot bow. Do you hunt?"

Lucas nods. "I will be this year."

"Great. Then I'll see you both in a week." He looks back at me. "And you can bet your ass I'm gonna win that date."

After he walks away, I smile at Lucas, who's still all masked up, and tell him, "I got you and Alex something, so when you get back, check in your glove box. I'll be setting up at camp." I reach out and give his hand a squeeze. "See you later."

* * *

I'm pulling out the cupcakes I made earlier as Jade sets plates on the counter, Phoebe stirs the chili, and Becca dumps ice in an ice bucket that Aunt Josie let us have—when she turned a blind eye to us carrying beer out the back door—that says "*Budweiser*" on it as the guys walk in.

The people we invited from the game all begin whistling and cheering. The entire team lights up. Well, everyone except Lucas.

He's looking at me, and he looks incredibly uneasy. I assume he's grieving the loss of all we planned for tonight, but it is what it is. I smile and hold up the cupcake with his Jersey number on it and the piped white frosting that says, "*ROCK STAR*," and grin big and stupidly. His lips twitch as he walks toward me, and I set his cupcake back on the platter.

"Cheer up, buttercup." I hip-check him and start to walk past him.

He grabs my hand. "We need to talk." Then he pulls me outside.

Once outside, he lets go of my hand and pulls the

necklace out from under his hoodie. "First of all, I love the necklace. Thank you."

I smile. "You deserve—"

"You don't have to pretend with me, okay? It's killing me, Tessa. I know I deserve for you to be pissed. I deserve it. So, stop holding back. Give me what I deserve."

Confused, I tilt my head.

"You held it together at the game after she told you. And even though it was a mistake and you and I aren't together anymore, I respect you enough that I want to explain. I want you to know I was fucked up."

When realization hits, the pain from what he's saying hits me so hard that all I can manage to say is, "Oh."

He begins, "It meant nothing."

It meant nothing? It. Meant. Nothing?

"You slept with her?" My voice squeaks, and I swallow bitter tears. "Again? When? Why?"

After his nod, he frantically tries to explain, but I hear nothing but the blood boiling inside of me. When he finally closes his mouth, I manage to force a smile, which I am sure looks more like a sneer, and say, "Okay, then." Then I turn to walk away.

"Tessa, wait," he says, grabbing my elbow.

I jack it away and turn. "Do. Not. Touch. Me."

"Tessa, baby, it was just—"

I hold up a hand, telling him to stop. "Lucas, I'm not sure what you want me to say. Should I congratulate you on your ability to manage stress by getting high? Or give you an *atta boy* because women throw themselves at you?" I bark out a disgusted laugh. "Although I would hardly call *that* a woman?" At this moment, I realize the sound of blood boiling happens right before rage happens. "Or maybe I should scold you on your problem controlling this?" I step to him, reach down, grab his dick, and squeeze so damn hard as I stare him dead in the eyes. Then I let go and step back. "You have a problem. A couple of them, actually. But I'm not yours, and you are absolutely not mine."

I turn to leave, and he again grabs my elbow.

"Don't you touch me. You make me sick."

"Tessa, I love you. I'm sorry."

The fact that I know him well enough to know he believes that calls pity for him and makes me realize I'm fucking pitiful myself.

"I still want you to be okay. I care deeply for you, and I will pray, Lucas, that someday you can see how wrong you are about your feelings for me if you could do that. If you could *fuck her*. Our friendship was never a friendship, because I loved you so much more than that, no matter the hurt it caused me. But that's where I was wrong. I said one thing and wanted something else desperately. I was hurt then. Now I feel betrayed and disgusted at myself. You should be ashamed of yourself; I certainly am ashamed of myself. You won't lie to me again, because now that I know you've lied to me, and yours—"

"I've never lied to you, Tessa."

I turn and walk toward camp, huffing, "I suppose not. How very noble of you."

I walk inside and find Jade.

She looks at me and immediately asks, "Tessa, what's wrong?"

"Tell Tommy that Lucas needs a friend right now." I clear my throat. "And Jade, right now I need to fall apart, so can you meet me at the pond after you see that Tommy takes care of Lucas?"

CLEANUP CREW

Chapter Thirty Four

LUCAS

Tessa stayed with her mother for two days. The first day, Sunday, was Halloween, and I went with Tommy to his church, just to give her a break. When I returned later that afternoon, she was gone. From what I gathered, from all the kids who showed up on the Ross's family's porch, Tessa was missed by more than just me. All the little ghouls and goblins asked where she was. John or Alex explained she took Kendall and Jake out with Maggie.

John and Alex also treated me no damn differently than they ever had. I have a suspicion they don't know, and that pisses me off because she should be able to count on them, and I am single-handedly fucking that up.

The next day, at school, she didn't have to avoid me. I came into class last minute and left first. Lunch and study hall, I spent a lot of time at the gym.

After school, I spent three hours with Coach Saville and the guidance counselor, applying for colleges. To be honest, they did everything for me. I just sat there, numb.

When I leave school, Sadi is in the parking lot, pulling up right next to my vehicle.

She steps out of her car, and I brush past her.

When she grabs my arm, I pull it away.

"You do not want to deal with me right now, Sadi."

"Real mature," she huffs.

I turn and point a finger in her face. "*Mature*? *You* want to counsel *me* on maturity?" I snap my mouth shut, not wanting the vile things dancing on the tip of my tongue to drip out, so I give it to her straight. "As the girl carrying my child"—I hit myself in the chest—"*I* do not want to let loose on you, but you listen, and you fucking hear me, Sadi. You *will not* win against me, and I do not want my win to cause my kid to live a life where he or she is stuck in the middle of an eighteen-year battle, so you better back the fuck down and start by understanding that I have no choice but to live at the Ross's, so get that you're hurting me more than you're hurting Tessa with your bullshit, and that is not something you want to do."

She slaps my finger away. "You don't hold the cards, Lucas," she says as she turns and walks away. "Keep in mind that I can end it whenever the fuck I want to."

"You think I don't know that!" I scream at her. "Yet you stood there the other day, dealing out demands, and think I give a shit knowing that! How about you leave me the fuck alone until you're actually holding that card and save the threats. Because, until then, there isn't a damn thing I can do. You fucking taught me that."

"I hate you!" she yells back as she slides in her car.

"Yeah, well, you're not alone!" I yell back, sliding into mine.

I hate me, too.

* * *

When I pull in, I see Tessa walking inside with Chewy and silently thank a God, who doesn't listen to me, that she's back.

Once inside, she avoids me, and I resolve to not thank God again. I mean, who am I to thank Him, anyway?

We eat, have small talk, and watch TV. Tonight, it's *The Nanny*. I sit and pretend to study, but all my focus is on Tessa as she helps Jake study his spelling words.

I learn that Tessa has tryouts tomorrow and test the communication waters, in front of her family, by telling her, "Good luck. Or is it break a leg?"

"Either works," she says. "And thanks."

The morning ritual is the same, and we even take Kendall and Jake to school together. But when we drop them off, I ask her if she wants to talk, which is fucked up.

When she doesn't say a damn thing and I make another attempt, she cuts me off with a firm, "Don't."

She comes home from school and studies, completely fucking ignoring me, which I deserve, unless anyone in her family is around, then she is all bullshit smiles or wearing headphones.

When Kendall asks her what's wrong, she tells her that she has call-backs, and that seems to ward off the questioning.

I get a bit pissed that they don't see what she's doing, but I also get why they don't. She's got a routine down, and she's comfortable in it, and so do they. I'm the one who's leeching off them.

I had no intention of signing up for basketball after what Coach Jones said, but there is no way I can come home after school and look at the clock for six hours, so I sign up. I also sign up to coach at the weekend intramural camp for the elementary kids this weekend so I'm not hanging around the house, wishing my life is something it's not.

Friday night, Alex spilled those beans, and she announced she got the lead and that her practices start at six every night and go on until nine, starting Monday. I felt some sort of relief, not just for me. For her.

Basketball ends at five, and I know damn well I could fuck off for an hour so that she isn't forced to see me, and that I'm not forced to see her. So, that's what I do, and I do it for a week.

After practice, Alex, Ryan and I either shoot hoops in the barn or guns out back. Tommy's in love and not around as much. I'm happy for him, but I miss him, too. Truth be told, we don't hang much at his place and, obviously, I'm on Ross arrest, so I'm not home at all.

I figure out that Tessa never told anyone about Sadi. More than once, I want to, hoping they will kick me out, but if they don't, an awkward situation would be even worse, so I always talk myself out of it. Jade and Tommy know, of course. Tessa made sure Tommy knew, because typical Tessa wants me to have someone to talk to.

Saturday night, Josie called and asked that Tessa train me at the restaurant. I was tired from being dragged around by the kids, but also wanted to be around her and, forced or not, I wanted a conversation with her. So, she taught me how to run the restaurant's dishwasher, and I pretended not to get it the first time, which was pathetic, but it kept us there in close proximity for four hours.

Little did I know that just put me in a front row seat to watching the only girl I ever loved slip farther and farther out of my reach.

* * *

The next week, Tessa stayed with Maggie two days again, and then it was like a rerun of a shitty TV program the rest of the week. Life severely sucked, but it sucked a little less because at least she was in my life. Soon, very fucking soon, that would be gone too.

Dad and I made the decision to stay the course for college, because one never knew what Sadi would do. So, sometimes I would daydream about that, but the star of that dream wasn't even football anymore. It was Tessa in the stands, smiling at me.

Saturday morning, I woke up at the ass crack of dawn and headed up to the camp, knowing that Tessa always cleaned it the weekend before hunting season began. I decided that was one thing I could take off her plate. Alex made it sound like she did it after cleaning the house, so I thought it was in the afternoon.

When she walks in, I'm on the counter, shirt off, sweating because I started a fire when I got here, washing windows. She looks at me with disdain, but I let it roll off my back, smile, jump down, and ask, "Hey, Tessa, did you come to help?"

Tessa forces a smile. "Yep, I do this the same day every year."

"I know, Alex told me. He mentioned you came up in the afternoon, so I came up early this morning. I thought I could get it done so you didn't have to. You do everything at the house. I thought I should pitch in since you have to deal with my sorry ass for the next two months."

She avoids eye contact by looking around. When she sees the black frame around the cardboard that she had written "*Doe Camp*" at her birthday party, sitting above the fireplace on the mantle, her eyes stall.

"You like it?" I cross my arms and lean against the counter. "I thought it deserved a frame."

"Looks good." She looks away as she takes a deep breath, carries a bag over, sets it on the counter, and begins unloading the cleaning supplies that she brought with her.

I reach over and grab a bottle of Clorox to mix in with the soapy water that I intend on using to wash down the walls as she grabs for the Pine-Sol, and our hands touch. Both of us freeze, and then she closes her eyes. I notice her inhale deeply and force myself to pull my hand away.

When she opens her eyes, I hold my hands up in the air. "My bad. It won't happen again."

She looks at me, expecting me to move, and I try, but for some reason, I just can't do it.

I close my eyes and whisper, "Tessa, I can't move right now, so you're going to have to."

She ducks under my arm and walks around to the other side of the counter where she begins organizing the products.

"I'll give you a minute, and then you can leave and I'll clean, or we just get it done so we can both leave."

I watch as she walks outside, leaving the door open, as she heads around to the back of the truck and opens the tailgate. When she comes back in, she is carrying two bags. She walks to the opposite side of the counter, sets the bags down, and begins unloading groceries.

"Are there more in the truck?"

"Yeah, a couple more bags."

I bring them inside, kicking the door closed behind me.

She calls behind me, "You may want to leave that door open. It's hot as hell in here."

When I head back to open the door, I walk out, knowing that I am on the brink of losing my shit.

I walk to the creek, squat down, and wrap my arms around my knees. I have messed up everything, and that is on me. It's my penance to pay. I have broad shoulders for a reason—to lug my shit around. But she doesn't. I also have strong arms. Arms that were made, and ache, to lift someone else up. No, fuck that, not someone else—her. I messed that up. I messed up something that could have been so right.

I try, in vain, to hold back tears, because I am not one to cry, though I have more lately than I have my entire life.

I hear gravel crunch beneath her feet. Then, out of the corner of my eye, I see her shaking out one of the area rugs. Then I see her freeze.

I quickly slap away the tears and hear her inhale a sharp breath. I look out of the corner of my eye and see her covering her mouth, pain evident in her eyes.

I take in a deep breath and say, "I'm so sorry, Tessa."

"Lucas," she whispers, "please don't cry."

"I have never felt this sort of pain. I feel like my heart is literally breaking into pieces, and then I see you and feel the hate you have for me. I can't even give you the space you deserve. I fucked up."

In a flash, she is by my side, crouching down and wrapping her arms around me. I stiffen.

"Tessa, don't."

When she doesn't let go, I wrap my arms around her and whisper, "I am so sorry."

"I don't hate you, Lucas," she whispers.

And I feel like a dick, because I'm immediately slapped

with the realization that her words are true. I am kicked in the gut with the knowledge that she doesn't hate me. Just like me, she's in love with someone she can't have. Unlike me, she doesn't deserve to be burdened by that.

She let's go, leans back so she's sitting on her heels, and then we're knee to knee. *And yes, that, too, fucks with me.*

"I want to be your friend. It's just going to take some time. Sorry."

"You have nothing to be sorry for, Tessa."

"Okay, you're right. I'm perfect. You are lucky to have me as a friend." Tessa forces a smile. "But Lucas, I'm lucky to have you, too." She stands up. "Because, without you, it would take me all day to get this place clean." She reaches down and grabs both my hands, pulling me up. Then she wipes my face with her sleeve and nods toward camp. "Let's get this done, okay?"

When I nod, she turns around, shaking her head. "And will you please put a shirt on?"

Inside camp, Tessa puts on her headphones and pushes play on her Walkman.

I tap her on the shoulder. "Share your music?" Then I pull the Walkman out of her hand and hit eject.

"Lucas," she says as she reaches for the tape.

I look down at it and read her writing out loud, "*Fuck off LL*? Never heard of that group before."

"Give me the tape, or I'm going to head out of the friendship zone and go back to ignoring you."

"You do know that I am now going to spend the rest of my life wondering what songs are on there, right?"

Her face pinkens. "I was mad."

I laugh. "Can we listen to just one song?"

"You're so damn conceited that you think you're LL?" She stomps her foot, and I laugh harder.

"Yeah, okay. My bad. I'll just put my ego back on the

pedestal it's been on for the past couple weeks and—"

"Seriously, Links." She laughs. "Shut up."

"Fine, you win. I'll go grab some music."

I head outside and grab the mixtape that I made then walk back in. I may not be one to wear my heart on my sleeve—hell, I didn't even know what the phrase meant until a few weeks ago—but I managed to make my first fucking mix tape, and on it, every single song that reminds me of Tessa Ross.

The label on mine is no less embarrassing as hers. But, unlike her, I don't give a shit if she sees it. Hell, I *want* her to know ... but that, too, is selfish.

As the first song begins, I grab my shirt and pull it on, followed by my hat, so I can cover my face that has got to be turning red right now.

"Country, huh?" she says with a shit-ass grin on her face.

I toss a cleaning rag at her. "Let's get this place cleaned up."

After, "I'm in a Hurry" by Alabama plays, which was the first song I heard around Tessa. Then "Hey Jealousy" plays, and she sings along with it. I wonder how long it will take for her to figure out it's from her notebook. Then I wonder how long it will take to figure out the significance of the song that she wrote in her book on the same day as our first kiss.

When "Eternal Flame" comes on, she finally looks at me then quickly away.

Over the music, she says, "You wanna get the loft, or do you want me to?"

"Loft was the first place I cleaned." *Because I knew I didn't want to be in my own head too long before I went up and remembered the night you and Toby had a heart to heart and talked about me.*

While we clean, we are lyrically reminded of our short-lived romance that has turned into a tragic love story. We exchange knowing glances; some with smiles, and some with sadness. Regardless, it's the truest love I have ever felt just the same.

The music stops after "Please Forgive Me" by Brian Adams, drilling a proverbial knife in my heart as I'm emptying the bucket of soapy water out the back door.

"I'm hungry, are you?"

She shakes her head.

"You haven't eaten shit in two weeks, Tessa."

She shrugs. "I haven't been playing sports. I don't need to consume as many calories."

"Okay, as your friend, I am telling you that you've lost weight. Before you know it, those are going to disappear." I point to her boobs, and she slaps my hand.

We both start to laugh.

I push out my bottom lip. "Come eat lunch with me, please?"

"Fine."

I can't help but grin as I quickly pack up the bag with her cleaning supplies, and then we head out.

I get to the door first and open it, and she slides in. Then I walk around and open the door behind mine, setting the bag in, then hop in.

I wait for her to buckle. When she doesn't, I look at her.

"What?" she asks.

"Buckle up, baby."

She rolls her eyes.

"Sorry. Buckle up, TT."

We drive into town and stop at the pizza place. I order for both of us and, while we wait for the food, I grab her a carton of milk, because I notice she's been skipping breakfast. Opening it, I pop a straw in before setting it down in front of her.

She looks at me weirdly, and I wink. "Does the body good."

"Overstepping," she mumbles.

"Not a way your male friends talk to you?" I ask.

Straw between her lips, she looks up and rolls her eyes as she shakes her head.

"Good to know." *And it is.*

I walk over and grab plates, napkins, and some plastic silverware, bringing it back to the table and setting a plate and napkin in front of her.

"Order's up," the goofy kid behind the counter yells.

I go retrieve it.

Setting down the chicken salad sub and two slices of cheese pizza, I then unwrap the sub and set half on the plate in front of her, hoping she eats something.

Looking down at the plate, she exhales a deep breath, picks up the half sub on her plate, and takes a bite. As she nibbles, I inhale my half. Just like her, I haven't felt much like eating lately.

When I'm done, I sit back and watch her pick at hers. When she looks as if she's getting frustrated, I lean in and whisper, "Tessa, just eat what you can."

To that, she takes a huge bite and begins chewing loudly and obnoxiously. I can't help but laugh. And I'm glad I do, because I'm graced with a smile, a genuine one.

"That good, huh?"

She rolls her eyes and takes a smaller bite before setting it down. "I think I'm going to get the rest to-go."

She heads over to the counter and asks the kid behind it, "Can I get this wrapped up to-go?"

"Anything else you want, Tessa? My number maybe?" the little shit asks.

"You got a better chance of seeing God, Jimmy."

Laughing, Jimmy, the little shit, wraps it up and hands it to her.

Glaring at him, I stand then fix my face real quick when Tessa comes back, because I'm sure that's not how a *friend* acts and, right now, even though I don't deserve it, she's on board to be that, so I'm hell-bent on walking the thin line without fucking up this time.

Once outside, I ask, "Who was that?"

"The boy I'm going to give myself to first," she whispers.

Yeah, fuck that.

I scowl at her. "Not funny."

She grins. "You're my friend, right? So, maybe we shouldn't be able to talk about stuff like this. What do you think?"

"First, I think you need to realize you don't date little Jimmys; and second, I think, why not?"

"Because it makes your face do that." She points at me then gets in my vehicle.

I walk around to get in and don't bother asking what my face is doing. I already fucking know.

I slide in, buckle my seat belt, and look over at her.

Her arms are crossed, and she's looking at me like she's expecting me to say something, so I ask, "What?"

"What to you?"

I reach over, grab her seat belt, and buckle it.

"You're a little obsessed with my seat belt."

"You're the one who wakes me up screaming every night after that dream you have." I start the vehicle.

She huffs, "I haven't had that dream in a couple weeks."

I glance over at her and lay out the truth, "You've had it every night."

"Oh, I didn't know." She looks down.

"The first night I left it alone, the next day, Kendall asked me why I didn't help you anymore. She looked at me like she was pissed. You know, a lot like you do most of the time." I shrug, and she looks up at me. "So, I've come in every night at about 2:30 in the morning. You really don't remember this?"

She shakes her head, and a wave of blonde covers her blue eyes. I have to stop myself from reaching over and pushing it behind her ear. "Well, we have had some fantastic conversations."

"About what?" she asks.

"I'll never tell."

"That's not fair." She looks away from me and out the window.

"No, what's not fair is the things you say and ask me to do to you while you're sleeping."

She swings her head around and demands, "Like what?"

"You getting mad, TT?" I joke, and she narrows her eyes. "Let's just say you're in safe hands, even when I have to pull them away from your body. You're an absolute dream in your sleep."

"Has anything happened?" she asks softly.

"No, baby. I would prefer you to be coherent, but my hands have been very close to your heart for many nights, and you won't let them go." I sit back in my seat. "You also say some pretty sweet things in your sleep. Fucked with me for a couple days, wondering how you could say all that and go back to hating me as soon as the sun came up."

"Hey, Lucas?" She swallows hard.

"Yes, Tessa?"

"I'm very embarrassed, but thank you."

I grip the steering wheel to stop myself from taking her hand.

"Do I talk about what's bugging me?" she asks.

"Just four people in an accident. That's all you've said besides you love me. And you make me promise to be safe."

"Every night?"

"Every. Single. Night."

"How long does it last?"

"Until I hold you, kiss you, and you fall asleep." I now look out my window.

"So, when do you leave my room?"

"When I wake up an hour or so later."

"I'm sorry," she says then sits up straight, no longer curling into herself. "Can you do me a favor?"

"Anything," I say.

"Can you wake me up next time?"

I nod. "If I have to."

"Thank you."

She looks down, and I see her cheeks begin to blush. I wonder if she's remembering some of the shit she's asked me to do, and those things include her. As much as I want her to know, so that she maybe gets that I'm not as big a dick as she thinks I am, not with her, anyway, I reassure her, "Tessa, that's all, okay?"

"You sure?"

I nod then quickly bring the subject back to safer grounds. "So, you're not playing basketball?"

"I was going to try to do the musical and play ball, but then I got the lead."

"So, that's where you go every night?" I laugh, as if I didn't know that already. "*Evita*."

"That's me." She smiles.

"I can't wait to see you on stage. Who is the lead guy?"

She starts laughing. "The pizza boy."

I shake my head. "No shit?"

"None."

"Maybe now is a good time for me to give you some advice about boys, since I'm your friend and all."

"Okay, let's start with the pizza boy," she suggests.

"No, that won't work. He would bore you to death. He's the exact opposite of me—I mean, of what you need."

"So, what do I need? And hold up, do you really want me to meet someone like you, my ex?" she asks.

"That's two questions, and we are not talking about your ex. He pisses me off," I joke.

"Okay, then what do I need?"

"Well, let me see … Let's start with the obvious. Someone who likes sports. You're competitive and would be so bored with a science geek or a boy who sings and dances on stage as a way to meet girls. You need someone who is fit, because you apparently like boys that are in shape."

"Oh yeah? What makes you think that?" she jokes.

"There's only three guys I have seen you look at twice; that LL guy—he's smoking hot." I wink, and she shakes her head. "GI Joe, although he's way too old for you. And that Benji character. However, if you can kick his ass at archery, you would easily tire of him." Tessa smiles, and I continue, "You need someone who likes music and can move." I grin.

"Yeah?" She smiles back.

I nod. "They have to be intelligent, because you are. And they have to be able to make you laugh. Your laugh, Tessa, it should never be stopped. It's infectious. It has to be someone who shares your values and loves family. Someone to let you explore who you are and, when you're ready and sober, have enough inner strength to allow you the time to explore them without just taking you right there because that's how hot you are."

She looks down and shakes her head.

"They have to love to talk, or at least love you enough to listen. They need to enjoy every part of you; from your perfect face, flawless skin, tight body, eyes they could sink into forever, and your soft, thick hair that just begs their hands to touch it, to your wit, and voice, and even your little tantrums. If they don't crave you every second of every day, they don't deserve you. If they succeed in life and don't search for you to share that with them, they don't deserve you. If they don't need you by their side during every part of life, they don't deserve you. If, when they fuck up, they don't love you enough to let you go, they don't deserve you."

I pull my hat down and try to hide the feelings, the desire, the fucking need inside me, but not only that—to shield me from seeing the same damn thing from her.

When I notice her breathing change, her leaning a bit closer, as her empty hands flex, I know damn well I need to get us back to the farm where others are around every corner, to keep her safe from me, and from herself.

I turn on the vehicle and throw it in reverse as an all-too-familiar car zips in and parks directly behind me.

Sadi jumps out and begins pounding in my window, screaming, "What the hell is going on?"

"Holy buzz kill," Tessa sighs out, and I would laugh but that would cause Sadi to seriously lose her shit.

"Just had lunch with my friend, Tessa. You two have met, right?"

"So, does she know?" she screams.

I glare at her. "She knows everything, absolutely everything."

Sadi looks past me and at Tessa. "He's having a baby with me, farm girl!"

Tessa leans forward and plasters on a fake as fuck smile. "I'm well aware of it, Sadi."

"Then what the fuck do you think you're doing with him?" she yells.

"He just told you, we had lunch. We're friends. Do you understand that? Shit, Sadi, I was hoping you and I could be buddies. Hell, I thought we were well on our way with all that crying you did on my shoulder and the shocking locker room confessional. I really was hoping we could all hang out sometime. Oh, and I was hoping for an invite to the baby shower," Tessa says, visibly shaking, trying the best she can to hold it together.

Sadi then yells, "Fuck you, white trash. I wouldn't invite you to a rock fight."

At this point, I'm ready to get out and drag her back to her car, but Tessa leans forward and gives it right back.

"Hey, Sadi, do you have any parenting books? You should know that all this stress is not good for your baby. So, if you give a fuck about that little life growing in your belly, you may try to get into a yoga class or find something to teach you how to relax. Lucas and I are friends. I plan to stay that way, and you need to accept it. I'm not like you; I'm not going to fuck someone's boyfriend, so you have nothing to worry about. And he'll be a good dad if you don't drive him over the edge, so just leave us the fuck alone."

"Tessa," I whisper, "don't waste your breath."

"Lay with pigs, Lucas, and you'll start smelling like them!" Sadi screams.

Tessa unbuckles her seat belt and screams back at her, "I think that's bullshit, or he'd smell like a crazy ass whore!"

Blue Love

I reach across the console and grab Tessa's shirt, holding her inside the SUV. "Sadi, move your car now."

For once, Sadi listens.

We sit in my SUV while Sadi peels out of the parking spot.

"You okay?" I ask, knowing damn well she's not.

"Fuck no!" she yells. "Who the fuck is she? The farm girl remarks were already getting old and now white trash?"

"I'm sorry she's trying to make you feel bad, and I'm sorry I brought you into this mess." I take her hand, and she stiffens. "This is okay, right? I'm trying to comfort you now."

"Yes, as a matter of fact, why don't you go pull in her front lawn so I can fuck you on the hood of your SUV, so that stupid bitch can watch!"

As soon as the words leave her mouth, she looks like she wants to gobble them back in.

"Will that make you feel better?" I ask, trying not to laugh.

Tessa looks at me and lets out a breath.

"I mean, Tessa, anything I can do to help, I will. It would be my honor, because there's nothing I'd rather watch than you come."

She pulls her hand away and covers her face. Then her body shakes in silent laughter as I back out.

Instead of going straight through the four-way stop, I swing right.

"Where are we going?"

"I'm only doing what I was asked." I joke. "Now try to calm yourself down until we get there. Play some music."

She leans forward, turns on the radio, and hits shuffles on the disc player.

"Now sit back and try to relax, okay?"

She nods as Tesla's "Love Song" begins. Then she shakes her head, leans back, and closes her eyes. It isn't until I pull into my driveway that she opens her eyes.

"I'll be right back. I need to grab a few things."

"Do you need help?"

I say it like it is, "No, thank you. We're friends and all, but I don't think I would trust myself with you in my bedroom, unsupervised."

Inside, I grab a few things. I've been slacking and not taking care of things at home, and that's not cool because no one else is around to do it.

When I open the door to get back in my vehicle, she asks, "What's this?"

"Banking stuff and bills that need to be paid." I turn on the SUV and turn around in the driveway.

When I pull out, she asks, "Where are we going now?"

"Do you have plans?"

Tessa shakes her head.

"Good. Can we go grocery shopping together?"

She nods. "Sure, I guess."

A mile or so down the road, I start to slow down and point to a house. "I want you to check out the third house on the left, up here."

I watch as she looks at the tiny white ranch with a small garage attached to it that sits on a quarter acre of land.

"Okay ... why?" she asks.

"That's Sadi's house. She lives there with her mother and little shit brother. Her mom works two crap jobs to be able to pay the mortgage and provide for her very spoiled, expectant child. Sadi is mean as shit to her. Should I turn around and park on the front lawn?" I joke.

"She lives close to you," Tessa mumbles.

"Yes, she does. I used to pick her up for school every morning, and she blew me all the way there."

"Wow, TMI."

"No, Tessa, that was honesty, the basis of our relationship. Sadi's not nice, funny, kind, or caring. I was always with her for a release, and companionship, I suppose, even though it was shitty. When she got pregnant after missing her pills, the ones I took her to get every month, I knew I wanted more than that for my child. She was pissed, because she would have responsibilities. She hit me a few times, and I got sick of her shit, and we broke up often. I tried to love her ... well, the best I knew how, and she just whined and took pity on herself. It got old. Then she broke up with me again, and I swore that was the last time. I called the girls to come over, she drove by and saw one of their cars. She stopped, stormed in, and walked in on our um ... party." I adjust my hat. "The rest, you already know. My point here was not to tell you all that to piss you off, but rather show you that you have absolutely no reason to get upset when she makes the farm girl cracks. All right? She has nothing on you. Nothing."

"You're truly a beautiful person," she whispers then slaps her hand over her mouth.

I take it and pull it away. "And you, Tessa Ross, made me that way in less than three months. The day I saw you getting out of the pond, the very first time, I knew I wanted you. The way you seemed annoyed with me was not a reaction I ever got from any girl, which made me want you more. You were a challenge. And then I found myself offering to do hay just so I could see you again. That day, I truly saw who you were, and I believe that day was the day I knew I loved you."

I clear my throat then continue, "Now all this shit is happening, and I ended up fucking up again, but everything happens for a reason, I guess. Or maybe it doesn't. Maybe that's just something people say to feel better about their situation. Regardless, I now know what I have to do for my child. I have to try to figure it all out and make life okay for that little life so that he or she can someday, God willing, know love, and maybe be half as amazing as you. And that means I lose what I want more than anything in this world."

"Would you please pull over?" Tessa says, her voice pained.

I immediately pull off the road. "You okay?"

"No!" she yells. "I'm not okay. I'm crushed, and I'm even more in love with you now than ever. I just want to scream, and cry, and ... I don't know. I need this pain to go away, Lucas. I love you, and it hurts so much."

Watching tears fill her eyes, I try to figure out how to make it better. The only thing I can come up with is, "I can make it easier for you. I can make you hate me. I'm good at that."

She throws off her seat belt, climbs over the console, sits on my lap, and hugs me so fucking tightly as she silently sobs. All I can do is hug her back.

A good time later, maybe an hour, a day, but not the lifetime I wish I could have with her, she sits back, kisses my cheek, and whispers, "I could never hate you."

As she climbs off my lap, I ask, "What can I do?"

"Be the best you can be, and be my friend, always."

"Done." I grab her hand.

* * *

On our way home from grabbing groceries, and me buying out the store, because I've yet to put any food in the cupboards or fridge since moving in, Jade calls and asks if I know where Tessa is.

"She's right here. You wanna talk to her?"

"No, I want you to bring her to camp."

"Will do. Give us ten."

I hang up and look over at Tessa. "Jade wants you at camp."

"Is she okay?" she asks with genuine concern.

Having already talked to Tommy this morning, I know what is up, but I don't want to take that away from them.

"Yeah, I'm sure she's fine."

Sore maybe, I think to myself, *but fine.*

I drop Tessa off next to the pond where Jade is waiting for her. Then I head back to camp to let them have some girl time.

As I stock up some cupboards with chips, pretzels, nuts, and snack foods for the hunting crew, I see them walking toward me then head outside because I do not need a recap of their first time.

Sitting on the back porch, I hear Jade hiss, "I hate that girl."

Tessa whispers back, "That girl is going to have Lucas's baby. I want her to be okay. So, I'm going to ask you to be nice to her. If she sees kindness, maybe she can be a decent mom to her child, to Lucas's child. It's part of Lucas, and I love him, Jade. I know he can be an amazing father."

I never deserved you.

"You're going to be nice to her?" Jade snorts.

"I'm going to tolerate her. It pretty much depends on how much shit I can take, but for him, I'll try."

Jade sighs. "You need to move on. I think that would be easier for you both."

It stings, but I know she's right. If someone else was good to her, how could I ask for anything else? Tessa's happiness is just as important to me. Hell, even more so than my own.

Opening Day

Chapter Thirty Five

Tessa

Feeling like I haven't slept in weeks, I head downstairs, tying my hair up in a bun before I begin the task of making sausage gravy. While the sausage cooks, I whip up some biscuits and put them in the oven. Then I set to making the gravy.

Once I've dumped it into the crockpot, I make another batch, this time with venison sausage, and double it, because who knows how many will be showing up to eat before heading to camp, where they will spend a week together.

Once all of that is set, I walk into the living room and open the VHS cupboard, grab *Bambi*, turn on the TV, put in the video, and plop on the couch, where I sit and watch

Blue Love

it, as I do every year while waiting for the hunters to show up at the house.

They always show up at the house on opening day, and then, depending on how many there are, of course, decide who stays at camp.

One by one, they begin to trickle in. Lucas is with Alex. I have to stop myself from laughing at his change in headgear. More specifically, how orange replaced white. It's not hard to stop myself from laughing, since he still looks freaking hot regardless of the color.

"What is she watching?" Lucas asks Alex.

"*Bambi*. She's watches it every year on opening day since she was four." Alex rolls his eyes. "She doesn't like hunting, but she likes guns and bows. Weird, huh?"

Lucas walks over, sits down next to me, and must just realize I'm awake. "Good movie?"

Smirking, I wink, and then I get back to the task of ignoring the men.

"Good morning Tessa." I look up as Ben walks in. "Please tell me that's venison sausage in the blue crockpot."

"Nope." I give him a dirty look, lift my nose, and turn back to the TV.

"You guys out, because I can fill your whole freezer within the next few days," Ben jokes as he flops down on the other side of me.

I smack him in the gut.

Laughing, he asks, "Hurt your hand, Ross?"

At that, Alex laughs, and I catch Lucas trying not to do the same.

"You see, the secret behind it is that, once the momma gets nailed, baby gets it immediately."

I sock him again.

"What, Tess? That's the humane thing to do. Godawful

listening to those fawns blat as they walk around the scary fields alone."

"I am totally going to kick your ass."

Ben smartly jumps up off the couch, but the damn fool continues.

"I mean, seriously, Tess, the thing would starve by itself, or freeze to death."

"Someone needs to tell him to shut his mouth."

Ben doesn't take the hint. "Best tasting venison—nice, young, and tender."

I jump up off the couch, intent on smacking him upside the head, when Alex grabs me.

"You've got ten seconds to get out of this room before I let her go."

Again, Ben doesn't listen. Instead, he grabs me and gives me a bear hug while laughing. "You are going to be a lot of fun this week."

"You have ten seconds to step away before I open a can of whoop ass." I laugh.

"Let's go," Alex says as he walks into the kitchen, and Ben follows, grabbing plates and food.

Lucas, however, does not.

"You sleep okay?" he whispers.

"No, I feel like garbage," I admit.

He feels my head. "You don't feel warm."

"Not garbage like ill. I feel like I didn't sleep. It's your fault," I whisper.

"Sorry, baby."

* * *

Jade helped me carry in the crockpots full of beef stew for lunch at camp. Then, since Uncle Jack will be preoccupied, she heads out to see her man on the sly.

I hurry around camp and plug all four of the crockpots in, and when I hear voices outside, I walk out on the back porch, where I see Alex, Lucas, and Ben walking into the clearing, from the woods.

Ben is all smiles as he says, "Hey, Tessa, did you warn Bambi I was coming today?"

I shake my head and ask, "Anyone get a deer yet?"

"Lucas got four doe. In my opinion, they were too small, but hey, to each their own, right?" Ben goads.

I look at Lucas, who shakes his head.

"No, but seriously, he had a shot and, for some unknown reason, he didn't—"

"Okay, I'm already bored of this deer talk," I cut him off, smiling inside.

Ben claps and rubs his hands together. "And bow season has just begun."

Ignoring his egging me on, I look at Alex. "Lunch is warming up. Give it twenty minutes. If you can't wait, there's sandwiches in the cooler. Have fun."

I then look at Lucas. "Can I talk to you?"

He nods and begins to walk toward me as I begin to walk toward the truck.

Once beside me, I ask him, "Do you like it? Hunting? Because you don't have to, you know."

"It's fine. I'll try it. Who knows, after I've done it once, I may like it." He suppresses a smile.

"Nice, Lucas." I roll my eyes. "I'm working tonight. Are you still planning on it?"

"Yes. Why?"

"I just wondered." I look at him, contemplating whether or not to dip a toe into what could either be quicksand or a quick fix.

"What's going on, Tessa?"

"I can't sleep, and I am tired. I just thought maybe … you could … help me out."

"Tessa …" he sighs.

"What?" I stomp my foot. "I'm tired and irritable."

He looks at me, eyes narrowed, and nods once. "Give me a minute."

Then he walks back to camp and yells in, his eyes on me, "Hey Alex, Tessa just reminded me we have to work tonight. I'm going to take off, okay?"

"Sure, man, see you later. We'll probably stop by for dinner," Alex replies.

"Bye, Ben. See you later." I wave.

"Bye, Ben." Lucas waves, mocking me.

I grab his hand and tug him toward the truck.

* * *

Heart beating a mile a minute, I bravely reach over and place my hand on his thigh.

"Tessa, what—"

"Lucas, don't. I need this," I whisper as I run my hand up his leg until it's right below his dick.

He hits the gas, and we speed down the road. I watch as he grows harder and harder.

As soon he parks, I grab his face and kiss him. He kisses me back.

When I start to reach down his pants, he hisses my name in warning. "Tessa."

"Let me make you—"

"Baby, this is not what friends—"

"Lucas, I'm exhausted. We can, so shut up and kiss me."

Half an hour later, after I got him off, and he did the boob thing and took me there, too, we walk inside, and I feel a hundred times better. Lucas must, too, I think as I run to the bathroom.

When I come out, Lucas walks down with a laundry basket, and I flop down on the couch, content, happy even.

I hear the washer start and when he walks out, I grab his hand and pull him down.

"Tessa, I'm not sure—"

"I'm tired." I yawn. "Let me sleep, please?"

I scoot forward and pat the spot behind me. He lays down, and I scoot back against him as he pulls a blanket off the back of the couch and throws it over me.

"Thank you, bud." I sigh.

* * *

I feel Lucas move out from behind me, and I pull the blanket up around my neck and dose back off.

When I wake, he's still not back, so I get up and walk out to the kitchen where I find him looking out the window.

He turns and grabs something off the counter, along with a glass of water, and walks toward me, face unreadable as he hands them to me.

"Feeling better?" he asks, stepping back to lean against the counter and crosses his arms.

"Yeah, a little." I toss the ibuprofen in my mouth then wash it back.

His brows knit. "What was that all about earlier?"

I look down and raises a shoulder. "I guess I missed you."

He lifts his chin. "Question?"

"You're on a roll. Go ahead."

"How did you get to camp?"

"Jade dropped me off."

"Why didn't you drive?" he asks, voice less dad and angrier mom.

"I wasn't feeling well?"

"Why, Tessa?"

He walks over to the garbage and reaches in, pulling out the bottle that I tossed in there earlier and setting it on the counter.

"I though you tasted like cinnamon and not minty fucking fresh earlier. Now I know why."

I cross my arms over my chest and glare at him.

Voice raised, he says, "I asked why, Tessa."

I raise mine right back. "Because I can't sleep, because you're all telling me what I need in a guy when I know damn well what I need, and I can't have. Because life fucking sucks, Lucas! And because I can!"

"Come on, Tessa; what else you got?" he yells back at me.

"Fuck you!" I turn to walk away, but he grabs my arm, stopping me. "Let me go!" I scream at him.

He wraps his arms around me, holding me in place. I attempt to wiggle away, but he pulls me up.

"Let me go, dammit!"

He carries me into the living room, and shame, guilt, and anger come together and combust. I start to cry.

"Just let me go."

Lucas sits down, pulls me with him, and whispers, "I need you to be okay."

"Well, that's not going to happen. It's going to get ugly, Lucas. I promise you that," I sob out.

"Tessa, I need you to be safe."

I laugh. "Oh, I will be."

"I'm so sorry," he whispers again.

"Stop saying that!" I try to get up, but he holds me tighter, pissing me off. "I'm pretty sure this wasn't part of some evil plan, not on your part, anyway. It's my life and, right now, it sucks."

I finally get free, run to the bathroom, and lock the door. I shower, hoping this headache from drinking a quarter bottle of Schnapps or the stress of being so fucking in love with someone I can't have yet can't get away from subsides.

He wants me to meet someone else, someone deserving. *He* should have been that someone. *He* should of because he told me he loved me, and I know he did.

I wrap a towel around me and walk out, passed him and up the stairs.

I grab a pair of tight jeans and a button-down shirt then put them on. I leave a few extra buttons undone so I could expose "the girls," so maybe I can find the guy, the one who deserves me, and then maybe he'd feel how I do, knowing I'm never going to be his, and he's never going to be mine.

Walking down the stairs, I see him pacing and walk past him. I open the fridge, grab a PBR, and pop the tab. Lifting it to my mouth, he snatches it. I laugh and walk to the bathroom, again locking the door, and start doing my hair. I even put on makeup.

When I walk out, he's standing in the middle of the living room, hands shoved deep in his pockets.

I turn in a circle. "Do I look okay? Am I showing enough skin? I'm thinking maybe I'll catch the eye of someone at the bar tonight. You'll be there. Maybe you could pick out the lucky guy I fuck tonight, because I'm so ready for that next step." I laugh.

I expect him to get pissed. Instead, I see hurt in his eyes.

I look away, not wanting to get sucked into feeling someone else's pain and ignoring mine.

I step to him as I unbutton my shirt then let it fall from my shoulders. "Unless, of course, you want to fuck me now." Then I unsnap my bra, and he turns away.

I reach around him and shove my fingers down the waistband of his jeans. "Come on, Lucas; don't turn your back on me. Shit, in a few months, maybe less, I will catch up to your dozen. Then will you want me?"

He pulls my hand out and storms past me and into the bathroom.

"Twelve will be nothing compared to what I'm going to do, and it certainly won't take four fucking years!"

I walk out to the kitchen and grab a bottle of whiskey. Twisting it open, I drink some down because this … this feels good. Angry feels good, not caring feels good, and …

Lucas pulls the bottle from my hand, and I let him.

I grab the truck keys off the counter and walk to the door. As I open it, he slams the palm of his hand against it, closing it.

"I need to go to work, Lucas. I get to sing tonight."

Lucas opens the door and takes my hand, leading me to his SUV. He opens the door, and I climb in. Then he buckles me in, which makes me laugh.

When he pulls out, he turns right.

"Wrong way, *baby*." I laugh as I look at the clock on his dashboard. "Look at that, we have an hour to kill before we have to be there. Maybe you could drop me off at the pizza shop and I can go fuck Pizza Boy. He can be my starter dick.

"Someone will want me, Lucas. I have thrown myself at you, and you sure don't want me. But you go and *fuck* her! Sorry I can't live up to your ideal of what's fuckable." I wish I could stop, I wish I could just shut up, but it just keeps coming. "Don't worry; I'm going to work on that!" I scream, and then the tears begin to fall again.

Blue Love

Lucas doesn't say a damn thing, and all I want is him to fight with me, or maybe I really just want him to fight for me.

At the four-way stop, he turns left, and I slap the tears away and again yell at him, "Where are we going?"

"To see your mother," he replies calmly.

"Fuck you. I'll jump out." I start to unbuckle my seat belt.

He jerks the vehicle over and parks on the side of the road, right across from the school.

When I try to open the door, he reaches over and slams it shut.

I turn on him, ready to give him hell, and see him wipe tears off his face. Then he grabs his phone and dials it.

"We're across from the school." He pauses before saying, "Of course."

I curl up into a ball and cry, because I hate him, and I love him, and there is no way that is normal.

He's ruined me. I hate him.

"I hate you so much."

"Good."

"I hope—"

"Shut the hell up, Tessa! Just shut up!"

I jerk my head up and scream at him, "Fuck you!"

"Not even if you beg," he sneers.

I spit in his face.

Jaw clenched, nostrils flaring, he opens his door with one hand and wipes his face with the other as he gets out and slams the door so hard the vehicle shakes.

A few minutes later, lights shine from behind, and then my door is swung open.

"Your mother's here."

"I'm not going with her."

"Get out, Tessa."

I lift my face and look at him. He looks disgusted.

I feel my lip start to quiver and know I'm going to cry, and not because I'm sad, but because I'm pissed.

I push him away and get out. Then I get in the back seat of Mom's Chevy.

I hear Lucas say, "I'm sorry about this, Mrs. Ross."

She hugs him and says, "You and me both, Lucas. Thank you."

When Mom gets in the car, she says not one word, and I am totally grateful.

When we walk into her apartment, I am shocked when I see my grandmother is here from Massachusetts.

She tells Kendall and Jake, "Give us a few minutes," and they walk into the living room and shut the door.

Grandma Violet looks at me sternly and asks, "Have you slept with that boy?"

Pissed that this is the first thing she's said to me in months—hell, she hasn't even called since Mom and Dad split—I shake my head and tell her, "No, Grandma, but I sure did try."

She slaps me across the face. "Shame on you."

"Mom!" my mother gasps.

I turn, grab the phone, and walk into the closet-sized bedroom. Shutting and locking the door, I dial Lucas's number. He answers but doesn't say anything.

So, I do.

"I hate you."

"I know."

"No, Lucas, you don't, but I promise you will."

"That's the plan."

"Who the fuck do you think you are?"

"Your ex, Tessa. Welcome to the club."

I hang up, bury my face in the pillow, and cry until I pass out.

RUNNING

Chapter Thirty Six

LUCAS

I fed Josie some lame-ass shit about Tessa being sick and promised to keep up with the dishes. She was cool with it. Hell, she didn't even question whether I could or couldn't.

As I worked, I listened to chick after chick butcher songs that Tessa would have nailed had she not gotten fucked up and lost her damn mind. All of which, was my fault. But fuck if even knowing that, I'm still livid with her. I cannot fucking believe she spit in my face.

Plenty of women have slapped me across the face—hell, even my mother when I hid her stash or dumped booze down the drain—but never has anyone spit in my fucking face until now. That was a first for sure.

A couple hours into my shift, Alex walks in and asks where she is. I give him the same story that I gave Josie, except he doesn't buy it.

"She didn't seem ill at camp, but she did seem off."

I grab a towel and wipe my hands as I turn and look at him. "Do what you will with this information, Alex, but I told Josie the same thing I just told you, so ..." I shrug.

"Go on," he says, leaning against the island.

"She was drunk and acting crazy. And before you get pissed at her, I promise you it's my fault. It's because of the shit I have brought into her life. I didn't know what else to do, so I tried to take her to your mom's. She threatened and then actually tried to jump out of the vehicle. I pulled over and called Maggie. She met us on Main Street."

He runs his hand through his hair.

"I'm taking off for a couple days, going to stay with my dad. Then I need to talk to the judge and convince him that I can stay at home. I can't do this shit to her anymore, Alex. I love her, and me being there is fucking shattering her."

On the brink of breaking down again, dipshit walks in and asks, "Where's Tess?"

Thank God Alex answers him because, straight-up, I know Ben wants to fuck Tessa, and I know damn well, if she keeps on this path, she'll do it to spite me.

"She didn't feel well, so Lucas took her to Mom's," Alex lies. "I'll be out in a minute, okay?"

Alex waits until Ben leaves the kitchen then turns back to me. "You sure you can miss school, man?"

"I've only missed two and a half days. If you could get me the assignments, I think I'll be okay."

"Sure," Alex says. "You know this isn't your fault, right?"

I shake my head then shrug. "Then, whose is it?"

* * *

On the highway, my phone rings and I answer.

"I just came home, and you're gone."

It's Tessa and, yeah, it's good to hear her sober voice, but I'm still pissed at her.

She continues, "You told Tommy, and Jade didn't even tell me. So, in case you were wondering, that didn't feel very good. What else did you tell them, huh, Lucas?"

"Told them the truth. I'm going to visit my Dad."

I hear her sniff.

"Well, you need to come back," she demands.

I don't say a damn thing.

"Did you hear me, Lucas?" she snaps. "Seriously, can you answer me?"

"Connection's clear. I didn't hear a question. What's up, Tessa?"

She begins to cry. "I'm sorry, Lucas. I'm so sorry."

I make damn sure I let zero emotion out when I reply, "It's all good, Tessa."

"When will you be back?" she asks.

"In a couple days." *And hopefully, I won't be coming back to the farm.*

"I want to see you now." Tessa's voice cracks.

"Sorry, Tessa. Court-ordered visitations are part of my life." *And will be for a long fucking time due to the fact I'll be the one demanding them from my kid's mom.*

"You hate me?" she asks.

"No, but you told me you hated me—or no, *fucking* hated me—then you spit in my face." No holding back the anger there. *Oops, my bad.*

"You took me to my mother, drunk," she snaps, and it pisses me off.

"You were acting like my mother on a bad night."

She gasps then whispers, "You're being mean."

"Yep. Just like you were when you asked me to you drop you off to the Pizza Boy so he could fuck you."

"You're trying to make me hate you," she whispers.

"It'll happen, anyway."

Pissed again, she raises her voice. "You know, I wish I recorded the stuff you said to me when I finally talked to you after two fucking weeks that started this shit again. I was doing fine."

"I wish you recorded it, too, because you're certainly not living up to your end of that conversation. What happened to your rules about being friends, Tessa?"

She huffs, "Oh please, I certainly wasn't alone."

"Yeah, well, it's kind of hard to say no to hand job."

"So, in the yearbook under weaknesses, will yours say *Sadi begging to be fucked and a hand job* or just—"

"You're acting like a crazy ex," I cut her off.

"And you just shattered my already broken heart."

And that shatters mine, but it has to happen.

"Anything else, Tessa?"

"Drive safe when you come home ... asshole," she whispers softly.

"Will do. Is that it?"

"No."

"Then let's have it. Come on, TT. Let me have it. Get it out of your system now."

"I love you!" she cries.

"Dammit, Tessa." I take a deep breath then say, "Goodbye."

* * *

Thankfully when I get to my Dad's, the house is empty. I run up to my room and into the bathroom, where I kneel down and try to steady my breathing, but even that doesn't help ease the tearing pain that will not go away inside my chest.

This is what heartbreak feels like sober. It sucks.

* * *

TESSA

I fell asleep before the guys came home from day two and woke up from that awful dream, when unfamiliar hands and an unfamiliar voice was trying to calm me.

"Tessa, wake up, sweetheart." He sits next to me and pulls my head on his lap.

"I'm sorry," I whisper, completely and totally embarrassed.

"Tess, girl, you need to wake up." Thankfully, he starts to stand.

"Please don't go. She needs you," Kendall says, startling him.

"Care to explain?" he asks, and I think, *Please don't.*

"She has bad dreams since Sadi started being mean."

"Sadi?" he asks.

Kendall sits up. "New girl at school. Just hug her, talk to her … Just make her stop crying."

"Little Ross," he begins.

"Kendall, my name is Kendall. Just hug her or something."

"Should I get your dad?"

No! I scream inside.

"No. She wouldn't want to upset him. Just …" Kendall sniffs. "Just help—"

"Okay, kiddo, does she have a favorite song?"

"Pearl Jam." Kendall sniffs again. "She likes Pearl Jam."

So, he sits there and sings to me, and he sings well.

* * *

Stretching, I feel a body beneath my head then hear a voice.

"Hey, Tess, good morning."

I flail and sputter, "Hello. Oh Jesus, I'm sorry."

Ben smiles. "From what I understand, it happens often."

"Did I …? I mean, can you tell me what happened?"

When he tells me, I'm relieved that it was just what I remember and that there was no kissing or any of the other stuff that Lucas said I did to him.

"What did you sing?" I ask, not remembering the song, just that he had a good voice.

"'Small Town,' a Pearl Jam song." Ben laughs. "Little Ross told me you liked them."

"I love that song." I yawn as I sit up.

"Well, maybe we need to try playing music at night," Ben suggests.

"Did I kiss you?"

He smirks and shakes his head.

"You know I'm a train wreck, right?"

Ben grins. "We can fix that. What time do you have to be at school?"

"Eight. Why?"

Ben laughs. "It's seven fifteen."

"Where's Alex?" I ask, jumping up and running toward the door.

Ben follows me down the stairs. "I assume in the woods. Get ready. I will take you to school."

I shower and dress. Then, as I'm drying my hair, Ben walks in, sits on the floor, and starts feeding me fruit.

When I'm done drying my hair, I start to put it in a ponytail.

"Are you crazy?" Ben he grabs the scrunchy. "Leave it down, Tess. It's gorgeous." He runs his hand through it. Then he takes my hand and pulls me out of the bathroom, into the kitchen, and grabs the bagel and water bottle off the counter, "Let's get you to school."

He opens the car door for me and shuts it. When he gets in, he doesn't tell me to buckle my seat belt. He hands me the bagel.

"Eat this."

By the time I get to school, I've finished.

"Thanks for last night, this morning, all of it," I say, getting out of the truck.

He gets out, too, hurrying around to give me a big hug.

"Whore," Sadi sneers as she walks by.

"Good at it," I yell to her retreating back as Ben steps away.

"Really?" He laughs.

"No, not really. Ben, you should know I'm far from that. I have kissed two guys, and I've never had sex." I shrug. "So, no, I'm not a whore, but if that's what she needs to think, then I'll let her."

"What's her name?" Ben asks, and I tell him.

"Same chick Kendall mentioned?"

"There is only one, so … yep."

"Hey, Sadi!" he yells "Check this out!"

Ben draws me into him, pulls my hair back gently, and

then he kisses me. A slow, soft kiss, too. His lips taste like mint, and he is a damn good kisser.

"That makes three, and they say the third time's a charm." He pulls me toward him and kisses me again. "Do you have to go to school, or can you stay home and do that with me all day?"

"Ben, that was ..." I shake my head. "I have to go to school."

He grins. "When are you done?"

"Three."

"Okay, I'll see you then," he says.

* * *

Inside the school, I run to the pay phone, drop in some quarters, and call him. He doesn't answer, so I leave a message.

"I woke up screaming last night, and you weren't there. He was. Kissed the boy when he dropped me off at school today. You weren't there. Probably tonight, when I scream in my sleep, I'll be thinking of you and do more than kiss the boy. That should make you very happy. And maybe, by then, I won't hurt each time I kiss the boy because I'm missing you."

Then I hang up.

* * *

Carrying a hangover and heartbreak in the same body is exhausting, but I manage this while also managing to avoid any run-ins with Lucas's past ... and future.

At the end of the day, walking out of the hell that my senior year at this high school is, I see Ben waiting by his big truck in the distance and, unlike Lucas when he sees me, he has a huge smile on his face. And, just like Lucas, his smile falls and his head snaps right, now scowling at Sadi, surrounded by her bitch posse.

Fuck this, I think as I walk toward him.

"You're Tessa's new friend?" Sadi asks him.

"You're the bitch that was talking shit to her this morning?"

I slow down and allow myself to enjoy seeing him give her just the tip of what she deserves.

Sadi smiles. "Well, that's no way to talk to a lady."

He crosses his arms and looks around. "I'm looking around, and yet I'm not seeing a lady."

He looks toward me and nods in my direction. "My bad. I see one now."

Sadi huffs, "What's your name?"

"That's none of your business," Ben sneers.

"The farm girl seems to get all in my business. My man is living at that farm now, so I'm just returning the favor by trying to get to know hers." When she sees me coming, she points at me. "Keep her away from him, and I just may leave her alone."

Ben looks back at her and shakes his head. "Lucas is a big boy. I think he can take care of himself."

She rubs her belly. "In a few short months, he'll be taking care of more than just himself."

Ben throws his head back and chuckles. "Oh, now I see. You're pregnant?"

"Yep, and he and I will be happy as long as you take care of the trash." Sadi flashes teeth.

The look he gives her would force a normal teen girl into a freaking eating disorder. "You know that's no way to keep a guy, right?"

She narrows her eyes. "Well, now that's none of your business, is it?"

I finally step in. "Hey, Ben, is she bugging you?"

"No, Tess, she isn't. I feel sorry for her skank ass, though. And even more sorry for our friend, Lucas." Ben glares at Sadi as he takes my bag then pops a kiss to my cheek. "You ready to go?"

"Oh, look at you two. Someday, you'll probably be raising pigs together on that farm of yours," Sadi says.

I shake my head as I turn to get into Ben's truck but leave her with a dose of reality. "And you'll be living with your momma in a dump, with a baby that Lucas didn't want as he ruins his life for a bitch like you."

When my hair gets yanked and she grabs my face with her other hand, digging her nails into my cheek, I fight the instinct to pound the piss out of a pregnant bitch.

Her hands are suddenly pulled off me, and Ben yells, "Get in, Tess; she isn't worth it."

I turn and watch him lift her off her feet and carry her back to the bitches standing there, watching. He drops her at their feet and demands, "Now act like fucking ladies and care for your bat-shit crazy friend."

He walks back and opens the driver's door, pushes the seat forward, and then pulls out a first-aid kit.

Thinking it's a bit overkill, I flip down the visor mirror and look at myself. "You have got to be fucking kidding me." A few more inches, and she would have reopened the wound still healing from my field hockey game. Instead, I have a new injury.

Now at my door he says, "Turn around and let me clean that up." When I turn, he cringes. "Sorry, Tess, this is gonna sting, but I don't want to see you catch whatever it is that rabid bitch may have."

He's right; it stings.

As he steps back, I thank him, and he leans in and kisses me.

"Thanks, Ben."

Sliding in the driver's side, he asks, "So you and Lucas—"

"We're not a thing." *Not anymore.*

"Damn, I feel sorry for that kid, and for Lucas."

"Me, too," I whisper.

Ben puts the vehicle in drive and pulls out of the parking lot. Through the rearview mirror, I see Sadi's friends placing hands on her belly and gushing. Apparently, the cat's out of the bag.

When we approach the four-way stop, Ben turns and looks at me. "Is he sure she's pregnant?"

"What do you mean? He had sex with her, and I guess she showed him a test results." I shrug.

"I mean, has he been to the doctor with her?"

"I don't think so."

"As crazy as her ass is, I can't believe he slept with her. He should have more proof than a damn stick that she may or may not have pissed on."

Butterflies stir things up in my stomach, the bad butterflies, and I feel like I'm going to get sick.

As soon as he puts the truck in park, he jumps out, runs to the passenger door, and opens it.

Kissing my forehead, he asks, "You wanna go to camp and see what I got today?"

We have left high school drama and arrived back at hunting camp. I laugh to myself. "Does it have horns?"

"No, spots and a pacifier still in its mouth." Ben laughs, and I smack him.

Stomping toward the house, I call behind me, "Then no. I have to get ready for rehearsal, anyway."

"When do you get home tonight?" Ben calls from behind me.

Opening the door, I call back, "About nine!"

"See you then." Ben laughs then asks, "Hot tub date?"

I look over my shoulder. "I'm mad at you, remember?"

He winks. "You'll get over it."

As soon as I walk in the house, I grab the phone and hurry to the bathroom, where I call Lucas. It goes directly to his voicemail.

"I got jumped today. You need to come home and put that bitch on a leash." I hang up then lean in closer to the mirror so I can get a better look at my face.

A few minutes later, I'm fixing my hair when the phone rings.

"Hello?"

"Who jumped you, Tessa?"

Lucas.

"The same girl you need to come back to and put a leash on. Who else? Sadi."

"Are you all right?" he asks, voice shaking in anger.

"No." My voice breaks.

His tone softens. "What happened, Tessa?"

I tell him the entire story, and he says nothing.

After a brief moment of silence, I ask, "Lucas, have you gone to the doctor with her?"

"No, I didn't need to. She showed me—"

"What if she's not really pregnant?"

"Tessa, I wish that were true."

"Okay, well, I just think you should do that," I suggest softly.

I wait a few beats before he responds.

"You going to be okay?"

"Are you?"

"I have to be, and so do you."

"Okay, then. I miss you, and I'm sorry for the other day, truly." Then I whisper, "Can you please come home?"

"I will see you soon, Tessa. Later."

Blue Love

* * *

I got my ass chewed and threatened to be grounded by mom, which is laughable because all I do is go to school, come home, and go to rehearsal. My fun? Working at Aunt Josie's bar. Then I went to rehearsal. It was a nice reprieve, getting to pretend to be someone I'm not, taking on their angst and heartache, allowing me to leave mine behind.

When I arrive home, the kids are already in bed, and Dad and Alex are probably still at camp. I decide to skip dinner and go to bed.

I set an alarm for eleven p.m.; that way I will hopefully wake before that reoccurring dream happens. I'm not worried the alarm will wake Kendall. She clearly sleeps through almost anything. Or, at least, I think she sleeps through most of it. But Lucas did say she scolded him when he stopped coming in. Either way, it's better for me to wake up and possibly disrupt her sleep that way than it is for her to see me in a different man's arms. Well, I guess any man's arms, for that matter.

I wake with my eleven o'clock alarm to find Ben standing in the doorway. "You missed our hot tub date."

I laugh. "I'm not getting in a hot tub with a Bambi killer."

He holds up a tape. "Might have a solution to your sleep problem."

I pat my bed. "Then I guess you can come in, Bambi slayer."

Ben pops the tape in the boom box next to the bed.

Alex leans in my room and asks, "Did Ben tell you he got a six point today?"

I look at Ben then back to Alex. "No, he told me he killed Bambi."

"Your sister's hot when she's pissed. I couldn't help myself." Ben chuckles.

We all laugh.

When the music begins, it's soft. No electric guitars, no loud base, just soft.

I look up at Ben. "What is this?"

"Just a mix of music that'll put you asleep, Tess." He taps the doorframe a couple times before walking away.

After Ben leaves my room, I give it a few seconds to make sure he's in bed, and then I open the nightstand drawer and pull out Lucas's mixed tape that I kept from the other day when we cleaned camp. Putting it in, I cry myself to sleep.

* * *

I'm dreaming ... and he's here.

He's sitting on my couch, my legs resting across his lap, and dream Tessa sits up. She crawls across the expansive couch, closing the space between us. She touches his face while whispering a prayer.

"Don't wake up, Tessa, don't wake up."

Dream Tessa sits on his lap and pulls his shirt over his head, wanting and needing to remove the barrier between them. She kisses the place above where his heart beats and whispers, "This should be mine."

In the dream, he hugs her tightly and makes a sound that tells her he, too, is in pain.

Then dream Tessa whispers, "I love you, Lucas. Run away with me."

Dream Lucas hugs her even tighter.

"I love you. Please don't ever leave me again."

Show Me

Chapter Thirty Seven

LUCAS

The week flew by fast and, as luck would have it, Benji left once I returned. Might have had something to do with me making sure that he saw me walking into her room and carrying her downstairs when she woke up crying.

But Friday, after basketball practice, the dipshit is back.

I watch him get out of his jacked-up truck. You know, the kind the guy in the locker room with the smallest dick drives. That kind.

Jade, Tessa, and Phoebe are too busy putting together charcuterie boards and vegetable trays to notice, and I don't give them a heads-up, because I want to see how she reacts to him without a heads-up.

When he walks in, all googly eyes and smiling, he immediately says, "Hey, Tess, did you miss me?"

I watch her look up, and her eyes come to me first, as they should, and then to him.

She doesn't address the question, which gives me more satisfaction than it should. She simply says, "Hey, Ben, how was your trip up?"

"Well worth it." Ben winks at her then looks at me.

Being the dick I am, I wink at him.

He shakes his head slightly and looks at me like I'm a joke.

I look at Tessa, and she must have caught my wink, because she is looking down and silently giggling.

Refocus, the one-winged angel on my shoulder reminds me. Only one winged because any angel sitting on my shoulder has to have fucked up enough to be sentenced with such a punishment. Should note that there is no horned monster on the other shoulder, because God knows I'm already full of the devil.

I walk by and reach around her, grabbing a piece of cheese off her board and whispering, "Damn, Tessa, could you at least look at the poor guy? This is painful to watch."

She laughs.

Before popping the cheese in my mouth, I whisper, "Now let's see your moves."

"Sorry about that." She smiles big and beautifully as she ... looks him over.

I hate it. *But that doesn't matter*, One-Wing reminds me.

"Only thing I've seen you in is a football uniform and orange or camo. Oh, and no bloodstains today, either. You look good, Ben."

"Didn't notice that a few days ago?" he says, amused as fuck.

"My bad." She shrugs.

"Much better," I say louder than I realized, and everyone looks at me. I shove a carrot into one of the dips she made earlier and shrug. "Needed a little something more."

She looks down, trying to hide her smirk.

"I brought my bow," Ben says, pulling off the stupid knit cap he has on then rubbing his saggy-ass hair. "Want to take a walk?"

"It's kind of dark out, don't you think?"

"Uh-huh." He smiles.

Fucker.

"You want to shoot in the dark?" Tessa asks, confused, which is adorable unless you're the one in love with the lamb you are basically tossing into the lion's den. Well, in the case of Benji, I suppose it's more a lion cub.

"Not really." He laughs. "But I do need to grab some more stuff out of my truck. Walk with me?" He grabs her hand and pulls her out the door.

I stand at the sink, getting a front row seat as I wash the dishes.

"He's cute," Phoebe says, but it's more a question.

"You think?" Alex asks.

"I mean, not like you, but—"

Alex chuckles as he walks toward me. "You're good, Phoebe."

Standing beside me, he grips my shoulder. "What do you think?"

"I think all right looking. But he's a cocky little sh—"

"Pot meet kettle." Jade snickers.

I look back at her and throw some eye darts. "Where's *your* boyfriend?"

She smirks. "Working."

I roll my eyes and look back out the window as Ben pulls a bunch of shit from his ride. "Anyone tell him there's no room at the inn until I get the judge to change his mind?"

"He's here for the weekends until the season is over," Alex says, turning and leaning against the counter.

I glance at him. "What?"

He nods to the sink. "You've washed that same plate three times. So, right now, you're basically rubbing your own nose in shit by looking out the window. If you want her, then—"

"She deserves more than I have to offer."

Alex lifts a shoulder. "Who says?"

"Me. I'm going to college and will use my savings from busting my ass for Dad this summer to pay for childcare. Weekends, I'm not playing. I'll have my kid in a house where I will be making sure my mom's not hitting the pipe or getting wasted. I won't have time for anything more than that. And if I dared to have a relationship, Sadi would make damn sure that the girl would get so sick of her shit that—"

"That's up to the girl," Phoebe interrupts me.

"No, Pheebs, that's up to me." I turn and poke myself in the chest. "Never in a million years would I want that for her." I throw my thumb over my shoulder. "She gets better, and if dipshit's a steppingstone to better, then I'll deal."

"Aw … man," Phoebe whispers. "I wanted to hate you."

"She may need you to, so don't stop."

When Tessa walks in, followed by Ben and half his belongings, I walk into the living room and see Kendall sitting alone.

I nod to Jake. "He sleeps sounder than you."

She smiles at me, and I notice something different.

"You got braces?"

"Yeah, yesterday." Her smile falls, and she looks down. "Tess didn't notice."

I sit on the other side of her and throw an arm around her shoulders. "That would be my fault, Kendall. I've caused some problems, and I'm sorry."

She looks up at me. "Does she like Ben?"

"Do you?"

Her face legit catches fire.

"Kendall …" I sigh.

"No." she scowls. "I don't like him."

I would call bullshit if she wasn't a middle school girl who just got braces and thinks her sister doesn't notice her anymore, but even I'm not that much of a dick.

I squeeze her shoulder. "Me either."

She looks up at me and smiles.

"I'm gonna wake up Jake, and we're going to bed. You should go back out with Blue Valley's senior class and enjoy all the senioritis going on around here." She pops a kiss to my cheek then whispers, "I'm Team Lucas."

A little shocked at the show of affection, although I shouldn't be—she is a Ross, after all—I still manage to tell her, "And Team Lucas is Team Tessa, even if it means he's not good enough for her." I return the cheek kiss then stand up. "Night, Kendall."

"Night, Lucas."

When I walk out to the kitchen, Tess asks Ben, "Do you play pitch?"

"Sounds super fun, Tessa. Can I play?" I ask, grinning obnoxiously.

"Of course." She smiles.

We all sit down at the table. Dipshit sits next to Tessa, and I sit across from her.

"So, Ben," I ask, "do you have a girlfriend?"

"No." Ben smiles at Tessa, seemingly oblivious to the fact that everyone can basically see him drooling.

"Okay, so we all know how to play, right?" Tessa asks.

"Nicely." Ben smiles at her then looks at me and chuckles.

"Of course. Lucas will be my partner, and Becca will be yours, got it?" Tessa asks as she shuffles the cards.

"Ben, have you *ever* had a girlfriend?" I ask, making sure I hide every bit of sarcasm from my voice.

"A few. How about you?" Ben leans forward and pretends to be excited about sharing. *Fucker.*

Tessa laughs as she deals the cards. "A few, as well, huh, Lucas?"

"Not really. Only dated two, just fucked the others." I pick up my cards. "Two to you, Ben. And tell me, how long did you date your girlfriends?"

Ben laughs. "Um ... Let's see ... one for a year, and the others for about six months."

"Did you have sex with them?"

Tessa covers her face. "Oh. My. God."

Ben laughs as he winks at her. "Yes, actually. Sorry, no pictures or videos to share."

Tessa gives me a what-the-hell-are-you-doing look.

I look back at Ben. "You play basketball?"

"Yep, love the game. You?"

"Football is my thing." I lay down the king of clubs. "But I think you already know that."

"I do." He looks back at Tessa. "You playing any winter sports?"

"Nope, I'm up to my elbows in *Evita*." She smiles.

"Come again?" Ben laughs.

"It's our school musical."

"Tessa has the lead," Becca explains as she lays down the Jack of clubs.

Blue Love

"You sing?" Ben asks.

Tessa nods. "I do."

"Awesome. I play guitar." He lays down the queen.

I give Tessa's foot a shove under the table, and she looks at her cards.

"Do you go to church, Ben?" Becca asks.

"Yep, not as much as I should, but I do." Ben smiles politely at Becca.

I throw down the opposite Jack and the ace. Then I push back in my seat and stand. "We're done now."

"No, man, we play to fifteen." Ben points at my seat. "I'm not done with you yet."

I grumble, and Tessa laughs.

"Hey, Lucas, can we do this?"

I look at her and nod. "Absolutely."

"Good." she says. "I like this game. So, Ben, do you dance?"

"A little." He smirks. "I bid three."

"I go four," I immediately outbid him.

Tessa and Becca laugh.

I lead with the queen of hearts and smile at Tessa, who looks terrified. She throws the two, Ben has a seven, and Becca cannot follow suit. Next, I throw the king of hearts, Tessa the ten, and Ben the eight. Tessa looks at me and giggles. I throw six, Ben throws a Jack and smirks, Tessa throws the ace.

"Good play, Tessa."

When the game is over, I excuse myself to use the bathroom.

As soon as I leave the room, I hear Ben ask, "So, Tess, how long did you two date?"

"Not long."

"Long enough? I mean, are you done with it?" Ben asks.

"Yes, but we're still friends."

"That's what all the rabid bitch shit was about?" Ben asks, and I immediately stop and continue listening.

"Yep."

"So, he fucked you up."

"Long story, but it's over."

"Good. He's not going to get all crazy on me, is he? I would hate to have to kick his ass in front of you." Ben chuckles, and I want to walk right the hell back out there and let him try.

She laughs. "No, he's a good guy."

Liar.

"Go for a walk with me?"

"Sure."

I hurry to the bathroom and crack the window so I can hear the shit. And yes, that's fucked up, but I never once said I wasn't.

"I have to tell you, Tessa; I have been crushing on you since I was about five."

"Oh yeah?" she asks. "So, where were you three months ago?"

Ouch.

"Last time I was here, you said you and he weren't a thing."

"We weren't."

"Guess I shouldn't have assumed you hadn't ever been."

She doesn't say anything.

"Let me know when you're available, and if you're interested."

"I'll definitely keep that in mind," she says, voice shaking a bit. "In the meantime, tell me about yourself, Ben."

"Let's sit on the deck and chat. Then you can ask me anything you want. I'm an open book."

Good. If they sit there, I'll still hear them.

"Okay, favorite subject?" Tessa asks.

While being a fucking creeper, I find out that Ben's favorite subject is science, his favorite color is green, his favorite sport to play is basketball, he loves water sports, music, racing dirt bike, hanging out with his boys, he went to church camp every summer until his sophomore year, his parents are still together, none of his relationships ended badly; all were, in fact, because the girls moved. He didn't feel the need to keep in contact with them but was always friendly when he saw them. *I'm surprised the dipshit didn't say he liked long walks on the beach and quiet, romantic candlelit dinners.*

"Your turn, Tessa. I want to know everything."

She feels comfortable enough with him to tell him pretty much everything.

When they walk inside, I hurry to beat them to the kitchen where Alex invites him to stay at the house and join them in the hot tub.

I feel a large furry ass on my feet and look down as Chewy looks at me, then at Ben and back at me, as if to ask if I'm gonna let this happen. I scratch behind his ear, and he lets out a sigh.

"If Tess doesn't mind, I would love to."

"Sounds like fun." Tessa smiles at him.

"Let's go get changed," Ben says, and he and everyone else hurries to get changed.

"We'll meet you guys there."

"How's it going?" I ask, starting to clear the table.

"All right," Tessa says quietly.

"Cool."

She moves in front of me. "I'm in no hurry, Lucas. I'm still not over my ex."

"I'm all right, Tessa, okay?"

She stomps her foot. "Then go get ready for the hot tub."

"Okay."

* * *

When Tessa walks down the stairs, I can't help but laugh.

"What?" she asks.

"That's a lot of clothes for a hot tub. Let me grab you something more appropriate." I bound up the stairs, and she follows me.

"Fine, but I really feel like you're trying to whore me out."

Already rummaging in her drawer, I toss some more appropriate swim wear. "You're going to a hot tub, not scuba diving."

When I turn, her naked back is to me, and I watch as she pulls the bikini top over her head. She stomps her foot when she can't get it tied, and I step up to her.

"Let me get that."

"Jesus, Lucas, you're really—"

"I just want you to be happy." I tie it then kiss the top of her head. "Perfect."

She turns and looks up at me.

"Go, Tessa. I'll be out in a few minutes."

After I change and grab some drinks, I head out. Before handing her the can of diet Pepsi, I open it, then hand out the others.

When I step in, Tessa puts a towel over her face, sinks down, and leans her head back against the padding.

"So, you guys hunting all week?" Ben asks.

"I'll go out before school and after practice," Alex answers.

"How about you, Lucas?" Ben asks.

"I'm not sure yet. This is my first year. Gotta see how I like it."

"You'll like shotgun better than bow hunting."

Ben looks at Tessa. "You still cry if someone shoots a doe with a bullet, or just get bent with arrows?"

"Yes." She smiles. "Actually, no."

"Yes, she does." Alex laughs. "She just doesn't try to beat us up anymore."

She takes the towel off her face and splashes Alex. Then she looks at me, then my chest, and promptly puts the towel back over her face. "Tunes, please."

The song "Two Princes" by The Black Crowes starts playing.

When Ben laughs, Tessa's foot comes out of the water and she kicks, splashing him.

Being ever the attention whore I am with her, I ask, "Tessa, why aren't you singing tonight? You always sing."

"Come on, Tess. Let's hear you sing," Dipshit chimes in.

"Seriously? Is this eighth grade? I'm good with just relaxing."

When the song ends, she takes the towel off her head, sits up, and then takes a sip of her soda. "You boys need to be up early; don't stay out here too late." She then stands up and climbs out, tiny round and rock-hard little ass on display.

"Do you know how disturbing it is to watch you two checking her out like that?" Alex asks.

"If she wasn't your sister, you'd be doing it, too." Ben chuckles.

"All right, that's my cue. Lucas, you can close this up, right?" Alex asks.

"Yep, see you inside."

"Well, this is uncomfortable." Ben rolls his neck.

"I don't think so." I rest my head back.

"As soon as you left the game, I asked Tessa how long you two dated. Then that shit with Sadi at your school happened. I should have caught on, but didn't."

"She and I are friends. As long as you're a good guy, I'm cool with that. I just want her to be happy, man. She's special."

"What happened with you two?" Ben asks.

"She didn't tell you?"

"No."

I open my eyes and tell him, "She deserves better."

"Says you or her?"

"Me," I say curtly.

"All right. Then no rush here."

"Good. She deserves the best, Ben."

"Agreed." He sticks out his hand, and I cave by shaking it. "You sure you're done?"

"Yes." *As if I have a choice.*

"Okay, I don't want to be the rebound. I can wait." He leans back. "You live here, man?"

"Only until after the holidays."

* * *

When we walk inside, Tessa is sitting in the living room, looking through an album.

"Sure, go ahead, check it out." Ben chuckles.

What kind of douche brings a photo album to hunting camp?

"Mom wanted me to show Maggie." He sits next to her, and I want to call bullshit.

"You have a band?"

Ben chuckles. "Sure do."

"You sing?"

"Some of the songs, but I also play the guitar. You'll have to come see us sometime."

"I'd like that."

Ben shows her his mother, his ex-girlfriends, and some pictures of him being crowned homecoming king. She laughs and looks back at me as I rinse off the same fucking plate.

"Hey, Lucas, Ben was homecoming king, too." She laughs.

"Cool. Three for three, Tessa." I mess up her hair as I walk by.

"What's that about?" Ben asks.

"He's talking about Toby, possibly my future husband." She laughs. *Ouch.* "He was my date to homecoming. He was homecoming king three years ago."

"Nice, Tess, you deserve royalty."

Dipshit thinks he's Mr. Romance.

* * *

She wakes up, like always, at two thirty in the morning. I head in, and as I promised her, I try to wake her.

"Tessa, you're okay. Wake up."

"Everything okay?" Dipshit says from behind me.

"Yep. She does this every night. She has for a few weeks.

"Tessa, wake up. You're okay. Everyone is fine."

She starts crying, and my instinct is to pick her up.

I look back at Ben. "You wanna take care of this?"

"Sure, I guess." I know Ben already has experienced in this, since he's the boy she talked about in the message she left.

"Works best if you pick her up."

He does, and she grabs the back of his head and starts crying into his shirt.

"You may want to talk to her and try to calm her down."

Ben sits down. "Tess, wake up, girl."

She opens her eyes, and he says, "She's awake."

"No, she's not. She'll probably kiss you," I warn him, *and probably say my name.*

She does, and it feels like a gut punch.

He slowly pulls away. "Dude, this is odd."

"I can leave." Then I decide, *Fuck that.* I reach over and shake her. "Tessa, wake up. Tessa, wake up!"

Tessa jerks up and looks around in confusion. She looks at Ben then at me as I am now kneeling before her. Her eyes get wide when realization hits.

She pushes us both aside. "Excuse me." Then she runs downstairs.

* * *

She's in the bathroom, crying, when I open the door and walk in. "You awake now?"

"Yes, I'm awake," she snaps, looking all sorts of angry and confused.

"Are you mad at me?"

"Yes!"

"He heard you and walked in as I was trying to wake you. I told him to pick you up, and he did. You kissed him," I explain.

"I what? And you let me?" she snaps.

"Tessa, it may have been worse if you were kissing me in front of him." I run my hand through my hair. "Or not. I don't know. What the fuck did you want me to do?"

"I don't know ... Get Alex?" She starts crying.

"That would be a bit odd—watching you shove your tongue in your brother's mouth? Yeah, no."

She looks up, and we both start laughing and Chewy pushes himself up off the ground across the room, walks over and lays beside us like all is well in the world, but it's not.

I wipe away her tears and tell her, "Sorry, baby, I didn't know what to do."

"This needs to stop. I need to know why I am doing this."

"On a positive note, you didn't ask him to do the things you asked me to do." I chuckle.

She slugs me.

"You good?"

"I have to pee."

I nod and walk out the door.

When she walks upstairs, I hear Alex ask, "You okay, Tessa?"

"I guess I have kind of been freaking out at night. Ben, I'm sorry I shoved my tongue down your throat. However, as Lucas kindly pointed out, at least it wasn't Alex who I tried to assault."

"Tess, you don't have to be sorry. I really enjoyed it," Dipshit jokes, and I hear a smack.

"I'll grab my stuff and sleep in here tonight," Alex huffs. He then walks in, grabs his pillow and a water bottle off his nightstand, and then back across the hall.

"So, what are you gonna do if she tries to put the Sleeping Beauty moves on you?" Dipshit asks.

"Dump this bottle of water over her head."

Time To Stand

Chapter Thirty Eight

TESSA

I wake up early, shower, take Chewy out and make breakfast while listening to my headphones.

Because of my very own dance party, I miss Ben and Alex walking in.

Alex does me a solid by hip-checking me.

I stop dancing immediately and pull off my headphones.

"Good morning, Tess," Ben says. "You look rested."

"I am."

"Remember anything from last night?" he asks.

Embarrassed, but whatever, I nod. "I do." Then I plate up breakfast for them, and they eat.

Lucas walks into the kitchen, opens the fridge, and grabs the milk. "Good morning."

"You going to school today or hunting?" Ben asks.

Lucas answers, "I need to go to school."

"You going to take Tess to school?"

"I can." Lucas nods.

"Good, because I wouldn't want to run into that Sadi thing again. She told me she was pregnant right before she went all rabid dog on Tess. You do know there is anal for that kind of girl, right?"

I slap my hand over my gapping mouth, and Lucas looks at me.

"Not my thing."

"Maybe it should be." Ben stands up and cleans his plate.

"So, Ben"—I try not to laugh—"you're into anal, huh?"

"Hell no. I am not here for this shit." Alex stands then walks straight out the door.

"I'm into all sorts of things." Ben winks. "I like anal about as much as I like shooting Bambi. See you later, Tess." He pops a kiss to my cheek. "Maybe we can talk about it more when you are done with practice."

* * *

We ride to school together in silence. Tension is thick as hell between us, and I want to slice it right open.

"So, you don't like ana—"

"Tessa. Please don't," he cut me off.

I grin and look out the window. Then I pop in a tape.

"Wanna hear one of my new favorite songs?"

"Sure, Tessa," he says in that monotone voice he's been using around me lately.

"It's by Divinyls." I bite back a laugh as I push *play*.

"It's not a new song, Tessa," he says through clenched teeth.

"It's all new to me, Lucas." I laugh, crank it up, and begin singing. "'*I don't want anybody else, when I think about you, I touch myself.*'"

As we pull into the school parking lot, Lucas turns the volume down. And, when he parks, I jump out, laughing.

"You coming?"

"Not yet," he sneers, eyes all dark and hooded.

I lean back in and look down at the crotch of his pants. "You need some help?"

Lucas throws his head back against the headrest and snaps, "Go away. Now."

Sadi walks by and hears him. She smirks and hurries to get behind me.

"How's your face, farm girl?"

Lucas immediately jumps out and quickly walks between us.

I throw up my middle finger. "Mine will heal. Yours, however, will look like that forever."

I look at Lucas. "I think Ben was on to something, but maybe after you shove it in her ass, you could gag her with it, so she learns to shut the fuck up."

Sadi lunges toward me, and he grabs her arm. I walk away.

"I told you to leave her the fuck alone, and I wasn't joking. She and I will be friends. You and I will be nothing, Sadi. Do you get it? Baby or not, you and I will be *nothing*."

When he catches up to me, he asks, "You okay?"

I look down to see if things have calmed down ... in his

pants. "You look better. Well, not better. Just more ... relaxed. That was fast, Lucas. Dead puppies?"

"No, her fucking voice," Lucas huffs.

We both burst out laughing as he opens the door and looks back at where I stand just looking at him. *My Lucas.*

"What?"

"For a few minutes, you looked happy again." My eyes begin to heat up. "I miss that."

He nods to the open door as the first bell ring.

As I walk in, I swear I hear him whisper, "Me, too."

* * *

Ben is in the parking lot, changing his shirt, when I walk out of school.

"Picking me up shirtless, Ben? Isn't it a bit cold out for that?" I ask as he walks toward me.

He bends down and kisses my cheek. "Didn't think you'd like Bambi blood all over me." Ben laughs as he slides his sweatshirt the rest of the way over his head. "Your friend, Sadi, is watching," he whispers. He then picks me up, tosses me over his shoulder, and walks toward the truck. "Wave at her, Tess."

Laughing, I do just that.

"That show would have been more effective if you had left that damn sweatshirt off."

"Tess, have you checked out my ass? Effect enough." Ben opens the door and drops me in. "Shit, Tess, you haven't even looked at my ass? When you get there, feel it. I've been told it's kind of nice."

"By lots of people?"

"A couple, but mainly my mom," Ben jokes.

"You are a lot of fun to be around, Ben. Is there a serious side to you?"

"Are you ready for there to be?" Ben asks, and then he heads around and hops in the driver's seat. "Yes, I can be serious, but I love to have fun, and I really like to make you laugh, Ross.

"Relationship talk; I already told you about the three long relationships I have been in. They were all based on friendship first and trust. I have slept with three girls. Well, not really slept, actually." He winks. "I've only actually slept with you. I'm very busy and active. My attention is easily distracted, so I'm very busy in bed, as well."

My brows jump up.

"Just being honest."

"So, if you're easily distracted, how does that work then?"

"There are hundreds of ways to please someone." Ben cocks his head to the side. "Busy is a good thing, I like to try and learn new things," He pauses and watches my eyes. "However, as much as I love to be distracted, I prefer the person I'm with to be completely focused on me. I have issues when it comes to that. When I love or make love, it's me and her in bed, and in each other's heads. There is no other way for me."

When we pull into the driveway, he turns off the engine, jumps out, runs around, and opens my door. For some reason, I can't look him in the eyes.

"Can't look at me, huh?" He chuckles. He has a good laugh. "Good. That's step one. See you tonight, Tess. Oh, and when I walk away, you could give it a look." He kisses my forehead and leaves his lips there for a bit longer than a quick peck, and I close my eyes. Then he walks away. When I open my eyes, he laughs, "Tess, another missed opportunity."

* * *

Blue Love

After doing my homework, I close my book and look out the window. The sky is getting darker, the leaves all changed, and the trees are nearly bare. This happened seemingly overnight, and somehow, I missed that change in the midst of my life doing the same.

I throw the Shake 'n Bake chicken I prepped earlier in the oven with the baking potatoes. Then I grab my running shoes and head for the door. When I step outside, I watch as Lucas pulls in.

He quickly hops out of his vehicle and asks, "Going for a run?"

"Yep, dinner's in the oven," I tell him as I stretch.

"I talked to Sadi today." He kicks at the ground.

"How did that go?" I ask as I jump in place a bit.

Lucas smiles sadly. "You're distracting my thoughts."

"Sorry. Walk with me. Let's talk."

"But you wanted to run."

"I would rather talk to a friend, and Jade has been very busy lately."

"So I've heard, over and over again." Lucas smiles.

"Your smile ... God, Lucas, I love your smile."

He frowns. "Sorry."

"Don't be sorry. It makes me happy."

We walk for a bit in silence, and I look at the reds and burnt orange colors of the trees. They look like they've caught fire. I would love to be holding his hand and walking toward the fire instead of feeling like the fire he started inside me is about to be drowned.

I decide to rip off the Band-Aid, open the dam, and ask, "So, let's hear it; what happened with Sadi?"

He looks at me and sighs. "You sure?"

I nod.

"Well, I think it bothered her a lot when I yelled at her

this morning, because she actually apologized. I told her that I thought we should go to counseling. You know, to learn how to deal with each other for the baby." He stops and looks at me. "Should I stop?"

My throat feels like it's tightening. "No, go on."

"She agreed, so I'm going to find someone and go once a week until we can get to the point where we can be civil to each other." He stops again, searching my eyes.

I swallow back the constricted lump. "I think that's a good idea, Lucas."

"She also agreed to allow me to go to the doctor appointment in three weeks if things go well with the counselor."

I force a smile.

"Do you want to sit and talk?"

"Nope, we can walk."

God, I hope we can, because all I want to do is run, scream out my frustrations, and cry for a month, maybe longer. He is going to be with her once a week, talking to her about feelings. He is going to her doctor appointments with her, and he's having a precious little baby with her. All the things I knew—God, how I knew—but suddenly, surrounded by fire, it all seems so real.

I remind myself that *I* encouraged this, that it's the right thing for him and his child, and yes, the girl who is so fucked up it's almost scary. But this is coming from a girl who knew herself, who had strong morals and a set path, who was on the brink of crazy herself. I knew I was going to either fall apart or be here, picking up sand-sized pieces of my heart, trying to put it back together for maybe ... ever.

Breathe, Tessa, I tell myself. *Be strong. He's doing the right thing. Let him. Be his friend. Just breathe.*

My foot catches a rock, and my ankle turns. So, right there, trying to stand strong, I fall.

Tears come immediately.

Lucas squats down beside me and swallows back his own tears. "You okay, Tessa?"

"No. It hurts." I curl into a ball and bury my face in my knees as tears pour onto them.

"Let me help you up."

"I can do it. Just give me a minute." I bat away tears and look up at him.

He's trying to be strong, and what sucks the most is I know he's hurting, just like me. Maybe even more.

He reaches out and begins rubbing small circles on my back, and I can't fucking breathe.

"Sorry, Tessa, does that hurt?"

"Yep." *Everything hurts.* "So, what else happened with her?"

"She told me I needed to move out of here," he answers quietly.

I feel my hands begin to shake. "And what did you say?"

"I told her I'd work on it, but it may be two more months."

I take a deep breath. "So, are you working on it?"

He shrugs. "I think I should."

"Oh," I say, and the tears fall harder.

"I know you don't want help up, but we should really get you back to clean up that leg."

I didn't even realize I'm bleeding. The pain in my leg is nothing compared to my shattering heart.

I lift my shirt to wipe my face and look down at my knee. Then I exhale and shake my head.

He stands and reaches out his hand. I take it, and he pulls me up.

I pull my hand away. "Thank you."

"Can you walk?"

"I'm going to have to figure it out," I say, forcing the first step.

"I can't let you limp all the way to the house, Tessa."

"Well, that one, you're just going to have to figure out." I force a smile.

THE END OF BOOK ONE

New Love releases November 11th, 2021

Books by MJ Fields
MJ FIELDS

THE LEGACY SERIES FAMILY OF BOOKS
(Recommended reading order)
The Blue Valley series
Blue Love
New Love - November 11th
Sad Love- November 25th
True Love- December 9th

Coming in 2022
Wrapped In Silk
Wrapped In Armor
Wrapped In Us

Stained
Forged
Merged

Love You Anyways

THE STEEL WORLDS

(Recommended reading order)

The Men of Steel Series
Jase
Cyrus
Zandor
Xavier
Forever Family
Raising Steel
Or get the
Men Of Steel complete box set

The Ties of Steel Series
Abe
Dominic
Eroe
Sabato
Or get the
Ties of Steel complete box set

The Rockers of Steel Series
Memphis Black
Finn Beckett
River James
Billy Jeffers
or get the
Rockers of Steel complete box set

The Match Duet
Match This!
ImPerfectly Matched!
or get the
complete duet

The Steel Country Series
Hammered
Destroyed
Wasted
or get the
Steel Country complete box set

Tied in Steel series
Valentina
Paige
Gia
or get the
Tied in Steel complete box set

Steel Crew
(Generation 2)
Tagged Steel
Branded Steel
Laced Steel
Justified Steel
Tricked Steel
Busted Steel
Smashed Steel
Marked Steel
Maxed Steel

The Norfolk Series
Irons
Shadows
Titan

Timeless Love series
Unraveled
Deserving Me

Hearts So Big
Couture Love

The Caldwell Brothers Series
(co-written w/ Chelsea Camaron)
Hendrix
Morrison
Jagger
Visibly Broken
Use Me

Holiday Springs
(co-written w/ Jessica Ruben)
The Broody Brit: For Christmas
The Irresistible Irishman: For St. Patrick's Day

Standalones
Offensive Rebound

About the Author

MJ Fields is a USA Today bestselling author of contemporary and new adult romance novels. She lives in New York with her daughter and smoochie faced Newfie, Theo.

When she's not locked away in the cave, she enjoys spending time with her family, listening to live music, watching theatre, singing off key, dancing to her own beat, listening to audio books, and reading— of course.

Forever Steel!

Join MJ's mailing list:
https://mjfieldsbooks.com/newsletter

Thank you

It takes an Army and that's no joke.
A huge thank you to the army of amazing and beautiful,
talented and hard working babes who worked hard to
makes this series shine, from the outside in.
<3

Cover designer, Amy at Q Designs
Editor, Kris at C&D Editing
Proofer, Asli Arif Fratarcangeli
Beta boss, and new member of the team, Brittni.
Sister from another mister, and legacy series historian,
Jamie.
My little ball of Florida sunshine, Geissa.
To my merch queen and forever friend, Diane.
My Street Crew, sounding board, book lovers, and friends.
Wrangler, pusher, friend, my almost daily call, right hand,
online shopping budy, cheerleader, and PR babe, Autumn
To my reader group… we'll have virtual tissues and
lengthy FB live chats over this book <3

You all are the best, and I love working with you all.
So much love.

Thank you to those who
LOVE this series and allowed me to rewrite it with… umm … minimal … -ish … stress and threats.
Love You Anyway,
MJ

Made in the USA
Columbia, SC
01 November 2021